FIC   Krich, Rochelle
       Majer.

       Speak no evil.

$21.95

DATE			

Speak
No Evil

Other works by Rochelle Majer Krich:

Angel of Death
Fair Game
Nowhere To Run
Till Death Do Us Part
Where's Mommy Now? (aka *Perfect Alibi*)

Speak No Evil

ROCHELLE MAJER KRICH

THE MYSTERIOUS PRESS

Published by Warner Books

A Time Warner Company

Mysterious Press books are published by Warner Books, Inc.,
1271 Avenue of the Americas, New York, NY 10020.

 A Time Warner Company

The Mysterious Press name and logo are registered trademarks of Warner Books,
Inc.

Printed in the United States of America

First printing: February 1996

10 9 8 7 6 5 4 3 2

Library of Congress Cataloging-in-Publication Data

Krich, Rochelle Majer.
    Speak no evil / Rochelle Majer Krich.
      p. cm.
    ISBN 0-89296-584-3 (hardcover)
    1. Women lawyers—California—Los Angeles—Fiction. 2. Serial
 murders—California—Los Angeles—Fiction. 3. Los Angeles (Calif.)—Fiction. I.
Title.
   PS3561.R477S64 1996
   813'.54—dc20
                            95-40541
                              CIP

For Mimi and Sol—
with much love

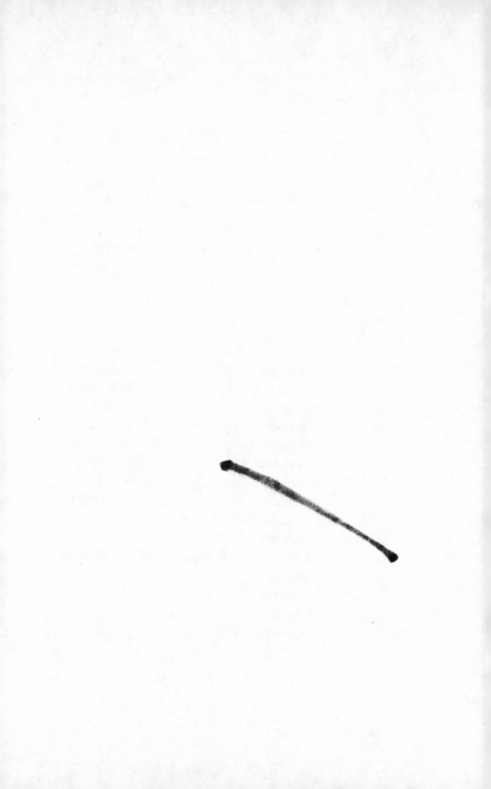

Acknowledgments

My thanks to the many people who provided background and information for SPEAK NO EVIL: Maynard Davis, criminal defense attorney; Jim Vickman, attorney at law; and Carolyn Yamaoka, court reporter, Santa Monica Court House. I am indebted to Renee Korn, Los Angeles Deputy District Attorney, Criminal Courts Building, for graciously giving me entree to her courtroom and sharing with me her wealth of knowledge. Most especially, I am grateful to Mary Hanlon, Deputy District Attorney, Santa Monica Court House, for our new friendship and for her patience in providing me with an insider's view of the intricate workings of the criminal justice system. Any mistakes in the novel are mine.

Special thanks to my editor, Sara Ann Freed; my agent, Sandra Dijkstra; and her associate, Katherine Miller, for their insightful suggestions and enthusiasm.

Author's note: This novel is a work of fiction. While it takes place in Los Angeles, California, and makes reference to actual places and buildings, none of the characters or events are real; they are all a product of my imagination, and any resemblance to real persons or actual events is totally coincidental.

Speak
No Evil

Chapter One

The witness, a slim, waiflike woman dwarfed by her surroundings and by fear, sat rigid on the stand, her tightly locked hands resting on her lap like a paperweight that would keep her from floating away. Her tongue made darting, stealthy sweeps of her upper lip, and her eyes avoided the defense counsel table and the attorney who was about to cross-examine her.

The woman had every reason to be nervous, Debra Laslow thought with a surge of sympathy as she shifted on the hard, cushionless bench in the spectator's gallery. Being questioned by Madeleine Chase was like having Hannibal Lecter for a dinner guest. The attorney's hand was resting familiarly on her client's shoulder, and she was whispering in his ear, probably reminding him what Debra reminded her own clients:

"Look interested, but not worried. Don't react to anything the witness says. No anger, no scowls. Don't bite your nails. Don't fidget. Don't slump."

According to a reliable source, Madeleine had warned a

client charged with rape that if he smirked at the witness or anyone on the jury, she'd castrate him herself.

"What did the client say?" Debra had asked the source.

"'Just get me off, bitch.'"

There were many stories about Madeleine.

The witness pushed a section of straight brown hair behind her ear—a sign of nervousness Debra thought must have pleased Madeleine, whose honey-blond hair, arranged in her trademark French twist, drew attention to her dramatic good looks.

Madeleine rose. There was something sensual about the fluid movement of her limbs as she slid out of her chair; there was something artificial, too, as if she'd practiced the move to create just the right effect on the people filling the rows behind her, watching her. She closed the single button of a beautiful dove gray Donna Karan suit jacket that Debra had almost bought at Saks and passed the prosecution table. She detoured in front of the jury box and ran her hand along the railing, caressing the dark wood, then approached the podium and smiled at the twenty-seven-year-old woman whose credibility she was about to destroy.

"Miss Parnell, isn't it a fact . . . ?"

A half hour later the judge declared a recess. Debra exited the courtroom and the adjoining small foyer and stood to the left of the wood-grain door. Several minutes later Madeleine emerged, swinging her charcoal gray alligator briefcase. She looked unruffled, unlike the witness she'd reduced to uncertainty and tears with a skill that had aroused in Debra admiration and a flash of uncomfortable envy.

Madeleine made her way down the low-ceilinged hall, followed by a *Los Angeles Times* crime reporter Debra recognized. She waited until he'd abandoned his prey; then, suppressing a flash of nervousness intensified by the perpetual gloominess of the hall's dim fluorescent lighting, she caught up with Madeleine. She was surprised, as always, to see that she and Madeleine were the same height—five feet five inches. From a distance Madeleine seemed taller, more imposing.

"Can I speak to you, Madeleine?" She kept her voice low, but it sounded unnaturally loud as it echoed off the brown ceramic-tiled walls. A handful of people were nearby—some standing, some sitting on the uncomfortable dark brown plastic benches that lined the walls; the *Times* reporter was hovering within earshot.

Madeleine stopped. "I was surprised to see you in the courtroom, Debra. So what did you think of my cross?" She smiled.

"Very effective." Debra returned the smile, resisting an impulse to smooth her shoulder-length, wavy dark brown hair, which was never as sleek as Madeleine's. "I was filing a motion and knew you were here. I need to speak to you, in private. Can we go somewhere for a few minutes?"

"Sorry, I have an appointment." Another smile. "You can call me later. Unless you want to talk now?"

Was it Debra's imagination, or had the reporter inched closer? She hesitated, then said, "When we had lunch two weeks ago, I mentioned I'd applied for the opening at your firm. I was turned down, and I wondered if you'd heard why."

The letter had arrived at home yesterday. Debra, anxious to leave her firm, had been sharply disappointed and stunned, because everything—the initial interview, the fancy dinner in the fancy restaurant with the partners, the subsequent conversation—had been so promising.

Madeleine sighed. "We're the top firm in the city because we're so selective. The fact is, Debra, when the partners asked me about you, I suggested they could do better. Sorry, but I assume you'd want the truth." Her tone was matter-of-fact, her gray eyes cool, unblinking, but the pull of her lips betrayed triumph.

Debra stared at her. "You wished me good luck," she said softly. Her face stung with humiliation and anger—at Madeleine, for her duplicity and cruelty; at herself, for having been gulled by Madeleine's "Let's be friends" phone call into believing that after years of being ruthlessly competitive and nasty and confrontational, the woman had changed.

"I wish opposing counsel good luck, too. They need it." Her eyes traveled dismissively from Debra's face to her taupe suit, then back to her face. "James Brand is doing seven years, isn't he? Poor man. I'm sure you gave his case your *very* best." She shook her head.

Debra clenched her hands. "No one could have gotten Brand off. Not even you." Don't rise to her bait, she told herself.

Madeleine answered with another smile. "Face facts, Debra. You're a mediocre attorney with unrealistic expectations. You've been trying to compete with me since we were at UCLA Law. It was pathetic then. Now it's annoying."

"You really have a problem, don't you?" Debra turned to leave.

"I'm just being honest." Madeleine raised her voice. "Better lawyers than you are scrambling for jobs. Stay with the firm that hired you, and be grateful. By the way, do they know you're scouting around?"

Anxiety stabbed at Debra. Turning back, she said, "No wonder people dislike you, Madeleine. Aside from your parents, I can't imagine anyone putting up with you, and they didn't have a choice."

Madeleine flinched. Debra was sorry the minute she spoke the words, sorry even before she remembered that Madeleine had grown up in foster homes until the Chases had adopted her. Hot with embarrassment, she reached out a tentative hand. "I'm sorry. I didn't mean—"

"Being a rabbi's daughter hasn't taught you any values, has it? You're a mediocre person as well as a mediocre lawyer."

Anger or hurt—maybe both—had flooded Madeleine's face with color. She turned abruptly and walked away. Debra watched her for a moment, waiting for the briefcase to resume its confident swing, but Madeleine was still clutching it against her side as she turned right toward the bank of elevators.

Crossing Santa Monica Boulevard, Wilshire winds past the dense, dark green copse that guards the privacy of the exclusive Los Angeles Country Club and meanders toward Westwood. Every turn reveals lofty condominium towers, a testament to the engineers who triumphed over seismic impediments to build them and to the wealthy who own them. At night the towers take on a magical, Fantasyland appearance, the shrubbery and trees flanking their lobby entrances illuminated with strands of tiny, twinkling lights that mimic the stars and create the illusion of heaven on earth.

Late that October evening Debra stood under the hunter green canopy outside the elegantly furnished locked lobby of one of the condominium towers, her fingers hesitating on the shiny brass plaque just below Madeleine's bell. The courthouse confrontation had nagged at her all day. She'd tried phoning Madeleine at home. The line had been busy for over an hour; when Madeleine had finally answered, Debra had hung up, suddenly uncertain of what to say. She'd decided that in person was better, if more difficult.

So she'd driven to Westwood. Partly because her father had tried to instill forgiveness and sensitivity in his children. Partly because the tightness around Madeleine's thin, unsmiling mouth and a fleeting look of hurt Debra had often noticed in her cool gray eyes had aroused her pity for the driven attorney who won case after case but seemed, with it all, unhappy. Debra regretted having brought additional hurt to those eyes.

Or was she here to exact satisfaction, to prove she wasn't mediocre? Madeleine's comment had rankled.

Wondering if she was inviting more insults, Debra pressed the bell. To her right the lights of a tall ficus winked encouragement. She pressed the bell again and held her finger against it longer this time, wincing at its strident twang. Still no answer. She remembered a Jewish maxim her father often quoted: "A good intention is considered as if it were an action." Telling herself she'd fulfilled her obligation, she turned and headed down the flagstone walkway to the street.

Approaching her were an elderly couple led by a leashed white Shih Tzu with a rhinestone collar. Debra stepped aside and smiled at the dog and its owners. The man and woman eyed her, wariness stamped on their faces. The dog emitted a low growl. They were reacting to her presence with the ingrained distrust toward strangers that everyone who lived in the city inhaled daily, along with the smog, but she felt transparent, as if they knew she was relieved that Madeleine wasn't home.

She sensed the couple's gaze as she made her way to her Acura. The dog growled again. Maybe she'd phone Madeleine tomorrow, at her office.

But in the morning Madeleine was dead, and Debra was left with good intentions and the whisper of regret.

Chapter Two

"She was shot to death in her condo last night," Glynnis said, fixing her gleaming brown eyes on Debra. "In her chest, they said." The dark-auburn-haired secretary shuddered and crossed her hands against her ample bosom, as if protecting herself from a similar fate.

Debra stared openmouthed at Glynnis and felt a wave of nausea at the bloody image that flashed through her mind.

"It was on the radio this morning. Didn't you hear it?"

She shook her head, too stunned to speak. She rarely listened to the radio news; after spending ten or more hours a day submerged in the grittiness of criminal defense, she preferred the balm of strings and flutes, of Beethoven and Mozart and Bach.

"I'll let you know if I hear an update," Glynnis promised, pinching off a barely yellowed leaf from the creeping Charlie on her desk.

Walking to her office, Debra was overcome with sadness, with regret for things unresolved. With fear. As soon as she was at her desk, she phoned Susan Clemens, a defense attorney. The two had become close friends working in the public defender's office.

"I heard," Susan interrupted when Debra started telling her about Madeleine's murder. "I talked to her just two days ago. God, I can't believe this!" She sighed. "I didn't like Madeleine. Hell, nobody did! But it's awful she was killed."

Both women were silent for a moment. Then Debra said, "I wonder who killed her."

"One of her clients? A witness she trashed on the stand? To tell you the truth, either thought scares the hell out of me."

It scared the hell out of Debra, too. Anyone who practiced criminal defense was aware of the inherent dangers of representing people accused of violence—people who can easily become the enemy. During her three years as a public defender before coming here to Knox and Cantrell, Debra had earned the hostility of several opposing witnesses and some of her own clients. "You deal with too many crazies," her brother, Aaron, told her frequently. He'd probably phone her as soon as he heard about the murder and urge her again to switch to a safer law practice.

"Maybe it was someone from Madeleine's personal life," Debra said. "Or maybe a burglar pushed his way into the lobby when she unlocked the door, then forced her at gunpoint to let him inside her condo." Her mind refused to play the scene to its grisly end. Was Madeleine dead when Debra was standing outside the lobby doors at ten-thirty? Or was the murderer inside her condominium at that very moment? In Debra's memory, the strident twang of the bell, so annoying the night before, seemed suddenly urgent, plaintive.

"Maybe." Susan didn't sound convinced.

"I'd better get to work. Got to rack up those billable hours." Meeting the monthly quota of hours that can be legitimately billed to clients was a razor-edged pendulum swinging over the head of everyone who worked for a private law firm. No billable hours was one of the things Debra missed about working in the public defender's office.

"Don't we all." Susan groaned. "Speaking of work, it would be strange going to Blackmeyer now, wouldn't it?"

Blackmeyer, Henderson, and Tobacznik was Madeleine's firm. "They turned me down," Debra said, deciding not to mention the courthouse quarrel. She realized with a flutter of anxiety that the police might learn about the confrontation from the *Times* reporter (he could use it to score points for future leads) and about her visit to the condo from the couple with the dog. Police, she knew, often latched on to the most visible, not the most logical, suspect. She considered phoning them, then wondered if she would be borrowing trouble.

"Cheer up, Deb. There are other firms. In fact, there's going to be an opening here. Mark Bentheim—he's an associate—just told me he and his wife are moving to Colorado."

"Talk about perfect timing." Most defense attorneys practiced alone or with one partner; among the larger L.A. defense firms, Susan's had an excellent reputation. And Susan often mentioned how happy she was with her work and her colleagues.

"You'd love it here, Deb. The partners are fair. There's room for advancement. The bonuses are great. And there are no Richards, thank God," she said, referring to a senior associate at Debra's firm who was making Debra miserable. "Of course, the hours are impossible—so what's new?"

"No kidding." Debra missed playing tennis every week, seeing art exhibits, browsing in bookstores, going to the latest movies. (Thank God for video, she often thought.) But she'd accepted the long days, and weekends, of private practice. And Susan's firm sounded like a place where she could be happy. "Working together would be wonderful, wouldn't it?" she said, buoyed for the first time in two days. "Thanks, Susan."

"Don't thank me until you get the job. And you'd have to swear not to show me up!" Susan laughed. "Send me your résumé. Mark plans to tell the partners on Monday. The minute he confirms he's leaving, I'll take the résumé to the senior partner. In the meantime, behave yourself at Knox and Cantrell. And good luck with your prelim. It's next week, right?"

"Tuesday." Her client, Timothy Lassister, was a twenty-two-year-old charged with possession of cocaine and with one prior to which he'd pled guilty and received a reduced sentence and probation. The case hinged on the legality of the search that had revealed the cocaine.

This would be Debra's first solo prelim at the firm—and, if the judge denied her 1538.5 motion to dismiss, her first trial. She'd been hired because of her acquittal record in the public defender's office, but for the seven months she'd been here, aside from representing several clients at arraignments, she'd been stuck studying case law, writing motions and briefs, and accompanying the other attorneys to plea sessions, dispositions, prelims, and trials. It was a ridiculous waste of her time and experience. It was one of the reasons she wanted to leave.

"I'm working on the opening for my motion in front of Judge Fogel," Debra said. "How does 'Four score and seven years ago' sound?"

Susan laughed again. "Quotable. Don't forget—you have to yell at Fogel. He's practically deaf."

After hanging up the phone, Debra removed her personal floppy disk from her desk drawer, inserted it into her computer, and printed a copy of her résumé for Susan. Then she spent the day on her motion, double-checking her precedents against the printouts of the relevant case law she'd accessed via her computer through her Lexis program.

At 4:30 she shut her computer and placed the Lassiter file in her briefcase. Sundown, and the Sabbath, would begin at 5:39. In normal traffic Debra's house on Citrus was a twenty-minute drive from the firm's Century City address. If she left now, she could drive by the Beverly Boulevard post office drop box and mail her résumés before the day's final pickup: one to Susan; eight others, which she'd been holding until she heard from Blackmeyer, to other firms.

She had pulled her office door shut when she saw Richard Dressner, Jeremy Knox's forty-two-year-old protégé and Debra's appointed mentor, approaching her. He was six feet tall, had thick, dark brown hair that he slicked back, keen brown eyes, a sharp nose, aggressive jaw, and full lips. He worked out regularly so that he could look wonderful in his suits and shirts, all Armani. His eyeglass frames were Armani, too. His ties were Hugo Boss; his cuff links, signature Chanel. Debra knew all this not because she was an expert on men's fashions, but because he made a point of telling her.

"Let's talk strategy about Lassiter, Debra," Richard said, gesturing in the direction of his office.

She didn't need to talk strategy. She had three years' experience as a public defender and didn't need babying. "I can't, Richard. I have to leave."

"Another early Friday?" He smiled. "Maybe I should become Orthodox, like you."

This Sunday night, the last in October, daylight savings would end, and next Friday Debra would leave work even earlier by an hour and four minutes. She tensed but forced herself to return the smile. "Any time Monday is fine."

"My calendar's full on Monday." He frowned. "This is your first trial, Debra. Lassiter's an important client."

"I'm fully prepared, Richard." She smiled again and tapped her briefcase, wondering what he would say if he knew about the résumés inside. "Don't worry. And have a nice weekend," she added as he turned and walked away.

In her first interview with the firm, Debra had explained that as a Sabbath observer, she'd have to leave early on many Fridays and miss certain days every year, that she was willing to work late every day and come in on Sundays and Christmas and New Year's. Jeremy Knox, the partner who had first interviewed her, had assured her that her religious observance wouldn't be a problem. He'd noted the specifics in her contract.

Richard was fully aware of the terms of Debra's employment. Though he was Jewish, he clearly resented her being observant and enjoyed harassing her in many ways whenever he could. He was the primary reason Debra hated her job and wanted to leave.

She stopped at Glynnis's desk on her way through the reception room. "Have a nice weekend, Glynnis."

"You, too, dear." The secretary smiled, then rearranged her face into a grave expression. "The boyfriend found the body, by the way. Lots of blood. You know what else?" She glanced at Debra expectantly.

"What?" Debra asked, more out of politeness than curiosity.

"I just spoke to Cynthia, Madeleine's secretary—we're friends, you know? She overheard the police talking when they checked Madeleine's office." Glynnis's voice had dropped to a whisper. She leaned forward. "She heard them say the killer cut out Madeleine's tongue." Glynnis shivered. "Isn't that the most repulsive thing you ever heard?"

Chapter Three

Janey Schultz was slicing carrots when the clack *from the hallway told her the dead bolt was being slid open.*

The bands constricted around her chest. Inhaling sharply, she tightened her grip on the knife handle and brought the blade down with ruthless swiftness onto the helpless carrot. Beads of perspiration dotted her upper lip.

"Dad's home," Ruth Schultz announced, entering the kitchen.

Janey nodded. The bands had loosened, but her lips were dry and she felt lightheaded. "I wish you wouldn't stare," she said, brushing the orange strips into the fluted glass bowl. "I'm fine."

"I know you're fine, honey. I was just thinking how pretty you look." She picked up a slivered carrot. "These are so professional. Julia Child couldn't do better."

A moment later her father was in the doorway. Janey wanted to run to him and let his strong arms comfort her as they always had, but something kept her rooted to the linoleum.

"*Smells good in here,*" *Norman Schultz said.* "*So how are my two best girls?*"

"*I'm fine,*" *Ruth said.* "*Janey's fine, too, right, sweetheart?*"

With an abrupt movement, Janey buried the tip of the knife in the cutting board and left the kitchen, passing wordlessly in front of her father, who had stepped aside to let her by.

"*It's the TV bulletins about Madeleine Chase,*" *her mother whispered to her father.* "*They've been showing them all day.*"

"*Shit! Can't that woman stay dead?*"

Her parents' whispers followed her to the living room and settled around her as she slumped against the sofa cushions. She clicked on the television with the remote control and switched channels until she found an old I Love Lucy *episode.*

Miss Schultz, isn't it a fact that everything you've testified to in court today about the defendant is a lie?

"*You'd think Janey'd be relieved,*" *Norman said.* "*After the hell that bitch lawyer put her through.*"

Isn't it a fact that you were angry at the defendant?

"*I guess it brought back everything,*" *her mother said.*

Isn't it a fact that on the day in question . . .

Janey raised the volume until Ricky and Lucy and Ethel and Fred and the braying canned laughter drowned out the voices in her head.

Ten minutes later they were all seated around the table. "*So did you go to the employment agency today?*" *her father asked.*

She had dreaded the question and his forced, casual tone and the painful smile that pinched his square, kind face. "*I wasn't up to it.*" *The vein at the side of her neck was throbbing. She lifted a finger to her throat and massaged the spot where the knife had pressed against her skin.* I'll kill you if you scream.

He took Janey's hand. "*You're nineteen years old. You won't go to school. You won't look for a job. Don't let what happened ruin your life. Don't let them do that to you.*"

His love was a terrible, crushing burden. "Please," *Janey whispered. Her hazel eyes flooded with tears.*

"*She needs time, Norman. She's getting better every day. Isn't that right, sweetheart?*"

"*I'll help you, but you have to take the first step,*" *her father said softly, linking his fingers through hers.* "*Promise me you'll go tomorrow. Do it for me.*"

"*I saw him today.*" *She blinked rapidly. Her breathing accelerated.* "*He was watching the house, waiting.*"

Norman exchanged a sharp glance with his wife. "*He's not watching you, baby,*" *he said as carefully as if he were stepping around land mines.* "*It seems real, but it isn't. I wish to hell I could make it go away.*"

"*This time I know I saw him. Will you call the police? Please, Daddy? I won't be able to sleep tonight. I know I won't.*"

"*Janey, the other times we called, he had a solid alibi. He wasn't anywhere near here.*" *He spoke patiently, slowly.* "*The doctor explained what's happening to you. You're—*"

"*I hate Dr. Fenneman!*" *She wrenched her hand free.* "*She never believes me. You don't believe me. No one believes me!*"

"*Don't do this to yourself.*" *Ruth left her seat to stand behind her daughter. She stroked Janey's long, dark blond hair.*

"*I want to believe you, baby. I do. It's just that . . .*" *His voice trailed off in bewilderment and frustration.*

"*He's the one who lied, he and Madeleine Chase! But I'm the one who has to stay locked up in my own house! I'm glad she's dead! I wish he was dead, too! I wish they were all dead!*"

"*You don't mean that!*" *Her mother's hands moved to Janey's shoulders.* "*It's wrong to talk like that, sweetheart. Tell her, Norman.*"

Norman sighed. Without looking at his daughter he said, "*Your mother's right.*" *He clenched his fork and stabbed the meat on his plate and ate in silence.*

"*So will you call the police, Daddy?*"

Chapter Four

"May God make you like Sarah, Rebecca, Rachel, and Leah . . . ," Rabbi Ephraim Laslow intoned softly in Hebrew as he stood with Debra in the archway to his son's dining room.

She always kept her eyes closed as her father placed his hands on her head and recited this Sabbath blessing upon his return from Friday evening services. His hands were strong and beautiful, with long, slender fingers that could have belonged to a musician or an artist and had served him well as a scholar and teacher and parent. His hands transported her back to her childhood, where she was a four-year-old sitting on his lap. They tickled her and formed magical, shadow creatures on her bedroom wall and guided her through the mysteries of the *aleph bet.*

"'May God bless you and safeguard you. . . .'"

She kept her eyes closed when her father blessed her because she wanted to feel enveloped by the solemn beauty and promise of the words and because, though seven years had passed and Debra, like her father and brother, had made small adjustments to her mother's death, and though the Sabbath was a day of serenity and joy, she knew there were tears in her father's eyes, just as there were tears in hers.

"'May God turn His countenance to you and establish peace for you.'" He kissed his daughter's forehead. "*Gut Shabbos,* Debra."

His lips were soft and his beard, which he'd kept after the thirty-day mourning period for his wife, tickled her skin; she'd grown accustomed to the sensation and almost liked it. "*Gut Shabbos,* Dad."

"So how much time did you have when you came home today?" he asked, his voice a mixture of fondness and admonition. "Twenty minutes?"

She smiled and inhaled the yeasty fragrance of the braided challahs warming in the oven. "Twenty-eight."

She'd raced home, grateful as always to Blanca, the Salvadoran housekeeper who came every Friday. Debra didn't cook or turn on electricity on the Sabbath, so she'd boiled water in the electric samovar for tea and set the *"Shabbos* clock"—a timer that turned her lights off on Friday night and back on late Saturday afternoon. She'd showered and put on makeup. She'd spread a white cloth on the breakfast room table. Finally, her blow-dried hair still damp, she'd placed two candles in the brass holders she'd bought when she'd moved out of her father's house almost a year ago. After lighting the candles, she'd covered her eyes, recited the blessing, and welcomed the Sabbath and tranquillity into her home. Then she'd walked to her brother's house.

Ephraim Laslow frowned and shook his head. "What happens if you're stuck in traffic when *Shabbos* starts? You'd have to leave your car and walk home. It could be miles."

"I'm careful," she said, knowing he was right.

"Hey, I'm starved!" Aaron called from the head of the table.

"You'd think he hadn't eaten all day." Debra's sister-in-law, Julia, smiled and lightly punched her husband's abdomen, then adjusted the white lace mantilla on her head.

Aaron and Julia often invited guests; tonight it was just the four of them. Sometimes they ate Sabbath meals at Debra's, more often at Julia's, whose schedule—doing bookkeeping Monday through Thursday for a pediatrician—was easier than Debra's. Some weekends Debra and her father accepted invitations from respective friends to give Julia and Aaron time alone; frequently they all ate at Aunt Edith's, Debra's mother's older sister. As the only L.A. relatives—Debra's maternal grandparents lived in Brooklyn, her father's widowed mother in Miami—Edith and her husband, Morris, doted on Debra and Aaron and on Julia, whose parents lived in Baltimore.

Ephraim Laslow took his place at Aaron's right. There was no mistaking they were father and son, Debra thought as she sat down next to Julia. They were the same height—five feet ten inches—and had the same pleasant, though not exactly handsome, faces with firm chins and intense brown eyes that looked straight at you from behind tortoise frames. (The Laslow eyes, Debra's mother, Anne, had called them. Though Debra resembled her mother more than her father, she had the eyes, too; her mother's had been hazel.) Aaron's brown hair looked darker because her father's hair, which had receded mildly, and his trim beard, were sprinkled with gray.

The beard gave him a distinguished air. Aaron occasionally talked about growing a beard, too. Julia and Debra had stopped voicing their dissension because they didn't believe he'd do it, just as they didn't believe him when he threatened to give up teaching Jewish and secular history in high school—something he loved—to pursue a more lucrative career.

Aaron led the singing. He was a tenor to her father's baritone, and Debra enjoyed listening to their harmony as they sang *"Shalom Aleichem"* to greet and bid farewell to the special angels who protected Jews as they returned from synagogue on Friday night. When the two men sang "A Woman of Valor," Aaron gazed at Julia with the same rapt adoration that shone in his eyes when he serenaded her at their wedding.

Julia returned his gaze. Aaron was thirty-three, two years older than Debra; Julia was thirty. She was petite and slim and had amber eyes and hair the color of ginger. All four of them—Debra, Aaron, Rabbi Laslow, even Julia—used to joke about the freckles her children would inherit, but after six years and a multitude of examinations and expensive procedures, there were still no children, and the joking had long ago stopped.

Debra's father and Aaron made kiddush on the wine, then recited another blessing on the challah. Between each course there were more songs and a discussion of the week's Torah reading, punctuated by casual conversation.

"I meant to ask you, Deb," Aaron said after he'd taken a few bites of roast chicken. "Any news about Madeleine Chase's murder?"

She shook her head "No." For the last hour she'd managed to block out the gruesome image of Madeleine's severed tongue. Now the image was back. She was queasy again and didn't want to talk about it. And maybe Glynnis was wrong—the radio news update she'd heard on her way home hadn't mentioned the mutilation.

"It's horrible," Julia said, her voice a half whisper. "I couldn't believe it when Aaron told me she was killed last night."

"Why are we talking about murder?" Her father's eyes flashed his annoyance. "That's a topic for the *Shabbos* table?"

"Madeleine and Debra were at UCLA together," Aaron

said. "Remember her, Dad? Debra talked about her all the time."

"I remember." Ephraim Laslow nodded. "It's a terrible tragedy. Still, it helps nothing to engage in idle gossip."

"But Dad—"

"Koh ribbon olam . . . ," he began, keeping time to the Chasidic melody by slapping his palm against the table.

Aaron knew when to stop. He joined in. Debra forced herself to sing but did little more than mouth the words. Madeleine's brutal murder had violated the sanctity of her Sabbath, and she was somber throughout the rest of the meal.

Her father, Aaron, and Julia escorted her home. The family lived within blocks of each other—Debra on Citrus; Aaron and Julia, five blocks west in a duplex on Detroit near Beverly; their father, in another Detroit duplex closer to Third—but with all the crime, Debra worried about walking at night. Some people, she'd heard, refused to go anywhere Friday nights; others hired armed guards to accompany them when they were invited out. Debra found both solutions extreme and disheartening, a flag of surrender to those who would imprison the city's occupants with fear. Walking along the quiet, empty, tree-lined streets, she hoped that the special Sabbath guardian angels who had accompanied her father and brother home from shul were doing overtime.

"You're so quiet, Debra," her father said. They were half a block ahead of Julia and Aaron. "Because of Madeleine Chase?"

"Yes." When she didn't continue, her father didn't prod. Rabbis, like psychologists, she thought, knew how to listen and wait; though her father had given up his pulpit several months after his wife's death, he still counseled couples and young adults. And his own children. "We quarreled yesterday, the same day she was killed," she added after a moment.

Her father sighed. "People quarrel, Debra. It happens."

"I said something unintentionally hurtful, Dad. I'm sure people overheard. I tried to apologize, but she wasn't home. Now she's dead, and I can't stop thinking about what I said." The words had tumbled out in a rush. She looked straight ahead; she couldn't bear to read disappointment in her father's eyes.

They walked in silence, interrupted only by the call of the crickets. Finally her father spoke. "In the strictest sense, Debra, Jewish law instructs that if I insult someone in front of ten people to the point that he pales, and he dies before I can make amends, I must gather ten males and take them to the deceased's grave and ask forgiveness." He put his arm around her. "We all say things we regret, even to those we love. *Especially* to those we love. There were words I said to your mother that I wish I'd never uttered. Mercifully, the memory dims. Ask forgiveness of Madeleine, Debra. Learn from your mistake, and forgive yourself."

Her father was only partially right. There were impatient, self-centered words Debra had thoughtlessly tossed at her mother that she, too, wished she'd never spoken. Seven years later, they still made her wince when she allowed herself to remember.

Chapter Five

"Two police detectives are here to see Miss Laslow," Glynnis announced Monday morning. Poking through a narrow opening between the door and the conference room, her head seemed disembodied, a Medusa-like tangle of mahogany curls. "They said it's important, or I wouldn't have interrupted."

"What's this about?" Richard half swiveled toward Glynnis but kept his eyes on Debra.

"They wouldn't say."

It was Madeleine. Debra told herself not to worry—the police would be talking to everyone who had interacted with the dead woman—but her stomach muscles tightened. Not knowing whether to stay or go, she faced the head of the large oval black walnut table for instruction from Jeremy Knox, the firm's fifty-seven-year-old silver-haired senior partner.

"Glynnis, please inform the detectives that Miss Laslow will be with them shortly," Jeremy said. "Have them wait in reception."

"Yes, sir." She removed her head from the doorway and pulled the door shut.

"Embezzling again?" Charles Graystone drawled in an undertone near Debra's ear. "How many thousands did you take this time?"

"Two hundred, and I'm not sharing." She smiled, but her thoughts were on the police who were waiting for her.

Charles, thirty-four, was a three-year associate at the firm. He was tall and lean, with handsome chiseled features and close-cropped black hair; he was married and had two little girls whom he adored. He and Debra shared, among other things, their "only" status at the firm—he was the only African American; she, the only woman—a fondness for Ben & Jerry's ice cream, and a dislike of Richard.

Richard was diagonally across from Debra; he always sat as close as possible to Jeremy, who seemed oblivious to the failings so clear to Debra and Charles. At the other end of the table was Anthony Cantrell, the fifty-two-year-old business manager. Unlike Jeremy, who was tall and distinguished and reminded Debra of Gregory Peck, Anthony was short and portly and dyed his hair a ridiculously unnatural black—Hercule Poirot without the mustache and sometimes, from what Charles had told her, without the "little gray cells."

"Can we continue?" Richard pulled up his monogrammed cuff to check his Movado watch. "I have appointments."

"Where were we?" Anthony fiddled with his bow tie. "Oh, yes. The facsimile machine. Many firms bill clients . . ."

Ten minutes later Debra collected her papers, picked up her coaster and mug, still half filled with not-so-hot chocolate, and left the conference room ahead of the others.

Sitting in reception was Stan Cummings from West L.A. He was in his forties, tall and stocky, with frizzed salt-and-pepper hair, a square, pockmarked face, and a flattened, heavily veined nose. Debra had cross-examined him on more than one occasion, and he was always thoroughly prepared, concise, unflappable. She'd enjoyed the challenge, and they'd developed a mutual respect.

With Cummings was a young detective with thick, longish blond hair, swimming pool blue eyes, and a lean, athletic build. Both men stood at Debra's arrival; Cummings performed introductions.

"Ms. Laslow, Detective Wraith and I are investigating the murder of Madeleine Chase," Cummings said in his customary low-keyed voice. "We understand you knew her?"

Debra's back was to Glynnis, but the keyboard was silent, and she knew the secretary was watching intently, her antennae fine-tuned. "Why don't we talk in my office."

Her office was small and filled with the usual furnishings—a walnut desk and credenza, a gray tweed armchair, a tall wood-tone file cabinet, and three bookcases crammed with the expensive legal tomes—some used, some new—that she'd accumulated over the past nine years. In the corner in a brass planter on the slate gray carpet was a Chinese evergreen that, with fluorescent lighting and Glynnis's superintendence, survived Debra's occasional neglect. Her diplomas from Barnard and from UCLA School of Law hung on the pale gray textured wallpaper next to a lithograph of Jerusalem by a contemporary Israeli woman artist. Debra's father and Aaron and Julia had presented it to her to celebrate her joining the firm. At least it won't leave a mark on the wallpaper when I take it down, Debra had thought when she'd decided to leave her job.

She sat behind her desk and, careful not to topple the photo of her family, placed a stack of folders on her keyboard to make room for her coaster and mug. "Madeleine and I were in the same class at UCLA Law School," she said after the detectives had settled themselves on two gray tweed chairs in front of her desk.

"You've been friends ever since?" Cummings asked.

"Acquaintances. Our paths crossed occasionally, and we belonged to the same professional organization." It was strange, this role reversal—Cummings asking questions instead of answering hers. Debra straightened a stack of papers.

"Which organization is that?"

"WRIT. Women's Rights in Toto. It helps women attorneys network." It also offered support and advice in crises in what was still very much a male-dominated field.

"We understand that you saw Ms. Chase last Thursday at the downtown courthouse," Wraith said. He was leaning against his chair back and had crossed one leg over the other, revealing the scuffed toe and worn sole of his boot.

"Yes." She went into "defense" mode and obeyed the instruction she gave her witnesses—don't volunteer information. She raised the mug of chocolate to her mouth, gratified that her hand wasn't shaking, then remembered her manners. "My breakfast," she said, gesturing with the mug. "Would you like some coffee?"

Both men declined the offer.

"Did Miss Chase seem agitated?" Cummings asked.

Debra shook her head and took a sip.

"Did she mention being threatened by anyone?"

"No. But that doesn't mean she *wasn't* being threatened. In our line of work, that's not uncommon."

"Our line of work, too." Cummings's smile deepened his jowls. "What about Miss Chase's personal relationships? Can you tell us anything that could help in our investigation?"

"No. As I said, we weren't really friends. Do you have any idea who killed her, Detective Cummings?"

"We're pursuing several possibilities."

From Debra's experience, that was a euphemism for "no."

"What did you and Ms. Chase discuss on Thursday?" Wraith asked.

She could tell from his too casual tone that he knew the

answer—from the *Times* reporter, no doubt—and regretted not having phoned the police over the weekend. In a matter-of-fact voice she said, "I'd applied for a position at several firms. Madeleine's turned me down, and I wanted to know if she knew why."

"Did she?"

He was watching her carefully, and she could tell he knew the answer to this question, too. "She told me she advised the firm not to hire me. My firm doesn't know I'm planning to leave, by the way. I'd appreciate your not letting that get out."

Wraith nodded. "Some friend. You must've been pretty angry, huh? I would be."

His smile was meant to be disarming. "Yes, I was." She took refuge in another sip of chocolate.

"You argued?"

"I expressed my opinion of her action. She expressed hers. I don't see how this is relevant to your investigation," she said, allowing her irritation to show.

"We're trying to establish a complete background on Miss Chase," Cummings said. "We want to get a picture of her activities and state of mind that day. We appreciate your cooperation."

"I'm happy to cooperate, but I have no knowledge of Madeleine's activities that day or her state of mind. Has the coroner established a time of death?" She much preferred asking questions, she decided, to answering them.

"Judging from the stomach contents and other factors, between seven P.M. and ten P.M. Thursday," Cummings said. "Miss Chase left her office at six-thirty. Her boyfriend called her at ten. She didn't answer, so he assumed she'd gone out. He called again several hours later. When she still didn't answer, he drove over and had the manager unlock Miss Chase's door."

"I tried phoning Madeleine after eight o'clock that same evening, Detective. Her line was busy for over an hour."

Cummings nodded. "That helps pin down the time." He noted the information. "Do you remember when you first tried calling?"

"No. Sorry."

She tensed and, holding her breath, waited for Wraith to ask why she'd phoned Madeleine, but he didn't. Debra didn't tell him; nor did she tell him she'd stood outside the condominium building at ten-thirty that night. She felt guilty but worried that, given her confrontation with Madeleine, they'd suspect her motive for wanting to see her.

And according to the detectives, Madeleine had been dead by ten, half an hour before Debra had arrived. She hadn't seen anyone or anything suspicious.

"Thanks for your assistance, Miss Laslow." Cummings stood and handed her his card. "If you think of anything else that could be relevant, please give me a call."

"Of course." She placed the card in the desk's center drawer.

The detectives left. She felt more shaken than she cared to admit and needed a friendly ear. Charles, she knew, was with a client. She phoned Susan's office and learned that Susan was in court. And Judge Claire Werner, her close friend and mentor, was still on vacation.

Debra had hung up the phone and was standing at the filing cabinet when Richard entered her office a minute later.

"What's with the cops, Debra? Everything okay?"

She wondered if he'd eavesdropped. "Fine, thanks. They wanted to know if I knew anything about Madeleine Chase."

"Right. You said you went to law school with her." He rested his hand on her shoulder. "This must be tough on you." His thumb massaged her neck.

"I'm okay." She shut the file drawer, casually moved her shoulder out from under his hand, and walked around her desk.

He followed her, positioning himself on a corner of the desk, lifted her mug and took a sip. "Cold." He grimaced. "I'd cut down on the chocolate, Debra. You don't want to ruin that body." He smiled.

"Cut it out, Richard." This was not the first time he'd commented on her body; each time she'd voiced her displeasure and changed the subject. She turned her head to the computer screen. "Would you excuse me, please? Timothy Lassiter's coming at eleven and I have notes to prepare for my motion tomorrow."

She'd instructed her client to bring his courtroom wardrobe for her approval, and they were going to review his testimony. She was also going to try again to dissuade him from taking the stand. He had a cockiness—part fear, part affluence—that could alienate the judge in the pretrial motion to dismiss. It would certainly alienate the jurors if the case went to trial.

"Ten to one the old man comes with him," Richard said. "Good thing Lassiter wasn't here earlier. I don't think he would've appreciated seeing his son's attorney being questioned by the police, do you?" He picked up a folder from her desk.

"It's not as if they brought handcuffs." She took the folder, angered by his presumption and anxious about the folder—it contained another copy of her résumé and a cover letter to one more firm she'd considered over the weekend. "I thought you had appointments all day."

"I do. I wanted to make sure you were okay. And I'd like to hear your arguments for the motion. My last appointment's at five. I'll be done by six-thirty. We can have dinner, review the key points. Pick a nice kosher restaurant." He smiled.

She'd had a "business" dinner with Richard a month after joining the firm. The dinner had been mild on business, heavy on the details of his two-year-old divorce, sexual innuendo, and touching—her arm, her waist, her knee. "Thanks, Richard. Dinner isn't necessary, but if you want, I'd be happy to do it here."

"*Do* it?" He smiled knowingly.

She pretended not to understand his meaning. "Go over the motion." Madeleine, she knew, wouldn't have tolerated his behavior. Neither would Susan.

"I don't know about you, but I think better on a full stomach. And we may have to work late into the night."

Debra shook her head. "Thanks, but I don't think so."

"Why not?"

"I don't want to complicate our working relationship."

"Hell, Debra, I'm offering dinner and my expert advice. I'm not asking you to compromise your virtue." He leaned toward her. "Yet." He grinned and pulled back.

"I don't think it's a good idea."

"I think it's a *great* idea."

"I'm sorry, Richard."

"I'm too much of a goy for you, is that it? Not kosher enough?" He sighed. "You know, Debra, you'll never get ahead in this firm—or any firm, for that matter—if you're not part of the team." He slid off the desk. "That's expert advice, too, Debra. It's free. I suggest you take it."

She didn't answer.

He walked to the door. When he turned, his eyes and mouth were hard, unsmiling. "I'm the one who told Jeremy and Anthony you're ready for this trial, Debra. I'm the one who convinced Lassiter you'd get little Timmy off. For your sake, I hope I didn't make a mistake."

Chapter Six

The kosher dairy restaurant on Pico was filled with familiar faces. Debra exchanged hellos with friends of her father and smiled as she greeted Sharon and Felice, two women she'd known from childhood, and their respective husbands, Mark and Myron. The M and M's, Aaron called them.

"You look great," Sharon said after Debra had admired pictures of both women's children. "New hairstyle?"

"Not really." It was the style she'd worn for years—shoulder length, brushed back from her face, no bangs. *Don't hide your pretty face*, her mother and father had said. She was conscious of the fact that her hemline, at just above the knee, was an inch or two shorter than strict modesty permitted.

"So how's private practice?" Felice asked.

"I love it," Debra lied.

After trying unsuccessfully to dissuade Timothy Lassiter from testifying, she'd spent several hours preparing him for his testimony. She couldn't decide who was more annoying:

Timothy's controlling, patronizing father or Timothy, with his bratty cockiness.

("Let's get on with this crap," he'd told her when she'd suggested that for his court appearance he unpunk his bleached blond hair, wear a conservative suit and tie, and remove his four earrings—a gold dagger, a crescent, an anvil, and a diamond stud. Then he'd said, "Hey, Debra, I heard a lawyer got herself killed last week. Maybe it's 'cause she didn't get her client off. Could start a trend." He'd grinned and his father had said, "Oh, for God's sake!" and Debra, feeling a surge of fear tinged with sadness for Madeleine, had asked, "Is that a threat, Timothy?" and stared at him until he muttered a nervous apology.)

Myron shook his head. "I'll never understand why any lawyer would go into criminal defense. I mean, how can you defend someone you know is guilty?"

It was clients like Timothy who sometimes made Debra wonder the same thing. "Someone has to protect the rights of the individual," she said. She smiled and hoped she didn't sound annoyed—she'd been asked that question countless times—at shul, at dinner parties, on dates. "And they're not all guilty."

"Yeah, sure," from Mark.

"But what if they *are* guilty?" Myron asked.

"They're still entitled to have their rights protected."

In her junior year at Barnard, while studying for the LSATs, eager to champion the innocent, Debra had been troubled about defending clients who might be guilty. She'd understood what she'd read: "that the way we find truth and protect the innocent in an adversary system of justice is by putting the government to work." Still, she'd had doubts. And she'd worried that defending someone guilty would conflict with Jewish law. On her first night home during semester break, she went to her father for advice.

He was in his usual spot—a worn, crushed green velvet

seat at their fruitwood dining room table, surrounded by mountains of books that camouflaged the scratches in the dulled veneer.

"In the Judaic system there are no defense attorneys, Debra, no prosecutors," he said in answer to her question. "The burden lies on eyewitnesses—a minimum of two—to present convincing testimony to the judges that the accused committed the crime."

Debra nodded. "Who questions the witnesses?"

"The judges. And they can do so aggressively." From one of the bookcases that lined the room, he removed a gilt-edged, oversize volume of the Talmud. He thumbed through the text until he found the page he wanted, then sat down and positioned the book on the table between himself and Debra. "You read," he said.

Most Orthodox girls didn't study the Talmud in high school, but Debra had cajoled until her father, who refused her little, had agreed. For four years she'd sat with him and untangled a few of the many intricately entwined skeins of Talmudic discourse and arguments that gave both of them hours of pleasure and provided her with an incomparable preparation for her law studies.

Her Aramaic was rusty, the passage unfamiliar. She read slowly, stumbling at first, then found her rhythm. Her father, who knew vast amounts of the Bible and the Talmud by heart, interrupted gently several times without looking at the text to make corrections.

"Very nice," he said when she'd completed the section. "Now tell me what you learned."

She was his pupil now, not his daughter. "In a discussion about capital punishment, the great sages of the Great Court during the Holy Temple era related that the court was called a 'killing court' if it executed one person in seventy years." She'd heard this before and found it fascinating. "Rabbi Akiva and Rabbi Tarfon exclaimed that were they part of

the Great Court, no one would ever be convicted of a capital crime because they would so thoroughly investigate and
question the witnesses that they would become completely
confused about their testimony." This second part was new
to her and opened the door to ethical possibilities.

"Excellent, Debra." Ephraim Laslow smiled his pride.

Debra smiled, too. "That's the credo of criminal defense
lawyers, you know. Witnesses are fair game, even if they're
telling the truth. Does this apply only to capital crimes?"

"Maimonides applied this to cases where the penalty in-
volves corporal punishment. Of course, the rabbis were discussing judges, not attorneys, so this doesn't help you." He
shut the tractate.

Debra chewed on her bottom lip as she thought. "In the
Judaic system, judges are officers of the court. In the American system, *attorneys* are officers of the court. So couldn't
one argue that attorneys can question the witnesses thoroughly? And that as an officer of the court, I can try to in-
validate witnesses' testimony in the best interests of my
client?"

"You're stretching, Debra." Her father shook his head, but
he was smiling, just as he'd smiled so many times before
when she'd untangled one complex thread. Then he held
up a finger, and his expression was serious. "With one stip-
ulation. 'Righteousness, righteousness shall you pursue.'
Judges—officers of the court, Debra—must pursue righteousness only *through* righteousness. The end cannot justify the means."

Not the carte blanche she'd hoped for—and not the tenet
espoused by defense attorneys who felt it was their duty to
obfuscate the truth within the rules of evidence. But it was
enough to overcome her qualms. Any lingering reservations
dwindled in law school, where she learned to distrust the
system and the police, most of whom she then saw as
brutes, and while clerking for a judge, when she dealt with

Fourth Amendment cases that hinged on civil rights viola-
tions by law enforcement agents. "Due process" became her
badge of honor. She was an idealist, determined to protect
the downtrodden, the individual.

Three years in the public defender's office exposed her
primarily to individuals who were habitual criminals, individuals who, for the most part, weren't downtrodden but
trod on others. She was disenchanted. The police were no
longer all brutes. Her idealism dimmed; her badge of honor
was tarnished. When she was offered a position at Knox
and Cantrell, she grabbed the opportunity to escape the
morass of human misery and deal with what she'd hoped
would be a better class of defendant and a cleaner class of
crime—white-collar crime where corporations, not individuals, were the victims and no one really got hurt.

And, yes, she'd admitted to herself and to her brother,
Aaron, when he'd prodded, she'd been tempted by the significant increase in salary. What was wrong with that?

So here she was. But instead of dealing with tax evasion
or embezzlement or securities fraud, she was defending
Timothy Lassiter. Not someone she'd want to have dinner
with, but someone whose rights she believed had been violated.

Debra engaged in small talk with the two couples, declined their offer to join them, and after exchanging
promises to get together soon, followed the waitress to her
table. She was fond of both women and felt a tug of wist-
fulness for the intimacy the three of them had shared.
They'd attended the same schools. They'd compared grades
and bra sizes, exchanged clothes and confidences. Debra
had been their bridesmaid, and they'd paid condolence calls
while she sat shiva for seven days with her family to mourn
her mother's death from breast cancer. Six months later
they'd consoled her when she broke off her engagement to
Barry. (She'd been on the rebound when she'd rushed into

the relationship, desperate to fill the void and dull the pain her mother's death had left; luckily, she'd realized before the invitations were printed that she didn't want to spend her life with him.)

Gradually the three women had drifted apart, and Debra had formed new friendships, mostly with single women. Sometimes she felt isolated in what was essentially a family-oriented community; sometimes she sensed that Sharon and Felice questioned her having chosen a career over marriage and family. They still invited her for dinners and called her to fill in for a fourth at their weekly tennis game and set her up on dates, but they'd told Aunt Edith that Debra was "too picky."

Debra loved the practice of law (if not her present job), but she hadn't chosen career over marriage and a family—she hoped one day soon to have both. And she wasn't "too picky."

She ordered angelhair pasta, then scribbled on a pad while she waited for her meal.

"Debra Laslow, right?"

Looking up, she saw a tall, attractive man in his thirties with straight brown hair and hazel eyes. He was wearing wire-framed glasses. And a black suede skullcap. "Do I know you?"

"Jeff Silver. You don't remember me, huh? Not great for the ego." He smiled. "We met half a year ago at a weekend event."

Debra smiled back. "Ojai or Palm Springs?" She didn't enjoy singles' weekends—she felt like a piece of meat on display—but attended them to prove to her aunt Edith and the rest of her well-meaning family that she was trying. And because you never knew.

Another smile. "The Westin Plaza in Costa Mesa. A seminar for attorneys on legal ethics. Okay if I sit down?"

She nodded and waited until he was seated. "What firm are you with?"

"No firm. I quit three years ago and took up writing."

"Am I talking to the next John Grisham?" She took a sip of water.

"Not unless he's switched to nonfiction. I'm researching a book on the legal system. Plus I teach at a local law school to pay the bills. What kind of law do you practice?"

"You don't remember everything about me?" she teased.

"I remembered your name. I remembered that you were intelligent and very pretty. I intended to phone you."

"Why didn't you?" She was enjoying the flirting and saw from the corner of her eye that Sharon and Felice were watching. She pictured the headlines in the next shul bulletin: DEBRA LASLOW MEETS MAN. STAY TUNED.

"I lost my nerve. So now I have a second chance." He smiled again. "Are you busy tomorrow night?"

"I don't know anything about you."

"Thirty-six years old. Born and raised in Chicago. B.A. from Michigan. Law degree from Northwestern. Moved to L.A. three years ago. Parents are happily married. Two sisters, both married. No nieces or nephews yet." He smiled. "So how about tomorrow night?"

"I'm presenting a motion to dismiss in the morning. If I win, I treat my friend Susan to dinner. If I lose, she's treating me."

"Wednesday, then? Thursday? Name the day."

He was good-looking and charming; Ted Bundy, the notorious serial killer, had been, too. "What shul do you go to?"

He raised an eyebrow. "You want to check me out, huh? I don't blame you." He mentioned an Orthodox synagogue in West Los Angeles. "No skeletons in my closets. For that matter, not many closets. I live in a one-bedroom apartment half a mile from shul."

What the heck, she thought. She wrote her phone number on the back of her business card and handed him the card.

He turned it over. "Knox and Cantrell. Criminal defense, right? So are you as good as Leslie Abramson?"

"Absolutely." She smiled. "I just haven't had a high-profile celebrity case to get my name in the papers. Yet."

"You're probably better off. That attorney who was killed last week, Madeleine Chase?" When Debra nodded, he said, "Her name was in the paper all the time. Maybe being well-known isn't always such a good idea."

"Maybe," she said quietly.

"Hey, I didn't mean to put a damper on things." He shook his head. "I finally get up the nerve to ask you out, and I talk about murder. Real smart."

She smiled. "It's okay."

The waitress arrived with Debra's pasta.

"I'd better get back to my carrot cake before the cream cheese frosting molds." Jeff pushed back his chair and stood. "I hope you win your motion. I'll phone you tomorrow night."

Her aunt Edith would *kvell*.

Chapter Seven

"I know the rabbi of that shul," Aaron said. "Jeff Silver, huh? Let me make some calls."

"Aaron Laslow, private investigator." Debra smiled. She loved her brother and was generally amused and touched by his protectiveness. "It has a certain ring to it."

They were in the den. Aaron was at his desk, his elbows resting on a stack of history papers he was grading. Julia was on the brown leather sofa next to Debra, her legs curled under her, working on a needlepoint canvas that would serve as the front panel of a bag for Aaron's prayer shawl. The cinnamony aroma of freshly baked apple pie wafted into the room from the kitchen.

"So what's he like?" Julia asked.

"Tall. Nice looking. Good sense of humor." Debra picked up a handful of peanuts from the bowl on the teakwood coffee table. "Ten to one he's got a wife and six kids stashed away somewhere."

She cast a quick, anxious look at her sister-in-law to see if the reference to children had troubled her, but Julia was smiling. Four months ago her gynecologist had scraped her uterine lining clean of scar tissue. "I can't promise anything," he'd cautioned. Maybe this month, Debra thought, there would be good news.

"Excited about your prelim tomorrow?" Aaron asked.

"Definitely. And nervous." She always was. After winning her first trial, she'd been assaulted by the visual aura that always preceded her tension-caused, pounding migraines; when the judge had polled the jury, Debra had seen flashing neon zigzag lines in front of the faces of the nine men and three women who had handed her a victory.

"You'll win." Julia threaded a crimson skein.

"I'd better. If I lose, Richard will probably use it as an excuse to fire me." She hesitated, then described the morning confrontation. "Don't tell Dad, okay?"

"What a slime!" Julia's eyes flashed her anger. "You could sue him, Deb. You could sue the firm, too. A legal secretary won seven million dollars 'cause she'd complained that one of the partners was sexually harassing her and they didn't do anything."

"Kind of excessive, don't you think?" Aaron wrote a comment on one of the papers with his red felt-tip pen.

"An appeals court trimmed off a few million," Debra said.

"Still not a bad settlement. I'll bet she's thrilled."

"She deserved it!" Julia put down her needle. "The jury obviously wanted to send a strong message. Are you saying sexual harassment isn't a serious offense?"

"Of course not. But four or five mil?" He leaned forward. "Did you tell Richard you found his comments offensive, Deb? Maybe to him it's just office repartee."

"No, I didn't tell him. But he knows I don't like it. He enjoys making me uncomfortable."

"My advice? Be more direct. Say, 'Richard, I don't want you making sexual innuendos. I don't want you touching me or referring to my body.'"

"I *want* to be direct! But I'm afraid he'll have me fired. That's what he's implied. So much for being a strong, independent woman." She sighed. "I've been doing pro bono work with Susan for a group that helps victims of rape and spousal abuse. It's kind of funny, isn't it—me telling women to empower themselves?" Lately she was as annoyed with herself as she was with Richard.

"Don't be so hard on yourself," Julia said.

"So preempt Dressner," Aaron said. "Talk to the partner who hired you. You told me he likes you."

"Charles warned me not to. He said Jeremy can hear no bad about Richard. Richard is the son he never had." She shrugged and scooped up another handful of peanuts.

"So what does Charles suggest?" Julia asked.

"That I kick Richard in the balls." The thought was tempting.

"Debra!" Julia shook her head and laughed. Debra laughed, too.

"Nice words from a rabbi's daughter," Aaron said.

"You asked." Sometimes she resented being a rabbi's daughter, having everything about her held up to public scrutiny—what she wore, what she did, what she said. In her adolescence her resentment had blossomed into mild rebellion—missing Saturday morning services; wearing excessive makeup and too short hems and sleeves; necking at R-rated movies with a senior from an all boys' Jewish high school. Wisely, her parents hadn't overreacted. "Anyway, your language isn't always so pure, Aaron." She smiled.

"I learned from my younger sister." He smiled, too, then stroked his chin. "So you can't go to Knox. But you *can* threaten Richard. Tell him you'll go public with your accusations."

"Me and Anita Hill. I'm the only woman attorney at the firm. It'll be my word against his. He'll blackball me, and no other decent firm will hire me."

"What about the secretaries? Maybe he's harassed them, too."

In addition to Glynnis and Barbara, whom Debra shared with Richard and Charles, there were Harriet, Anthony's secretary, and Rosemary, Jeremy's secretary. "I suppose I could check it out."

"What about Glynnis?" Julia asked. "She knows everything that goes on. Why not ask her?"

Debra groaned. "Glynnis *adores* Richard. She bakes him cookies. She takes his clothes to the cleaners. She'd lie down and let him drive his BMW over her if he asked." She smiled at the thought, then shook her head. "I'll wait it out till I get an offer from another firm. With any luck, that should be soon." She pushed away the bowl of peanuts. "Don't let me eat any more of these."

"Too bad one of your detective contacts can't come in and question him," Julia said. "Shake him up a bit."

"Too bad," she agreed. "Speaking of detectives, I was questioned today about Madeleine. It wasn't much fun. They'd obviously learned that she and I quarreled on Thursday." She explained what had happened.

"She really *was* a witch," Aaron said. "But why do you sound so nervous? You're not the only one who fought with the woman."

"No, but I'm probably the only one who drove to her condo the night she was murdered. I went there to apologize."

"That's just like you." Julia smiled and put her hand on Debra's. "I'm sure the detectives understood."

Debra hesitated. "I didn't tell them I was there. I decided they'd think it was suspicious after my fight with Madeleine."

Aaron frowned. "Debra, do you realize—"

"I know, I know. You don't have to tell me I was stupid."

"Call them now," Julia urged.

"And tell them I forgot?" She stood and picked up her purse. "Hey, I'm not really worried," she said, seeing the concern on Aaron's and Julia's faces; she regretted having told them. "I just hope the police find the killer and put him away."

In the kitchen she waited while Julia wrapped a generous portion of warm apple pie.

"Maybe if I eat the whole cake and get fat, Richard will stop lusting after me. What do you think?" Debra puffed out her cheeks, then grinned and kissed Julia's cheek.

Aaron walked her to her car and put his arm around her when she shivered at the cold. "By the way, Deb, I asked around and found a contractor to retrofit your house. Adam Bergman. He's calling you this week."

"That's great." She'd been meaning to call someone for months, since the earthquake. She opened the car door, placed the aluminum foil–wrapped cake and purse on the seat, and got in.

"And here I was nervous you'd say you didn't need your older brother handling your life." His sigh of relief was exaggerated.

"Sometimes I do. Sometimes I don't." She smiled impishly. "Thanks for finding the contractor, Aaron, and for listening to my woes." She fastened her seat belt and harness. "Don't tell Dad about the police questioning me, okay?"

"Or about Richard. Anything else I shouldn't tell him?" he asked, his voice serious again.

"That's it for now. I'll let you know when they arrest me. Lighten up," she said when he frowned. "This is no big deal."

"You're the expert on the law."

She read the worry in his eyes as he kissed her cheek before he closed her door.

* * *

The phone was ringing when she entered her service porch. She hurried to the kitchen, picked up the receiver, and tensed when she heard Richard's voice. Was he calling to take the Lassiter case away from her? To fire her?

"I'm sorry about the way we left things," he said. "I overreacted, and I don't want you brooding. You should be concentrating on Lassiter."

This was a switch. "I appreciate your calling, Richard."

"I have every confidence in you, Debra. You have a promising future with the firm."

"That's nice of you to say." She felt a twinge of discomfort, knowing she intended to make her future elsewhere. Had Richard taken a "pleasant" pill? Or was he nervous that she'd complain to Jeremy or Anthony? "Well, thanks again, Richard."

"Any points you want to go over? I have the time."

"No, thanks. I've got it nailed. I plan to go to bed early and get a solid night's sleep."

"Good idea. My ex always said satin nightgowns made her sleep better. I picture you in ivory. Or in black. Am I right?"

Once a sleaze, always a sleaze. "Gray sweats. Good night, Richard."

"What a waste! Can't you let a guy fantasize?" He laughed. "Get that sleep and go for blood in the morning."

She grimaced. It was an innocuous phrase, one she often used. Now it made her think of Madeleine.

Chapter Eight

"The Superior Court of Santa Monica is in session. The Honorable Judge Harrison Fogel presiding. You may remain seated."

Sitting at the defense table, Debra kept her eyes on Fogel, trying to read something from the white-haired jurist's body language as he climbed the steps and took his seat. He slapped a tall stack of folders onto his desk and opened the top one.

"Ms. Laslow!" Fogel barked.

"Your Honor." Debra reminded herself that Fogel was hard of hearing and prone to shouting, but her heart was pounding. She stood and motioned to Timothy Lassiter to do the same. He jumped to his feet as though she'd used an electric prod.

"Ms. Laslow, I've used the recess to consider your arguments and those of the district attorney. I've reviewed the authorities and the testimony of the police who searched your client's apartment." He adjusted his bifocals and glared at Timothy.

It's not good, Debra thought, steeling herself for disappointment. She reminded herself that this was just a motion. A jury trial was totally different. She was great with juries.

"I don't approve of drugs, Mr. Lassiter," Fogel said. "Drugs, in case you haven't been watching any television ads, young man, fry your brains. Did you know that?"

"Yes, sir." His voice quaked.

This was not the Timothy who had slouched and smirked in her office yesterday. He was clean shaved. His hair was neatly trimmed and several shades darker. No earrings. No smile. No attitude.

"But you don't believe it, do you?" The judge turned to Debra. "Your client doesn't deny possession of an illegal substance. He doesn't claim someone else put it there without his knowledge. Yet you want the Court to dismiss this case because you say the police had no right to open your client's kitchen cabinets and look for drugs, even though they had a pretty good idea they'd find some." He paused. "Which, in fact, they did."

Out of the corner of her eye, Debra saw that Timothy had paled and seemed on the verge of tears.

The judge leaned forward. "I wish I could deny your motion, Ms. Laslow. But I can't, and that irks the hell out of me."

Elation coursed through her. She bit the inside of her cheek to repress a smile and nodded solemnly.

"The Court finds that the police conducted a warrantless search. There was no consent to search. There was no illegal substance in plain view. The officers cited exigent circumstances, but the Court doesn't find that any existed. And the Court agrees with you, Ms. Laslow, that if Officer Hickman smelled pot on the individual who opened the door to let him in, he should have arranged for a deputy to maintain the scene and obtained a warrant before he began his search."

The judge stared at Timothy. "Mr. Lassiter, you're luckier than you deserve. If you appear in my courtroom again for possession, I'll make sure you get the maximum penalty. Case dismissed." He pounded the gavel.

While Fogel called the next case, Debra collected her papers, put them in her briefcase, then escorted Timothy to the spectator's gallery, where his father was standing.

"You did it, Debra! You're the best!" Timothy hugged her.

"I second my son's review." Lassiter shook her hand.

"Thank you." She faced Timothy. "I hope you'll follow Judge Fogel's advice."

He expelled a breath. "Are you kidding? I've learned my lesson. I'm staying clean."

"I'm glad to hear it." Though he sounded sincere, experience told her his newfound conviction, prompted by fear, might not last. But, she was his attorney, not his parent or his counselor.

Outside the courtroom Debra walked down the long corridor to a bank of pay phones. She called the office and asked Glynnis to inform Jeremy and Richard that she'd won her motion. She called Julia at work. She left a message on her father's answering machine—he was in the synagogue, leading his daily Talmud study group. Then she phoned Susan.

"Fogel rarely grants a motion!" Susan exclaimed. "Way to go, girl! So how do you feel?"

"Pretty damn good." Debra smiled. "Admit it. You're excited because you're getting a free dinner."

"How'd you guess?" Susan laughed. "I'm meeting with a client till six. Pick me up at seven, okay? And prepare to refinance your home—I love kosher food."

Still smiling at the image of Susan gorging herself—she was tiny and ate like a bird—Debra hung up and continued down the hall to Department M. Looking through the door's window, she saw that the courtroom was empty. She tried the knob; the door opened, and she entered.

The brown-haired clerk at the end of the room looked up

from his computer screen and smiled. "Hey, Ms. Laslow. How's it going?"

"Pretty good, Brian. Is Judge Werner in her chambers?"

He nodded. "Taking a break. She needs it—first day back from vacation and she's had a hell of a morning." He picked up his receiver, spoke into it, then said, "Go on in, Ms. Laslow."

Debra exited the courtroom through a door behind the clerk's desk and entered a short hall. She knocked on the door to her right, opened it, and stepped inside. Claire was standing in the middle of the room, her long legs slightly apart, exercising while holding small weights in both hands. She was wearing black shorts, a gray tank top, and a red sweat band across her high forehead and her helmet of glossy black hair.

"Preparing to arm wrestle the bailiff?" Debra asked.

She reversed the direction of her arm rotations. "Building up bone mass. And letting off steam." Her face was flushed; her forehead glistened with perspiration. Her topaz blue eyes were intense in their concentration.

"Why are you steamed?"

"Tell you when I'm done." She swung her hands high above her head, brought them to her sides, then walked to a cabinet, where she stored the weights. "I'm going to put on something more befitting a woman of my stature." She smiled and stepped into a small bathroom.

While Claire changed, Debra looked around the room. She loved coming here, scanning the hundreds of volumes of jurisprudence that occupied the floor-to-ceiling, built-in bookcases, volumes with so many fascinating facts, so much knowledge, so much wisdom. There were diplomas and certificates on the walls and a massive calendar filled with Claire's neat handwriting in red ink.

Debra was contemplating following in Claire's footsteps and donning the black robe that vested her with so much authority and responsibility. She'd mentioned her plans to Claire, who had offered encouragement but had added a warning.

"Being a judge can be rewarding, Debra. It can also be terribly frustrating. Sometimes you know that though the law is being upheld, justice has been denied. Sometimes you lie awake all night, plagued by doubts—are you making the right decision? Are you about to ruin a life, break up a family?"

"How do you deal with that?" Debra had asked.

"I pray for guidance. I'm not a churchgoer, but I tell myself that if I've allowed one of the bad guys to slip through the cracks, or if the system has, God will even the scales."

"And that reasoning helps you?"

Claire had smiled. "Sometimes. Other times I take a stiff drink and tell myself I'll take over for Judge Wapner on the *People's Court.* More pay, less stress."

Debra had met Claire three years ago. She'd tried several cases in her courtroom and had always been impressed by her fairness and quiet authority. Claire had made the first overture outside the courtroom; Debra had been flattered and pleased. The friendship had blossomed.

The two women had much in common: They both loved the law. They were both single—Claire was divorced with no children—and commiserated over the difficulty of meeting intelligent, eligible men. They both had widowed fathers and had lost loved ones to cancer; Claire's sister, Lee, had died six years ago at twenty-four. Lee's death, she'd told Debra, had destroyed her father, already mourning his wife, and added stress to her own troubled marriage. A year later Claire had moved back to Los Angeles from San Francisco. Debra was aware that she was drawn to Claire as a replacement for her mother, just as Claire probably saw Debra as a substitute for her sister.

Claire's room, decorated in green and burgundy, was feminine, but not frilly. Other judges kept family photos in their chambers, but there were none on Claire's large walnut desk or on her ecru walls—she'd told Debra once that she found it imperative to keep her personal and professional lives separate.

"In these chambers, Debra, I can't be swayed by emotion. I can't function effectively when I'm reminded by a photo or other memorabilia that I'm someone's daughter, someone's sister, someone's friend, someone's lover. In these chambers I'm a judge."

The judge emerged from the bathroom wearing a black skirt, a peach blouse, and black suede flats. "How are you, Debra?"

"Fine. I suppose you heard about Madeleine Chase?"

"That's all everybody's talking about. It's horrible. Scary, too." Claire's eyes had clouded. "So what brings you to the courthouse today?"

"Fogel just granted my motion."

"Your motion?" Claire frowned, then shook her head. "I forgot it was today! Congratulations!" She hugged Debra. "Fogel's tougher than I am."

Debra smiled. "You don't look like someone who just had a week's vacation. So why are you steamed?"

"My first day back, and I had a confrontation with Nancy Argula. She's furious with a ruling I made yesterday. The jury found the defendant guilty of stealing a slice of pepperoni pizza from picnickers. He's had two priors—shoplifting and forging a check. Nancy bumped up the misdemeanor to a felony because it was his third offense—which is by the books. I gave him three to five. She's insisting on life."

Debra nodded. Three strikes you're out. Under California law, a third conviction for a felony, violent or nonviolent, mandated a life sentence. The law's intention was good—to rid the streets of violent criminals. In practice, it was clogging the courts with hundreds of cases that normally never went to trial, cases in which the accused pled guilty in exchange for a reduced sentence. Now third-time offenders feared plea bargaining unless they were guaranteed that the third offense would be lowered to a misdemeanor. Which didn't make law enforcement people happy. The law also often targeted offenders who posed no threat to society and added them to an already overcrowded prison population.

"What's Nancy's position?" Debra asked.

"That the defendant is a career criminal who will commit more crimes unless he's put away. She argued that he terrified the people from whom he stole the pizza." From a makeup bag in her desk drawer, Claire took out a lipstick and a blush.

"But does she honestly think that warrants life?"

"She does. Legally she's right. I don't feel good about what I'm doing. But how the hell can I sentence the man to life because he was hungry and helped himself to a slice of pizza?"

"You're right. It's ridiculous. What happens now?"

Claire applied lipstick and blush. "Nancy will appeal. She's also threatened to have me brought up on charges of judicial misconduct."

The idea of Claire being guilty of judicial misconduct was ludicrous. "Think she'll do it?"

"The public wants criminals put away." Claire walked to a coat tree in the corner of the room and removed her black robe. "So do I, but the punishment has to fit the crime. This law is preventing us from doing what we were appointed to do—use judicial discretion, mete out justice." She slipped her arms into the sleeves of the robe. "You'll probably be reading about me in the Metro section."

"My name may be next to yours. Two detectives questioned me yesterday about Madeleine."

"Really?" She pulled the robe's zipper up halfway. "Did they say they had any leads?"

"Just me." Debra told her about the courthouse confrontation.

Claire frowned, then said, "It's routine, Debra. Forget about it. Forget about Blackmeyer turning you down, too. You'll get a position at a better firm," she said, returning to her desk.

"I hope it's soon. Richard is making me miserable." She hesitated. "About Madeleine . . ." She wanted to tell Claire that she'd driven to Madeleine's on the night of the murder, that she'd kept the information from the police. But Claire was a stickler for the truth. Debra hadn't told Susan, either.

"You feel guilty because you said something unkind to her hours before she was killed." Claire put her hand on Debra's shoulder. "Don't. She was murdered. That's terrible, but it doesn't change the fact that she was nasty. God only knows how many people hated her. She's alienated just about every DA and judge I know. Including me."

"Hating is one thing, Claire. Killing is another."

"Madeleine pushed a lot of people close to the edge. I can't count all the witnesses she demolished on the stand. And she was manipulative. I heard she was sleeping with Jonathan Blackmeyer."

"You're kidding!" Blackmeyer was the senior partner in Madeleine's firm. Debra was surprised Glynnis hadn't heard.

"Blackmeyer's secretary told a law clerk who told Brian. Madeleine threatened to tell Blackmeyer's wife unless he made her partner. Brian also heard that Madeleine's boyfriend knew about the affair and was angry as hell. So you see, the police have more suspects than they can handle. They're not interested in you."

"That's comforting." Debra smiled. "And I suppose I have nothing to worry about even if they are. Rumor has it you're soft on crime, Your Honor. If they try me for murder, you'll let me off, right?"

"If I'm still a judge." Claire pulled the zipper the rest of the way up. "Strange, isn't it, how we're all more concerned about Madeleine now that she's dead than when she was alive?"

Chapter Nine

"Something I can help you with?" Debra asked, struggling to filter the anger from her voice as she entered her office.

Richard was in front of her desk, his back toward her. When he turned to face her, he was smiling and holding a cellophane-wrapped bouquet of long-stemmed red roses. "Congratulations," he said, stepping toward her and handing her the flowers. "Your first victory of many."

"These are beautiful, Richard." She was embarrassed by her false suspicion and disconcerted by his gesture. She didn't want to feel kindly toward him. Bending her head down to hide her blush, she sniffed the flowers' heady fragrance. "Thank you."

"Thank Arthur Lassiter. He sent them."

"This is so sweet of him." She smiled with genuine pleasure and read the note tucked inside the cellophane: "I'm in your debt, Ms. Laslow. Brava on your flawless performance." She slipped the note back into the cellophane and hoped Timothy wouldn't require an encore.

"Lassiter thinks you deserve a hothouse full of flowers. Apparently, you made mincemeat of the cop's testimony."

"Hickman's a rookie. He made mistakes when he arrived at Timothy's apartment. I got him to admit them on the stand." She'd felt a twinge of sympathy for the red-faced policeman, but sympathy hadn't deterred her from scoring points at his expense for her client. Neither had Hickman's increasingly stony glare.

"And you won. Which is why I'm giving you a new client. Lassiter recommended him and thinks you'd be perfect for him."

Talk about instant reward. Debra wondered whether the punishment for disappointing Arthur Lassiter would have been as swift. And what form it would have taken. "Who's the client?"

"Kenneth Avedon. Ask Glynnis to find a vase for the roses. Then come to my office and I'll tell you the details."

Richard's office was larger than Debra's, and though the western view from the ninth-floor room wasn't spectacular—the Century City towers blocked the ocean and everything leading to it—at least he *had* a view. His desk—a black granite slab on a travertine base—held a telephone, a Rolodex, a daily calendar, a leather box of personalized notepaper, and one folder centered on the black leather desk mat. His computer was on his credenza.

"I never have more than one folder on my desk," he'd told Debra on her second day at the firm. "I want the client to feel he has my undivided attention."

"Who's Kenneth Avedon?" Debra asked when she was seated in one of Richard's black leather armchairs. She was pleased by the vote of confidence and Lassiter's demonstration of gratitude, but she felt uncomfortable. What would happen to the client when Debra left the firm?

"A Beverly Hills internist. From a wealthy family, Lassiter said. Avedon phoned just before you returned. He has surgery today and tomorrow morning. He'd like to meet with you tomorrow afternoon."

"What's the charge?" Her pen was poised over her yellow pad.

"Raping his receptionist. Lassiter says the charge is ridiculous—he's known Avedon since he was a little boy."

Little boys—even those from wealthy families—sometimes grew up to be rapists. "I hate rape cases," she said quietly, crossing her legs.

"Who doesn't?" Richard grimaced and leaned back against his chair. "You won two when you were a public defender, right?" When Debra nodded, he smiled. "That's what I told Lassiter. The timing's perfect. Now that Junior isn't going to trial, your calendar's more or less free."

"I still have the briefs and motions for Donovan and White." Richard had promised her she could assist if the cases went to trial.

"Avedon comes first. If you need help, ask Charles."

"Has Avedon been arraigned?"

"He's had a prelim and been bound over for trial. Trial date's set for"— Richard opened his folder and moved his finger down a sheet of paper—"Tuesday, November fifth. Two weeks from today. It's tight, but most of the pretrial work's been done. He's out on fifty thousand bail."

"I'll file for a continuance. Did he fire his attorney? Or did the attorney drop him?" Either possibility was troubling. So was Avedon's having been bound over for trial—the district attorney obviously had a decent case. Many acquaintance rapes never went to trial because there was no corroborating evidence.

"He didn't fire her, and she didn't drop him. His attorney was Madeleine Chase. I know," Richard said, seeing the shock on Debra's face. "It spooked me, too."

All roads lead to Madeleine. Richard didn't look spooked; she sensed he'd enjoyed startling her. "Wouldn't it make more sense for Avedon to have someone else at Blackmeyer take over?"

"Exactly what I asked him. He said he'd retained Madeleine because he'd been advised that having a woman for defense counsel is a plus in a rape trial."

A woman attorney interacting with the male defendant made him appear less villainous to the jurors. So much of trial work was appearances. "There are no other women attorneys at the firm?"

"Apparently none with significant rape trial experience. And Avedon intimated he wasn't eager to stay with the firm, given the notoriety surrounding Madeleine's murder. Lassiter knew of his predicament and mentioned you."

"I don't know." Debra stared out the window.

"Kenneth Avedon is coming in to meet with you. If he likes you and the firm, he'll retain you to represent him." Richard's tone had taken on a sharp edge. "What don't you know?"

Debra didn't answer. What could she say? That she'd loathed every minute of the two rape trials she'd successfully litigated? That her professional gratification had been overshadowed by her gnawing worry that she might be responsible for winning freedom for men who belonged behind bars? That she'd hoped, by entering private practice, never to have to try another rape trial again?

"I thought you'd be pleased, Debra. You keep saying that you'd like more courtroom exposure. That's why I gave you Lassiter. That's why I'm giving you Avedon."

"You're giving me Avedon because I'm the only woman here."

"Absolutely." He nodded. "If we had a client charged with a hate crime against an African American, we'd probably put Charles on it. And if we represented a company accused of wrongfully terminating an older worker, Jeremy would be lead counsel. It's not sexism. It's not racism. It's not agism. It's effective strategy that no law firm can afford to ignore."

Most firms tried to match attorneys to clients. Her resistance was illogical. "Does Blackmeyer know Avedon is leaving?"

"I just spoke with him. He isn't happy, but what can he do? He'll give Avedon his file—by law he has to, of course. We'll have the police reports and the notes from the district attorney."

"What about Madeleine's notes?" Unlike all the official documents, which legally belonged to the client, the notes were "attorney work product" and belonged to the attorney and, by extension, to the firm.

"Blackmeyer hasn't decided, and I didn't want to push. My feeling is he'll take a few days, then release the notes. Avedon will be here tomorrow at two-thirty."

"I'll see if I'm free." She hadn't scheduled any appointments for that time, but she resented Richard's presumption.

"You are. I checked your calendar."

What else had he checked? She felt a surge of anger. "Did Avedon tell you what happened?"

"No. Just that he's innocent."

"Aren't they all?" She capped her pen and stood.

Richard leaned toward her, his elbows on the desk. "Whether or not he's innocent, Debra, you're bound to represent him as zealously as possible and see that his rights are protected."

"I don't need a law school lecture, Richard."

"I think you do." He reached for his phone. "Enjoy the roses while you can," he said, swiveling sideways in his chair. "Unfortunately, delicate things don't last long."

On the way back to her office, while stopping to accept congratulations from Charles and Jeremy, she wondered whether Richard had been insinuating anything. Probably not. Aaron often told her she was overly analytical and sensitive to the nuance of words. "Typical of a lawyer who majored in English," he'd say.

Glynnis was in Debra's office, arranging the flowers in a cut-crystal vase she'd placed on the credenza. Even with her three-inch platform shoes, the top of the vase was almost as tall as she was. She smiled when Debra entered, then adjusted a twig of baby's breath and stepped back to observe the effect. "How's that?"

"Perfect. You have a magic touch, Glynnis."

The woman dimpled with pleasure. "Thank you, dear. I put the roses in tepid water with an aspirin. They'll last twice as long. Enjoy." She left the office and pulled the door shut behind her.

Tell Richard, Debra thought. She shuffled through a stack of message slips on her desk and saw one from Susan. Debra phoned her office. "Standing me up?" she asked when Susan came on the line.

Susan laughed. "Not when I'm getting free eats. My meeting is a little later, so I should be back around seven-thirty. Can we go to dinner at eight?"

"No problem."

"Why do you sound glum? You should be high after your win."

"I was. Dressner just gave me another client. A rape case." She drew a rectangle on the pad in front of her.

"Shit." Susan sighed. "I just finished one of those, remember? I got my client off on mistaken identity. You know what? We just got back the DNA results today—my guy *didn't* do it. Talk about relief. So what's with your guy?"

"He's been charged with raping his receptionist."

" 'He said, she said,' huh? You've got a better shot at acquittal than you would with a stranger rape. What's his story?"

"I'll find out tomorrow. That's when he's coming in." She

paused. "Susan, did you give the senior partner my résumé? I'm getting desperate."

"Not yet. Mark hasn't told him he's leaving."

She felt a twinge of anxiety. "He hasn't changed his mind, has he?"

"No. Mark will probably tell him today. Stop worrying, okay?"

"Okay. Have you heard anything new about Madeleine's murder?"

"*Nada.* You?"

"According to Claire's clerk, Madeleine was having an affair with Blackmeyer and threatened to tell his wife unless he made her a partner."

"Not surprising. Madeleine was ambitious. and she *did* have a nasty tongue. Oh, God!" Susan whispered. "I can't believe I said that! Every time I think about what Glynnis told you, I get sick."

"Me, too."

After saying good-bye and hanging up the phone, Debra turned on her computer and pulled up the Lassiter file to write a summary of the disposition of the case while the details were sharp in her mind. The monitor was a stabbing, electric blue. She reached for the knob to adjust the brightness, then frowned. The screen had been fine when she'd used it last night before leaving the office.

Richard had been in her office, delivering the roses. Checking her calendar. Had he been snooping through her files? She touched the side of the monitor. It was cool. Then again, she'd been in Richard's office for a while.

She checked her desk drawers. Nothing seemed out of order. She told herself she was being paranoid. Someone from the cleaning crew must have moved the knob while dusting the office last night.

She adjusted the brightness and began to type.

Chapter Ten

Susan's black Ford Explorer was in her driveway, and both sides of the street were filled with cars. Debra double-parked in front of the house and honked. A minute later she honked again, waited, then, feeling a little annoyed, drove down Croft and turned the corner, where she found a parking space.

She walked to Susan's house and rang the bell. She waited, rang it again, and, giving in to a surge of impatience, twisted the doorknob. She wasn't surprised when the door opened. Susan had probably gone next door to borrow something. She was always borrowing something, she'd told Debra—flour, eggs, tissues, detergent. "My neighbors now consult with me before they go to the market," she'd said, and laughed with a hint of ruefulness. Debra hesitated, then stepped into the hexagonal entry hall and shut the door behind her.

"Susan?" Feeling very much the intruder, she listened for sounds of occupancy—the flush of a toilet, the hum of a blow dryer, the tapping of Susan's heels on the hardwood floor of the back hall from the bedroom to the living room.

"Come on, Susan!" she called, raising her voice to fill the vacuum of silence and still her sudden unease. "We'll be late."

An unearthly yelp pierced her ears.

A small terrier bounded from the living room and leaped at her. Debra blocked her face with her arms. The dog dropped to the floor and darted into the living room.

"Susan?" she whispered, dropping her arms to her sides. She was weighted with a dread so heavy that she felt as though her legs had been nailed to the ceramic-tiled floor.

She forced herself to enter the living room. The dog quivered in the far corner, yipping, slapping the air with its tail, its black eyes staring at the huddled figure in the center of the room Susan had just redecorated in all white—"So impractical, it'll show everything, but damn, I love it!"—now stained with blood.

There was so much blood.

Bile rose in Debra's throat. She gagged. She clamped her hand over her mouth and, her legs trembling, inched closer to the body. Maybe it wasn't Susan, she told herself. She whimpered when she saw the thin, elfin Tinkerbell body and layered light blond hair.

A small, neat hole with a singed, blackened circumference marred the back of Susan's ivory silk blouse; blood was seeping out of the hole, forming a trail of capillaries. Debra bent down and lifted Susan's hand. It was warm. She felt for a pulse, knowing she would find none.

She put down Susan's hand with a gentleness that made no sense. She didn't want to see her eyes—green eyes always animated, always laughing, eyes now dead, unseeing. As she stood up, she stole a glance at Susan's face. That was when she noticed the pool of angry blood near Susan's mouth and something lying in the pool, something . . .

Susan's tongue.

Debra moaned. She doubled over, clutching her stomach, and vomited. She started to shake and staggered several feet before she collapsed in front of the white marble fireplace and buried her face in thick nylon pile whose fibers smelled of new carpet.

She heard the intensifying wail of a siren. The police. Thank God! she thought, and wondered who had alerted them so quickly. She tried to stand; her arms and legs were like rubber. Grabbing on to the andirons for support, she pulled herself to her knees, then to her feet.

"Police!" a male voice bellowed. The door slammed open. "Don't move!"

"She's dead," Debra said, her voice almost inaudible. Her breath was ragged; her throat was raw from retching.

"Drop the weapon!" a woman warned.

What weapon? Debra looked at her hands and saw that she was holding the andirons. My God! she thought. They—

"Drop it now or I'll shoot!"

She let the andirons fall with a thud onto the carpet.

"Raise your hands slowly and place them at the back of your head."

Her arms were leaden, her hands trembling. She did as she'd been instructed.

"I'll check the other rooms," the male officer said. Debra heard him cross behind her and out of the living room. She moved her head a fraction of an inch toward the female officer; the cold metal of a gun barrel at her temple stopped her. The woman's approach had been so silent that Debra hadn't heard her.

"Look straight ahead," the woman ordered, and withdrew her gun.

Strong, unkind hands moved beneath Debra's jacket and jabbed under her arms and along her sides. The same hands slipped under her vomit-splattered cashmere sweater, between her legs under her new suede skirt, inside her new suede boots. Patting, poking, probing. Debra bit her lip.

"Turn around slowly. Keep your hands on your head."

She obeyed and faced the uniformed officer, a stern-looking, blond-haired woman not much taller than Debra.

Walking toward them was a medium-height, thin African American male. "No sign of anyone else," he said. "The back door was open."

He aimed his weapon at Debra's chest while his partner searched under the front of her sweater and patted her waistband and panties, wrinkling her nose in disgust at the stench of the vomit. Debra was outraged, humiliated, terrified. She told herself it was their job to be suspicious and closed her eyes and pretended that this wasn't happening to her, just as she'd often pretended, when the pain was too unbearable, that her mother wasn't dying.

"Sit on the couch," the woman officer commanded Debra, motioning to a sofa at the end of the room.

Debra walked, robotlike, to the white cotton brocade sofa and sat down. "She was dead when I—"

"Remove your right boot."

Debra pulled off her boot, noting mechanically that it was bloodstained. She handed it to the officer and glanced at the partner. He had slipped on booties and was walking toward Susan's body, careful to avoid stepping in the blood. He lifted Susan's wrist.

The woman checked inside the boot and set it aside. Debra removed the other boot. The woman examined it, then returned both boots to Debra. "She's clean," she called to her partner.

He was walking around the body, Debra saw as she put her boots on. Soon he would be leaning over Susan. Debra could have warned him, but they wouldn't let her talk, wouldn't let her explain. So let him see. Debra turned her attention to the woman, who had asked her something. "I'm sorry," Debra said. "I didn't hear you."

"What's your name?"

"Deb—"

"Aw, jeez!" he exclaimed. "Aw, shit! This is sick."

Debra felt a small thrill of revenge, which quickly gave way to nausea. She swallowed hard. Tears flooded her eyes.

"What?" the woman asked, turning toward him.

He didn't respond. She removed booties from her pockets, slipped them over her shoes, and walked across the room to her partner. Her face whitened. She muttered something, then turned to stare at Debra. Even from across the room, Debra sensed her recoil.

Debra could not, for one minute longer, allow them to believe that she had done this. "Officer—" she began.

"I'll radio for the medical examiner and the wagon and the techs," the man said, and left the room without looking at Debra.

"We'll wait till my partner gets back," the woman said, returning to the sofa. Her voice and light brown eyes were stony.

Debra waited. Several minutes passed before the male officer reappeared. During that time, she had stared at the Abstract gray-and-blue lithograph over the fireplace.

"They're on the way," he told his partner. He turned to Debra. "I'm Officer Hemming. This is Officer Jenkin. We'd like to ask you a few questions." When she nodded, he said, "What's your name?"

"Debra Laslow."

"Do you have identification, Ms. Laslow?"

"In my purse." Where *was* her purse? She looked around but didn't see it. She had no recollection of having dropped it. "My purse is missing," she said, and saw the officers exchange glances. "Look, I know this seems strange, but as soon as I find it, I can show you my driver's license and business card. I'm an attorney."

"Do you know the dead woman's name?" Hemming asked.

Debra had become so caught up in proving her identity that she'd forgotten for a moment that Susan was lying dead, mutilated, not more than ten feet away. "Her name is Susan Clemens," she said quietly. "She's an attorney, too. She's . . . she was my friend." She pressed her hand against her mouth to quiet her lips.

"Was she married?"

Debra shook her head. "Her parents live in Houston. Her father's name is William Clemens." Someone would have to tell them that their only child had been murdered.

"Is that your Ford Explorer or hers?" Hemming asked.

"Susan's. My car's at the end of the block."

"There are several spots right in front of the house. Why'd you park so far away?"

"There were no empty spots when I arrived." What was the point of these stupid questions?

"So what happened here, Ms. Laslow?" Jenkin asked. "You two have a fight that turned ugly?"

"There was no fight!" She stared at their impassive faces, angered and sickened by the accusation, but reminded herself that the police didn't know her. Calm, not indignation, would help her best. "Susan was dead when I got here. I tried telling you that."

"Where'd you get the scratches on your face and hands?" Hemming asked.

Debra frowned. "What scratches?" She touched her cheek and felt the welts. She looked at her hands and was surprised to see the thin red parallel lines.

"Did she attack you first?" Jenkin asked. "Is that what happened?"

"I told you, she was dead when I got here." The officers

hadn't moved, but she felt as though they were looming over her. In the past she'd sympathized with clients who had been intimidated by the police; for the first time she shared their fear.

"How'd you know she was dead?" Hemming asked.

"I checked for a pulse."

"How'd you get in?" Jenkin asked.

"The door was open. We were going out to dinner. She was expecting me." Debra hesitated. "When I was in the entry hall, I sensed something was wrong."

"What was wrong?" Hemming asked, his tone sharper.

"I don't know. It was just a feeling."

"Did you see anyone near the house when you arrived?"

"No."

"Did you hear any sounds that would indicate that someone other than the victim was in the house?"

"No."

"So why were you holding the andirons?" Jenkin asked.

"I used them to support myself. I vomited after seeing Susan's . . ." She couldn't finish the sentence. "I collapsed. About the . . . tongue," she began, wanting to tell them that Madeleine's tongue had been severed, too, that the murders were probably connected.

"Why'd she scratch you?"

Debra's head was beginning to throb. "She didn't scratch me. I don't under— The dog! Susan said she'd been feeding a stray terrier. It scratched me. That's when I knew something was wrong."

"You didn't mention a dog jumping you. A moment ago you said you weren't sure why you had that feeling."

"I'm upset. It's hard to think clearly. I didn't remember the dog."

"But now you remember the dog." Jenkin's voice and eyes telegraphed her skepticism.

"That's correct," Debra said calmly, knowing she could not indulge in irritation.

"So where's this dog?" Jenkin asked, looking around the room.

Debra looked around, too. Where *was* the dog? "She was terrified. She must be hiding in the back of the house."

"I'll check," Hemming said. He left the room.

"What time did you get here?" Jenkin asked.

"Five minutes to eight. That's when I told Susan I'd pick her up." She could only imagine how she looked—her face was scratched, probably bleeding, and blotched with tears and nasal discharge; her clothes were bloodied; her sweater reeked of vomit. No wonder the police were suspicious. "May I have a tissue, please?"

"Soon," Jenkin said, and it was clear from her tone that "soon" meant whenever she felt like it, that she didn't much care about Debra's needs. "Where were you going?"

Debra named the restaurant. "We had reservations."

The partner returned. "No dog. No dog food or bowl." He looked at Debra with interest. "No purse."

"I told you—she's a stray. She scratched me."

"Susan scratched you?" Jenkin asked.

"The dog scratched me," Debra said, refusing to get angry, because that's what this bitch wanted. She wanted to rattle Debra, to get her confused.

"She scratched you because you were attacking Susan?" the woman asked. "Is that what happened?"

If the situation weren't so frightening, it would be ludicrous. "The dog scratched me because she was terrified," Debra said with exaggerated patience. "She probably ran outside when she heard your sirens." She didn't know why she was talking. They weren't listening to her. They didn't believe her.

"Where's your purse?" the woman asked.

Debra closed her eyes briefly and took a deep breath. "I

don't have to answer your questions. I know my rights," she snapped, allowing herself to feel anger. Anger was infinitely better than fear. Anger kept her from crying about Susan.

"Oh, yeah. You're an attorney." Her eyes gleamed with amused disdain. "So you know we can take you in for questioning."

"Not unless you arrest me. At which point I will demand to be allowed to contact my attorney. And I still won't answer your questions." She didn't have an attorney. She quickly considered the possibilities and decided she would call Charles.

"You're not under arrest," Hemming said. "If you have nothing to hide, why won't you cooperate and answer our questions?"

Debra turned her head and stared again at the fireplace.

"Why would someone cut out her tongue?" Jenkin asked.

Chapter Eleven

They arrested and handcuffed her and made her wait in the black-and-white police vehicle until a medical examiner's van, a crime unit, and two more uniformed police arrived.

She sat in the backseat, trying to keep the brutal images from playing over and over in her mind. Every now and then the tears would start again. She had never received the promised tissue; she wiped her eyes and nose with the back of her hand and wondered what had happened to her purse.

Finally they drove her to Wilshire Division on Venice Boulevard, just east of La Brea. Debra had been here often during daytime visiting hours to talk with clients. Though she would have liked to have someone corroborate her identity, she was relieved when she recognized no one on the evening shift.

She asked to use the rest room. A matron accompanied her; she uncuffed Debra so that she could use the toilet and wash her ravaged face, then clamped the metal bracelets back on her wrists.

She told them she wanted to phone her lawyer. They told her "soon." She told them she was entitled to make three calls within three hours. They gave her a quarter for the pay phone. Charles's home phone number was in her missing purse, but she thought she knew it by heart. She punched the numbers but transposed the digits and reached a non-English-speaking Asian man who hung up on Debra.

She asked for another quarter, but when she called Charles's number, she heard a busy signal. They told her she could try again later. They put her in a holding cell; she thanked God it was empty and sat on a cot for over an hour until they came for her and led her to an interrogation cubicle, where she waited another half hour before the door opened and a detective entered.

He was in his early forties, she guessed, about five feet eight inches with a slight build. He had thick, curly black hair, brown eyes hooded by bushy eyebrows, a short, squat nose, and thin, chapped lips. He was wearing a camel sports coat, brown slacks slung low on his hips, and a white shirt with no tie. He was holding her brown Coach purse.

"Detective Marty Simms," he told her. He sat across from her and placed the purse in the center of the small narrow wood table. "I understand that you tried to reach your attorney and that his line was busy. You want to try again now?"

"Yes. Where did they find my purse?"

"Where do you think they found it?"

She sighed. "It's eleven o'clock, Detective. I'm extremely tired, and I'm not in the mood to play games. I want to go home."

"You're an attorney, I see." He was holding her business card. "Knox and Cantrell, criminal defense. Pretty good firm, huh?"

"I told the officers who arrested me that I was an attorney. They treated me like a criminal. By the way, how did they arrive so quickly?"

"A neighbor heard what sounded like a gunshot. She thought it could've been a truck backfiring, but she went next door. The lights were on, but no one answered the bell. Both cars were in the driveway. She thought it was strange. She phoned the police."

Debra nodded.

"Look at it from the officers' viewpoint, Ms. Laslow. You're in the house with a woman who's just been brutally murdered. You're holding a weapon. You're covered with scratches. You have no ID."

"The 'weapon' was andirons. I vomited and collapsed after finding my friend murdered. I used the andirons to help me get to my feet. I explained that to the officers."

"Andirons have been used to kill people." He tapped a pencil against the table. "We found your purse in a neighbor's hedges. Any idea how it got there?" He watched her closely.

"I'd like to try phoning my attorney again now."

"No problem." He pushed his chair back. "Let's go."

Charles's line was still busy. Debra almost cried with frustration.

"You can try again in a while," Simms said. "I'll have someone take you back to the holding cell."

She didn't want to return to the cell. She wanted to go home, to get out of her soiled clothes, to shower, to sleep. She wanted to wake up in the morning and find out that all this had been a nightmare, that Susan was still alive. "If I answer your questions, and you're satisfied, will you let me go home?" she asked, knowing she was doing something she would never allow a client to do.

He led her back to the cubicle and made her sign a statement that she had voluntarily and with full knowledge waived her rights. "So how do you think your purse ended up in the neighbor's hedge?" he asked after he turned on a tape recorder.

"Susan's terrier." Sitting in the holding cell, she'd had ample time to contemplate the possibilities.

Simms smiled. "A dog took your purse? Did it go shopping?"

"The dog jumped me when I entered the house. I followed her into the living room. That's when I saw Susan." She blinked back tears and cleared her throat. "The dog must have taken my purse when she left. I wouldn't have noticed anything, not then."

"We haven't found the dog." He pulled at his bottom lip.

"She's probably too scared to come back. She's a stray."

"The victim had skin tissue embedded under her nails. You told the officers this dog scratched your face and hands. But there's no dog."

She decided she didn't like Simms. "The dog was there. Your officers frisked me. They didn't find a gun or a knife. Detective, are you aware that—"

"Here's a possibility. Just hypothetical." He leaned forward. "You fight with the victim. She scratches you. You shoot her, then cut out her tongue to make it look kinky, like some psycho did it."

"But I don't have—"

He held up his hand. "You leave, then remember something you should've taken care of. You dump the gun and knife and drive back, making sure to park out of sight. You're in the house when you hear police sirens. You don't want them to check your purse—there could be blood in it. You run out to the backyard, stick the purse in the neighbor's hedges, run back in. End of story."

"She was dead when I got there."

"Not a bad story, though, is it?" He smiled.

"If you like fiction." She cleared her throat. "Detective,

last week another attorney, Madeleine Chase, was murdered. I'm surprised you didn't know."

"I've got a news flash for you, Ms. Laslow. People get murdered in this city every day. Some of them are attorneys." He shrugged. "There are eighteen LAPD divisions, and we don't spend our days gabbing with each other on the phone."

Debra swallowed, then said, "Madeleine Chase's tongue was severed, just like . . . just like Susan's."

Simms scowled. "Why the hell didn't you tell me that right away?"

"I tried. You kept interrupting. I also tried telling the officers who arrested me."

Simms tapped his pencil against the table again as he studied Debra. "Maybe there's a connection. Maybe not. Did Ms. Clemens mention having trouble with any of her clients?"

"No one specific that I can recall." She was relieved that the questioning had taken a less personal turn, but she was still wary—maybe Simms wanted her to drop her guard.

"Was she dating anyone on a steady basis? Had she broken up recently with anyone?"

Debra shook her head.

"Did she have any personal enemies?"

"Everyone liked her." Unlike Madeleine, whom everyone had loathed. And they were both dead. *First, let's kill all the lawyers,* Shakespeare had said. Debra shivered.

"You cold?"

"Just tired. Can I go home now?"

"A few more questions. You told the officers you had a feeling something was wrong as soon as you entered the house. Why is that?"

"I told them—the terrier jumped me. And Susan didn't answer when I called." And last week another woman attorney had been murdered. Debra considered telling Simms that she'd gone to Madeleine's condo, then decided not to. There would be more questions, more suspicion masquerading behind the deceptive friendliness in his eyes.

"Okay. That's it for now, Ms. Laslow. I know where to reach you if I have more questions. Don't leave town without advising me." He smiled. "One more thing. Don't mention to anyone what you saw tonight. Especially the victim's mutilated tongue."

She felt another wave of nausea. "Of course not." She had no intention of discussing the gruesome discovery with anyone.

"I'll have someone drive you to your car after you're printed."

She frowned. "Am I still a suspect?"

"You touched the victim, the andirons. Probably other things. We need your prints for purposes of elimination." Simms stood up.

"Fine." She wasn't sure if he was telling her the truth. She leaned across the table and reached for her purse.

"We'll need that for a couple of days, Ms. Laslow."

"Is that for purposes of elimination, too?" She saw his smile and knew they would check for blood residue. So what? "What about my things? My car keys, house keys, my checkbook. Everything."

"You can have them. Thanks for your cooperation."

Debra stood. "I assume you'll be talking to the media. I'd very much appreciate your not giving them my name."

"I'll do my best."

Jeff Silver had phoned. Who was Jeff Silver? Debra wondered as she played back her messages when she returned home. Then she remembered: the man from the restaurant, the one she'd met at the legal ethics seminar. Her father had phoned to congratulate her on winning the motion. So had Aaron. Her aunt Edith had phoned, too: Would Debra please call her back tonight; it was very, very important. "Very, very important" meant a prospective date.

Another time she would have smiled. Now she was thankful that it was too late to return calls; the idea of talking to anyone filled her with exhaustion. There were other messages, but she would listen to them in the morning.

She undressed quickly and tossed her bloodstained clothes into the trash—they would forever remind her of Susan's gruesome death. In the shower she washed her hair and soaped her body, scrubbing the areas Officer Jenkin had touched. She avoided her scratched cheek, which had begun to sting. After she toweled herself dry, she cleansed the wound with hydrogen peroxide, then applied antibiotic ointment.

She was looking in the mirror, blow-drying her hair, when she thought she detected a blind spot on her cheek. A migraine? She turned off the blow dryer and checked her hands; there were blind spots on two of her fingers. She took two extra-strength pain killers from the medicine cabinet and downed them with water. The tablets wouldn't abort the visual aura that always preceded her migraines, but if she took them early enough, they would minimize the ensuing pain.

She slipped on a nightshirt and lay in her bed with her hands on top of her down comforter. The less she moved, the better. Sometimes she kept her eyes open; sometimes, like tonight, she kept them shut, observing with detached fascination the brilliant, pulsating arc of light that lengthened and widened until it filled the black screen of the private theater of her right eye.

The left side of her mouth and face and her left arm tingled with a needlelike sensation. That was normal, she'd learned. So was the occasional temporary aphasia—when that happened, she could think of a word but couldn't say it. She'd been a freshman at Barnard, talking long distance to her parents, when she'd first experienced an aphasic episode. Somehow she'd managed to finish the conversation without communicating her alarm. The next day a neurologist at Columbia Presbyterian had tested her and assured her that she had classic migraines, not a brain tumor as she'd feared.

Now, though there was no one else here, she tested herself as she always did. She thought of the word "house" and pronounced it aloud. "House," she repeated, comforted by the familiar sound. She thought of Susan's house and the word "body" and winced.

The arc of flashing light was receding and a dull ache beginning over her right eye when the phone on her night stand rang. The migraine had intensified her hearing, and each ring was an assault, but she made no move to pick up the receiver. After four rings the answering machine in the kitchen picked up the call. Even from the bedroom she could hear her brother's voice; the noise reverberated inside her skull.

". . . tell you that according to the rabbi, Jeff Silver's a nice guy."

She wished that she weren't spending the night alone, that she had someone with whom she could share her fears, someone with whom she didn't have to start new. Not Barry—she had no regrets, except for the fact that she'd hurt him and caused him and his family embarrassment when she'd broken off the engagement. He'd married a lovely woman, and Debra had been pleased to read an announcement in a recent alumni newsletter of their third child, a girl.

She had no regrets about Stephen, either; she'd dated him before Barry and had loved him intensely—too intensely, her parents had felt. "It isn't good when a woman loves a man more than he loves her," her mother had said. "Don't rush into anything."

"You're wrong!" Debra had lashed out against her mother, who was wise and selfless and was losing her battle against cancer. "You just don't want me to move to Philadelphia." Even as she uttered the words, she knew they were untrue. "I'm sorry," she whispered, kneeling at her mother's bed. "I didn't mean it."

Debra had cried. Her mother had squeezed her hand and told her she understood and loved her, but the words had hung in the air, and Debra could never retract them, just as she could never forget the words Stephen spoke when, standing at the door to her parents' duplex on the night before he returned to Philadelphia, as she worried how, with her mother's illness, they would make a long-distance relationship work, he said, "Debra, don't think I'm going to be pressured into marrying you because your mother is dying."

She said nothing and nodded when he told her he would call her from Philadelphia, and understood for the first time what her mother had meant. She would forever regret that silent acquiescence to his power over her.

She never heard from him again, not even when her mother died. She had always felt that a note would have been nice.

She thought about her mother and Susan and stared into the darkness.

Chapter Twelve

"Tighter," Karl Vaughan snapped. He sat on the brown vinyl bench in the health club dressing room, his gloved hands extended toward the young male attendant.

"You got it, sir." He began adjusting the laces on the right glove. "How's everything with the wife and kids, Mr. Vaughan?"

"Why?" He stared at the attendant.

The man blinked and tried a smile. "I haven't seen you in some time, me bein' away for nine months and all. Just thought I'd ask."

"Did they tell you that something is wrong with my family?"

The young man's face turned bright red. "No, sir. Absolutely not. It's just that you and me, we was kind of friendly before, and I thought . . ." He cleared his throat. "Sorry if I offended you, sir." He kept his eyes on the glove.

"You are not my friend. You are not my therapist. So I don't know why you presume a familiarity that doesn't exist."

"It won't happen again, sir." He gave a final tug and deftly tied the laces. *"How's that?"* He slicked back a shock of blond hair that had fallen over his brow.

"Better."

The attendant worked silently on the right glove. When he was finished, he looked at Vaughan. *"Is that satisfactory, sir?"* he asked, careful to keep his voice free of nuance.

"Quite."

Vaughan was sick of the questions. Everywhere he went there were questions—at work, at a party, at a professional conference, at the club. Even when people didn't ask, he knew they were looking at him. Wondering. Pitying him.

Poor Karl Vaughan. He had it all, and then . . .

He still had it all—a beautiful, loving wife and two daughters; a thriving medical practice; a five-million-dollar Beverly Hills house and everything that went with it.

He had it all, and he had nothing. Because the man who had robbed them had taken more than things. He'd stolen their innocence, their peace. And the monster was free, breathing the same air they were. Laughing.

Everything tasted like ash in Karl Vaughan's mouth.

Vaughan walked to the workout room. Passing the Lifecycle and the treadmill, he crossed the scuffed floor to the punching bags. To his left, a dark-haired man with a paunch was jabbing at another bag.

"How're you doin'?" the man asked, huffing.

Vaughan ignored him. Adjusting his stance, he slammed his right fist into the bag. The impact reverberated up his arm.

Poor Karl Vaughan.

He attacked with his left, then with the right again. He punched left, right, left, right, until his hands were pummeling the bag with a perfect, syncopated rhythm that blocked out the screaming in his mind and brought him an excruci-

ating, sweet release that filled his eyes with tears. When he was finished, he was panting, his body glistening with sweat.

"That's some killer punch you've got," observed his neighbor. "So who're you hitting?"

Vaughan smiled thinly. "Just keeping in shape."

After he showered, he put on his suit. He was strapping on his Rolex when he saw the attendant at the end of the narrow locker room. Vaughan approached him and saw apprehension cloud the man's face. The fact gave him no pleasure.

"Thanks." He handed the man the gloves and a twenty-dollar bill.

"Very generous of you, sir. I'm sorry about before."

Beneath the sycophantic patter, he heard something new in the attendant's voice. He saw it in his eyes, too. Pity. Someone had told him about poor Karl Vaughan. "You earned it. Sorry I blew up."

"No need to apologize, sir. Everyone has an off day."

Karl wanted to choke him.

In the car he heard a radio announcement about the murdered criminal defense attorney, Madeleine Chase. ". . . no arrests yet." Karl grunted and switched the channel. Fifteen minutes later he pulled the black Mercedes past the electronic gates and into one stall of the four-car garage. On the kitchen counter he found a note from Alicia:

Karl—I phoned your office; you'd already left. I waited till ten to have dinner with you. There's poached salmon in the fridge. Wake me when you get home.

He walked upstairs and entered his seven-year-old daughter's bedroom. The house had six bedrooms, but ever since it happened, his four-year-old had taken to sleeping with her sister. Alicia had checked with the therapist, who said it was normal. What was normal? he wondered. He felt his chest tighten as he studied his daughters' angelic faces. He left the room and returned to the stairs.

"Karl, is that you? . . . Karl?"

He heard the panic rising in Alicia's voice. He had no choice but to answer and walk to the master bedroom, but he stayed in the doorway.

"Are you coming to sleep?" she asked.

"Not yet. Don't wait up."

"I think we should talk."

She always wanted to talk about it. She needed to talk about it—that was part of the healing process, the therapist had explained. But what about Karl's healing process, goddammit? What about Karl's needs? What about the fact that he was sick and tired of talking about it?

What about that, Alicia? he wanted to yell.

He left the doorway without answering her. Downstairs, he sat in his study, nursing a glass of Glenfiddich, thinking about his daughters. Alicia said the therapist felt they would be all right, that they hadn't witnessed it, that they didn't really understand what had happened.

Most of the time, he didn't understand, either.

Chapter Thirteen

Someone was walking along the side of her house.

Debra was reciting the *Amidah*, a part of her morning prayers, when she heard the crackling of leaves being trampled outside her window.

She froze, then listened intently. It was possible she'd imagined the sounds; she was jittery because of Susan's murder and exhausted—the caffeine in the two tablets she'd taken (the equivalent of seven cups of coffee, a doctor had told her) had kept her up for hours before she'd finally fallen into a restless sleep.

She heard it again—heavy footsteps, human footsteps. Her phone was on the desk, within reach, but she wasn't permitted to speak during the *Amidah*.

A twig snapped.

Her heart beat faster. Forcing herself not to skip anything, she completed the prayer and then tiptoed to the back of the house. She heard a series of creaks. It took her several seconds to identify the sounds: someone was removing the framed screen to an access port that led underneath her house.

She stole to the central hall and made certain the door to the basement was locked, then raced to the kitchen. With a chef's knife in her hand, she picked up the phone receiver and punched 911.

The doorbell rang.

"Emergency operator. How can I help you?"

Debra hesitated. She replaced the receiver but took the knife with her to the front entry. She looked through the peephole at the man standing at her door. He was wearing jeans and a black sweatshirt; a black-and-silver Raiders cap cast a shadow over his dark blue eyes. His cheeks and nose were smudged with dirt.

"Yes?" She gripped the knife tightly, wondering how the person who had murdered Susan and Madeleine had gained access to their homes.

"Ms. Laslow? Adam Bergman. I left a message on your machine telling you I'd be by to measure your house. I'm all done."

She wished she'd listened to the rest of her messages. Feeling silly, her face flushed with relief, she unlocked the door and opened it. "Please come in."

He wiped his black leather athletic shoes on the hemp mat—"I don't want to track in dirt," he told her—and stepped inside. He towered over her. Even with his face smudged, he was very good-looking, she thought. She decided he was in his mid-thirties.

"Your paper," he said, handing her the *L.A. Times.*

"Thanks." She took it with her right hand. He was staring at her left hand and the long knife. "I was about to slice a grapefruit when you rang the bell," she said, embarrassed to tell him the truth. He would think she was neurotic. "Be right back."

She hurried to the kitchen and put the knife on the

counter. When she returned, he was standing in the empty living room.

"I love these high ceilings," he said. "Great molding, too." He had taken off his cap. Centered on his thick dark brown curly hair was a black yarmulke.

She didn't remember Aaron mentioning that Bergman was Orthodox. Not that it mattered. "It's what sold me on the house. The ceilings, I mean." She smiled to be friendly, though with Susan dead she didn't much feel like smiling. The facial movement pulled at the scratch on her cheek— with makeup on, it was barely noticeable. She bit her lip to keep from crying.

He smiled, too, deepening the fine lines around his eyes. "You want the house bolted and the cripple wall reinforced, right?"

"Right." Her voice was husky from unshed tears, and she thought how incongruous it was, almost disrespectful, to be discussing home repair just hours after Susan had been killed. "Could you check the foundation, too?"

"I already did. It has a couple of minor cracks, but I can patch them. I'll go out to my truck and write up an estimate."

While he was gone, she unfolded the *Times* and anxiously scanned the front and Metro sections but found no mention of Susan's murder. She poured orange juice into a glass and filled a bowl with cereal and banana slices, but after a sip of the juice and a spoonful of cereal, she found that she couldn't eat.

Bergman was back in five minutes with an invoice. "This estimate is good for sixty days," he told her.

She scanned the neatly printed description of what he planned to do: seven-inch bolts every six feet along the perimeter of the house to secure it to the foundation; half-inch plywood panels to reinforce the cripple walls. His fee seemed reasonable. He wanted three payments—the first on

commencing work; the second when he finished the bolt-
ing; the third upon completion of the job. She had enough
in her checking account for the first payment.

She looked forward to feeling secure in her home. "When
can you start?"

"Tomorrow morning."

She felt lethargic and almost phoned the office to say she
wasn't coming in but decided keeping busy would be therapeutic. Driving to work, she heard about Susan's murder on
the radio: ". . . shot to death in her Los Angeles home," the
announcer said. "According to LAPD Detective Marty
Simms, the body was discovered by another attorney, Debra
Laslow, who was taken in for—"

"Son of a bitch!" Debra swore aloud. Using her cellular
phone, she called Julia and, after telling her what had happened and assuring her that she was all right, asked her to
convey the message to her father and brother.

"I can't believe what you've been through," Julia said, her
voice somber. "Last week it was that other attorney. Now
Susan. My God, Debra, you don't think the murders are
connected, do you? Remember that guy in San Francisco
who killed all those lawyers?"

Debra remembered the killings well. She'd been in law
school at the time; like many of her classmates, she'd been
frightened and had fleetingly contemplated pursuing another, safer profession. "Ten to one it's just a horrible coincidence," she said, tightening her grip on the steering
wheel.

"Still basking in the glory of winning the Lassiter motion,
Debra?" Jeremy Knox said when Debra entered his office.
"That was nicely done." He beamed at her.

"Thank you." Winning the motion seemed to have taken
place years ago. "Jeremy, you should know that the police

questioned me last night in regard to a murder. The story was on the news."

Glynnis had heard. "It must've been horrible for you," she'd told Debra. "The shock and all. And to be interrogated like that." Curiosity had gleamed in her eyes. Rosemary, Jeremy's secretary, had avoided looking directly at Debra. So she knew, too.

"Who was murdered?" Jeremy asked quietly.

"Susan Clemens." Tears welled again in Debra's eyes. "She's . . . she was a criminal defense attorney and a close friend." She'd repeated the fact so many times to the police that she was able to recite them now in a neat, antiseptic summation that did nothing to convey the horror of what she'd seen only thirteen hours earlier; she felt as if she were talking about someone distant, not Susan.

"How terrible for you, Debra! And how tragic for your friend. We hear about murder all the time, but when it strikes close to home . . ." He sighed. "Do you need some time off?"

She shook her head. "Keeping busy will do me good. I'm worried that the firm will get calls from the media."

"I'd be surprised if we didn't. I've had my share of dealings with the media. I can handle them." He smiled. "I appreciate your telling me. Now put the matter out of your mind. You're meeting a new client today. Kenneth Avedon?"

"Yes. He's coming this afternoon."

"Arthur Lassiter speaks highly of him. And Arthur's enchanted with you." Jeremy smiled again. "Richard and I are both extremely pleased with your work, Debra. I hope you're as happy being here as we are having you a member of our team."

"Thank you." Should she tell him she wasn't happy, and why? Jeremy would talk to Richard; Richard would stop harassing her; she wouldn't have to leave. "About Richard, Jeremy. I have concerns—"

"He won't be bothered by the media attention, either. Richard will support you one hundred percent."

"That's gratifying to hear. Because sometimes," she said, carefully watching Jeremy's expression, feeling as if she were inching forward on smooth ice that could turn thin and brittle at any moment, "sometimes, I sense from some comments he's made that he's annoyed by my religious observance." She would begin with this, she decided, then broach the issue of sexual harassment.

"You stated your needs clearly when we interviewed you, Debra. Richard respects your religious observance. Why wouldn't he? He's Jewish, too." Jeremy stood, walked to Debra, and put his arm around her shoulders. "Richard may kid once in a while—that's his way. But he's told me how much he admires your work and how fond he is of you. And Richard, bless him, is never less than honest."

Charles was right, Debra thought: Jeremy was a superior attorney who led the firm with intellect, authority, and dignity, but he would never see beyond his illusion of Richard.

She understood about illusions. She'd had illusions about Stephen. Her father had had illusions, too. He counseled individuals and couples and had raised his children with wisdom and common sense, but he'd refused to listen to oncologists who had tried to dissuade him from driving his wife to Tijuana for a series of injections of laetrile, a substance extracted from the pits of apricots that he had convinced himself would arrest her cancer.

Her father had been motivated by desperation and love. Debra didn't know what motivated Jeremy; it didn't matter. She thanked him for his understanding and returned to her office, where, following her own excellent advice, she buried herself in her work so that she wouldn't dwell on the fact that a medical examiner was mutilating Susan's body to find out the exact cause of her death.

Chapter Fourteen

At eleven o'clock Glynnis informed Debra that Detective Marty Simms was here to see her.

"Please ask him to wait," Debra said. After being manhandled and humiliated and locked up in a holding cell, she'd felt intimidated by the police. This morning she was angry; having Simms cool his heels gave her pleasure and a measure of control.

She returned her attention to the brief on her computer screen. She began revising a paragraph, but her mind was on Simms—obviously he'd learned that Debra had known Madeleine. When Glynnis buzzed again, Debra asked her to show him in. She was clearing the screen when the door opened and Simms strode into the room.

"How can I help you, Detective?"

"You can start by not wasting my time." He glowered at her. " 'Course I'm just a city employee who gets paid shit to try to put the bad guys away. You're a hot-shot lawyer who makes ten dollars a minute to put them back on the street."

"Do you have a problem with the concept of criminal de-

fense, Detective Simms?" She felt infinitely better sitting at
her own desk, in her own office, than she'd felt sitting at
the small, scarred table in the police interrogation room.

"I have a problem with *you.*" He pulled a chair closer to
her desk and sat down. "You withheld information. We
were at Ms. Clemens's office and found something that be-
longs to you." From the inside pocket of his camel wool
jacket he withdrew a folded paper.

It was her résumé. She knew that even before he unfolded it and dropped it on her desk with the printed side
up.

"Funny you didn't mention last night that you'd applied
for a position at the victim's firm," Simms said.

"I didn't mention it because it isn't relevant."

"Uh-huh. So is it also not *relevant* that Detective Cummings from West L.A. questioned you just two days ago
about Madeleine Chase?"

"Cummings talked to me because Madeleine and I were
in law school together. He is no doubt questioning everyone who knew her."

"No doubt," Simms mimicked. "That still doesn't explain
why you didn't tell me about it."

"Am I still a suspect? If so, I'll have my attorney join us
before I answer any more questions. He's down the hall."
She placed her hand on the receiver, though she had no
idea whether Charles was in.

"You're not a suspect. Not at this time. I'm just curious."

Debra removed her hand from the receiver. "The truth? I
wanted to go home. If I mentioned that I knew her, you'd
draw incorrect inferences, and I would have been at the station all night answering more questions."

"You applied for a position at Ms. Chase's firm, too."

"I applied to several firms. I told that to Cummings."

"Just coincidence, huh?" His smile was a sneer.

"Just coincidence. In fact, Susan's the one who suggested that I apply for a position at her firm."

"And Ms. Chase nixed your getting hired by her firm, right? According to Wraith, you and the dead woman had words about it." He looked around the room. "Small office, no view. Guess you're not such a hot shot yet."

Now was the time to tell him she'd been to the condo. She opened her mouth to speak but lost her nerve. "Have you established any connections between Madeleine's and Susan's murders?"

He cocked his head and stared at her. "You're the connection, as far as I can see. Cummings says he didn't tell you Ms. Chase's tongue had been severed. Neither did Wraith. The media didn't know. So my question is, Ms. Laslow, how did *you* know?"

"My secretary heard it from Madeleine's secretary."

He eyed her for a moment, assessing her, then scowled. "I asked you not to discuss this with anyone. I hope to hell you've kept your word."

"I did. Obviously, you didn't keep *your* word. On my way to work, I heard the radio newscaster announce that you took me in for questioning."

He smiled. "You know what they say—it's not bad getting your name in the paper, as long as they spell it right." He shrugged. "I tried my best."

Like hell you did. "Well, I'll try *my* best to keep the information about the murders to myself."

Simms gripped the edge of her desk and leaned toward her. "You leak anything about the murders, I'll arrest you for interfering with a police investigation and make it stick. You got that?"

"I got that." She met his look with a defiance she didn't feel. "When can I have my purse back?"

"When we're finished with it." He picked up the résumé and slipped it into his pocket.

"I'd appreciate your not mentioning that I've sent out résumés to other firms. I haven't announced my intention to leave."

He shook his head. "You've got chutzpah, I'll give you that." He shoved back his chair and stood up. "If you think of anything else that isn't *relevant,* let me know." He headed for the door.

"Detective Simms," Debra said.

He stopped and turned to face her. "What?"

"I don't think this has any connection to the murders, but Madeleine and Susan were both members of WRIT. I'm a member, too."

He frowned. "What the hell is that?"

"Women's Rights in Toto. It's an organization of women attorneys. We network. We give each other advice. We're trying to help women get equal pay and equal promotions."

"Yeah, you women lawyers have it tough." He took a notepad and pen out of his pocket. "You have a number for this group?"

She flipped through her Rolodex, found the WRIT entry, and dictated the number. "By the way, Detective, did you find the dog?"

He put his pad and pen in his pocket. "Not yet." He walked to the door.

"There *was* a dog," she said to Simms's back.

He left the door open—just to annoy her, Debra knew. She got up to shut it, then changed her mind. Taking her purse with her, she walked down the hall to Charles's office, knocked on his door, and opened it. When she saw that he was talking into his Dictaphone, she started to pull the door shut.

"Hey, don't go." He clicked off the Dictaphone and walked around his desk to her. "I heard what happened, but I didn't want to bug you with a million questions." He rested his hand on her shoulder. "You okay, Debra?" he asked tenderly.

She'd promised herself she wouldn't cry, but his concern made her eyes tear. She squeezed his hand, feeling a rush of affection for him. "Not really. I feel pretty shaky. Do you have a minute?"

"Always."

She sat on one of his client chairs. He moved to his desk. Half sitting on the edge, his arms folded against his chest, he listened intently as she told him in her well-rehearsed sentences about finding Susan's body, about being searched by the police, being handcuffed, interrogated. When she was finished, her lips were trembling.

"Jesus, Debra! Why the hell didn't you call me?"

"I did, twice. Your line was busy."

He scribbled a phone number on a sheet of notepaper and handed it to her. "My pager. Call me any time. I mean that."

She took a dollar bill from her wallet and gave it to him.

"For my pager number?" He smiled as he took the dollar, but his dark brown eyes were serious.

"To retain you as my attorney and get your advice. Simms just left my office. He finds it suspicious that I sent résumés to Madeleine's and Susan's firms, and—"

"You're definitely decided on leaving?" He pursed his lips. "Don't let Richard win, Debra. You could have a great future here."

She shook her head. "I wish I could stay—mainly because of you, to tell you the truth—but Richard is making that impossible."

"Any way I can help?"

"Short of lobotomizing Richard or getting rid of him, I don't think so." They both smiled. "Thanks for offering, though. Anyway, Richard's not my main problem. Madeleine kept me from being hired by Blackmeyer, and we fought about it at the courthouse." She told him that she'd gone to Madeleine's condominium, that she hadn't informed the police, and why. "Last night I didn't tell Simms, either—I knew it would set him off. I didn't even tell him I knew Madeleine. He's mad about that, too."

Charles had maintained a poker face while she spoke. Now he sighed and shook his head. "Not smart, Debra."

"I know. I can't believe how badly I've handled this—I'm a lawyer's nightmare." It was a humbling experience that gave her new insight into her own clients who were less than forthcoming with the police. "Wilshire has my fingerprints. And I left prints at Madeleine's—on the brass plaque under her bell." A nice, smooth surface, perfect for finding latents. "And I was at Madeleine's a few weeks ago. I must have touched things when I was there."

He nodded. "Anyone see you the night of the murder?"

"A couple walking their dog."

He nodded again. "Did you tell Cummings you *weren't* there?"

"No. I didn't lie. I just didn't volunteer information."

"Who knows you were there? Anyone?"

"My brother and sister-in-law." She regretted having burdened them with the knowledge.

"My advice, Debra? Call Cummings and tell him."

"He'll think I killed her. He's talked with Simms, and there are too many coincidences, all involving me. I knew both women. I sent résumés to both of their firms. I was at Madeleine's condo, probably right after she was killed. I found Susan's body."

"But the murders aren't connected, Debra."

"Yes, they are." There was no way of softening this. "Susan's tongue was severed, Charles. Just like Madeleine's."

He winced. "I thought maybe Glynnis had heard wrong. You know Glynnis." He paused, then said, "That's sick,

Debra. I hope to hell they find the bastard who did this."
His skin looked pasty. "You scared?"

"Terrified. I'm trying not think about it." It was like trying
not to breathe. "If Simms finds out I was at Madeleine's that
night, he'll pull me in for questioning again. I don't want to
go through that. Plus my name will be in the papers, and
no decent firm will hire me."

"You're not letting me earn my dollar, Debra. Why'd you
ask my advice if you knew you weren't going to take it?"

"I needed to talk this out with someone I can trust. If I
told Aaron and Julia, they'd just worry." She sighed. "I know
you're right. I *should* call Cummings. I'll think about it."

"They're going to find out," he said quietly. "You know
that."

"But in the meantime, with any luck the police will find
the killer. And I can interview with a few firms. Anyway, I
don't think Simms really suspects me. He's giving me a hard
time because he doesn't like lawyers."

"So why the dollar?"

"In case I'm wrong."

When she returned to her desk, she phoned Susan's secretary, whom she'd met a number of times. "Joyce, this is
Debra Laslow," she said when the woman answered.
"Joyce? Are you there?" she asked when the secretary didn't
respond.

"I heard they took you in for questioning about Ms.
Clemens's murder," she whispered.

Debra heard suspicion, alarm, and a hint of curiosity in
the secretary's voice; she didn't blame her. "That's because I
found Susan's body. They wanted to know what I saw.
That's all."

There was another silence. Then Joyce said, "God, she
was so nice! Why did someone have to kill her?" She
sobbed quietly.

"That's why I'm calling," Debra said softly. "I want to find out what happened." She waited until the secretary stopped crying, then said, "Did Susan mention that she was frightened about anyone in particular?"

"The police asked me that." Joyce sniffled. "She received crank calls once in a while from clients who thought she should've done better for them. But I couldn't think of anyone specific."

"Did she keep a record of the calls?"

"Not that I know of. She *did* keep threatening letters. She laughed about them, but I know some of them frightened her. They scared the hell out of me."

Debra had received similar letters—"Dear Ms. Laslow, I'm in my cell, counting the days until I get out. You should be counting them, too, 'cause I'll be heading straight for your house. I've got lots of interesting things planned for you, you bitch. . . ."

"Where did she keep the letters?" Debra asked.

"Those that were written by clients or ex-clients, or by prosecution witnesses, she had me file with the respective cases. The others—letters from strangers—she had me put in a separate file—the 'Ugly Americans' file, she called it. She had such a clever way of phrasing things, didn't she?"

"Yes, she did," Debra said, feeling a fresh pang of loss. "Did she receive any angry letters about her involvement with WRIT?"

"Writ? Oh, you mean the organization? Not that I recall. The police want me to go through all her files and give them copies of any threatening letters I find. I should be doing that right now, but I can't seem to get started, you know?"

Debra knew. "Can I ask you a favor, Joyce? Would you make copies of the letters for me? I can stop by and pick them up."

"I can't. I'd be violating client-attorney confidentiality."

"What about the 'Ugly Americans' file? Those letters are

from strangers, you said, so you wouldn't be violating confidentiality."

"That's true, I guess. But I'm not sure the police would want me to give out any information."

"Joyce, I'm trying to find out who killed Susan. You want to help find her killer, don't you?"

"I need to think about this, okay? Look, I have to go, Ms. Laslow. There's so much to do."

"Can I call you in a day or so about the letters?"

The secretary's "Okay" was grudging, but it was better than a refusal. Debra thanked her and hung up the phone.

Madeleine no doubt had her own "Ugly Americans" file— probably a thicker one than Susan's. Debra wondered whether the files of both murdered women contained similar letters.

Chapter Fifteen

Kenneth Avedon arrived ten minutes late. Typical of doctors, Debra thought as she walked to Richard's office to meet her new client. From the experiences she'd had with some of her mother's physicians, she was prepared for arrogance, too, but Avedon was contrite with apology.

"I asked Blackmeyer's secretary to messenger over my files," he explained after Richard performed the introductions. "This morning she told me they need my written authorization before they'd release them. So I drove there on the way here and picked them up myself. Sorry," he said again, running his hand through his wavy, short blond hair.

"Not a problem." Richard smiled.

Especially since the meter is ticking, Debra thought. Five minutes later she and the doctor were in her office—she'd turned down Richard's offer of using his larger, more impressive room—and Avedon's files, two brown accordion envelopes, were on her desk.

She had studied Avedon in Richard's office, trying to get a sense of him from his physical appearance. He was tall and slim and had a boyish face with preppy good looks enhanced by his tortoise-framed glasses and the beige wool vest he wore under his sports jacket. He would look good on the witness stand.

"I feel guilty leaving Blackmeyer," Avedon said. "But under the circumstances . . . I assume Mr. Dressner explained?" He spoke in a low, pleasant voice that held a hint of nervousness.

"He did." She uncapped her pen. "Kenneth—"

"Ken," he corrected.

"Ken, I know this is difficult, starting over with a new attorney. I intend to read all the documents in your files, but I need to ask you questions you've probably answered more than once—to the police, to Ms. Chase. To others."

"Of course." He cleared his throat.

"Okay." Debra smiled encouragingly. "Tell me what happened."

"July twenty-third, a Tuesday, Penny and I went to dinner after work. Then she came with me to my apartment. We had sex, and she drove to her friend's house, where she stayed the night. Five weeks later the police arrested me for rape." He expelled a deep breath. "I wake up some mornings and still can't believe this is happening. It's so crazy!"

"Why did she wait so long to file charges?"

"She told the police she was ashamed and afraid to tell her parents. They're very strict. And when her parents found out, they didn't want her to press charges. They didn't want people to know."

That was often the case with rape victims. The woman's story was plausible. "What changed her mind?" she asked, studying Avedon.

"She says she couldn't live with it anymore, but I know she did it because she was angry when I became engaged."

Debra wrote down the words "revenge" and "scorned" and underlined them. "Did Penny have reason to assume you were interested in having a serious relationship with her?"

"I never gave her reason to. But she obviously did. She made it clear she liked me. We both knew it was going to happen."

"How did you know?"

He shrugged. "Eye contact. Sexual innuendos she made. Body language. She'd rest her hand on mine when she handed me a folder, brush up against me. Stuff like that."

"You didn't discourage it?"

"I guess I should have. But Penny's pretty and outgoing. She seemed to know what she wanted. I didn't think it was a big deal."

"When you had sex with Penny that night, were you involved with your fiancée?"

He crossed his leg. "Vickie and I were dating, but we weren't committed. She knows all about Penny. She supports me totally."

The fiancée was a plus. Debra wrote a few notes, then said, "Was this the first time you had intercourse with Penny?"

"Yes. She was a virgin. I was shocked. She'd talked as if she'd had experience with men. And she's twenty-one years old. Most women that age have had sex." He looked at Debra for confirmation.

Debra flipped a page of her pad and wondered what he would say if he knew that she was a virgin, too, that she was discussing with practiced nonchalance the intimate details of an act of which she had only book knowledge. "Did she tell you this before you had intercourse?"

"No. I wouldn't have done it if I'd known. She told the police she was crying the whole time, begging me to stop because she was a virgin. That isn't true." Avedon's face had colored. "She cried a little afterward, because she was scared.

That's when she told me. I think she wanted to make me feel guilty, responsible."

"You couldn't tell while you were having intercourse?"

"Not really. What with women using tampons nowadays . . ." He shrugged again.

"Did you use a condom?"

"She asked me to. I would've used one even if she had-n't."

Again Debra was pleased. The jury could be persuaded to view a woman's request that a condom be used as proof of informed consent. "Whose idea was it to go out to din-ner?"

"It was mutual. I'd said that maybe we'd go out to dinner one night and she said, 'How about tomorrow?' and I said fine."

Another plus. "Did you pick her up at her house?"

"No. Her parents keep her on a tight leash. She didn't think they'd approve of her going out with me, so she told them she was going out with a friend after work and spend-ing the night."

"How did she get to work?"

"Her car. She brought along a change of clothes."

"Did Penny have anything alcoholic to drink that night?"

"She had wine with dinner. In my apartment we had some drinks, too. She told the police I got her drunk. I didn't, but I'm worried about what the jury will think."

"Jurors are inclined to disapprove of women who initiate the date and have drinks. On the other hand, a recent Cali-fornia revision states that a rape is committed when a per-son is prevented from resisting sex because she's drunk or drugged. It doesn't matter who provided the drinks or drugs—the accused or accuser."

Avedon frowned. "How drunk is 'drunk'? Penny was defi-nitely aware of what she was doing."

"That's why some people don't like the revised law—it's

ambiguous. It may be revised again. Did you ask Penny out a second time?"

"Yes. She said no. She said she was worried that her parents would find out and would be very angry with her."

She capped her pen. "Ken, I'm sure Madeleine told you that cases like this boil down to the credibility of the two parties involved." *He said, she said,* Susan had called it just yesterday. Debra felt a surge of grief; with an effort, she pushed aside thoughts of her murdered friend, as she'd been doing all day. "You're not denying intercourse took place. You're saying Penny consented. There's no physical evidence to say otherwise, and since the act was private, there are no witnesses."

"They have an audiocassette." Avedon adjusted the crease in his slacks. "The police had Penny phone me four weeks after we went out and tape our conversation. The district attorney sent a transcript of the conversation to Madeleine. It's in the file."

Debra frowned. "I'll read it later. Tell me about the tape."

"We talked a while. She said she liked me but was confused about our relationship. Then she kept asking me, 'Why did you force me to have sex with you?' and 'Why were you so rough?'"

"And how did you respond?" Debra asked in a casual tone.

"I said something like, 'I'm sorry you're upset' and 'I didn't mean to be rough.'"

This was not good. "You didn't deny her accusations?"

"I thought she felt guilty because she'd lost her virginity and needed to blame someone. I didn't see the point in making her more upset. I just wanted to end the conversation."

"Did you at any point admit that you raped her?"

"No. When she said, 'Why did you rape me?' I said, 'I *didn't* rape you' and told her I was hanging up." He leaned forward. "The thing is, I don't understand why the tape's admissible. Isn't it a violation of my rights?"

"I'm sure Madeleine explained this to you."

"She said the judge would probably allow the jury to hear it. She talked about adoptive admissions."

"An adoptive admission is an acceptance by the defendant of what the other party is charging. The defendant is 'adopting' as true what the other party is saying by not denying it."

"But how can she tape me without my knowledge? How can she be allowed to try to get me to incriminate myself?"

"The Sixth Amendment applies only if you've been arrested or charged. At that point you'd have to be Mirandized—informed of your right to remain silent."

"But I was a suspect—the police had Penny phone me."

Debra shook her head. "Being a suspect doesn't count."

"Isn't it entrapment?"

She shook her head again. "I'll try to have the tape excluded, but I don't think I'll be successful. Still, you denied you raped her. The jury will hear that." They would also hear the adoptive admissions; Debra would have to explain them just as Avedon had explained them to her. "From what you've told me, I think we have a good chance at an acquittal."

"I didn't rape her. I hope you believe me."

Debra never asked her clients whether they were guilty; she didn't want to know if they were. That knowledge could hamper her from zealously refuting the evidence of the prosecution; it would also make her guilty of suborning perjury if the client lied under oath.

She looked at Avedon's clear gray eyes and nodded, and although it shouldn't have made a difference to her, she hoped he was telling the truth. "Let's meet on Friday after I review your file. I'd like you to see a psychologist we use. He'll administer a personality test. If everything goes well—

and I'm sure it will—he can testify that your profile is incompatible with a rapist's." She wrote the psychologist's name on a piece of notepaper.

"You're sure this is necessary?" Avedon said as he accepted the slip of paper. "I'm not worried. I just don't like personality tests. Or psychologists."

"Everything helps. I'd also like you to prepare a list of character witnesses—friends, family, your kindergarten teacher, your Cub Scout leader." She smiled.

"Madeleine asked me to do that. I'll bring it on Friday."

"Good." She nodded. "Also, I'd like to file for a continuance, Ken. Since you have a new attorney, I'm confident we'll get one."

"I'd prefer not to postpone the trial. Vickie and I want to get married on New Year's as planned. Mr. Dressner didn't seem to think it was a problem.

Not for Richard it wasn't. "It won't be a problem," she said. Two weeks gave her little time, but she had Avedon's file, and Madeleine, she was certain, had been thorough. Debra scanned her notes. "One more question. You said Penny spent that night with a friend. Did Penny tell her she'd been raped?"

Avedon shook his head. "She told the police she was too ashamed. The friend is religious, but not as religious as Penny's parents. They're Orthodox. That's why Penny thought they'd disapprove of me—I'm not even Jewish. I told all this to Mr. Dressner yesterday."

Debra felt her face becoming warm. "I guess he forgot to mention it to me. What's Penny's last name?"

"Bailor."

Penny Bailor, Debra repeated silently to herself.

Chapter Sixteen

"You set me up," she said, her voice just below a yell as she stepped into Richard's office. She yanked the door shut. "You knew the complaining witness was Orthodox. This gives you a kick, doesn't it?"

"Don't be ridiculous." His smile had disappeared. "We discussed the other day why you're the right attorney for this case. The fact that you're Orthodox is just another plus."

"But you didn't mention it to me."

"I thought you should judge the merits of the case without being hampered by outside factors. Obviously, I was right. You don't know this woman, do you?"

"No. But—"

"So there's no conflict of interest."

"Just because I don't know her doesn't mean she's not a member of the Orthodox community. We probably know people in common. It'll be awkward as hell for me, Richard."

"You're a professional, Debra. Live with it. Avedon is

yours." He opened the lid to his Rolodex and thumbed through the tabs.

"What if I said I don't want the case?"

He looked up at her. "That wouldn't be wise. If anyone should feel hesitant, it's Avedon. His first attorney is murdered. His new one is interrogated by the police about being at the scene of another murder. Not a situation to inspire confidence."

Her face reddened. "I spoke to Jeremy about what happened. He said he supports me completely, and that you would, too."

"I support you absolutely. What you went through must have been horrific. And if the subject comes up, I'll assure Avedon that your being questioned was strictly routine." He leaned back against his chair. "But support is a two-way street, don't you think?"

Jeff Silver phoned as she was leaving the office. "I figured if I couldn't reach you at home, I'd try you at work," he said. "Unless, of course, you're not interested. If that's the case—"

"No, not at all," she said quickly. "I haven't returned your calls because I've had a lot on my mind."

"You won your motion, right? How was the celebratory dinner?"

He was the only person in Los Angeles who hadn't heard, Debra decided. Hoping that this would be the last time she repeated what had happened, she told him about Susan.

"God, that's horrible!" he exclaimed when Debra had finished. After a short silence, he said, "Let me take you out tonight."

"I can't, Jeff. I'm exhausted." And not in the mood. The idea of going out with anyone so soon after Susan's murder seemed wrong.

"You've been through hell. You're emotionally drained. If you go home, you'll just dwell on what happened, right?"

"Right," she admitted, playing with the phone cord.

"So what time should I pick you up?"

On the way home she rented *It Happened One Night* at the La Cienega video Wherehouse, then stopped at her father's duplex. His car, an old dark brown Chevy Caprice, was parked in front, but that didn't mean he was home. He often walked the few blocks to the synagogue and back. "Why lose a parking space?" he always joked.

She used her key to let herself in. He was at the kitchen table, playing a solitaire game of chess. When he saw her, he stood up. She walked into his arms and buried her head against his chest and sobbed while he stroked her hair.

"Debra," he whispered.

She leaned against him for another moment, loving the smell of his starched shirt, the comforting, regular beating of his heart, then pulled away. "I got mascara on your shirt."

"That's what laundries are for." He smiled. "Everybody has to make a living." He took a tissue from his pants pocket and wiped gently beneath her eyes. "Julia said you're all right. Are you?"

"Things are complicated, but I think they'll be okay."

"I'm not a fragile old man, Debra. Don't try to protect me. If you need help, you'll tell me?"

"I'll tell you." She sat at the table and looked at the chess board. "I have a date tonight."

"One of Aunt Edith's young men?" He smiled and sat down.

"No." She told him about Jeff Silver.

"I hope Edith won't feel slighted. She tries so hard." His smile deepened. "She wants to introduce me to a nice widow."

"You should do it, Dad." He was so lonely. Seeing another woman take her mother's place in this house, at his side, would be odd and uncomfortable at first, but Debra wanted him to remarry—it was one of the reasons she'd bought her own home and moved out.

He shook his head. "I'm not ready. Not a day goes by that I don't miss your mother."

Debra nodded and took his hand. Sometimes she'd see a woman whose gait or hairstyle or slope of the shoulders would remind her sharply of her mother. Some nights her mother seemed so real in her dreams that waking brought with it the stabbing pain of fresh loss.

She asked him about his day and saw his eyes become animated as he described one of his students, a forty-three-year-old Iranian immigrant who was quickly mastering Hebrew and Talmudic discourse.

"The determination!" Her father shook his head. "What about you, Debra? You're not working too hard?" He moved his white bishop to attack the opposing queen.

"Actually, I have a new case. A rape case. The problem is, the complaining witness—"

"The victim, you mean?" He glanced up from the board.

"We don't refer to her as a victim," she said more crisply than she'd intended. "That would imply that my client is guilty. Anyway, the woman is from an Orthodox home, and that bothers me."

He nodded. "Either this woman falsely accused your client, or your client raped her. Can someone else take this case?"

"My boss says I have to take it. I met with the client today."

Her father nodded again. "You think he's innocent?"

"I think so. Even if he isn't, I have to defend him zealously. And in cross-examining the witness, I'll have to ask intimate questions. I'll be embarrassing her in public." It was what she'd hated most about trying rape cases; with the witness being someone from her own small community, she found the idea even more onerous.

"And you want to know whether by Jewish law you have a problem." He moved an opposing knight to block the bishop's attack, then looked up at his daughter. "Are you coming to me for an answer, Debra, or for a solution?"

"For a solution," she said, hoping she hadn't disappointed him. He was her rock, her strength. She'd turned to him more than to Aaron after her mother had died. Sometimes she wondered where *he* found comfort.

"And if I tell you this cross-examination is prohibited?"

"I don't know." She could imagine Richard's reaction if she told him she couldn't cross-examine Penny Bailor because of Jewish law.

"An honest response. Before you ask the question, Debra, you have to consider the ramifications of the answer." He moved his black bishop to attack the opposing queen's rook. "The commentaries prohibit humiliating someone in public. They compare the act to killing him."

She nodded.

"But the prohibition implies that the embarrassed party does not want or does not invite the embarrassment. By pressing charges, the witness is knowingly subjecting herself to potential humiliation." He stoked his beard. "So one could argue that she accepts the potential humiliation, and that removes the onus from your shoulders. You have your solution, Debra."

"So why don't I feel relieved?" Debra studied the board and moved her knight to take the bishop.

"If you take the bishop, you'll lose your queen." He returned the knight to its former position. "Sometimes, Debra, whatever move you make, you can't win."

Jeff picked her up in his black Sentra and drove her to a kosher restaurant on La Brea that featured European and Chinese cuisine and, according to Julia, the best desserts in the world. Debra hadn't eaten all day and she loved Chinese food, but when the pou-pou platter arrived, she had no appetite and had to force herself to taste the egg rolls and ribs so that Jeff wouldn't feel uncomfortable.

"Tell me about your book," she said. "What's it on?"

"The criminal justice system." He saw consternation in her eyes. "I know, I know. I said you needed a change of scenery. But I don't feel compelled to discuss my work." He smiled.

"No, tell me," she said, more out of politeness than interest.

"Not much to tell. I'm in the research stage. I talk to law professors, victims, convicts, district attorneys, criminal defense attorneys. I was a prosecutor before I quit practicing law."

"The enemy, huh?" She smiled, trying to lighten her own mood, but felt like crying. It was a mistake to have come tonight, she decided. "So are you going to interview me?"

He smiled, too. "If you want."

"Depends on the dessert. What's the title of your book?"

"Justice on Trial."

"Ouch." She grimaced.

"You have to admit the system doesn't always work. Guilty people walk all too often. Victims are abused by the process."

"The system's not perfect, but it's the best we have."

"You never have doubts about what you're doing?"

"Sure I do. But I really believe in the cornerstone of the system—it's better for ten guilty people to go free than for one innocent person to be convicted. And what's the alternative? Trial by torture? No trial? A police state?"

"Trial by truth would be nice. Where the lawyers can't play games with the facts. Take the motion you won. What was it?"

She told him, without giving names, about the Lassiter case.

"See what I mean? Your client possessed cocaine, and he got off. Right now he's probably back on the stuff."

"Maybe, but that's not my problem. He got off because the police screwed up and conducted a warrantless search. So maybe next time they'll do their job more carefully and make me work harder."

"Maybe." He nodded. "What if a woman killed her husband—would you tell her to claim she was abused by him if she wasn't?"

"No, of course not," Debra said, her tone sharp. "That's highly unethical. You can't invent a story for your client. You know that."

"You're saying attorneys *never* suggest defenses? What if a client's charged with hit and run? Can the attorney inform him of the legal defenses to his crime before asking for the facts?"

Debra hesitated. "I know that some attorneys would do that."

"So what kind of defense would they mention?"

She bit into the won ton and thought for a moment. "The lawyer might say, 'If you ran from the scene because you feared the other driver was going to kill you, you may be acquitted.' Then the lawyer might suggest that the client take a few days to think about why he fled before he tells the lawyer what happened."

"Is that what you'd do?"

"No. Lawyers can properly suggest a defense if the evidence doesn't exclude it, but one, I'm uncomfortable doing that, and two, if clients concoct a defense because the attorney suggested it, the client's going to get torn to shreds on the cross-examination."

"What's your approach?"

She took a sip of water. "Is this for the book?"

"Maybe." He smiled.

"I want to know all the facts. Then I put them in the best light and show that the government hasn't proved its case."

"What happens if your client's acquitted and offends again?"

"Thank God I haven't been in that situation. I've thought about it. I like what Alan Dershowitz tells his clients: 'Every dog gets one bite. Don't dream of calling me if you ever get in trouble again. Not only will I not represent you, I'll be on the other side.'"

Jeff nodded again. "What are you working on now?"

"A date rape." She sighed and picked up an egg roll.

Jeff frowned. "You think he did it, huh?"

"Actually, I have a good feeling about him. But I hate rape cases in general, and this one . . ." She shook her head. "The complaining witness is a young woman from an Orthodox family."

"So don't take the case."

"Not my option. My boss insists." She recalled the scene with Richard and tightened her lips.

"Tell him you've got a conflict of interest."

"I don't, really. I don't know the witness."

"You could tell your boss your family knows her."

She shook her head, feeling a flicker of annoyance at his insistence over what was none of his business. "Tell me about your family," she said to change the subject.

Over dinner he amused her with anecdotes about his family in Chicago; then she told him carefully selected, non-intimate facts about hers because she had learned to be cautious. He was bright and witty and physically attractive, but as he walked her to her front door, she admitted to herself with disappointment that though the evening had been pleasant, there was nothing electric about the way she felt toward him. Maybe it was the timing—her nerves were still jangled from the events of the past twenty-four hours. If he asked her out again, she'd say yes.

She'd brought Avedon's file home but decided she would deal with it in the morning. Lying in bed, she tried watching the movie she'd rented—she loved movies, especially oldies—but she couldn't concentrate. She caught the end of the eleven o'clock news, then turned off the television.

In the middle of the night, she dreamed she was in a room with a sheet-covered mound. She walked to the mound, leaving bloody footsteps behind her, and when she lifted the sheet, she saw Susan, whose open mouth was a black, empty hole. Debra screamed.

She woke up with a start, her heart lurching in her chest, the scream ringing in her ears. She switched on her night-stand lamp and left it on, the way she had when she'd been plagued by nightmares as a little girl, and finally fell into a restless sleep.

Chapter Seventeen

The hammering beneath the house started at eight in the morning. Debra was using the StairMaster in the spare bedroom when she heard the noise over the music coming through her Walkman earphones. She finished her daily thirty minutes and slow-down exercises, then showered and dressed.

She was applying makeup when the doorbell rang.

"Good morning," Adam Bergman said after she let him in. "No paper this time. Sorry." He smiled.

"I already took it in." The front page of the Metro section had carried an article about Susan's murder with a small photo of Debra. "Thanks anyway."

"My men will need electricity. Will you be home?"

"No, but there's a garage outlet you can use. I'll leave the garage open. You can lock it when you leave. I forgot to ask you—how long will the retrofitting take?"

"We should be done by Monday afternoon."

"That's great." She'd have to remember to transfer money

from savings to checking today. "By the way, Mr. Bergman—"

"Call me Adam."

"I'm Debra," she said, not unpleased by the shift to a first-name basis. "Do you do small remodeling?" When he nodded, she led him to an alcove off the living room. "I want to fix this up as an office with a desk and built-in bookcases." She'd decided to furnish the second bedroom as a guest room. And if she married someday and had children . . .

"Serious-looking books," he said, glancing at the stacks of tall, thick volumes on the beige carpet.

"I often bring work home from the office. I'm an attorney," she added, and hoped she didn't sound superior. She'd been using her laptop computer on the kitchen table and found it inconvenient to traipse back and forth through the living room to the alcove for another legal reference work she needed.

"You'll want to maximize space." He crossed the room and opened a door. "I'd eliminate this closet if you don't need it. You'll gain two and a half feet."

She nodded. "Okay."

"What kind of wood do you like?"

"Something that says library. Not too light, but not too cold and forbidding. And not too expensive." She smiled.

"Walnut or oak, maybe. Rosewood's beautiful, but that *is* expensive. What kind of law do you practice?"

"Criminal defense," she said, wondering at the non sequitur. She braced herself for the usual "Why would you want to deal with criminals?" question.

"I guess we can't barter, then. I need an attorney to set up a living trust for my parents." He smiled. "Let me take some measurements so I can give you a rough cost."

While he measured, Debra boiled water in a kettle and toasted a cinnamon-raisin bagel. She was spreading blackberry jam on the bagel when he entered the kitchen.

"Do you have a sheet of paper and a pencil?" he asked.

She took both from a drawer she'd allocated to odds and ends. He sat at the breakfast room table and sketched, his hands moving with swift assurance over the blank paper. The kettle whistled. She shut off the burner and took down her favorite mug. "Would you like some coffee or tea, Adam?"

"Coffee would be nice. Decaf, low-fat milk if you have some."

She prepared coffee for him, raspberry tea for herself. From a drawer in the built-in breakfront where she kept knickknacks, she took two mats and placed them on the table. She had to walk around him to get to the drawer, but he didn't seem distracted. He continued drawing, even when she brought the cups and saucers and bagel to the table.

"Would you like a bagel?" She felt awkward eating in front of him and not asking him to join her. "It's kosher. Sara Lee."

He looked up and smiled. "No, thanks. I had breakfast. No grapefruit for you this morning?"

"Grapefruit?" She frowned. It took a second before she remembered the knife; she wondered whether he'd known she was lying. She turned so that he couldn't see her face. "No, not today." She washed her hands, recited the benediction over bread, then returned to the table and took a bite of the bagel.

"Is this more or less what you had in mind?" he asked a minute later, pushing the paper in front of her.

It was exactly what she'd had in mind, she said. He told her the approximate cost—it was high but affordable. They agreed that he would come on Sunday with precise drawings and an exact cost based on two different types of wood.

"Thanks for the coffee." He stood up, folded the paper, and slipped it inside the pocket of his jeans. "I had bar mitzvah lessons with a Rabbi Laslow twenty years ago. Any relation?"

"My dad. He still gives bar mitzvah lessons."

She and Aaron had spent countless evenings and occasional Sunday afternoons at the gray-and-white-pebbled Formica kitchen table doing homework or playing games against the background of her father's musical rendition of the *trop*—the intricate cantillations used for the reading of the weekly portion of the Torah—followed by the agonized imitations of pupils whose voices croaked and screeched. She and Aaron had been forbidden to disturb the sessions, but sometimes she would inch open the door and peek at the gangly, pimply-faced adolescents.

Adam smiled. "Really? I remember sitting in the dining room, dying for the session to be over. Your mother always brought out a plate of home-baked chocolate-chip oatmeal cookies. I still think it was a bribe to get me to come back each week. Does she still bake those cookies?"

"My mother died seven years ago," she said, feeling sorry for Adam, whose smile had dimmed.

"That must be rough, no matter how many years have passed," he said softly.

She was used to having people avert their eyes, used to hearing awkwardness in their voices; she didn't blame them. But there was only kindness in Adam's voice and in the sudden intensity of his blue eyes, and she felt suddenly vulnerable.

"Let me open the garage," she said.

Her first stop was the Long Beach courthouse, where she attended the arraignment of a client charged with burglary. Then she drove to her office and thumbed through the thick stack of papers in Kenneth Avedon's files. She noted that Annette Prado had handled the preliminary hearing. Annette was a veteran deputy district attorney with Sex Crimes. She was tough, skilled, and ambitious, but not a monster—Madeleine Chase with a heart and a conscience.

Debra had tried two cases against Annette; she'd lost the first, won the second.

Thinking about the district attorney's office, Debra wondered about Claire and the pizza thief. She phoned Claire's chambers; while the clerk checked to see if Claire could talk, Debra began reading the police report of Avedon's arrest.

"Are you okay?" Claire asked, her voice husky with urgency when she came on the line a minute later. "I've been thinking about you ever since I heard."

Debra closed the folder. "I told you I'd make the Metro page before you, didn't I?" she said with feigned lightness. "Glynnis said you phoned several times yesterday. Thanks. I'm sorry I didn't return your calls."

"Don't apologize. And for God's sake, don't thank me. I was worried about you. And don't talk about it, unless you want to."

"It's too gruesome, too unbelievable, too—" She blinked back tears and cleared her throat. "I don't know what to worry about first, the fact that some psycho killed two lawyers, both of whom I knew, or that I may be a suspect."

"What are you talking about?" Claire's tone was sharp.

"A Detective Simms questioned me Tuesday night, and again yesterday. He doesn't seem to like me very much."

"Marty Simms? From Wilshire? He's testified in my court. Don't take his reaction to you personally, Debra. He doesn't like most criminal defense attorneys."

"So he indicated. How's the pizza man?"

"I'm still waiting for the ax to fall. Why?"

"Just wondering. You know Annette Prado, don't you? She's going to prosecute a rape case I'm trying."

"Debra—"

"I inherited the client from Madeleine, can you believe it? And the complaining witness comes from an Orthodox family. She's charged my client with date rape, so you can—"

"Debra! What the hell is wrong with you? You know better than to discuss this with me. What if you try this case before me?"

"You're right," she said, abashed. "I'm sorry."

Claire sighed. "I'm sorry, too. I shouldn't have bitten your head off. I'm on edge."

"Because of Nancy Argula?"

"That and my father. He drove his car into a lamp pole last night. Can you believe he had only a few minor bruises? So did the car. He's angry because I threatened to take the car away. He isn't supposed to drive at night. God, I wish my mother were alive to handle him!"

Debra knew there was friction between Claire and her father. He was in his late sixties and had some physical problems but insisted on living alone; Claire would worry less if he were in a retirement home. "He'll calm down, Claire."

"Probably. You have no idea how lucky you are to have a good relationship with your father. You're sure you're okay?"

"I'm fine."

"Good luck with your case, and with Annette Prado."

An hour later Debra had read all the papers in Avedon's file. She was pleased to see that what Avedon had told her yesterday agreed with the statements he'd made to the police and at the prelim. They didn't, of course, concur with Penny Bailor's statements. She hadn't testified at the prelim—with the passage of Proposition 115, she didn't have to; a police officer had done so on her behalf. The first time Debra would be able to gauge her credibility as a witness would be when she took the stand during the trial. That was a disadvantage. Debra reread all the documents and saw no mention that Penny Bailor had accused Avedon of using a weapon or threatening her with bodily harm. That was good news.

Among the witnesses Annette planned to call were Penny

Bailor, her mother, the detective who first interviewed
Penny, and Shira Frick, the girlfriend at whose home Penny
had spent the night of the alleged rape. Madeleine had
taken statements from Avedon's staff, including the receptionist who had replaced Penny, Avedon's fiancée, former
girlfriends, and several colleagues. She'd also interviewed
Avedon's next-door neighbor and the apartment's security
guard. The file contained all the written statements from the
defense and prosecution witnesses.

Debra phoned the district attorney's office and informed
Annette that Kenneth Avedon had retained her as defense
counsel.

"You're taking over for Madeleine?" Annette's voice betrayed surprise, then dropped almost to a whisper. "It's terrible about her murder. And Susan was killed just five days
later! It must have been horrible for you, finding her. I suppose it's just a grim coincidence, but still . . ."

It was no coincidence. Fear twisted inside her, and an
image of Susan, lying in a pool of blood, appeared in her
mind. She closed her eyes; the image was still there, would
probably always be there. "It's hard for me to talk about it,
Annette," she said, her voice trembling.

"Of course! I'm sorry, Debra." She paused, then in a businesslike tone said, "I assume you'll file for a continuance—
because of taking over for Madeleine, I mean."

"We don't need a continuance. And my client wants to
put this behind him. His wedding is set for New Year's
Day."

"In the prison chapel? I have to tell you, Debra, my witness is extremely convincing. And we have that tape."

"My witness is convincing, too. I read the tape transcript.
I'm not worried." Avedon's adoptive admissions *did* worry
her. She believed his explanation for why he hadn't denied
Penny's charges, but the jury would hear the admissions

and his lack of denial. And juries, she'd learned from experience, were unpredictable.

"We also have a shrink who will testify that my witness is suffering from rape trauma syndrome," Annette said.

Debra frowned. "I don't see any reports or statements to that effect in my client's file." Not all states allowed expert testimony on rape trauma syndrome; California did, as long as the prosecution could show that the complaining witness's behavior was consistent with that of someone suffering from the syndrome.

"Our psychiatrist examined her yesterday. I'll send you the report. What's your firm's address?"

She gave Annette the address and phone and fax numbers. "Would your witness be willing to have our psychiatrist examine her?" On a sheet of paper, she wrote, SHRINK RAPE TRAUMA SYNDROME?

"I'll ask her. Is your client going to testify?"

"I haven't decided." Even if she had, it wasn't information she'd share with Annette—she preferred to keep the prosecutor on her toes, guessing.

"By the way, Debra, are there any reports from experts or statements from witnesses that I don't know about?"

There were few surprises for attorneys in the courtroom. Under the terms of "reciprocal discovery"—also a result of Proposition 115—the prosecution was entitled to see statements and reports from all defense witnesses. "As far as I know, you have copies of everything I have."

"Unless Madeleine withheld a few goodies. Or took oral statements which she didn't record, so she could get around prop one-one-five. You wouldn't do that, would you, Debra?" Underneath the playful tone was a serious, steely edge.

"I would never do anything unethical, Annette," Debra said, which wasn't really an answer. "See you in court."

If Madeleine had taken oral statements and not recorded

them, they, like the identity of her killer, had gone with her to her grave.

"Here you are." Cynthia Ellis, the fortyish brown-haired woman who had been Madeleine's secretary, handed Debra a sealed gray envelope. "This is everything."

"Thank you." Debra had phoned Blackmeyer and asked him for Madeleine's notes. After a second's hesitation, Blackmeyer had agreed—maybe, she guessed, he felt guilty over having rejected her after he'd practically offered her the position.

Guilt was fine if it produced results. An hour later she'd driven to the law offices to pick up the notes. She'd felt a twinge of regret mixed with envy when she entered reception, an area three times as large as that of Knox and Cantrell.

"Is Mr. Blackmeyer in?" she asked now. "I'd like to thank him."

"He's unavailable."

Either that, or the senior partner felt uncomfortable seeing her. Or maybe, since he'd been having an affair with Madeleine, he wanted no contact with anyone who had known her or her secrets. "This must be terribly difficult for you," Debra said in a tone hushed with sadness and respect.

"It's been hard. The shock. Police coming and going. Clients phoning, worried about what's going to happen to them." Her eyes brimmed with tears.

"You liked Madeleine very much, didn't you?" Debra said quietly.

"No, I didn't. You're surprised that I'd say that, aren't you?" A wry smile played around her thin lips. "She was demanding. She didn't mince words if she wasn't satisfied with my work. But she was a terrific lawyer, and she did whatever it took to win."

"I suppose she received letters from people angry with her."

"Tons." The smile deepened. "To tell you the truth, I think she was proud of them in a strange way."

"Did she save them?"

"The ones from clients, she did. I made Xerox copies for the police. The anonymous hate letters—and there were a number of those—she'd rip those up and toss them into the trash. I think she did it to show me and the world that she wasn't afraid." The woman hesitated, then leaned toward Debra. "But she *was* afraid."

Debra felt a prick of excitement. "How do you know?"

"She'd tape the letters up again when no one was looking. At least she did one time—I saw a retaped letter on her desk when I came into her office without knocking. It looked like a small jigsaw puzzle. When I asked her about it, Ms. Chase was furious."

"When was that?"

The woman's brow was furrowed. "Two weeks ago?"

"Do you know what Ms. Chase did with that letter?"

"No. The police asked me that, too. They searched through her desk and files." She neatened a stack of folders on her desk.

"You don't happen to know what the letter said?"

"I don't read other people's mail, Ms. Laslow." Her voice had turned frosty with indignation.

"I didn't mean to suggest you did," she said in a soothing tone. "I thought Ms. Chase may have discussed the letter."

"She didn't. And I don't pry." Her face red, the secretary stood, lifted the stack of folders, and held them against her chest. "I have to photocopy some papers. Excuse me, please."

"I'm sorry. It's just that—"

"I don't know anything about the letter." She crossed the room to the photocopy machine against the far wall.

The lady doth protest too much, methinks, Debra decided.

Chapter Eighteen

A large sign on her front lawn advertised BERGMAN CONSTRUCTION. Debra was startled by the sign—it disturbed the smooth expanse of green—but as she pulled into her driveway, she decided she liked the idea that anyone passing by would know there was activity around the house.

She walked into the backyard. Adam had locked the garage as she'd asked. Though it was dark, she could see from the reflection of the light above the circuit breaker system on the back wall that his men had neatly stacked the plywood and other materials.

"Debra?"

She turned, startled, and saw Adam walking toward her. "I thought you'd gone," she said. She hadn't noticed his truck parked in front; then again, she hadn't looked for it.

"My guys blew a fuse, and I didn't want you coming home to a house without electricity. Sorry. The breakers on the back wall seem okay. Do you have some elsewhere?"

She felt a flash of annoyance, but he was so good-looking, and his smile was so apologetic. "There are breakers in the service porch. Whoever wired this house put the garage, the bedrooms, and the kitchen on the same circuit. I'll check."

"You'll need a flashlight," he said, showing her the one in his hand.

She had a moment's hesitation about entering a dark house with someone who was, after all, a stranger; then she decided she was being silly and unlocked the side door. He followed her inside and aimed his flashlight at a cabinet above the washing machine while she took down a box of plug fuses and placed it on the dryer. She found the labeled breaker she needed and unscrewed the fuse, then reached for the box of fuses just as Adam did. Their hands met. She drew hers away quickly, flustered. He handed her a fuse. She felt his eyes on her as she screwed it into place.

The panel light on the machine flicked on. "Success." She smiled.

"Most women I know aren't this handy."

"I wouldn't call this 'handy.'" She returned the box of fuses to the shelf and shut the cabinet door. "And living alone forces you to be independent." She switched on the service porch fixture and blinked at the glare of the fluorescent light.

"Are you divorced? If it's none of my business, just say so."

It was none of his business, but she shook her head and said, "Never married."

"Me either."

The conversation was too personal. So was the way he was gazing at her. "Thanks for the moral support and the flashlight."

"Sorry again about the fuse."

"Better today than tomorrow. I would have been frantic,

rushing home at the last minute from work, trying to get ready for *Shabbos* and having the breakers blow."

"That's the second thing I like about being self-employed. My day is over when I say it is. I don't have to explain to anyone."

Debra thought about Richard and almost sighed. "What's the first?"

"I love my work." He smiled again. "See you tomorrow."

She still loved the law, but it had been a long time since she'd loved her work. After Adam left, she changed into slacks and a sweater, listened to her phone messages, then checked the mail. More bills, including the mortgage. There was a lingerie catalog and a slim envelope from Hoffinger, Bailey and Tchuck, Attorneys at Law. With nervous fingers, she tore open the envelope and unfolded the letter inside.

They wanted to meet with her. Could she please call to arrange for an interview?

An interview was not a job offer, she cautioned herself as she walked to the breakfast room, but she was tingling with elation. She tossed the other mail onto the table and tucked the letter and envelope behind a divider in her attaché case.

She had stopped for a slice of pizza on the way home but was suddenly hungry again. Rummaging through the freezer, she found a package of split-pea soup. She slit open the plastic pouch and was about to heat the soup in the microwave when Jeff phoned.

"You sound high," he said after they'd exchanged hellos and a few pleasantries. "I take it your date rape case is shaping up?"

"It looks promising." She hesitated, wondering if telling him was premature, but she wanted to share the news with someone. "Actually, I'm excited because after sending my résumé to a number of law firms, I'm finally going to interview with one."

"You're not happy where you are?"

"I'm having problems with the senior partner's fair-haired boy—dark-haired, really. This is confidential, Jeff."

"Don't worry—I won't put it in my book." He laughed.

"So which firm are you interviewing with?"

"Hoffinger, Bailey and Tchuck."

"Hoffinger's a good firm. Is that your first choice?"

Blackmeyer had been her first choice, Susan's firm a strong second. Debra didn't want to mention either and have to deal with questions. She named the other firms, then said, "I haven't decided yet which one I prefer. How's your writing coming along?"

"Limping." He laughed. "I spent the day thinking about you. I had a great time last night, Debra. I thought we'd go out Saturday night."

She'd had a nice time, too, even though there had been no magic. She thought about Adam Bergman, and her reaction when their hands had accidentally touched, and said, "I'd like that."

They talked for half an hour. After she hung up, she returned calls to her father and to several friends who'd phoned to express concern—and natural curiosity, she guessed—about the Metro article. Then she phoned Aunt Edith and apologized for not having returned her calls sooner.

"As long as you're all right, Debra," her aunt said. "The paper made it sound like you were going to jail."

Marty Simms appeared in her mind. Debra shook her head to dislodge the image. "I'm not going to jail, Aunt Edith."

"Of course not!" she exclaimed, and with no transition and with a directness and singularity of purpose that awed Debra and made her smile, Edith told her about a thirty-seven-year-old dermatologist her friend Bernice knew. "Divorced, but no children. If I tell Bernice to give him your number, he can still call you for this Saturday night."

"I have a date Saturday night," she said, feeling almost guilty about ruining her aunt's well-intentioned plans.

"Someone else fixed you up?" Edith's voice held pleasure, surprise, and a hint of pique. "What's his name?"

"Jeff Silver. Aaron checked him out. How's Uncle Morrie?" she asked to change the subject. "And Jenny and the kids?"

She listened for a few minutes while her aunt talked about her grandchildren; then she said good night. Her last call was to Aaron. "Sorry I didn't phone yesterday," she told her brother. "I wasn't up to talking."

"That's okay. I understand." He sounded distant, detached.

Debra frowned. "Something's wrong. I can hear it in your voice. Problems at work?"

"Work is fine."

"Then what?" When he didn't answer, she asked again.

"Julia got her period." His tone was flat, emotionless.

She was overwhelmed with disappointment for Julia, for Aaron, for all of them. "I'm so sorry, Aaron." She bit her lip and was silent for a moment, not knowing what else to say. "Can I talk to her?"

"Not now. She's crying, and I don't know what to tell her, Debra. We really thought that this time . . ." His voice trailed off.

"Is there anything I can do?" There was another silence. "Have you thought about in vitro, Aaron?" she finally asked.

"Have you thought about where we'd get the money?" He sighed. "It's at least ten thousand dollars per attempt."

"I could lend you the money. I'd be happy to do it."

"The hot-shot criminal defense attorney saves her poor older brother? No thanks."

"You know that's not so." He was frustrated, pained; he needed to lash out at someone. "You'd lend me the money if I needed it," she said softly. "That's what families are for, Aaron."

"I know. I'm sorry I snapped at you. It's just . . . I have to go to Julia, Debra. See you tomorrow night."

"Call me if you need to talk," she said, but he had hung up the phone.

She was no longer hungry, but the split-pea mix, now defrosted, had oozed through the slit she'd made into the bowl. Still thinking about Aaron and Julia, she heated the soup and brought it and a roll to the breakfast room table.

She spotted the lingerie catalog under the stack of mail. She pulled it toward her and flipped through the pages showing beautiful, sexy women in beautiful, sexy garments.

One of the pages was folded vertically. She unfolded it and saw that someone had drawn a red asterisk next to a photo of a tall, leggy model with wavy dark brown hair who was wearing a slinky, spaghetti-strap, ivory satin nightgown that skimmed her body and exposed the top half of her full breasts.

There was another asterisk next to the photo below. In this the same woman was lying on her side, her head propped up on one hand; she was modeling a lacy black bra and matching high-cut bikini panties.

"Definitely you," the person had scrawled in the margin.

Debra tore out the page, filled with fury and disgust at Richard—she *knew* it was Richard—and a flutter of unease. She was about to crumple the page, then decided to keep it. Maybe she would show it to Jeremy.

But Richard would deny that he'd sent the catalog.

And she couldn't prove that he had.

Chapter Nineteen

Avedon had brought a typed list with the names, addresses, and phone numbers of people who would testify to his solid character.

Debra slipped the list at the back of his folder. "I've read all the documents and statements in your file, Ken. I've also obtained Madeleine Chase's notes."

She'd felt strange reading the handwritten, ghostlike communication. Madeleine had assessed Avedon—"strong witness, highly credible, good-looking, highly sympathetic." She'd also scribbled cryptic comments—"6 yrs.?" and "G.P.?"—in the margins of one of the pages. Neither comment seemed relevant to Avedon, who was an internist, not a general practitioner. Debra had asked him about them; he'd shaken his head and said he didn't know what they meant.

"So what do you think?" Avedon asked now.

"As I explained, the jury will decide who's more credible—you or Penny. The prosecution will present her as a wholesome young woman—a virgin—from a devout background whose only flaw was poor judgment in going out to dinner with her employer—a wealthy internist who plied her with liquor and then raped her."

"She was willing." Avedon's chin jutted forward. "She was all over me when we got to my place. Do you think the jury will believe her?"

"You're a doctor—respected, clean-cut, financially secure—not the typical rapist. On the other hand, Ken, many people—and remember, jurors are only people—envy doctors and think they're arrogant and wouldn't mind seeing them brought down a notch."

"Wonderful," he said, his tone glum.

"It's just something to be aware of." Debra flashed a reassuring smile. "Penny claims she waited to press charges because she didn't want to deal with the trauma and shame of testifying, of having everyone know she'd been raped." That's what Debra had read in the police report; that's what she'd verified when she'd phoned the officer, a woman Debra had dealt with on previous rape cases, who had first interviewed Penny. "From what you've told me, you feel she pressed charges because her fantasy about marrying you blew up when you became engaged to Vickie."

"That's exactly what happened." He nodded vigorously.

She glanced again at Madeleine's notes and the word "VIRGIN??" "You said Penny told you only after you had intercourse that she was a virgin and that you couldn't tell. Is it possible she lied?"

"Madeleine asked me that, too. It's possible. There was nothing to say she *was* a virgin. Why?"

"If we can prove she lied about being a virgin, the jury may believe she lied about being raped, too. That's an avenue I think Madeleine wanted to explore. But there are problems. One, we have to find a person or persons with whom she had sex before you. Two, even if we can prove she had sex, the judge may disallow the testimony because of the rape shield laws, which state that the complaining witness's prior sexual history can't be introduced."

"Madeleine told me. The laws aren't fair, are they?"

"They *are* fair. A lot of people still believe that a rape victim 'asked for it.' That isn't true. And the fact that a woman has had prior sexual activity outside of a marital relationship, or has even been promiscuous, has no bearing on whether or not she was raped. Rape shield laws prevent attorneys from putting her and her past on trial instead of the defendant."

"You sound passionate about this," Avedon said with a trace of discomfort. "I'm glad you're on my side."

"Sorry." She smiled. "I've seen some ugly abuse of victims on the stand. But I *am* on your side, Ken. And if Penny testifies that she was a virgin and we find evidence to the contrary, I'll argue to have that evidence submitted to the jury. The other thing—"

Her intercom buzzed. "Excuse me." She picked up her phone and said, "Yes?" and learned that Simms was here. "You know I'm with a client, Glynnis," she said, trying to sound annoyed in front of Avedon and not nervous, because of course Simms had discovered that she'd been at Madeleine's condo on the night of the murder.

"He insists on seeing you now."

"I'll be right out." Hanging up the receiver, she forced herself to smile. "Something's come up that needs my immediate attention. I'll be just a few minutes. I hope you don't mind."

Ken Avedon smiled and assured her that he didn't mind. Leaving her office, she was careful to pull the door shut behind her. Simms, she saw, was slouched on a chair.

"Is the conference room available, Glynnis?" She had no intention of talking within earshot of the secretary. When Glynnis nodded, Debra turned to Simms, who had approached. "Please come with me, Detective," she said with cool civility.

He followed her down the hall into the room. "Nice," he said, looking at the long oval table. He sat on one of the chairs and swiveled back and forth as he ran his hand across the table's smooth surface. "Is this where you have your power meetings?"

She remained standing. "I have a client in my office. He's not paying me to stand here and talk to you. What do you want?"

"How much?"

She frowned. "What?"

"How much does he pay you per hour? Two fifty? Three? Four?"

"That's none of your business."

"I'll bet it's a lot. How much do you think I make?"

"I'm not interested in comparing salaries, Detective. Do you have something to ask me? If not—"

"Where were you on the night Madeleine Chase was killed?"

She was prepared for the question, but not for the tightening in her stomach; she wondered if he sensed her tension. "I spent the evening at home until ten o'clock, at which time I drove to Madeleine's condominium to apologize for my part in our quarrel that afternoon." She noted with some pleasure the surprise that flashed across Simms's rugged face and the disappointment that pulled at his jowls. "I arrived at ten-thirty. I rang her bell outside the lobby several times, then left when no one answered."

"You didn't mention this to me or to Detective Cummings."

"Cummings told me Madeleine had been killed between seven and ten that night—half an hour before I arrived. I didn't notice anyone or anything suspicious at the scene, so I saw no reason to volunteer that information." She felt a sudden, overwhelming rush of relief; her animosity toward Simms ebbed. "In retrospect, I was wrong, Detective, and I apologize."

"Why didn't you just phone her?"

"I did, several times. Her line was busy. One time she answered, and I hung up. I got cold feet."

"So you drove out there. But you didn't go up to her condo?"

"Not that night. I was there two weeks prior, though, at a meeting of WRIT, the organization I told you about."

"A couple saw you that night and said you seemed nervous."

"I *was* nervous. I wasn't looking forward to apologizing to Madeleine—if you'd known her, you'd understand. And their dog was growling at me." Debra smiled.

Simms frowned. "Murder isn't funny, Ms. Laslow."

"I don't mean to suggest it is," she said, the smile gone.

"Cummings spoke to several of Ms. Chase's law school classmates. They all thought you were going to be law review editor, but she was selected."

"I was disappointed." She shrugged, pushing away the memories of Madeleine smirking, Madeleine gloating. "But I got over it."

"Right after that you applied to Blackmeyer and were turned down in favor of—guess who? Madeleine Chase."

"You're really doing your homework, aren't you?" she said lightly, but the tension had returned. "I wasn't unhappy about being turned down. I clerked instead for Judge Ramsey, then joined the public defender's office. You probably know all this."

"I know that Madeleine Chase screwed you out of being law review editor. She screwed you out of a job with the top firm in the city. Years later she did it again."

"I didn't like Madeleine, Detective. Then again, almost no

one I know did. But it isn't as though she ruined my life, or my career. Knox and Cantrell is an excellent law firm."

"If it's so excellent, why are you eager to leave?" Simms stood. "By the way, your purse has traces of Susan Clemens's blood inside. I'll bet the dog did it, huh?"

He walked past her, opened the door, and left the conference room. She would have liked to remain where she was, to assess her situation, but Avedon was waiting. She exited the room and saw Simms talking to Richard. The two men shook hands. Simms left.

Richard approached Debra. "This is beginning to feel like an LAPD division, not a law firm. I want to talk to you."

"Dr. Avedon's waiting for me," she said with feigned composure. "I'll come to your office when he leaves."

"Do that," he snapped.

She felt his eyes on her as she hurried down the hall, but her attention was focused on trying to remember what she and Avedon had been discussing when she'd left the office.

"Sorry," she said, smiling as she resumed her seat behind her desk. "That took a little longer than I anticipated."

"No problem. It gave me time to think." He leaned forward. "What if we can't prove Penny wasn't a virgin?"

"You said Penny told you she was a virgin to make you feel responsible, that her goal was marriage. It would be great if we could establish a pattern of behavior. Whom did she work for before you hired her?"

"An orthopedic surgeon. The information's on her job application."

"Is the doctor single?"

"I don't know."

"Let me check it out." Debra wrote a note on her pad. "Call me with his name, phone number, address."

"What if we can't prove there's a pattern?"

"We don't have to. We don't have to prove Penny wanted

to marry you, either. All we have to do is create reasonable doubt."

"What about her clothes? She was wearing really sexy black underwear. Madeleine said that would help us."

Debra had seen Madeleine's note to that effect. "We don't need to mention that, Ken." It was a sleazy tactic, one she preferred not to use.

"Doesn't it mean that she wanted sex?"

"No, it doesn't." Debra thought of the lingerie catalog on her counter and of the lacy underwear she'd bought on a whim because she'd wanted to feel good about herself.

"I still think we should bring in the underwear."

"Let's wait and see." She stood to indicate that the subject and the meeting were over. "Get me the name of the orthopedist."

She left the office at three-forty, but a three-car collision at the intersection of Beverly Boulevard and San Vicente kept her sitting in her Acura for twenty minutes, during which she felt frustrated and nervous and had to restrain herself from honking at the drivers in front of her who were as immobilized as she was.

When she stepped inside her house it was four-thirty—five minutes until the printed candle-lighting time—but she had eighteen additional minutes until sunset that she could use in case of emergency. She raced through her routine, happy that her father couldn't see her; two minutes before sunset, when she was about to light the candles, the phone rang. She could hear her mother's gentle admonition ("I'm going to light now, Debra; whoever it is will call back after *Shabbos*"), then picked up the receiver and was punished for her curiosity with Richard's brusque, angry voice.

"You were supposed to come talk to me," he said.

"I tried, several times. You weren't in your office." She didn't add that she hadn't been disappointed.

"The police dropping by is becoming a problem, Debra. It sets a poor image for our clients."

"No one saw Simms. Avedon doesn't know why I left the office."

"That's another thing—it was totally unprofessional of you to leave a client like that."

"Richard, I hear you. I apologize for today, and I'm perfectly happy to discuss this with you on Monday morning." She checked her watch—she had one minute left.

"Monday morning you'll find another excuse to avoid me."

"I'm not avoiding you, but I'm about to light Sabbath candles."

"Light them a few minutes later. Listen, Debra—"

"Richard, I have to go. I won't violate the Sabbath."

"There's nothing wrong with talking on the phone on the Sabbath, Debra. There's no work involved. That's the problem with Orthodoxy—it takes things to an extreme."

"I respect your point of view, Richard, but it's not mine. I'm hanging up."

"Debra—"

She hung up the receiver and struck a match. The phone rang again. She lit the first candle and after the fourth ring heard the answering machine click on. She lit the second candle and Richard's voice yelled, "Pick up the phone, damn it!" as she circled the candles three times and, with her hands covering her eyes, recited the blessing.

There was another series of four rings, then another. She tried not to hear them as she concentrated with her eyes still tightly shut on her weekly prayers—children for Julia and Aaron, solace for her father, continued health for Aunt Edith and Uncle Morrie ("Debra, answer the phone!") and Jenny and her husband and children. Her eyes teared as she added a prayer for the eternal rest of Susan's soul and, after a brief hesitation, Madeleine's.

The ringing stopped. Debra walked into the dark living room and checked the mail—she couldn't open any sealed envelopes on the Sabbath; she just wanted to see what had come. After returning to the breakfast room, she noticed that one envelope had been hand-delivered; written on the front was only her name, no address.

The flap hadn't been sealed. She pulled out a sheet of paper, and by the soft glow of the flickering, dancing Sabbath candles, she read the message:

"Get out of the way of Justice."

Chapter Twenty

The bar mitzvah boy was having difficulty with the trills in the cantillation. Debra winced in sympathy each time he foundered, his voice plummeting from a croak to a squeak, sometimes stopping altogether, at which point he was bombarded by a fusillade of well-intentioned but unnerving corrections from other male congregants. She recalled how nervous she'd been for Aaron during his public rite of passage into Jewish adulthood and thought about Adam Bergman, whom her father had tutored. She wondered what synagogue he attended.

Another mispronounced word invited another round of corrections silenced by a "Shah!" from the rabbi, who pounded on his lectern as the boy's mother, standing four rows ahead of Debra in front of the beige curtain on top of the wooden partition that separated the men from the women, dabbed at her brow and upper lip with a crumpled tissue.

"Poor kid," Debra whispered to Julia, who was sitting next to her, absorbed in the Torah reading; but Julia didn't respond. During dinner last night, though Debra had been preoccupied with the threatening letter, which she had no intention of revealing to her family, she'd noticed Julia's forced cheerfulness and the puffiness around her eyes, had heard a listlessness in Aaron's voice as he'd accompanied their father, who had sung the Sabbath melodies with joyous fervor as he always did, even the week after his wife's burial. "On *Shabbos,* one is not allowed to mourn," he'd reminded Aaron and Debra with a tremulous, hoarse voice as the tears had welled in his eyes.

Susan was being buried this morning. Marty Simms was probably at the funeral, speculating about Debra's absence. She felt fresh regret that she wasn't able to attend—the services were at Forest Lawn, ten miles away, and she couldn't drive on the Sabbath. She'd sent a note to Susan's secretary and asked her to forward it to Susan's parents in Houston.

Finally, the bar mitzvah boy finished, his last note a triumphant peal that elicited relieved cries of *"Mazel tov!"* from the men on the other side of the partition and from the women and children, who parted the curtains and pelted him with small, tulle-wrapped bouquets of candies, raisins, and almonds. The boy had covered his head with a prayer shawl for protection; around him squealing children dove to the carpeted floor, snatching up packets. In the aisle near Debra, a little girl who had thrown her bag into the men's section was wailing for its return. Debra found a packet on the floor beneath her seat and handed it to the little girl, who stopped crying with an abruptness that aroused in Debra a pang of envy for childhood, when most problems were quickly and easily resolved and candies or a kiss could make it all better.

Thirty minutes later the service concluded. Debra and Julia followed the others to the adjoining reception hall, where people exchanged traditional wishes of joy—God willing, we look forward to your happy occasions. Once or twice Debra was greeted with a second of uncomfortable silence, broken by "How's your job?" or "How's the family?" from people who didn't know what to say to Debra, whose fourth finger on her left hand was unadorned. Or to Julia, whose abdomen was flat after six years of marriage.

Those were the moments Debra dreaded, but they were rare, and she didn't let them prevent her from coming here on Saturday mornings and holidays to participate in the services and hear the universal melodies to ancient words that uplifted her and gave her a feeling of connection to her community and to her roots, a feeling she often found diminished during the week.

She sensed that people were looking her way—talking about her and the Metro article, no doubt. She couldn't blame them. One older woman in a curly medium brown wig was blatantly staring. Debra spooned egg salad onto her plate and walked to her father and her aunt.

"You look beautiful," Edith said, offering her cheek to Debra, who kissed her aunt and inhaled a whiff of the White Linen her mother had always worn. Aunt Edith was shorter and plumper than her sister, Anne, but her features reminded Debra strongly of her mother—the long, oval face and high forehead; the short, thin nose and hazel eyes with amber centers; full lips that curved easily into a smile; long, reddish brown hair that, outside the house, was tucked beneath a hat or beret or covered with a wig of the same color. Seeing her aunt always filled Debra with a gentle, not unpleasant ache that she almost welcomed.

"Where's Julia?" her father asked.

"With Aaron, I guess. I like your suit, Aunt Edith. You lost weight, didn't you?" she asked, knowing that the question would please her aunt, who was constantly dieting.

"Size eight." She smiled. "Uncle Morrie was thrilled until I told him I'll have to get a whole new wardrobe."

"You're the lawyer?" asked a voice behind Debra.

Still smiling at her aunt, Debra turned and faced the woman who had been staring at her just minutes before.

"You're Debra Laslow, right? They pointed you out."

People would sometimes approach Debra for free legal advice. "Nothing big," they'd assure her. And if it *was* "nothing big" and she could answer easily, she'd preface the advice by cautioning that she was speaking as a friend, not an attorney. "I'm Debra Laslow. How can I help you?"

"Ma, let's go," said a short bearded man who had approached. He put his hand on his mother's shoulder.

She shrugged off his hand. "You're the one who's going to say my Penina's a liar."

Debra frowned, bewildered. "I'm sorry. I don't—"

"Penny," she hissed. "My daughter. Don't pretend you don't know."

Debra blanched. Her aunt said, "What's going on?" and Debra quietly told Penny Bailor's mother that she was sorry, but she couldn't discuss this with her.

The woman faced Ephraim Laslow. "You're her father, they said. A rabbi. You think what your daughter's doing is right?"

Rabbi Laslow put his arm around Debra. "My daughter," he began, but was cut off by the son, who whispered, "Ma, not now," and steered his mother away. A few seconds later mother and son were swallowed by the noisy crowd, and Debra was profoundly relieved that no one else had heard.

"Imagine, coming up to you like that," Aunt Edith said. "Why is she so angry?"

Ephraim Laslow turned to Debra. "You're all right?"

Debra nodded. "I'll wait outside."

She left the hall and was exiting the building when she heard someone say, "Ms. Laslow!" She knew it was Penny Bailor's brother and was tempted to hurry down the stairs to the street, but he was already at her side.

"Stuart Bailor," he said, introducing himself in a polite,

subdued voice. "I wanted to apologize for my mother. She shouldn't have attacked you, but you can understand why she's so agitated."

"I understand." She smiled to show she was sincere and wondered whether Penny Bailor's mother had sent the warning note.

"Good." He nodded. "Is there any way you'd consider not defending this man, Ms. Laslow?"

Debra's smile froze. At least the mother was more direct, she thought, and said, "I've made a commitment to my client." She looked around and saw only two little girls swishing their crinolined skirts.

"Commitment's important." He leaned forward, his hands in his jacket pockets. "Of course, you know what they'll say—'If an Orthodox Jew is defending this guy—'"

"Mr. Bailor—"

"'If an Orthodox Jew,'" he repeated, his voice shrill enough to attract the attention of the little girls, "'if an Orthodox Jew is defending this guy accused of raping an Orthodox Jewish woman, the woman must be lying.' That's what I would think."

"Mr. Bailor, I don't mean to be rude, but it's inappropriate for me to talk to you like this." The little girls, she saw, had returned to their conversation.

"The jury will think Penny's lying," Stuart Bailor said, visibly struggling for calm. "Do you think *that's* appropriate? Do you think that's fair to my sister?"

"The jury will make its decision based on all the evidence. The district attorney handling this case is highly competent."

"My sister's life will be ruined if they say she . . . did this . . . willingly." The brother was blushing. "You know the community. What chance will she have of getting married?"

*   *   *

Jeff took her to see a Kevin Kline film in Century City and for dessert at the Pico restaurant where they'd met.

"You're a little quiet tonight," he remarked after the waitress brought their orders. "You didn't like the movie?"

"I loved the movie." She hesitated, then said, "I had an upsetting encounter at shul. It's been on my mind." She told him what had happened, told him, too, about the note she'd received. "I think the mother sent it, or the brother." Or Penny herself?

"Did you ask the brother?"

She shook her head. "He'd just deny it." She tasted the hazelnut cheesecake with the caramel sauce—it was her favorite, but tonight it wasn't working its magic.

"So drop the case."

She looked up at him, startled. "Because the witness is Orthodox?" she asked, feeling stirrings of anger. During lunch she'd received the same "What do you need this for?" advice—from Aaron, from Aunt Edith and Uncle Morrie. Only her father and Julia had come to her defense, and Debra had sensed that her father had done so halfheartedly.

"Because of the note," Jeff said. "I don't like it."

"It's just a stupid piece of paper." A stupid piece of paper she hadn't mentioned to anyone in her family, a paper whose words frightened her and made her look over her shoulder and wonder.

"Then why are you so upset?"

"Because even though the complaining witness is lying, I feel bad for her family." She swirled her fork in the caramel sauce. "Can we change the subject, please?"

"Fine with me."

They talked about law school, about books they'd recently read, about their childhoods. Again she found him funny, bright, attractive; again something was missing. When he walked her to her front door, she let him kiss her, thinking maybe that would make the difference, but the sensation of his lips against hers was pleasant, nothing more, and she drew quickly away.

"I've never gone out with a rabbi's daughter before," he said at her abrupt movement. "Is this a religious thing or am I rushing you?"

Though physical contact between unmarried people was proscribed, Debra had kissed before. She believed in the authority and wisdom of the proscription and envied the innocence and moral fortitude of people like Aaron and Julia, who had first touched, in private, after their wedding ceremony; but she had come to terms with her fallibility and set careful boundaries for herself.

"Both," she said.

She spent Sunday morning going through her closets for items to take to Aunt Edith, who was collecting used clothing for Russian Jewish immigrants.

Adam arrived at eleven-thirty, wearing dark olive green slacks and a brown-and-olive-green sweater and no sports cap. She'd been about to eat a tuna-fish sandwich; she offered to make one for him—offered hesitantly, because she found him extremely good-looking (better looking than Jeff, she had to admit, and more physically exciting), and she sensed again from the way he looked at her that his interest in her was becoming personal and breaking bread together a second time would lend a domestic air to what was, after all, a business relationship.

"Tuna sounds great," he said.

They sat in the breakfast room, eating the sandwiches while he reviewed the plans he'd drawn for her library in the alcove. She had thought about ash veneers for the built-in bookcases and the desk that would extend perpendicularly from the wider wall but agreed with him that bleached oak would give the small room a lighter, more open feeling. She told him she also needed partitions and extra shelves in her bedroom closet, wondering whether she was searching for reasons to have him around.

"We can do that at the same time," he said. "It shouldn't be too expensive—just materials and labor."

"When can your cabinet maker start on my office?"

"I'll be starting the project myself Tuesday," he said, and she knew she'd been right. She was concerned but flattered and told herself there was a definite advantage to having Adam build the cabinets himself—she wouldn't have to worry about leaving strangers in her house while she went to work.

She gave him the second payment, then walked him to the front door, where she saw a folded sheet of white paper that someone had slipped under the sill. Her expression must have alarmed him, because he asked what was wrong as she picked up the paper and opened it and read an advertisement from a gardening service.

"Nothing," she said, her heart still racing. "I got a warning note on Friday to drop a case I'm handling. I thought it was another one." She smiled to show that she was all right.

He nodded. "I don't blame you for being nervous, especially with those lawyers getting killed and mutilated."

She stared at him. "What do you mean?"

"Sorry. I thought you knew." He sounded uncomfortable and shifted his weight to his other foot "On the news on my way here, they were talking about the latest attorney who was killed. They mentioned that her tongue had been severed." He said the last sentence in an undertone while looking somewhere over her head.

Simms must be furious at the leak. She hoped he wouldn't blame her—she'd told only Charles and had done so in confidence. "I knew about the tongue," she said, and saw the surprise on Adam's face. "I found the second victim, Susan Clemens. She and I were good friends. You didn't see my name in the papers?"

He shook his head. "That must have been gruesome for you," he said quietly. "Whoever's doing this is really sick, Debra. You should consider getting an alarm system or bars."

She nodded. "Did the news report say anything else?"

"Just that all three women were killed the same way."

"*Two* women, you mean."

"Three," he said, his eyes and voice filled with apology for what he was telling her. "Another one was found dead this morning."

Chapter Twenty-one

*Emma Banks stepped out of the shower and tow-
eled herself dry. It was her third shower of the day and the
third time that, wearing her navy terry-cloth robe, she
padded down the hall into her bedroom and checked the
miniblinds, even though she knew they were shut.*

*Her furniture crowded the room, which was much smaller
than her old bedroom—the entire apartment was much
smaller, one bedroom instead of two with a tiny kitchen, and
the rent was much higher; the space between the dresser and
the foot of the king-size bed was so narrow that she had to
stand sideways to open the drawer to take out fresh underwear. Andrea and Bill had said, "Why don't you get new
furniture, Mom?" but she'd chosen everything together with
Harry and lived with it during the thirty-two years of their
marriage and for the first five years of her widowhood, so
how could she bear to part with it?*

It was bad enough that she'd had to move.

*The lights in the bedroom and the rest of the apartment
were still on even though it was two o'clock in the afternoon.*

Emma knew she shouldn't be wasteful, not with water (she'd told the apartment building manager she'd pay for that, too) and not with electricity, not now that her job was in jeopardy. She supposed she could shower less often and open the blinds during the day and try to sleep with the lights off at night, but the thought filled her with panic, and when she placed her hand on her chest, she felt the urgent beating of her heart.

She wasn't ready.

She buttoned the waistband of her pants. They were tight; so were most of her clothes. She'd gained eight pounds this month, which was strange, really, because last month she'd lost ten pounds and everybody at work had said, "You lost weight, Emma!" and Andrea had said, "You're skinny as a rail, Mom," and Emma didn't understand why it was that sometimes she felt like eating and other times the thought of food repulsed her. Last night she'd devoured two pints of ice cream and a bag of potato chips after finishing a frozen dinner and a bowl of soup. She hadn't even been conscious of eating everything, had been amazed when she'd seen the empty cartons and bags on the kitchen counter.

Now the pantry was almost bare. She had enough money in her checking account for two weeks of groceries, but if she lost her job, she'd have to dip into savings, and there wasn't all that much there, even with the insurance from Harry's policy; the earliest she was entitled to Social Security would be three years from now, when she turned sixty-two, and she wouldn't get full benefits. After Harry died she'd gone back to work to fill up the lonely hours; now with the higher rent, she needed the income. She couldn't remember if she'd told that to her supervisor, Mrs. Wolenski.

She checked the windows in the living room and dining ell, opening the locks and shutting them again. She did the same for the front door, which she could see from her bedroom. That was one advantage of having a compact apart-

ment, that and the fact that there weren't many closets. She used to tell Harry that you could never have enough closets, but she didn't feel that way, not any more, and she always left her closets open, even though Andrea and Bill told her she was being neurotic.

At the kitchen sink she drizzled Joy into her palm and lathered and rinsed her hands and arms up to her elbows, enjoying the warm water and the squeaky clean feeling. She tried not to think about her meeting on Friday with Mrs. Wolenski. Though she had reviewed the conversation in her mind a hundred times, she still couldn't understand why she was being warned. Mrs. Wolenski had spoken about Emma's frequent absences and her inability sometimes to focus properly, which caused her to make mistakes that other people had to undo; and Emma proved to Mrs. Wolenski that the absences weren't frequent and promised she would try harder to focus and would Mrs. Wolenski please give her a little time, after everything that had happened? And that was when Mrs. Wolenski had told her that she, Emma, was making some of the other people at the agency uncomfortable because she was sad all the time and sometimes started crying, out of the blue, and no one knew how to deal with that. And Emma had said she'd try not to cry and what had happened to compassion? And Mrs. Wolenski had said, let's see what happens next week.

Next week was tomorrow.

She heard a noise at the door and checked the lock again, then checked the windows. Really, the apartment wasn't bad; it was clean and newly painted and the beige carpets worn but freshly shampooed, and she did have a utility room with her own washer and dryer so she didn't have to go downstairs to the basement to do her laundry. But she missed her old place and her neighbors and the shops and found herself wishing all the time that she could go back.

But then he would find her again.

Chapter Twenty-two

Monday morning Debra found a sheet of paper tucked behind her windshield wiper. She yanked it out, annoyed by the proliferation of advertising fliers, and was unprepared to see the same warning—"GET OUT OF THE WAY OF JUSTICE." This time the writer had printed in large capital red letters, as if the words themselves hadn't conveyed enough threat.

Her chest constricted. With her briefcase in her left hand and the note in her right, she half ran to the backyard, where Adam was talking to one of his men. He didn't hear her above the high-pitched whine of the electric saw, and she had to yell "Adam!" twice before he turned and walked toward her, quickening his pace as he saw the terror on her face.

"What's wrong?" he asked, his eyes and voice telegraphing urgency and concern.

She showed him the message, careful to hold the paper by its top corner. "Did you see anyone leave this on my car?"

Her voice was shrill even to her own ears, and she made no effort to hide her panic, unlike yesterday, when she'd tried to mask the terror that had snaked through her at the news that another attorney (Kelly Malter—Debra heard her name countless times during the day) had been killed. Adam had offered to stay, but though the thought of being alone in the house had filled her with dread, she'd felt compelled to pretend she was all right. After he'd left, she'd secured all the windows and doors and phoned her family. She'd pretended with them, too—she didn't want them to worry about her. It had been a relief when she finally spoke to Claire and was able to voice her panic.

Adam shook his head. "Let me ask my men." Reaching for the sheet of paper, he showed surprise, then quick understanding, when she moved it out of reach.

She watched him approach the worker he'd been talking to; the man listened, narrowed his eyes, shook his head. He disappeared from view. A moment later the whining of the saw stopped, then resumed. The worker reappeared and shook his head again.

Adam returned to Debra. "Neither of my men saw anything, Debra. Maybe one of your neighbors did. I'll help you check."

They spent twenty minutes talking to the people up and down the block, many of whom Debra had never met. She wasn't really surprised to learn that no one had seen anything.

Simms placed both notes on his desk, which was crowded with papers and blue vinyl loose-leaf notebooks. One of the notebooks was labeled CLEMENS, SUSAN; Debra knew it contained reports and graphic photographs of Susan's body.

"What happened to this one?" Simms pointed to the crumpled paper on the left.

"That came first. I didn't think it was serious, so I threw it out." She'd retrieved it from the trash, placed both notes in a plastic bag, and driven to the station where she'd been interrogated less than a week ago. Simms had been surprised to see her and told her so as he'd escorted her from reception to the partitioned area where he worked.

" 'Get out of the way of Justice,' " Simms read aloud, then glanced at her. "What's the reference?"

"It may be to my new client." She told him about her confrontation with Penny Bailor's mother and brother. "I don't know if they sent the notes. If they did, I don't want to press charges," she added quickly. "I just want them warned. But what if the notes were sent by the person who killed Madeleine and Susan?"

"And Kelly Malter." He tapped his pencil on his desk. "Did you apply for a position at her firm?"

Deutsch and Contreras—Debra had heard that name on the news countless times, too. "Yes, I did." Bracing herself for Simms's next comment, she said, "I told you I applied to most of the top firms in the city—ten, in fact. It's not exactly a criminal offense. And I didn't know Ms. Malter."

"I had WRIT fax me their membership list. She's a member."

"WRIT has a large membership. I've never met her, although I learned at last night's emergency meeting that she was a member." Over half the membership—private attorneys, public defenders, prosecutors, judges—had attended the session at the home of the organization's president. Claire had been there, sitting next to Nancy Argula. Annette Prado had been there, too. Debra had gone over to the petite, olive-skinned woman and said hello.

"Three women attorneys, all WRIT members, murdered— I don't blame you for calling a meeting. With so many bright women in one room, I'm sure you figured out who's doing the killings."

"Actually, we came up with two theories," she said, ignoring his sarcasm, wondering if he disliked women or attorneys or both, or just her. "The three murdered women were in private practice. The killer may be a male who went over the edge because he's been frustrated in his legal career and is blaming his failure on the increased number of women in private law firms."

Simms raised his brows. "So this guy's knocking off women attorneys to open up slots for himself?" He laced his hands behind his head and leaned back against his chair.

"It's not a rational action. He's killing to express his anger, to take revenge."

"How does he choose his victims?"

They'd discussed this at the WRIT meeting, too. "He targets a top woman in each firm. Maybe he's seen her name in print. Maybe he applied to one or more of these firms and was rejected."

Simms scribbled something on a small pad in front of him. "And you think he could be targeting you. Are you one of the top women in your firm?" The sarcasm was heavier now.

What was his problem? "I'm the *only* woman. And my name's been in the papers lately." This morning's Metro section had not only linked all three murders, but had mentioned again that Debra had discovered Susan's body and been questioned by the police.

"What's the second theory?"

"WRIT endorsed a woman running for city council and came out against her opponent, Henry Osterhaus. Osterhaus was on the board of directors of an electronics corporation, where he sexually harassed women. WRIT encouraged his victims to press charges. Osterhaus was forced to resign from the corporation and drop out of the election. He wrote really nasty letters to WRIT."

"Spell his name," Simms said, his tone crisp, businesslike.

Debra spelled it for him. "We're not accusing Osterhaus.

We're saying he's a possibility, especially since all three victims were WRIT members." The *Times* had already gleaned that information, too, and printed it.

"Were you active in this campaign against Osterhaus?"

"Not especially. Susan was—she was very active in combating sexual harassment. I think Madeleine was active in the campaign, too. And the entire membership supported WRIT's actions. Our names were listed in a newspaper ad sponsoring his opponent."

Simms wrote down the information, then said, "And now you say you've received two threatening notes."

"I *did* receive them. The first one came in an envelope, but there was no stamp, no post office markings. Just my name, written on the front. The second was on my windshield."

"And no one saw anyone deliver either of these notes?"

"That's correct."

"And if we check for fingerprints, we'll find yours on both notes, is that right?"

"Yes. I had no reason to be careful not to leave prints. Are you suggesting I sent these notes to myself?" she asked, injecting coldness into her voice.

"Why would I suggest that?"

She knew from his cat-and-mouse tone and smile that he'd implied exactly that. "Madeleine's secretary told me Madeleine recently received a threatening note. Susan's secretary said Susan received a number of letters, but I don't know how recently. And I don't know about Kelly Malter." Debra had asked people at the meeting, but no one had known.

"Are you an attorney or a detective, Ms. Laslow?" he said, the angry glint in his eyes belying his bantering tone.

"Three of my colleagues have been murdered. Everyone I know is frightened, including me—and I'm the only one, as far as I know, who's received these notes."

"Which, as you said, may refer to your new client. 'Get out of the way of Justice' could mean get off the case."

"The quote ends with 'She'—meaning Justice—'is blind.' " Debra had looked it up. "The notes could be from the Bailors. Or from a psychotic male attorney warning me I'm next, or from someone angry at WRIT. Can you find out if Kelly received one?"

"McCormack from Beverly Hills PD is handling her homicide. I'll ask." Simms's tone was grudging. "And we'll test both notes for prints. We have yours on file, so we can eliminate them."

She couldn't tell from his expression whether his last comment was a reminder that she'd been a suspect. "Thank you," she said, standing. "What about checking to see if a male attorney has applied to the law firms where the victims worked, and maybe to other firms as well?"

"Believe it or not, Ms. Laslow, the thought occurred to me."

He was right to be annoyed. "I'm sorry. I'm just so anxious, because of the notes. You can understand that. Is the police department setting up a task force to handle the investigation?"

"They're talking about it. So have you given any thought as to how Ms. Clemens's blood found its way into your purse?"

"Obviously the dog transferred blood from the carpet to the inside of the purse."

"Obviously." He squinted at her. "Were you aware that Ms. Chase had scheduled a lunch appointment with your boss for the day after she was killed? She'd written it on her calendar."

Debra stared at Simms. "With Mr. Knox?"

"With Mr. Dressner. He confirmed it. I'm wondering why she was planning to meet with him." He looked at her for an answer.

"I have absolutely no idea," she said, trying to gauge from his voice and eyes what he was thinking.

"Maybe she was going to tell him you'd applied to her firm." Simms spun a mug on his desk. "From what I've heard, she was nasty. Maybe she wanted to get you in trouble."

Debra didn't answer.

"According to someone who witnessed your confrontation with her the day she died, she implied she was going to do just that."

"I don't recall that," she said, recalling all too clearly.

"Then," Simms continued as if she hadn't spoken, "you told her it was no surprise no one liked her. Do you recall *that?*"

Debra sighed. "We've gone over this before, Detective. I didn't like Madeleine, but I didn't kill her."

"You went to her condo after making sure she'd be there by phoning and hanging up—you didn't mention it to Detective Cummings at first, probably because you didn't realize the phone company records would show that you called."

"I went to apologize in person. I thought—" She stopped. "This is ridiculous! What motive would I have to kill Madeleine?"

"We've gone over *that* before, too." He smiled. "Revenge?"

"And what was my motive for killing Susan, who was my close friend? And Kelly Malter, whom I didn't even know?" It occurred to Debra that Simms might be baiting her, pretending to suspect her just to irritate her or worry her.

Simms smiled again. "Let me know if you get any more notes."

Chapter Twenty-three

The office of Melvin Volkand, the orthopedic surgeon Penny Bailor had listed as a reference for Avedon, was
located in the Cedars-Sinai medical towers. Debra parked in
a lot and walked along Third Street to the patio between
the east and west towers.

She hated coming here. Seven years had passed since
she'd last brought her mother for chemotherapy, but she
was assaulted by memories—her mother's brave smile; her
slim hand, attenuated by weakness, resting on Debra's arm;
her voice soft with unnecessary apology because she
couldn't walk faster. The lobby was crowded with people of
varying ages. Debra could smell their fear—or maybe it was
her own.

Volkand's suite was on the tenth floor; her mother's oncologist was on the seventh. The elevator stopped on three
and four and five and six. When the doors slid open on
seven, Debra's stomach lurched and she wondered, as she
often did, what she would say if she came face-to-face with
the oncologist, who, after her mother had told him Debra's

father had located a cancer specialist who had developed a new, experimental drug, had said, "So, Mrs. Laslow"—Debra could still see his arrogant sneer as he sat behind his desk— "So, Mrs. Laslow, what wild goose chase are you on now?"

Debra's mother had been silent; so had Debra, because how do you speak back to a man who had appointed himself a god? And the god, with cruel satisfaction in his eyes, had said, "To try this new drug, Mrs. Laslow, your red cell count has to go up, and who knows when that will happen, if ever?"

At home her mother had cried, and Debra had consoled, and the red cell count had gone up, and the other oncologist, a kind, caring man who had made no promises, had at least given them the gift of several months of cautious hope.

Melvin Volkand, M.D., was a disappointment—he was short and portly and in his fifties, clearly not someone Penny Bailor would pursue even if he weren't married.

"What's this about?" Volkand asked when Debra entered his paneled office. "You made an appointment—for which you were half an hour late, by the way!—and I assumed you needed medical care. Then you tell Donna you want to talk to me about Penny Bailor."

"I'm sorry. I had an emergency." Debra sat down in front of his desk. "I'm representing Dr. Avedon, who is charged with raping Ms. Bailor. My client is innocent," she added, seeing the shock on Volkand's face give way to repugnance. "I'm trying to find information for his defense." The firm used a private detective—a retired cop—to help with investigations, but Debra had wanted to speak to the doctor herself.

"Well, I have nothing to say about Penny, except that she was a fine receptionist, and everyone liked her. I was sorry to let her go, so if you've come to find out otherwise, you're out of luck." His tone was brusque, almost angry.

"Why did she leave, do you know?"

"No, I do not," he snapped. "I assumed she was going back to school until Avedon phoned me for a reference."

"I noticed that you have an associate, Dr. Sanger. If he's in, I'd like to talk to him."

"That's entirely up to Dr. Sanger." Volkand stood in dismissal. "My office will, of course, bill you for this appointment and for the half hour you kept me waiting."

Dr. Sanger, Debra learned from Donna, the thin, petite Asian receptionist, was with a patient.

"How old is he?" Debra asked.

"In his early thirties. But he's very competent." She smiled.

Debra showed the woman her business card, then repeated what she'd told Volkand. "Is Dr. Sanger married?"

The smile disappeared. "I can't answer personal questions about the doctor. And I've never met Ms. Bailor. You'll have to wait until Dr. Sanger can see you." The receptionist slid shut the glass partition.

A half hour later Debra met with Eric Sanger. The associate was tall and gangly and unmarried. And reluctant to discuss Penny.

"I really don't want to get involved," he admitted. "Plus, I have nothing to tell you." He checked his watch.

"Did you ever go out with Ms. Bailor?"

"A couple of times. Dinner and a movie. Nothing serious." He shrugged.

"Who initiated the dates?"

"Who?" He frowned. "I'd have to say she did."

"Did you have sexual relations with Ms. Bailor?"

"Hey, come on!" The doctor's face colored.

She felt a tingling of excitement. "I could subpoena you," she said with calm authority, thought she wasn't sure she could subpoena Sanger, since his testimony might not even be admissible.

"The answer is no, we didn't. Not what you wanted, huh?"

Not at all what she'd wanted. "I want the truth, Dr. Sanger."

"The truth is that Penny is a nice girl who comes on like she's very sophisticated, very with it, but she's not."

"Did you engage in any physical contact with Ms. Bailor?"

"God, you lawyers have a way with words, don't you?" He laughed. "We kissed. And we did some other stuff. But no sex. I thought Penny might get the wrong idea."

"The wrong idea?"

"I wasn't interested in a serious relationship. I told her that, and we agreed not to go out again."

"So when you said the dates weren't serious, you meant on your part, is that right?"

"I guess. Right," he added, clearly uncomfortable.

"And you sensed she *was* interested in a serious relationship?"

"Well, yeah. She told me she liked doctors. What the hell, we're nice guys, aren't we?" He smiled.

"And how long after you told her you weren't interested in a serious relationship did she quit her job here?"

"I don't remember exactly. A month? Something like that." He checked his watch again. "I have a patient waiting. If you have any more questions, you'll have to phone me."

And you won't be in, Debra thought. "You may be called to testify for the defense, Dr. Sanger." She handed him her card, which he took gingerly, as if it were contaminated.

Before Debra left, she spoke with the X-ray technician, Yvonne, who confirmed that Penny Bailor had liked doctors.

"She said she hoped to marry one," Yvonne told Debra. "I said, 'Good luck, honey. Don't we all?'"

Debra handed out another card. "If you think of anything else, please call me." Not exactly what she'd wanted, she thought as she walked back to her car, but not a total disappointment.

Adam was loading his equipment into his truck when Debra pulled into her driveway at four-thirty. He reached her as she was getting out of the car, and she was startled to realize how pleased she was to see him.

"Did you show the police the notes?" he asked.

"Yes. They're following up on them." She shut the car door.

"You're home early, aren't you? Are you okay?"

"I had a terrible headache." The migraine had struck in the afternoon, and after the aura had receded, she'd been assaulted by ferocious pain over her right eye. "It's better now, but I decided to leave early. Thanks for asking."

"I'm concerned."

He was staring at her, and he spoke with a simple intensity that made her heart beat faster. "Is the cripple wall shearing completed?" she asked, to depersonalize their conversation.

"All done."

"You'll want a check."

He followed her inside to the kitchen and stood while she leaned over the counter and made out the final payment.

"Thanks." He folded the check and pocketed it. "If you don't have plans, would you have dinner with me tonight?"

"It's nice of you to offer, but I'm exhausted. I think I'll make it an early night." She *was* exhausted; she also had reservations about going out with him. *Because he's a contractor and you're a lawyer?* Aaron would say. But that wasn't it.

"Another time." Adam smiled again. "I checked the locks on your front and side doors. The front door's fine. I'd change the side door lock. It's too easy for someone to break in."

The thought unnerved her. "Could you take care of that for me, please?" She'd been on edge all day, extremely alert when she'd left the office and aware of everyone around her—in the hall, on the elevator, in the underground parking structure. WRIT was mailing letters to all the law firms in the city, asking them to provide security, but Madeleine, Susan, and Kelly hadn't been killed in their offices—they'd been killed at home.

"I'll install a new lock in the morning," Adam said.

She accompanied him to the front door and locked it behind him, regretting for an instant that she'd turned down his invitation. The house seemed larger, emptier; her heels echoed on the hardwood floor.

There were the usual messages on her answering machine—her family, some friends. Jeff had phoned several times—he'd heard about Kelly Malter and was concerned about Debra. Could she please call him as soon as she came home?

A secretary from Hoffinger, Bailey and Tchuk had left a message, too. Mr. Tchuk would like to postpone his interview with Debra and would phone to reschedule.

Don't call us; we'll call you.

So much for that position. Hoffinger et al must have seen her name in the Metro. By now, every firm she'd applied to was probably aware of her notoriety. Jeremy had promised support, and she believed him, but would that support be eroded by continuing media reminders of Debra's involvement with Susan's murder, by the fact that she was still being questioned by the police? And what if Richard convinced Jeremy that Debra was a liability? She wanted to leave the firm, but only if she had another offer. Richard had been out of the office all day, so she didn't know whether he was still angry about Friday's phone call.

A rustling noise outside the kitchen window alarmed her. She stood still, listening, then heard a cat's meow, but the knot of tension remained in her stomach. She didn't know why she was worrying about her career—in view of the fact that a maniac was killing women attorneys, her career paled in significance. So did the fact that Marty Simms considered her a suspect. She supposed it was human nature to worry.

Her head began to throb again. She wondered whether Simms was playing games with her. On an impulse, she phoned West L.A. Division and asked to be connected to Laurie Besem, a homicide detective with whom she'd become friendly when she'd been in the public defender's office.

"How are you, Debra?" Laurie asked when she came on the line.

"Nervous, like most of the women attorneys I know. Terrified, actually."

"The slashed tongue murders, you mean. It's really kinky."

"You probably know I found Susan Clemens," Debra said.

"Yeah, I heard that."

Was it her imagination, or did Laurie sound strained? "I've been talking with Marty Simms from Wilshire. Do you know him?"

"Sure. He was at West L.A. before he transferred to Wilshire."

Definitely strained, Debra decided. And wary. "Does he have anything particular against criminal defense attorneys?"

"He doesn't like them for the same reason most cops don't—we work our asses off to put criminals behind bars, and you guys do your best to put them right back in society."

"Does he dislike women?"

"It's no big secret. Marty's mom abandoned him and his sister to take up some career. His father took it hard and drank. Marty raised the sister. So he has a hard time with career women."

"Does that go for women cops, too?"

"That goes for everyone. He tried giving me a hard time when he was here, but I didn't take any shit from him."

"I think he dislikes me."

Laurie laughed. "Hell, he doesn't like me, either. So what?"

"He's implied that he suspects I'm involved with these murders. He's playing games with me, right?"

Laurie was silent a moment. "Marty takes his work seriously."

"Has Stan Cummings said anything to you?"

"Debra, I can't discuss this. I'm sorry, okay?"

"Laurie, you know I didn't kill anyone. Do they have any leads?"

"We're investigating several possibilities."

"Including me?" When Laurie didn't answer, Debra asked, "Should I get a lawyer?" She was half joking, half serious.

"It's always good to have a lawyer," Laurie said, her tone light. "Look, I'm sure this is just routine, but if you have questions, you'd better ask Stan. I have to go."

Debra listened to the dial phone, lost in thought, then returned Jeff's call.

"Are you okay?" he asked when he heard her voice. "I thought about you every time they had another bulletin about the murdered attorney. I think you should show that note to the police."

She hesitated, then told him about the second note. "I took both notes to the police. They said they'd follow up."

"I sure as hell hope so! Do you want me to come over? I can be there in ten minutes."

The thought was tempting, but she was drained and wanted to go to bed. "Thanks, but I'll be all right."

"Call if you change your mind. I don't care what time it is."

She promised she'd call and said good night. She made certain both doors and all the windows were securely shut, then went into the bedroom and changed into her night-gown. Claire phoned; she wanted to make sure Debra was all right.

"I've been better," Debra said. "Richard sent me a sexy lingerie catalog, Hoffinger rejected me, and Detective Simms thinks I'm a murderer. Oh, yeah, and did I mention there's a psycho killer loose?"

"What's the matter with you, Debra! Why are you letting Simms get to you? You didn't kill anyone."

Debra was startled by the vehemence of Claire's tone. "Hey, Your Honor. You sound kind of edgy yourself."

"Am I? Sorry." She sighed. "Who *isn't* tense these days? I'm just so worried about you, Debra. Do you want to move into my spare room until they find the killer? You'd have total privacy."

"Thanks, but I want to stay home." Aaron and Julia had made the same offer. So had her father. "How's your dad?"

"Talk about tense. He's more grumpy than usual. I guess that's good news—it means he's completely recovered."

They spoke a while longer, then hung up. Debra was pulling down the comforter when the phone rang again. It was the Bailors' rabbi. Would Debra meet with him to discuss Penny's situation? Debra politely but firmly explained that she was committed to her client and hung up before the rabbi could press her.

That night she dreamed again about finding Susan mur-dered, but when she neared the body and lifted the blood-ied sheet, the face she saw wasn't Susan's.

It was her own.

Chapter Twenty-four

"I worried about you all night," Jeff said as he stepped inside Debra's entry.

She'd been surprised to find him at her door at eight-thirty in the morning, and though she was touched by his concern, she was troubled by the intimacy it implied and by the rapid escalation in the way he viewed their relationship. He was leaning toward her, and she knew he was going to kiss her. She didn't want to be kissed and moved out of reach as Adam appeared in the living room.

"The new lock on the side door's installed, Debra," he said, looking at Jeff, who was studying Adam with interest.

She introduced the men to each other, making a point to identify Jeff as "my friend" to Adam.

Jeff said, "I thought I'd drive you to work and pick you up, Debra. I make my own hours, so it's no imposition. And I won't have to worry about your safety."

"Thanks, but I don't think so." Needing an escort sounded melodramatic, and she wasn't a helpless damsel in distress.

"Sounds like a good idea, Debra," Adam said. "Especially after those notes."

"You know about the notes?" Jeff asked.

She could hear the resentment in his voice. "Adam was here yesterday morning when I found the second one," she said, annoyed that she felt compelled to explain.

"So how about it?" Jeff asked. "My chariot awaits."

She shook her head. "I need my car during work hours. And I'm not worried about being safe during the daytime. None of the women were murdered at their place of work." So far, she thought.

"What if I follow you home? You could call me fifteen minutes before you're ready to leave. I could check out your house, make sure no one's lurking around. Why take chances, Debra?"

She was about to say no, then thought about Madelaine and Susan and Kelly. They had come home alone, at night, to empty houses. "I keep erratic work hours. I don't want you waiting for my call."

"Here's my pager number." Adam handed her a card. "If Jeff's not available and you're nervous, you can always reach me."

"I'll be available," Jeff said, scowling at Adam.

My heroes, she thought. She would have found this comic if the reason behind her need for protection wasn't so serious. Adam said, "Nice to meet you, Jeff," and, "Be careful, Debra," and disappeared into the alcove. Debra got her suit jacket and attaché case from the bedroom, then walked with Jeff to her car.

"How will this Bergman guy lock up?" Jeff asked, opening the driver's door for Debra.

"I gave him my key. He'll drop it in the mailbox when he leaves." She got into the car.

"Obviously you trust him. You know him a long time?"

"A week. He did the retrofitting on the house. Now he's

converting an alcove into an office. My brother recommended him, and it turns out my father gave him bar mitzvah lessons. Small world, isn't it?" She fastened her seat harness.

"From the way he talked, I thought you had a personal relationship. Kind of presumptuous of him to offer to escort you home, isn't it?"

She felt herself becoming angry, though she wasn't sure why. "I know you and Adam about the same length of time, Jeff. He's concerned about me, just as you are."

His face reddened. "You're right, and I'm sorry, Debra. Just jealous, I guess. You'll call me when you're ready to come home?"

"If I'm nervous, I will. And I really appreciate the offer."

He shut her door. She turned on the ignition, backed out of the driveway, and headed toward Beverly Boulevard. As she was turning left at the corner, she looked in the rearview mirror and saw his Sentra behind her. She waved good-bye.

Madeleine had done an excellent job in soliciting statements from the key witnesses for the defense, but Debra needed to meet with them herself, to get a sense of the people behind the words.

At the restaurant on Wilshire Boulevard where Kenneth Avedon had taken Penny that Tuesday night, Debra spoke to a ponytailed waiter named Chris who confirmed that Penny had been affectionate toward Avedon, "putting her hand on his, that kind of stuff." No, Penny hadn't been drunk, but she'd been "happy, laughing." Avedon, Chris told Debra, frequented the restaurant. Chris had never seen Penny before; he'd noticed her because she was very pretty.

"Do you remember who was sitting next to or near Dr. Avedon and Ms. Bailor?" Debra had seen no statements in Avedon's file from other couples who had been in the restaurant that night.

"Nope. The other lawyer asked me that. The place was crowded that night. Anyway, the doctor and his date were sitting in that booth." He pointed to Debra's right. "So they had some privacy."

Debra questioned the other waiter and two waitresses, all of whom vaguely remembered Penny and the doctor but could offer nothing more about her behavior.

From the restaurant Debra drove to Avedon's Beverly Hills office on Bedford near Dayton. She interviewed the staff, including the new receptionist Penny had trained. She also saw a color snapshot of Penny stapled to her employment application. She was very pretty, with long, thick, curly blond hair, blue eyes, and a pouty mouth. Debra could see why Avedon had been attracted to her and why the waiter had remembered her. She checked the references on the application and wrote down the names, addresses, and phone numbers of nonfamily members Penny had listed. She also copied down the phone number and address of Penny's high school; it was the same all girls' school Debra had attended. She wondered if Penny had worn the same blue-and-green-plaid uniform skirt and hated it as much.

"You've had a busy morning, haven't you?" Richard asked, entering Debra's office. "I came by a few times."

She had expected curtness, if not hostility, but he sounded genuinely friendly. "I've been talking to witnesses for Avedon," she told him. "I think it looks good." She waited until he seated himself, then filled him in on the details. "One minor setback—Annette Prado phoned. Penny Bailor declined to be examined by our psychologist. It's disappointing, but not surprising."

Richard nodded. "Do you have their shrink's statement?"

"Annette promised she'd fax it today. Avedon met with

our psychologist—I have the results of the personality test and the psychologist's statement. It's very positive."

"Excellent." He nodded again, then said, "That was shocking news about the other woman attorney being killed, and that all three were murdered by the same person. You must be frightened, Debra. Do you have a security system at home?"

She shook her head. "I'm thinking of getting one." Adam probably knew about alarm companies. She would ask him.

"Good." He crossed his legs at the ankles. "Not that a security system helped Madeleine. The killer got into her lobby."

"Maybe he followed her home and forced his way into the lobby when she opened the doors," she said, wondering again why Madeleine had planned to meet with Richard. "Or maybe he got someone else to buzz him in."

"Or maybe Madeleine knew the killer and let him in. Or let *her* in—the killer *could* be a woman, according to Simms." He looked at her with interest, then said, "I saw that they mentioned your name in the papers again."

A knot formed in her stomach. "I can't control that, Richard." She stood and walked to her bookcase for a reference book she didn't need. Had Simms intimated to Richard that she was a serious suspect?

"I didn't say you could. Why are you so defensive?"

She turned and looked at him. He seemed sincere. "Sorry. I'm on edge. And our last conversation wasn't exactly pleasant."

"You hung up on me," he said without anger.

"I had no choice. The Sabbath was starting."

He walked over to her. "I don't think God would mind if you used the phone on the Sabbath, or had a cheeseburger or lobster or worked on some of the Jewish holidays the way most Jews do."

"I've more than compensated for any time I've taken off. Why does Orthodoxy bother you so much? Are you threat-

ened by it?" She couldn't understand him—she was friendly
with Jews who were Conservative, Reform, unaffiliated; all of
them always treated her religious observance with respect.

"It's outdated, holier than thou. Why won't you have dinner with me?" He had moved closer and was standing next
to her.

"Don't confuse the issue, Richard."

"It's the same issue. You won't go out with me because
you think you're a better Jew."

"That's not true. You're interested in a casual physical relationship. I'm looking for someone who shares my beliefs
and lifestyle."

He shook his head and sighed. "You're so damn repressed! You could be a very sexy woman, Debra, if you let
your hair down." He reached both hands toward her hair
and smiled when she stepped away. "Did you like the catalog I sent you?"

"No, I did not," she said, surprised by his admission. She
opened the reference text.

"You have to agree that model looks like you. I'll bet you
fill out a bra even better than she does."

She slammed the book shut. "Don't talk to me like that!"

"See what I mean? You're repressed because of your religion."

"I don't enjoy your references to my body or your dirty
jokes. It has nothing to do with religion—no women I
know enjoy that. I don't want you touching me or sending
me underwear catalogs or making sexual allusions or—"

"Or what? You'll tell on me?" he said, mimicking a little
boy's whine. "Or maybe you'll quit?" He cocked his head,
and now the smile was sly, amused. "You won't quit—not
now. With your notoriety, there isn't a firm in the city that
would hire you."

She wished she could resign this very minute, but he was
right, and she had payments to make for her mortgage and

car and for the remodeling she'd just started and for clothes she hadn't even worn. She couldn't afford moral outrage or dignity.

"I have a lot of work to do, Richard," she said.

"If I were you, I'd rethink my attitude, be friendlier to the boss." He leaned forward so that his lips almost touched hers.

She didn't flinch. "Is there an 'or else'?" she said, and stared at him until his smile slipped into a frown and he left her office.

The lights in her breakfast and dining rooms were on when she pulled into her driveway. It was past eight o'clock, but she thought for a moment that Adam was still inside, working on the alcove, and realized with disappointment that his truck wasn't in view.

Up and down the block street lamps doled out circles of light. She stared through the windshield and side windows at the darkness that surrounded her, searching for shadowy figures. Leaving work, she'd checked the elevator before entering it, and after exiting on the second floor of the underground parking structure, her keys ready in her hand, she'd been keenly aware of everyone around her as she'd strode with feigned assurance to her car and regretted having phoned Jeff and told him that she didn't need him to escort her home. She regretted her decision again now as she unlocked her car, locked it quickly, and, carrying a few grocery bags, hurried to her side door, wondering whether she was being cautious or paranoid and when all this would end.

On the kitchen counter she found a note from Adam— he'd turned on her electric timer so that the lights would be on when she came home. "Hope that's okay," he'd written. "See you tomorrow."

She checked the alcove; the tarp Adam had spread on the floor was filled with plaster debris and old lath. With the closet gone and new drywall installed, the room looked considerably larger. She contemplated phoning Adam to tell him she was pleased with the progress and thank him for setting the timer for the lights but realized that what she really wanted was to hear his voice. And she would be sending the wrong signal.

She listened to Mozart on her portable CD player while she prepared and ate a light supper. When she was washing the dishes she returned phone messages (this was becoming a ritual, making reassuring calls to her family and friends) and again turned down offers from her father and Aaron and Julia and Aunt Edith to move in with them until "the police catch this man and put an end to these horrible killings." They didn't even know about the notes she'd received.

Julia had sounded better. She'd voiced her disappointment about not being pregnant and had said, "This is another month." Debra couldn't tell whether the optimism was feigned or real.

She went from room to room, checking to see that the doors were locked and the windows latched before she turned off the lights in the front of the house. She changed into her nightgown and watched Letterman in bed for a while; when she felt herself becoming drowsy, she clicked off the set with her remote control, turned out her lamp, and, pulling the comforter over her shoulders, said her prayers. She hoped the nightmare wouldn't recur.

The sound of breaking glass woke her. Earthquake! she thought. Her heart was pounding as she jerked to a sitting position, but she quickly noted that nothing was shaking.

The sound had come from the front. She listened intently but heard only the beating of her heart and the thrum of a car engine. She turned on the nightstand lamp and looked at her clock radio—it was 1:38. She stepped into the shoes she always kept under her bed (a precaution she'd taken after the last earthquake) and walked down the hall, turning on lights along the way.

When she entered the living room, she inhaled sharply. The picture window had been shattered; large shards of glass and smaller fragments littered the hardwood floor, reflecting the light from the recessed ceiling fixtures. Debra hugged her arms as she stood shivering in her nightgown from fear and from the chilled air that had invaded the room through the gaping hole.

She spotted the brick that had splintered the window; secured around it with a rubber band was a sheet of paper. Stepping carefully around the glass, she neared the brick but was careful not to touch it. Even before bending down, she could see that the message printed on the face of the note was the same:

"GET OUT OF THE WAY OF JUSTICE!"

Familiarity did nothing to lessen her fear. She walked into the breakfast room and picked up the receiver to phone the police, then decided she didn't want to deal with them at two o'clock in the morning. She could phone her brother and spend the night at his house; she had the key to her father's house and could let herself in—he was a heavy sleeper and wouldn't be disturbed by her arrival. But she didn't want to alarm them, and she wasn't sure she wanted to tell them what had happened. They would insist that she move in with them, and she wasn't prepared to admit defeat or sacrifice her independence.

She shut off all the lights she'd turned on and returned to her bedroom, telling herself that whoever had shattered her window had done so to warn her and would certainly not return tonight, that the window's jagged opening would prevent anyone from using it to enter her house.

She'd taken a knife from the kitchen; she slipped it under her bed and wished she had a gun.

Chapter Twenty-five

"What happened to your window?" Adam stared at the shattered glass.

Debra told him. "The police were here. They took the brick and note, but I doubt they'll find any prints." Two uniformed officers had arrived at 7:20, forty-five minutes after she'd reported what was by then no longer an emergency. She'd half expected Simms to show up—her house on Citrus south of Beverly was under the jurisdiction of Wilshire Division; when he didn't, she'd asked one of the patrolmen to give him the brick and note. "Can you give me an estimate for a new window, Adam?"

He nodded. "In the meantime I'll remove the broken window and board up the opening with plywood."

"That would be wonderful," Debra said, grateful that he was here. "Let me know how much I owe you for that."

He shook his head. "No charge."

"Don't be silly. It's material plus your labor."

"I have the plywood, which I can reuse. The labor's no big deal. Tell you what—if you're worried about my time, you can repay me by having dinner with me tonight." He smiled.

"That doesn't sound like good business," she said, trying to make light of his invitation.

"Let me worry about that. So how about dinner?"

"I wouldn't be good company." It was a lame excuse, and she knew from his eyes that he thought so, too.

The truth was that she felt drawn to him, and that made her nervous—for a long time she'd been wary of becoming seriously involved. "Maybe it's not because of what happened with Barry," Julia had suggested a while ago. "Maybe you're afraid that if you become close to someone else, you'll lose that person just like you lost your mom." That's not it, Debra had insisted; sometimes, though, she wondered whether her sister-in-law was right.

"I'm considering following your advice and getting an alarm system," she said now to fill what had become an uncomfortable silence. "Could you recommend a company who installs them?"

"I know a few. I'll get you their numbers."

His tone was friendly but more professional; she felt an inexplicable sense of loss and decided that turning him down had been stupid. "On second thought," she said, "dinner sounds nice."

She spent the morning in Culver City attending the arraignment of a client charged with drunk and disorderly conduct. From there she drove to a gun store on Olympic and, after holding various weapons in her hand, selected and paid for a Colt thirty-caliber revolver.

"You'll need a basic firearm safety certificate," the salesperson said. "Twenty dollars for a lifetime certificate."

To qualify for the certificate, the salesman explained, Debra had to correctly answer twenty-three out of thirty questions on a firearm and handgun safety test; she could first watch a two-hour video in the store if she wanted. She took the test and passed, then filled out the necessary California State paperwork. She'd known that there would be a fifteen-day waiting period before she could obtain the gun. Fifteen days in the abstract had seemed reasonable. Now it seemed interminably long.

"I saw in the paper that you were questioned by the police," Avedon told Debra that afternoon. "Not much fun, is it?"

His tone was noncommittal, and she couldn't tell from his facial expression what he was thinking. "Ken, if you have any reservations about my representing you, believe me, I'll understand. Richard or someone else can take over."

He shook his head. "I want *you,* Debra. You understand more than most attorneys what it's like to have to defend yourself against something you didn't do." He leaned back against his chair. "Are we going to talk about my testimony? I'm a little nervous about all this."

"That's understandable." She smiled to reassure him. "Just answer the questions honestly and simply—don't volunteer any information, not to me and not to the district attorney when she cross-examines you."

He nodded.

"I may not even have you take the stand. It'll depend on how Penny comes across." And how damaging the tape would sound.

"What day would I testify?"

"If a courtroom's available, jury selection will start Tuesday. The judge—"

"What do you mean, 'available'?" He was frowning. "The trial's scheduled. I hope this isn't going to drag out."

"I hope so, too. Sometimes all the judges are tied up hearing cases that are taking longer than anticipated. Your preliminary hearing was on September ninth. By law you're entitled to a trial no later than sixty days after you've been bound over. This Tuesday, November fifth, will be the fifty-seventh day, so we'll probably get priority." When he nodded, she said, "If jury selection is completed on Tuesday—again, that depends a lot on the judge—the judge may or may not have the State give its opening statement that same day or on Wednesday."

"Are you giving an opening statement?"

"Yes. I don't always, because an opening statement locks us into a defense. But since our defense is that the complaining witness is lying for ulterior motives, I want the jury to have that on their minds when they listen to the State's witnesses." She folded her hands. "The State plans to put on five witnesses. That should take up Wednesday and Thursday and most of Friday. So my guess is that if you testify, it'll be Monday or Tuesday."

She had partially scripted the questions she planned to ask Avedon; she posed some of them now and was pleased with the forthright, earnest manner in which he answered. She reminded herself that he was "testifying" in the comfort of her office; some witnesses—she'd had her share of these—performed brilliantly in her office, then froze on the stand. She sensed that wouldn't happen with Avedon, and her confidence was bolstered by the fact that Madeleine had made the same assessment.

After familiarizing Avedon with the kinds of questions she would ask, she posed questions she envisioned Annette Prado asking. Again, she was pleased with the doctor's responses. "Just remember to tell the truth, and you'll be fine," she told him.

"What should I wear?" Avedon asked when they were done.

"What you have on is fine." She glanced at his dark taupe suit and beige vest. With a flash of fondness that surprised her, she thought about Timothy Lassiter and his four earrings. She wondered how he was doing.

After Avedon left, Debra phoned Wilshire Division and was connected with Marty Simms.

"Too bad about your window," he said. "We'll try to get prints off the note or the brick. We're still waiting for results on the first two papers you brought me. By the way, why'd you wait till morning to phone the police?"

"I didn't see the point in calling at one-forty. Did the officers find out if any of my neighbors saw who did this?"

"Nope. Apparently, your neighbors are heavy sleepers."

Apparently. "Have you had a chance to investigate the theories we talked about yesterday, Detective?"

"We've begun preliminary investigations."

"What about Osterhaus? Have you—"

"Hey, don't push." His voice had taken on a surly edge.

"Madeleine was murdered on Thursday, Susan on the following Tuesday—five days later—and Kelly Malter on Sunday, five days after that." Debra had made the realization some time last night, after her window had been smashed. "Five days from Sunday is Friday—two days from now. I don't want to be the next victim, Detective. I think you can see why I'm anxious."

"Actually, I see a lot. Talk to you soon, Ms. Laslow."

She could picture the smirk on his face. She hung up the receiver, then walked to the secretary's desk. "Glynnis, do we keep files on people who applied to join the firm?"

"Lawyers, you mean? We keep applications for a year. Mr. Knox and Mr. Cantrell like to have a record, in case a position opens up—like it did before you joined. Did you want to see one of the applications?" Curiosity stamped her face.

"Could you please photocopy *all* the applications for me, Glynnis? And please put them in a folder."

Thirty minutes later the folder was on Debra's desk. She thumbed through the papers—there were fifty or more—and put the folder in her attaché case. She didn't know whether the police had obtained the names of attorneys who had applied—and been rejected—for positions at Madeleine's, Susan's, and Kelly Malter's firms; Simms's line about "preliminary investigations" had sounded vague. Debra wanted to access those names herself, but she was certain that none of the dead women's secretaries would release the information; Debra didn't blame them. She would have to talk to the firms' senior partners and explain her exigent need.

Blackmeyer first, she decided. She phoned and, after asking for an appointment with Jonathan Blackmeyer, learned that he was unavailable for the rest of the week. So, she discovered with two more phone calls, were the senior partners of Susan's and Kelly's firms. I'm persona non grata, Debra realized.

She returned her attention to her legal pad and the motion she was drafting to introduce Penny Bailor's past relationships if in fact the information became relevant—if they could prove she'd lied about being a virgin. At first Debra had difficulty concentrating, but she reminded herself that Avedon was her client and deserved her best effort.

She hoped Marty Simms was giving his best effort, too.

Adam in a sports jacket and slacks looked even more handsome than he did in jeans. She hoped he hadn't noticed her stare when she opened the front door. Then again, he'd been staring, too, and she'd flushed with pleasure under his gaze and his softly spoken, "You look beautiful." She'd dressed with great care. She'd wanted to look right, hadn't wanted to overdo; she'd settled on a rayon challis print skirt and a pale yellow cashmere sweater.

There was a taupe Buick in front of her house. She assumed it was Adam's but he crossed the street to a dark green Infiniti. He caught the surprised look in her eyes as he opened the passenger door. "Were you expecting the truck?" he asked with an amused smile.

"I wasn't sure," she said, coloring at the admission. "The truck would've been fine," she added as she sat on the plush tan leather seat.

"Maybe next time." He smiled again and shut her door, then walked to the driver's side and got in.

He took her to a restaurant on Third Street with French cuisine and steep prices. She hoped he didn't feel he had to impress her, but he ordered the stuffed breast of veal without even glancing at the oversize menu, and she realized he'd been there before. She ordered the veal, too. The waitress brought a bottle of white wine and filled their glasses.

Debra had worried that aside from the remodeling work he was doing for her, they would have nothing of shared interest to talk about. She'd prepared a mental list of conversation openers—"Tell me about your family, your job, your life"—so she was surprised to find herself answering his questions instead of asking her own; surprised, too, that by the time they were halfway through with the veal, she was revealing information she generally didn't reveal— Aaron and Julia's childlessness; her concern about her father's loneliness; her own ambivalence about her job; her continuing grief for her mother.

She paused and shook her head. "I don't know why I'm telling you all this. I guess it's because you're a very good listener. You should have been a psychologist, or a lawyer." She smiled.

He laughed. "No thanks. I'm perfectly happy with what I do."

"What made you decide to become a contractor?"

"My previous job. I have an MBA. I was on the executive track in a corporation that sells medical equipment. I had stock options, the works. I hated it." He studied her face. "Are you surprised because I hated the job, or because I have a graduate degree?"

She felt herself blushing and lifted her wine goblet to hide her face. "You must think I'm a terrible snob."

He smiled. "Most people have the same reaction—they just don't admit it. My parents were horrified when I quit the job, especially since I'm their only child. 'Why work with your hands when you can work with your mind?' my dad kept saying. He was Willy Loman to my Biff."

"What does your dad do?"

"He's an accountant. He's a lot happier now that he sees me earning a decent living, but he and my mom still say, 'All that college wasted.' " Adam shrugged. "I still use my mind. I read more now than I did when I had the job. I'm more relaxed." He took a sip of water. "I sound a little defensive, huh?"

"A little." She smiled. "I'm constantly put on the defensive about my career—'What's a nice Jewish girl like you doing defending criminals?' You learn to live with the comments."

"What's a nice Jewish girl like you doing defending criminals?" he asked, then laughed when she groaned. "Is your family supportive?"

"I think they'd prefer my practicing a different kind of law—entertainment, tax, corporate. Something safer. Not divorce law," she added. "Did you know that divorce lawyers are targets of a disproportionately high percentage of violence or threats of violence from their clients or the contesting spouses?"

"Makes sense." He nodded. "All that unleashed anger. I guess your family's especially concerned because of the killings, and because of the notes you've received."

"They don't know about the notes." She saw Adam's raised brows. "They'd panic and insist that I move in with them."

"Maybe that's not a bad idea."

"I'm considering it—I'm definitely sleeping at my dad's Friday night." Though she could phone the police on the

Sabbath in case of emergency, she would feel more vulnerable alone in the house, more apt to panic at every strange noise. Friday would also be five days from the date of Kelly Malter's murder. "But I resent being forced from my home."

"I don't blame you. What about the alarm system? Did you have a chance to phone anyone?"

Adam had given her three names; she'd phoned the one he'd recommended most. "They're sending someone in the morning to give me an estimate." She paused. "I hate guns, but I bought one today. I won't have it for fifteen days, but in the meantime I plan to go to a shooting club to practice." Adam was looking at her with interest, and she wondered what he thought about his date.

"I don't blame you for taking precautions. The police haven't learned anything about the notes?"

She shook her head. "The notes may not be connected to the murders. I'm trying a date rape this Tuesday, and the complaining witness comes from an Orthodox family. Her family may be sending the notes."

"Debra—"

"Are you going to ask me why I don't drop the case? Everyone else has, except for my father."

"Now *you're* sounding a little defensive." He smiled. "I was going to offer to lend you my gun until you get yours. And I can go with you to shooting practice and give you some pointers."

It was her turn to be surprised. "You have a gun?"

"I bought one after the riots—I wanted to feel I could protect myself and my parents if there was another riot. Of course when I thought about it rationally, I realized a gun doesn't do much against a Molotov cocktail." He smiled grimly. "If I had kids, I'd get rid of the gun. You hear about too many tragic accidents with guns in the house."

"I thought I'd go shooting this Sunday afternoon."

"Sunday's fine. Two o'clock?" When she agreed, he said, "What about my gun? Do you want to borrow it?"

"What if I told you a detective from Wilshire Division suspects that I could have killed these three women?"

He stared at her, then smiled. "You're joking, right?"

She shook her head.

"I'm still not worried. Do you want to borrow it?"

Technically, it was illegal. But fifteen days was a long time to wait. "Let me think about it."

They ate for a while in a comfortable silence that she felt no need to fill. Over dessert he told her about his family and about some of the houses he'd remodeled and the homeowners who'd driven him crazy with indecision. After dinner he drove to Rodeo Drive, and they walked along the exclusive Beverly Hills street, stopping to ogle outrageously priced merchandise, wondering which shop had been used to film Julia Roberts in *Pretty Woman.* The air was cool and brisk; against her protests he slipped his jacket around her shoulders. She liked the way it felt.

When he took her home, she was surprised to see that it was past midnight. She'd had a wonderful time and for five hours had been able to forget about her problems, problems that flooded her with sharp suddenness when he pulled up in front of her house and she saw the boarded-up living room window.

Adam came inside to make certain the house was secure; she waited in the living room, and though she didn't think someone was hiding in one of the rooms, ready to attack her, she was relieved when he returned several minutes later and told her that everything was fine.

Jeff had left a message on her machine. She would phone him in the morning, though she wasn't sure what she would say.

* * *

Simms entered her office at ten o'clock on Thursday morning. "Do you know a Wesley Pratt?" he demanded in his usual surly tone.

She mouthed the name, then shook her head. "Should I?"

"He's an attorney."

He was almost smirking at her, and she started to snap, "There are lots of attorneys," then realized why he was so smug. *Simms had found him!* Last night she'd written a list of the names on the applications Glynnis had photocopied. She didn't recognize Pratt's, but the fact that he hadn't applied to Knox and Cantrell didn't mean anything.

She inhaled sharply. "Wesley Pratt has been rejected by the other firms? That's it, isn't it?" she asked with growing excitement and grudging admiration for Marty Simms, whom she didn't like but who had, after all, done his job very, very well.

"He's an attorney," Simms said, "who was found dead at seven-thirty this morning by his maid. His tongue was severed."

Chapter Twenty-six

"Pratt worked for Stein and Mulcahey. Do you know the firm?"

Debra felt pressure building at her temples. "Stein and Mulcahey," she told Simms, "is one of the top criminal defense firms in the city. And before you ask, yes, I applied there, too." Now that a male attorney had been killed, nothing made sense. Her head was beginning to throb; she could barely concentrate. She desperately wanted Simms to leave.

"Just another weird coincidence?" Simms picked at his lip. "Where were you last night, Ms. Laslow?"

She stared at him, thinking how absurd it was that she was worried about being killed and he was playing stupid games with her. She wished Charles were here, not in court. "You obviously dislike me, Detective," she said with forced calm. "You've decided to harass and intimidate me, and I don't know why."

"Timothy Lassiter likes you a whole lot, doesn't he? When he's coked up and gets behind the wheel of a car and kills someone and you bail him out again, he'll like you even more."

She frowned. "What does Lassiter have to do with this?"

"Hickman, the officer you trashed on the stand, is the son of a cop friend of mine. I heard the next day all about your fine performance." He clapped his hands.

She knew her face betrayed her surprise; she kept her voice impassive. "I was doing my job. Hickman didn't follow procedure. Next time I'm sure he will." Her eyes narrowed. "You're abusing your authority. I plan to report this to your superior."

"Go ahead. You asked me why I don't like you—I told you. That has nothing to do with why I'm here. I'm pursuing all angles of the investigation."

"Which investigation—Susan's murder or Wesley Pratt's?"

"Both. Pratt lived in the Larchmont area—that's in our division. So where were you last night?"

"I don't have to answer your questions, Detective, but I will do so voluntarily. I went out to dinner with a friend. We left at seven-thirty. We returned at twelve forty-five."

"Your friend's name and phone number?"

"Adam Bergman." She took out her wallet and dictated Adam's business number from the card he'd given her.

"So you could have left your house again?"

"I could have, but I didn't."

"Before she was murdered, your friend Susan phoned West L.A. and left a message for Detective Wraith. You remember Wraith, don't you?" Simms's tone was snide. "He questioned you about Madeleine Chase's murder."

Debra frowned. "What's your point, Detective?"

"The message was that she had information about Madeleine's murder. When Wraith returned her call, Ms. Clemens told him she'd been mistaken. 'About what?' Wraith asked. She wouldn't say. The next day Ms. Clemens was dead. Interesting, don't you think?"

It *was* very interesting, and troubling. Why hadn't Susan mentioned anything to her? "Wraith just remembered this now?"

Simms raised his brows. "Did I say that, Ms. Laslow?"

"You never mentioned this before."

Simms smiled. "See, that's where you're confused. I don't share information with you. You share it with us."

She ignored his sarcasm. "Assuming that Susan spoke to Wraith, I still don't see the significance. She thought she had information. She realized she was mistaken. That's why she didn't tell me about it," Debra said, thinking aloud.

"Maybe she didn't tell you because *you* were the relevant information."

"Is this another one of your fictional hypotheses?" She realized she was gripping the edge of her desk and relaxed her hands, wondering again whether Simms was serious.

"She suspects that you killed Ms. Chase. She phones the station, chickens out because you and she are good friends. Maybe she asks one too many questions and you know she suspects you. Maybe she confronts you and tells you to turn yourself in. In any case, you figure you have no choice but to kill her, too."

Let him rant, Debra thought.

"You're smart, so you slash her tongue and make it look like there's a psycho going around killing attorneys. And you send yourself notes to make it look like you're the next target."

Debra cleared her throat. "And I choose my targets at firms where I applied, drawing attention to myself?"

"I said you're smart." Simms leaned toward her. "Because of course you'd argue that if you were guilty, you wouldn't have done that. You'd argue that someone was setting you up."

"If you're so sure I'm the killer, why haven't you arrested me?" She had a sudden thought. "Where's your partner?

Why do you always question me by yourself? That's not department policy."

"We're short-handed, and my partner's pursuing other leads."

It was a reasonable answer, but she sensed from the tightness in Simms's voice that she'd touched a chord. "Could it be that no one else wants to waste time on your fantastic theory? Or maybe you're here alone because this is a game."

Simms's face had reddened. "No game, Ms. Laslow. I'm thorough. I'm tenacious. If you're guilty, I'll nail you."

"And if I'm not?" she asked quietly. "Have you checked into Osterhaus's alibis for the murders?"

"We're doing that." Simms pulled at his lip again. "He's angry at WRIT, all right—told me he'd like to see every member jailed. But why would Osterhaus kill a male attorney?"

"To throw you off track." He was making her jumpy—one minute treating her like a suspect, the next minute like a confidante. Was that his game? "Or maybe he isn't the killer. Maybe the killer is an attorney—male or female—who's been turned down by criminal defense firms and wants revenge. That still fits."

"Maybe." Simms's tone was noncommittal. "We're pursuing all leads."

"There are other possibilities." Debra had considered several since Susan's murder. "The killer could be someone angry against criminal defense attorneys in private practice because he felt betrayed by his own attorney. Or maybe he's enraged because he thinks they earn too much money and waste the taxpayer's money."

Simms snorted. "If that's the case, we'd have to question ninety percent of the population."

"Someone sent me threatening notes. Someone smashed my front window. Has it occurred to you that I may be the next victim?" She was trembling with frustration—why wouldn't Simms believe her?

"But you *weren't* the next victim. Somehow, I wasn't surprised." He smiled, enjoying the moment, then pushed back his chair. "You know the routine, Ms. Laslow. Don't leave town."

She had an illogical urge to take her lithograph of Jerusalem and disappear. But that wouldn't solve her problems.

She stared at the wall and thought about what Simms had said—that Susan had phoned the police—and recalled suddenly that Susan had told her she'd talked to Madeleine two days before the murder. Had Susan remembered something revealing from that conversation? Something connected to Osterhaus or WRIT?

Or maybe Madeleine had mentioned receiving a threatening letter, and then Susan had received a similar one. . . .

It was just like Susan not to tell Debra about the note—she wouldn't have wanted to alarm her. And then she'd reconsidered and decided that, in fact, she had no information for the police. So there had been nothing to tell.

Debra phoned Susan's secretary.

"I can't give you copies of those letters, Ms. Laslow," Joyce said before Debra even asked. "I'm really sorry, but I don't want to get into trouble with the police or with my employers."

Debra couldn't really blame the woman. "Joyce, did Susan ever get a letter that said 'Get out of the way of Justice'?"

"Not that I recall. But it's possible."

"She spoke with Madeleine Chase a few days before Madeleine was killed. Do you have any idea what they talked about?"

"No. How would I? I wish I could help you, Ms. Laslow. Really I do."

Charles came into Debra's office an hour later, shaken by the news about Wesley Pratt. Had Debra heard? She told him about her conversation with Simms.

Charles frowned. "Damn it, Debra! You shouldn't talk to Simms if I'm not present."

"You're right." She sighed. "But I didn't kill anyone, so of course I don't believe he seriously thinks I did."

"What would you do if a client behaved like this?" He shook his head. "Next time, if you can't reach me, just keep quiet."

She promised that next time she would.

She told Glynnis she had several appointments and would be back within two hours. Her first stop was at Blackmeyer. Cynthia Ellis tightened her lips when she saw Debra approach.

"If it's about that letter—" the secretary began.

"It's not about the letter. I don't blame you for being cautious." She smiled to show she was sincere. "Cynthia, I've received two threatening letters, both of which said 'Get out of the way of Justice.' And the other day someone threw a brick through my front window."

The woman eyed her warily. "I don't know what you want."

"Someone's killing lawyers, Cynthia. I'm scared and I need your help. I'm trying to figure out the connection between the murders, to figure out who killed Madeleine and the others."

"Why don't you leave that to the police? They were here the other day, asking for the names of male attorneys who were turned down for positions here. Then a short while ago a detective called and said he also wanted the names of women attorneys who were turned down."

That was gratifying news—if Simms was following up on

her suggestion, he clearly wasn't convinced that Debra was the killer. "I can't wait for the police to find the killer. I'm terrified that he may be planning to kill me, just like he killed the others." She didn't add that the notes could have been sent by someone from the Bailor family, though she knew that was still a distinct possibility. "Will you help me?"

Indecision played across her face. "What does it involve?"

"I need to know what cases Madeleine worked on over the past six months." Debra had chosen six months because it seemed reasonable—not too limiting, not too far in the past.

Cynthia shook her head vehemently. "I can't give you clients' files. I'd lose my job."

"I don't want the files or clients' names. I want to know the types of cases—burglary, driving under the influence, murder. The disposition of the case—acquittal, plea bargain, conviction, hung jury, mistrial. And the date each case was adjudicated."

The woman looked puzzled. "How will that help you?"

"I'm looking for a pattern—maybe each of the slain attorneys lost a similar type of case." She could forward the information to the police; they could obtain the names of the clients involved. "I have to try *something*. Can you get me the information?"

"It'll take time, figuring out which cases Ms. Chase worked on. I'll have to go through all the files."

Debra waited. Pushing, she knew, would be counterproductive.

"Okay," Cynthia finally said. "I'll have it for you tomorrow."

From Blackmeyer Debra drove to Susan's firm. Joyce was clearly uncomfortable when Debra entered the reception room, but Debra assured her quickly that she hadn't come to pressure her about the threatening letters Susan had received, that she'd come for help that wouldn't jeopardize the secretary's job.

"I don't want names," Debra repeated after she explained what she needed. "I don't want you to compromise a client's confidentiality."

Joyce finally agreed to help Debra. Kelly Malter's secretary agreed to help, too. So did Wesley Pratt's secretary. Debra would have the case descriptions and dispositions from all four attorneys tomorrow afternoon.

When Debra returned to her office, she found a curt note from Richard on her desk: "HAVE DONOVAN BRIEF ON MY DESK BY END OF DAY." No "please." No explanation for the sudden urgency for a brief Richard had asked her to prepare "when you have the time."

He was punishing her for her lack of friendliness. She didn't much care; in fact, the work kept her from dwelling on Simms and his insane accusations and wondering what, if anything, the four legal secretaries were uncovering for her.

Debra spent the day reading case law and writing the Donovan brief. At six-thirty she took the final draft to Richard's office. He wasn't in; she left the papers on his desk.

Jeff phoned her just before she was leaving work. He'd heard about Wesley Pratt. "I left a message on your machine last night," he told her. "When you didn't call back, I drove by your house to make sure you were all right. What happened to your window?"

She didn't know how she felt about his driving by her house. She supposed she should appreciate his concern, but uninvited, it felt cloying. She told him about the vandalism. "The police are checking into it," she said, wondering if that was true.

"I hope this convinces you to drop the rape case, Debra."

When she didn't answer, he said, "Do you want me to follow you home tonight?"

"No, thanks. Charles—one of my colleagues here—is walking me to my car. I'll be okay."

"I can meet you at the house and check things out before you go in, make sure everything's safe."

"Adam's there—he's working on my alcove office." He'd offered to wait till Debra came home, and she hadn't put up any resistance. "I'm having an alarm system installed this week."

"That's good," Jeff said without enthusiasm. "What about having dinner with me tonight?"

"I'm really not up to it, Jeff. Thanks for asking."

"Sure. Saturday night, then? A movie?"

She hesitated, then said, "To tell you the truth, Jeff, I've enjoyed our evenings together, but I'm not sure we're right for each other." How do you tell someone there's no magic?

"Funny, I thought things were going well. Was it because I kissed you the other night? Am I coming on too strong?"

"It isn't that, Jeff. I have to go now."

"Debra, wait. Look, I'm disappointed that you feel this way—I won't lie. But I'd like us to be friends. Is that okay?"

"Of course," she said, though she didn't know if that was possible.

"For one thing, I'd like to show you the outline and first few chapters of my book. I'd appreciate your honest feedback. And I *mean* 'honest'—I can take your criticism." He laughed.

"I'd be happy to read what you've written." She felt hesitant about continuing the relationship, but how could she say no?

"Is Sunday night okay?"

"I'm going to a WRIT meeting at the Sportsman's Lodge in the Valley." Because of the murders, the board was anticipating a large turnout for this second emergency session and had decided to meet in one of the hotel's conference rooms instead of a private home. "Monday night's out—my trial starts Tuesday. Depending on how things go, maybe we could have coffee on Tuesday night."

"That would be great, but let's make it dinner. I'll call you Monday at work. Promise me you'll be careful, Debra."

That was an easy promise to keep.

Chapter Twenty-seven

On Friday morning an armed guard greeted Debra at the door to reception. It was about time, she thought, and wondered if it was just coincidence that the guard had appeared only after a male attorney had been murdered. This morning the alarm company salesperson had measured the house and counted doors and windows and told Debra he'd fax a quote to her office for the cost of the installation before the day was over. A salesman from another company Adam had recommended was coming to the house on Monday.

Richard had left her another note: he needed a second brief by the end of the day. She booted her computer and worked without interruption. By two o'clock she was done. Richard wasn't in; she put the finished brief on his desk, put Avedon's file in her attaché case, and walked into reception.

"I have some appointments," she told Glynnis. She'd phoned the four secretaries and had been gratified to learn that the case lists were waiting for her. "I won't be back today. When Mr. Dressner returns, please tell him I left the brief on his desk."

"I'll tell him. Have a nice weekend, dear. And please be careful. It's getting so that I'm afraid to turn on the news."

Debra *was* careful. She was careful in the hall, careful in the elevator, careful in the parking structure. She was careful to check the backseat of her car before she unlocked the door and climbed in, careful to lock her doors immediately, careful to check her rearview mirror for cars that might be following her as she stopped by each of the firms and picked up the case lists, careful to look around her before she pulled into her driveway, before she exited the safety of her car, before she unlocked the side door of her house and stepped inside.

Careful, careful, careful.

She undressed quickly, showered, shampooed and dried her hair, then put on a skirt and sweater. In the morning she'd packed an overnight case; she tossed in some toiletries and the envelopes containing the case lists the secretaries had prepared for her.

Though she would be spending Sabbath at her father's house, she spread a white cloth on the breakfast room table; in the center she placed a vase with the roses Adam had left for her to find, along with a note that wished her "Good *Shabbos*."

Before she left she checked the mail slot. She ignored the bills and magazines—they would wait till she returned—and gave her attention to an eight-by-ten manila envelope. Her name had been typed in the center; someone had typed, "Superior Court of the State of California" and the downtown Temple Street address in the upper left-hand corner, but it wasn't an official envelope, and she knew to handle it with care. From the canceled stamps, she saw that it had been mailed yesterday. Using a letter opener and holding the envelope by a corner, she slit open the envelope and shook its contents onto the kitchen counter.

There were four newspaper clippings, one with a photo of Madeleine, one of Susan, one of Kelly Malter, and one of Wesley Pratt, whose face Debra had seen on the television news last night. There was also a grainy newsprint snapshot of Debra in profile pasted onto a sheet of white paper; underneath the photo someone had printed a caption:

The tongues of dying men enforce attention. . . .
Get out of the way of Justice.

She'd had to wait for her shaking to subside before she drove to her father's, so it was only five minutes before candle lighting when she parked near the duplex. Her father had obviously been looking for her arrival; he opened the door before she rang the bell, and she could see from his pursed lips and frown that he was upset.

"I'm sorry I'm so late." She kissed his cheek.

In her bedroom closet, still filled with clothes she'd left behind and the games and toys from her childhood, she hung up the suit she'd brought to wear to synagogue in the morning. Someone—probably the cleaning woman who came every other week—had taken off the white chenille bedspread and put on fresh bedding.

Her mother's silver five-armed candelabra and tray sat on the dining room table, which was covered with a white lace cloth frayed from innumerable washings. She felt her father's eyes on her as she lit and blessed the candles; when she removed her hands from her face and said, *"Gut Shabbos,"* he looked stern, sad faced.

He was unusually quiet as they walked a block and a half to Aaron and Julia's; he was quiet, too, when he returned with Aaron from synagogue, quiet throughout dinner, quiet on the walk home.

She changed into a nightgown and robe and went into the breakfast room to read the newspaper. Only a small light was on, and the room was cast in shadows. Her father was at the table. In front of him was a chess set, but he was staring at the wall.

Next to the chess set she saw a manila envelope addressed to Rabbi Ephraim Laslow. In the upper left-hand corner someone had typed, "Superior Court of the State of California."

"When did it come?" she asked, her heart leaden.

He turned and looked at her. "Today. You got the same clippings?"

She nodded. He looked suddenly old, frail.

"But you weren't going to tell me." When she didn't answer, he said, "I lost your mother. I don't want to lose you, too, Debra."

"I'm sorry, Daddy," she whispered, her eyes filled with tears. "I'll be okay. I promise." She put her arms around him and kissed the top of his head.

They talked for a while before he went to sleep. Debra tried to sleep, too, but gave up after an hour and returned to the breakfast room, taking with her the lists from the secretaries.

Following Debra's request, each secretary had made three columns: CASE; DISPOSITION; DATE OF FINAL ACTION. Having no idea what pattern she was searching for, Debra studied the lists, beginning with the one prepared by Cynthia. She studied the lists a second time, then a third; when she was finished, she'd learned only that in the space of six months, each attorney had tried an impressive number of cases and won a majority of those cases.

She paid attention to cases that had ended in convictions and those in which the client had pled to a lesser charge; no pattern emerged. She was hampered by the fact that on the Sabbath she couldn't write or make any notations; technically, she shouldn't even be studying the lists—work on the Sabbath was forbidden, except in life-and-death situations. But this was a life-and-death situation, she thought, glancing at the manila envelope at the end of the table. Even her father would agree.

The secretaries had compiled the lists by going through the attorneys' files in alphabetical order and noting cases that had been handled within the time frame Debra had indicated; that explained why the cases weren't listed in chronological order or by type of charge. Debra wished she could use a computer to regroup the information by type of charge and by the date of the final legal action. She tried to do so mentally but soon gave up.

Maybe six months was too wide a time frame. The murders had started a little over two weeks ago; there had been four murders within two weeks. Something had triggered them. She rubbed her eyes and studied the lists again, focusing this time only on cases that had seen final legal action within the past six weeks. Again she concentrated on convictions. Kelly Malter's client had been convicted three weeks ago of burglary. Wesley Pratt's client had pled to second-degree manslaughter. Madeleine and Susan had won acquittals for their clients.

She scanned the lists again, searching for a similarity among the type of charge that each attorney had tried last before his or her death. Again she saw nothing.

At some point she thought about Susan's "Ugly Americans" file and the letters from people irate with her for defending criminals. Maybe the killer was one of these "Ugly Americans"; Debra had suggested as much to Simms yesterday.

Yawning, she searched Madeleine's list. During the past six weeks Madeleine had won two cases—one of them, an insurance fraud case, had been decided two days before she'd been killed. Susan had won an assault with a deadly weapon a week before she'd been killed; and three weeks before that, she'd won the rape case she'd mentioned to Debra. Kelly Malter had won three cases in the past six weeks: armed robbery; driving under the influence; rape.

Debra stared at the paper for a moment, then pulled Madeleine's list toward her and ran her finger down the entries until she found what she'd been looking for: the other case Madeleine had won within the past six weeks was a rape case.

She told herself that she was jumping to conclusions, that it was late and she was tired, that she was desperate to find something where nothing was there; but her heart was hammering and her palms were sweaty as she pulled Wesley Pratt's list and ran her finger along the entries. Halfway down the page she found it: on Monday of this week, Pratt had won an acquittal for a client charged with rape.

Four attorneys had won rape cases. Four attorneys were dead, their tongues severed.

The tongues of dying men enforce attention. . . .
Get out of the way of Justice.

Debra was trying a rape case, too.

Chapter Twenty-eight

"It isn't that I don't love you," Dennis Wallace said, lying on his side of the king-size bed.

"I know." Nancy pulled the comforter past her bare shoulders, covering the thin-strapped black nightgown she'd chosen with care.

"You're angry, aren't you?"

"I'm not angry." She was angry, very angry.

"You weren't ready, now I'm not ready. Why isn't that fair?"

"It's fair."

"Then why don't you understand?"

She looked at him and saw that he was staring at the ceiling. "You think I let him."

"I never said that, Nancy."

"You don't have to say it. I can see it in the way you look at me. You're wondering all the time, aren't you? You believe everything that lawyer said."

"No."

"Last week when we went to that party, you said my dress

*was too short and too tight. It wasn't too short or too tight
when I bought it. You loved it when I bought it."*

He didn't say anything.

"You think I didn't fight hard enough, don't you?"

*"I'm trying to deal with this. Honest to God, Nancy, I'm
trying! I was hurt by this, too. You don't seem to understand
that."*

"I'm the one who was raped, Dennis!"

*"What do you want me to do, Nancy? You want me to find
him and rip his effing head off? Will that make you feel better?"*

*There was so much anger in him. It made her want to
scream, to punch someone. Last night he hadn't come home
until very late, and when he had, he'd refused to tell her
where he'd been.*

*"I want you to hold me when I need you to hold me, Den-
nis. I want you to make love to me without thinking about
what happened and making me feel that this was my fault.
Can you do that?"*

"I love you, Nancy. You know I love you."

"But it's not the same between us."

"No, it's not the same." His voice was filled with sadness.

"And it will never be the same, will it?"

Dennis sighed.

"I think you should move out," she said.

*He was silent for a minute. "Maybe for a short while," he
conceded. "Just till I can get my head on straight. It isn't that
I don't love you."*

Chapter Twenty-nine

It was possible that she was wrong. After her father left the house in the morning, Debra took out the lists and studied them with a mixture of horror, fascination, and dread that continued to weigh on her in the synagogue, where she had difficulty concentrating on the prayers, and later, during lunch at Aunt Edith's. Talk about the slain attorneys was conspicuously absent by some tacit agreement, just as it had been absent last night at Aaron and Julia's (her father's doing?); she forced herself to smile and to be animated and, conscious of her aunt's watchful eye, to take generous helpings of delicious food that held no appeal for her today.

"How's that young man you went out with?" Aunt Edith asked Debra, spooning cole slaw onto her plate.

"I don't think he's for me."

"No go, huh?" Aaron said.

Edith said, "So what about Bernice's person? Should she give him your number?"

"Actually, I met someone else. His name is Adam Bergman."

"Adam Bergman?" Aaron eyed Debra. "Why didn't you mention it last night?"

Debra shrugged. She turned to her father, who was sitting next to her. "You gave him bar mitzvah lessons, Dad."

"I hope he won't hold that against you." He smiled.

She was warmed by his smile—it was the first genuinely carefree expression she'd seen on his face all day. Though they hadn't discussed the contents of the manila envelope since last night, his fears (he didn't even know about her discovery) and her obligation to reassure him lay heavy on her mind.

"So what does he do?" asked Uncle Morrie, spearing a slice of brisket and lifting it carefully to his plate.

"He's a contractor. He did the retrofitting on my house. That's how we met. He has an MBA," she added, and was annoyed with herself for feeling she had to expand on his credentials.

"As long as he's nice." Edith smiled. "Don't eat so fast," she told her husband.

"Right," Uncle Morrie said, and Debra wasn't sure whether he was responding to his wife's first or second comment.

"Just remember, Deb, I get *shatchonus gelt.*" Aaron smiled. He was referring to the traditional monetary gift to a matchmaker.

"You'll take it out in trade," Uncle Morrie said, and everyone laughed, including Debra, though the remark wasn't that funny.

Later, while her father napped, she studied the lists again. She tried to let another pattern suggest itself, but she couldn't unsee what she'd seen last night. It was like the hidden animals in a puzzle picture, she thought—difficult to find, but once you saw them, they leaped out at you.

It was a mitzvah—a positive commandment—to enjoy the Sabbath; ordinarily Debra savored every quiet, tranquil moment, but today she found herself glancing at her watch, urging the minutes along so that she could phone Simms, feeling guilty about her impatience. She'd contemplated walking the two or so miles to Wilshire Division, but Simms wouldn't be there on a Saturday, and she couldn't bring him the lists, since carrying on the Sabbath was forbidden.

And she wasn't sure.

Her father came home from shul and recited the havdalah, the blessing that separates the Sabbath from the week; she held the lit braided candle high over her head ("Hold it as high as you want your husband to be," her family had teased when she was a young girl) and sniffed the allspice and cloves in the wooden, tower-shaped spice box. Her father doused the candle in the wine that had overflowed from the chalice onto a plate and, dabbing his fingers in the wine, touched them to his eyes, to show his love of the commandment, and inserted them into his pockets; wine spilled in the house takes on a blessed quality.

When the ceremony was over and she could call Simms, she decided not to. Instead, she phoned Claire.

Claire's condominium was in a security building on Oakhurst in Beverly Hills. Debra had been there several times before; she announced herself through the intercom and waited for Claire to buzz her into a lobby furnished with chintz-covered couches and oversize potted plants.

"You sounded so anxious on the phone," Claire said when she opened the door to her third-floor apartment. "I'm glad I was home when you called. I'm worried about you, Debra."

Debra followed Claire into a small, square living room and sat down on one of two cream-colored damask sofas that faced each other. She handed the folder to Claire, who sat next to her.

"What are these?" Claire asked, flipping through the lists.

Debra explained what information the lists contained. "I thought I might be able to detect a pattern that would explain why those four attorneys were killed."

Claire looked up quickly. "Did you?" Her voice was sharp with excitement and a hint of fear.

"I think so. But I could be wrong. So I want you to examine the lists yourself and see what you find."

"Why aren't the police doing this?" She sounded almost angry.

"Maybe they are. But I can't sit around and wait. I'm scared, Claire. The thought that someone's out there, that I'm next . . ." She closed her eyes and felt Claire's hand on hers; she bit her lip to stop from crying. "I received another threat on Friday."

She inhaled sharply. "The same note?"

Debra told her about the clippings. "My dad received the identical packet. This time there were two quotes—'Get out of the way of Justice' and 'The tongues of dying men enforce attention.' The second quote is from *Richard the Third.*"

Claire shut the folder. "Does that have significance to you?"

Debra shook her head. "Before I got the packet with both quotes, I thought the person threatening me was connected with the case I'm trying this Tuesday. I thought the family wanted me to drop the case and was making a dramatic point."

"But with the tongues quote, you think you're being threatened by the same person who killed Madeleine and the others and slashed their tongues." Claire's voice was somber, reflective.

"Maybe it's still the family of the complaining witness—

the slashed tongues thing has been all over the media. Maybe they're using it to frighten me into giving up the case."

Claire nodded. She picked up the folder and opened it again. "What am I looking for?"

"I want you to figure it out for yourself. That way I'll know if what I'm thinking is plausible."

Claire left the room and brought back a pencil and a pad of paper. She spread the lists on the wood coffee table and leaned over them, making numerical notations, crossing them out. Debra walked over to the fireplace and studied the lithograph on the wall and the framed photos on the mantel—Claire, in cap and gown, standing between her parents; Claire with her sister, Lee; Claire in her chambers. Debra strolled around the room, glancing at Claire every so often. When she returned to the sofa, she thumbed through an issue of *Architectural Digest,* but her eyes were intent on Claire.

Fifteen minutes later Claire stopped writing and leaned back against the sofa cushion. "I give up. I tried connecting types of convictions and got nowhere."

"I tried that first, too. Look at the acquittals."

"That was my next thought." Claire scanned the lists again. "Lots of acquittals. Pretty impressive—doesn't say much for the prosecution. I'll narrow it down to within the past two months." She ran her fingers down each page, writing as she found relevant entries. When she had finished scanning the last list, she looked at what she'd written.

She frowned and cast a quick, incredulous glance at Debra. Biting her lip, she scanned the lists again, then turned her attention to her pad, then back to the lists. When she looked up at Debra, her face was ashen.

"They all recently won rape trials. That's it, isn't it?" Her voice shook. "But why?"

Debra had thought about it for hours before she'd fallen asleep last night. "Someone—either a person related in some way to a rape victim, or a rape victim herself—is punishing the lawyers who get the rapists off. That's why the severed tongues."

Claire winced. "What do you mean?"

"I think the killer is saying that lawyers use their tongues to grill rape victims and put them through hell on the stand. To the killer, the tongue is a symbol of evil."

" 'Speak no evil.' " Claire shuddered.

Debra nodded. As a woman, she was repelled by the legal system that forced rape victims brave enough to testify to suffer humiliation as the intimate details of their lives were exposed to strangers in what invariably became a public rape. As a lawyer, she believed in every person's right to a fair trial and the obligation of the defense attorney to zealously defend her client.

"This is so bizarre, so grotesque," Claire whispered. She touched Debra's arm. "You have to tell Simms right away!"

"He'll think I'm trumping up some theory to push suspicion away from me." She repeated what he'd said on his last visit to her office, thinking as she spoke how insane the charges sounded.

Claire shook her head with impatience. "Obviously, Simms's dislike for you has colored his assessment of the murders. Do you think he believes what he's saying or is he just harassing you?"

"I'm not sure. Sometimes I think he's very serious, and that's scary as hell. I didn't do anything, for God's sake!"

"Show him the lists. Explain it to him. He'll believe you. My God!" Her hand went to her mouth. "You're trying a rape case this week! The notes . . ." Her voice trailed off.

"Simms can get the names of the complaining witnesses. The police will have concrete leads. Unless, of course, the killer isn't connected to any of these cases. In that case, it may take forever to find him."

"And in the meantime? What about your trial?"

"I can withdraw from the case, but I don't feel that's ethical. And what happens if everyone is too afraid to defend someone charged with rape? What happens to innocent people?"

Claire glanced at the lists on the coffee table, then said, "You realize if you win this case, he'll go after you."

"I realize that." The thought was numbing. The thought, when she allowed it into her mind, made her rigid with fear.

"You could say you have a conflict of interest," Claire said. "Knowing that if you win you might die, do you honestly think you can represent your client as zealously as you should? Isn't it possible that you won't do your best?" She gazed at her earnestly.

"I would hope that I'd do my best. You wouldn't drop the case if you were in my place, would you?"

There was a beat of hesitation. "Absolutely. I'd wait for the police to find the killer. That's what you should do."

"You're lying," Debra said softly. "You're saying that because you're afraid for me, aren't you?"

Claire's silence was an answer.

Debra phoned Wilshire and asked the desk sergeant to have Detective Simms call her at Claire's. While she waited, Claire brought a cup of tea for Debra and for herself.

Claire sat down. "I might be hearing your case, you know. The trial I'm hearing now is in jury deliberations. I expect a verdict on Monday. Most of the other judges are in the middle of cases or will be starting new trials on Monday. Do you—"

The phone rang. Claire hurried to the kitchen to answer it,

then brought the cordless receiver to Debra. "It's Simms," she said.

Debra took the receiver. "Detective Simms?"

"What's the emergency, Ms. Laslow? Another broken window? Some more newspaper clippings?"

"I think I know why someone killed the attorneys."

Simms expelled an annoyed breath. "We've been through this."

"You don't understand. I found the connection. All four attorneys were murdered because they won rape trials."

"Not a bad idea."

"I'm serious, Detective!" she snapped impatiently.

"Is this why you bothered me on a Saturday night? Have a nice evening, Ms. Laslow. And lay off the sauce."

"I can show you. I can prove it to you." She told him about the lists, explained how she'd made her discovery. When she was finished, he made her go over it again. Then he was silent for so long that she thought he'd hung up.

"Where are you now?" he finally asked.

"At a friend's. I can meet you at the station in twenty minutes." She would be sleeping at her father's—she was afraid to go home to an empty house at night—but she didn't want Simms to come there.

"Bring the lists," Simms said.

Chapter Thirty

She followed Simms from reception to his desk and sat down, handing him the folder with the lists and the manila envelope her father had received—she'd taken it along to Claire's and told her father she'd be turning it in to the police.

"What's this?" Simms said, touching the envelope.

"My father received that on Friday. It contains newspaper clippings of the four murdered attorneys, a snapshot of me, and a threatening caption. I received the same packet on Friday, too."

He opened the envelope, examined the snapshot of Debra, then slipped everything back and tossed the envelope onto his desk. He opened the folder and scanned each list. "Explain this again."

She repeated everything, pointing to the entries as she spoke. "I know it sounds bizarre," she said when she finished.

"Yeah." Simms looked at the papers, then at her. "I'm impressed, Ms. Laslow. Clever thinking."

She couldn't tell whether he was being sincere or sarcastic. "This would explain why I've been receiving threats. I'm starting a date rape trial this Tuesday."

He shook his head. "I'll never understand that—a woman attorney defending a rapist. How do you live with yourself?"

She clenched her teeth. "Everybody's entitled to a defense. And not every person charged with a crime is guilty."

"Your client's a saint, huh?"

"It's not my job to decide whether he's innocent or guilty. That's up to the jury." She paused, then said, "You could subpoena the client files and get the names of the complaining witnesses. Maybe one of them—or someone related to them—is the killer."

"You have an annoying habit of telling people how to do their jobs, you know that?" He glared at her. "I'll check into this."

He didn't sound convinced. "You don't see a pattern?"

"Oh, there's a pattern. The question is, did the killer murder attorneys because they won rape trials, or because he—or she—wanted to create an *artificial* pattern to lead the police in the wrong direction? Did he have a motive for killing only *one* of the attorneys and use the others as window dressing? See what I mean?" His eyes had narrowed and were riveted on her.

She saw exactly what he meant. He still suspected her—or wanted her to believe he did. "That sounds farfetched."

"Say a person kills someone out of jealousy or rage. He's frightened, he may even be sorry, but he can't undo the deed. And he doesn't want to spend his life in prison." Simms shrugged. "Desperate situations, desperate measures. You know what's interesting? Pratt and Malter received threatening notes a week or so before they were killed. Madeleine Chase and Susan Clemens didn't. Why is that, do you think?" When she didn't answer immediately, he said, "Cat got your *tongue,* Ms. Laslow? Or should I say 'dog'?"

She flinched and saw satisfaction on his face. "You have no respect for these dead victims, do you?"

"Sure I do. But I also have respect for the *living* victims."

She ignored his implication and said, "Madeleine received a threatening note but threw it out. Maybe Susan did, too. What did these other notes say?"

"Same thing yours did: 'Get out of the way of Justice.' 'The tongues of dying men enforce attention.' "

"Were you able to identify prints on the notes I gave you?"

"*Nada*—except for yours. The lab couldn't raise any others. No prints on the notes the other attorneys received, either."

"So whoever sent the notes wore gloves." When Simms didn't answer, she stood and slipped her purse strap onto her shoulder. "It occurred to me that whoever else is trying a rape case, or has just won an acquittal, is in danger, too."

"I already thought of that. I'll check into it. Your trial starts Tuesday, you said. That means it'll probably go to the jury the following week, right?" When she nodded, he said, "Maybe you'd better hope you lose."

The house looked undisturbed when Debra returned Sunday morning. She worked all morning on her opening statement and reread Avedon's file. At one-fifteen Adam arrived and took her to the Beverly Hills Gun Club. He'd brought along his own gun for her to use: a small .38 Smith & Wesson, similar to a number of weapons she'd handled at the gun shop.

He told her how to stand—feet slightly apart—and how to aim with both arms extended. Standing in the shooting range, she was surrounded by the acrid smell of gunpowder. Even with ear protectors on, the sound of each shot was deafening, and she was startled by the recoil action of the gun, which, on her first two or three attempts, seemed to lurch in her hand. She was startled, too, by the power that coursed through her.

On the way back to her house, she told Adam about the manila envelopes and the rape pattern she'd discovered. When he offered again to lend her his gun, she didn't refuse.

Looking around the conference room at the Sportsman's Lodge, Debra estimated that over a hundred women had shown up for the WRIT meeting. Two uniformed police—one man, one woman—spoke on safety tips: Don't go out at night alone. Don't enter an elevator before assessing the passengers. Always lock your car and look in the backseat before entering. Have your key in your hand before you approach your car. If a car is following your car, don't go home; go to the nearest police station. Never open your door to a stranger, even if he says he's with the police.

Debra hadn't learned anything new, but hearing the suggestions was always a good reinforcement. Not that she needed reinforcement—she was on guard all the time lately.

After the lecture, the officers answered questions—first from the podium, then informally. Debra spotted a number of women she knew. Annette Prado was across the room. She noticed Debra and waved, then mouthed, "See you on Tuesday."

Claire was talking to the woman officer. Debra walked toward her, exchanging greetings with other attorneys on her way. She waited until Claire had finished talking to the woman, then tapped Claire's shoulder.

Claire turned. "How are you?" she said in an undertone when she saw Debra. She touched Debra's arm.

"Okay, considering." She forced a smile to her lips. "I thought you were having dinner with your father tonight."

"I thought so, too, but when I phoned to tell him I was picking him up, he said he'd changed his mind." Claire shrugged. "Speaking about fathers, did you tell yours about your theory?"

Debra shook her head. "I don't want him to panic." She'd decided not to tell Aaron, either. "And what if I'm wrong? That's why I'm not saying anything to the others here tonight."

Claire was silent a moment, then nodded. "You're probably right. Any news from Simms?"

"I don't expect any until tomorrow, when he can contact the firms."

Another attorney came up to Claire. Debra excused herself and spoke with some of the other women she knew. Ten minutes later she left the conference with two of them. She'd attended weddings at the hotel, and each time she'd admired the natural beauty of the setting; walking now along the wood-slatted path that bridged several ponds, she ignored the ducks and trees and, hurrying to her car, saw no beauty, only danger.

She exited the parking lot, turned left on Ventura, and headed for the 101 freeway. From a radio traffic report she learned that there had been a collision on the southbound 101 near the Lankershim exit. She decided to take Laurel Canyon instead.

Stopping at the traffic light at Ventura and Laurel Canyon, she felt the beginning of a headache over her right eye. She studied the street sign. The letters were all there—her vision seemed all right. It was a tension headache, not a migraine.

She turned right onto Laurel Canyon and drove a mile until Mulholland, the crest of the mountain. Almost immediately the boulevard narrowed, and there was only one lane going in each direction. There were just a few cars ahead of her on the road, which had started to twist as it descended through the canyon. The area was shrouded in darkness, except for once in a while, when the headlights of an oncoming car would warn her of its approach.

Glancing at the next road sign, she was alarmed when she couldn't see all the letters. It was a migraine after all, she realized as she continued her descent. Her aura was starting, and there was nowhere for her to stop. In the rearview mirror she could see the headlights of the car behind her.

She felt a tingling of anxiety but told herself the drive was only another two and a half miles; if she was careful, she could make it out of the canyon and back into the city, where the narrow road would once again become a boulevard and she could pull over to the curb and wait until her vision returned to normal. She resisted the urge to accelerate, to outrace the advent of the blinding zigzag neon lights.

The car behind her was coming closer, its headlights two eyes, glaring at her. She was annoyed—it wasn't safe to drive faster, not because of her headache, but because of the winding, downward incline that made her keep her foot on the brake.

The car was coming even closer. She was angry now—what the hell was wrong with the driver? There was no way for him to pass her. She stayed a safe distance from her right, where the mountain wall looked harder and more unforgiving than it did in daylight.

She glanced in the rearview mirror again. It was a black or dark blue midsize car. She honked once, then again. By now her right eye was flooded with arcing lights. She swerved with each turn, to the right, to the left, to the right again; still the car was inching closer, hugging the tail of her Acura, and with a thudding suddenness that made her chest feel hollow and her lips tingle, she realized there could be a more sinister explanation for the car and the driver, who seemed intent on forcing her into the side of the mountain.

She honked again and, straining to see beyond the zigzag lines, made out a partial license plate: an initial number *1* followed by an *A*. The driver was wearing a hat, and she could barely see his face.

Now the car was almost on top of her. She released her foot from the brake and, gripping the steering wheel, let the car accelerate down the serpentine road. She turned a bend, then another. Ahead of her were the red taillights of a car that seemed to be moving slowly, so slowly that she would ram into it if it didn't move faster. As she approached, she saw that ahead of this car were others, and that they had all stopped for the red light at an intersection.

Her heart hammering with terror, she slammed on the brakes and, when she was inches away from the car in front of her, jerked the steering wheel to the right and drove several feet up the unpaved driveway of a house on stilts.

She turned quickly to her left and looked through the back window but didn't see the black car. She looked to her right—the car had pulled back and stopped. She tried again to see the license plate numbers, but by now everything was a blur, and she felt as if she were trying to read underwater.

A second later the intersection light turned green.

The black car whizzed by and disappeared.

Chapter Thirty-one

The women's section in the synagogue was empty when Debra arrived at seven o'clock Monday morning. She parted the curtains and watched a man remove one of the Torah scrolls from the navy velvet-draped ark. On Mondays and Thursdays someone would read from the weekly Bible portion, which would be read in its entirety on the coming Sabbath.

Mondays and Thursdays and Saturdays were also designated for someone who had to express special thanks to God for having been spared from a life-threatening situation. At the appropriate time Debra rose. She recited the blessing in Hebrew and listened as the men, one of whom was her father (he must have recognized her voice; he must be wondering), responded.

A short while later the service was over. Every few minutes Debra parted the curtains; when she saw that all the men except her father had left, she returned her prayer book to the bookcase and walked into the men's section.

Her father was at one of the tables toward the front of the

he had no choice—it was the king's order, and he had to arrest someone.

" 'Do this,' Rav Elazar told him. 'Go to a diner at four in the morning. If you see a man dozing while holding his wine cup, ask about him. He may be a young rabbinical scholar. He may be a laborer. If he is neither, he is a thief.' The matter was heard in the palace, and Rav Elazar was authorized to follow his own advice. He did so and arrested many thieves.

"Rav Yehoshuah ben Korchah sent a message to Rav Elazar: 'Vinegar son of wine! How long will you hand over the people of our God to their execution!' Rav Elazar replied, 'I am ridding the vineyard of its thorns.' To which Rav Yehoshuah answered, 'Let the Master of the vineyard come and get rid of His thorns Himself!' " Ephraim Laslow looked at his daughter.

Debra shook her head. "I don't understand your point. I'm not prosecuting anyone. I'm trying to protect my client's rights."

"You've appointed yourself a savior, Debra. There's an arrogance in your action, a stubbornness. You're championing not just your client, but all defendants and the criminal justice system. That's not your responsibility, just as it wasn't Rav Elazar's responsibility to apprehend thieves. God can bring thieves to justice. Society will take care of criminal justice."

He spoke with a sharpness she'd never heard before; underneath it she recognized fear. "My whole life you've taught me to be concerned about others, not just myself. My whole life you've showed me a Jewish history filled with men and women who risked their lives to save others."

"Yes, but they didn't do so with the *certainty* of losing their own lives." He leaned toward her. "There are only three conditions under which you must sacrifice your life: if someone says, 'I will kill you unless you commit an immoral sexual act' or 'I will kill you if you don't worship my gods' or 'I will kill you if you don't kill another.' "

"I know that, Dad." She spoke with a hint of impatience.

"Then you also know that if a pregnant woman needs a medical procedure that would endanger the fetus, the Torah instructs that she undergo the procedure and lose the fetus. If two people face certain death, each one has the obligation to save himself first."

Debra was silent.

Her father clasped her hand between his two. "I know this doesn't sound idealistic—I can see that you disapprove, that you're disillusioned. But the Torah is a document for living."

"You're giving me the halachic view, the law. But what about morality?"

"In Judaism there's no difference. Halacha and morality are one." He studied her face. "And if I told you—not as a rabbi, but as your father—to give this up, to walk away?"

"I'd have to honor your wishes."

"But you'd resent me." Sighing, he released her hand. "I won't tell you what to do, Debra. Not as a rabbi, not as your father."

She felt a twinge of disappointment and wondered whether she'd come here to be advised or to be told that the decision wasn't hers to make. "Maybe the threats aren't from the killer. Maybe someone from the Bailor family is using the murders—the reference to the slashed tongue, for example—to frighten me into withdrawing from the case. To frighten you, too."

"In that case, whoever is responsible is doing an effective job. I haven't felt this terrified, this helpless, since the doctors told me your mother's cancer was terminal."

"I'm sorry," she whispered, and stroked his cheek.

He nodded, then pulled over a volume of the Talmud

that was lying on the table, opened it, and stared at the pages.

"So in view of the fact that I'm the next target, I want a full-time, armed female bodyguard," Debra said in a quiet, determined tone to the white-faced men sitting at the conference table. "I want her to drive me to and from work. I want her to accompany me wherever I go. I want her to sleep in my house. Without the bodyguard, I won't represent Avedon tomorrow morning."

Charles squeezed her hand under the table. Like Adam, he'd been shocked by what she'd told him about the rape pattern, then incredulous, then alarmed and grimly supportive of her demands, even before she told him about the black car.

There was an uncomfortable silence, during which she wondered what the others were thinking. Anthony had been staring at her from the minute she'd started talking. Jeremy and Richard had stared, too—she could hardly blame them. Now they were frowning.

Jeremy nodded. "You're absolutely right, Debra."

For the second time that morning, she wasn't sure whether she was relieved or disappointed. Had they said "no" to the bodyguard, she could have withdrawn from the case and told herself that they, not she, had made the decision.

"You're sure about this rape pattern?" Richard asked. "It seems so crazy."

She couldn't detect sarcasm or hostility in his voice; he was certainly entitled to be skeptical. "I can't be positive, but Detective Simms thinks I'm right. He's asking a judge to sign subpoenas for the files of the four rape cases in question."

"What about police protection?" Richard asked.

"They can't provide that." She didn't add that Simms still suspected her.

"Why not file for a continuance until the police find the killer?" Anthony asked. "Given the circumstances, I'm sure the judge will allow one."

"That's fine with me." Debra nodded. It *was* fine. "But *you'll* have to tell Avedon. He's anxious to get this over with."

Jeremy said, "We can't allow a psychotic killer to derail the criminal justice system, Anthony. This time it's rape cases. Next time it'll be something else." He turned to Debra. "You'll have your bodyguard today. I'll have Rosemary make the arrangements."

"Debra doesn't need the bodyguard until the verdict is in," Anthony said.

Now it was her turn to stare. She felt another reassuring touch from Charles, who muttered, "Jesus!" under his breath while Jeremy glared at Anthony and said, "This isn't a time to pinch pennies."

"I'm merely making a practical suggestion." His face had turned pink. He fidgeted with his bow tie. "We do have a guard in the lobby."

"What if the killer moves up his schedule?" Richard said. "We can't afford to place Debra in any jeopardy."

She looked at Richard, but his eyes were on Jeremy and she couldn't see his expression. She wondered if he was supporting her or demonstrating loyalty to Jeremy, then decided it didn't matter.

"At the risk of annoying everyone with another practical question," Anthony said, "what if the police don't find the killer within the next few weeks? How long will we keep this bodyguard?"

"As long as necessary." Jeremy's tone conveyed finality.

She was still puzzling over Richard's show of support when she returned to her office. She phoned her father and told him about the bodyguard. "So that should put your mind at ease," she said.

"It does. But how long will they pay for a bodyguard?" her father asked, echoing Anthony's question.

She repeated what Jeremy had told her. Her father said, "That's good," but she could hear in his voice her own concern—what would happen if the police didn't find the killer soon? At what point would Jeremy decide that Debra's safety was becoming too expensive?

At eleven-thirty Simms phoned Debra to tell her he'd obtained four subpoenas—one for each file.

"So we should know today who the witnesses are," Debra said.

"Not '*we*,' Ms. Laslow. I can't tell you that."

Debra wanted to argue that her life was in jeopardy, that she was entitled to know; but the detective was right. "Would you give me the case numbers?" With the case numbers, she could obtain the transcripts of the trials from the hall of public records and learn the names of the complaining witnesses.

"I'll have to check with my supervisor."

"Once the cases have been tried, they're public record." She could get the information by calling all the DAs and asking which rape trials the four slain attorneys had handled, but that would take time.

"You're probably right, but I want to clear this with my boss. I'm not trying to stonewall you." Simms sounded sincere. "We checked the court dockets in L.A. County—there are five rape cases set for trial, but none till December. I'm going to phone the five attorneys handling the cases—three women and two men—and find out if they received any threats. Want to place bets?"

His sarcasm was back; she could picture his crooked smile. She hung up, then picked up the receiver to phone Claire just as Glynnis buzzed and told her Jeff Silver was on the line.

"I'm sure you're busy," he told her after they exchanged greetings. "I want to know if we're on for tomorrow night."

She didn't have the energy to be charming, but she didn't want to hurt his feelings. "We're on. Unless something comes up during the trial tomorrow that needs my attention."

"Okay. Do you want me to escort you home after work today? I keep offering, and you keep turning me down."

Adam had followed her to work that morning—she'd returned home after she'd gone to the synagogue—and escorted her to the elevator. "Thanks, but the firm is hiring a bodyguard for me."

"Just for you? Why? Did something else happen?"

With some reluctance, she told him about the packet and about the car that had tailgated her last night and explained what she'd discovered about the rape cases.

There was a short silence. Then Jeff said, "You're going to drop the rape case, aren't you?"

She could hear the shock in his voice. "I told you—the firm's hiring me a full-time, armed bodyguard. I'll be safe." What was safe? she wondered.

"Listen, I don't know you very long, and this isn't my business, but I don't think a bodyguard's foolproof protection. Why don't you drop the case? Or postpone it?"

"I appreciate your concern, Jeff," she said, trying not to allow her irritation to show. "But I've made my decision, and I don't want to discuss this anymore."

"But—" He stopped, then said, "Okay. Eight o'clock tomorrow night?"

"Eight o'clock is fine."

Richard had made several comments on the Donovan brief that needed Debra's response. She was working on them when Annette Prado phoned in the early afternoon.

"I wanted to make sure you got the shrink's statement,"

Annette said. "I forgot to ask when I saw you at the meeting last night."

"I have it." There had been nothing surprising in the psychologist's assessment, nothing Debra hadn't heard before, nothing that, with some luck, she wouldn't be able to refute.

"By the way, Debra, I heard that you got threatening letters. Is that true?"

This must be the real reason Annette had called. Debra wondered who had told her. "It's true. Detective Simms from Wilshire is checking them out."

"Marty Simms? He testified for me a number of times. He's one tenacious son of bitch. If there's something to be found about the letters, he'll find it."

"The Simms I know is with Homicide, not Sex Crimes."

"Medium height and wiry? Bushy eyebrows? A permanent scowl on his face? Always picking at his lips?"

That was Simms. An unsettling sensation fluttered through her stomach. "Yes."

"He was with Sex Crimes at the time. I heard he switched to Homicide. He really hated rapists—you could see it on his face. God, I loved having him on the stand!"

Debra felt physically ill. "How did he feel about the lawyers who defended them?"

"What do you think?" Annette laughed. "Why do you ask? Is he giving you a hard time?"

"You could say that."

"Don't take it personally, Debra. The victims really got to him, you know? I guess that's why he switched to Homicide—murder is gruesome, but the victims aren't there, looking you in the face, crying. It was probably the right decision for Simms."

"Probably," Debra said.

Chapter Thirty-two

The bodyguard—a tall, muscular, blond-haired woman in her late twenties named Nadine who had served in the Marines and was an aspiring scriptwriter—followed Debra home.

Adam was visibly relieved to meet Nadine and learn that she would be sleeping in the house. "Do you want to have dinner with me?" he asked Debra while the bodyguard was looking around the house.

She wanted to spend time with him, but she was too tense, too exhausted. "I need a good night's sleep before the trial tomorrow. How about Wednesday?" she asked before he could suggest Tuesday.

"Great." He smiled. "The guy from the other alarm company dropped off a quote—it's on the breakfast room table. Want to see how your office is coming along?"

She followed him to the alcove. The bookcase frame was completed; there were short cabinets on the bottom and room for four tall shelves above—she would need them for her legal texts. The desk had been partially assembled.

"It looks wonderful, Adam. So does the new living room window." She'd noticed it immediately. "Although I kind of miss the plywood look." She liked the way his eyes crinkled when he smiled. She liked a great many things about him.

"I'll call you tonight—but not late." He leaned toward her; she thought he was about to kiss her, but just then Nadine appeared. He pulled back and said good night.

After Adam left, the bodyguard secured the doors and windows; when the kosher Chinese restaurant delivered Debra's order—cashew chicken for Debra, pepper beef for Nadine—the ex-marine motioned to Debra to wait in the living room while she walked to the front door, her gun drawn, and demanded to see identification from the delivery man before she opened the door and slipped her gun into her holster. Later she checked the house again; when Debra entered the den to ask if she needed anything for the night, she saw the gun on the sofa, next to Nadine's laptop computer.

At 7:45 on Tuesday morning, Nadine drove Debra to the Santa Monica Court House in her dented white Honda Civic. "Whoever's threatening you knows your car," she'd said when Debra had suggested they take the Acura.

From the parking lot, the two women walked to the Main Street entrance of the courthouse. Debra felt odd being escorted by the bodyguard, but no one looking at them would know—Nadine's gun was hidden by the jacket of her burgundy suit.

Debra much preferred the Santa Monica or West L.A. courthouse and surroundings to downtown. Downtown was overpowered by tall gray buildings that blocked the sky, streets crowded with people hurrying past vagrants to their destinations, exhaust from buses and from cars whose drivers were honking angrily at each other; here in Santa Monica palm tree fronds brushed against the sky that always seemed more intensely blue, and Debra could smell the briny perfume of the Pacific Ocean, only blocks away.

"Cute sign," Nadine said, pointing to the sheet pasted to the glass door: NO SHIRT, NO SHOES, NO ENTRY.

Debra had seen the sign so many times that she no longer noticed it. She smiled in agreement and opened the door. Inside the lobby she placed her purse and briefcase on a conveyer belt that passed under a metal detector. Nadine surrendered her weapon, then followed Debra under a metal detector arch. Debra retrieved her purse and briefcase and waited for Ken Avedon in front of the elevators, where she'd told him to meet her at 8:20.

It was 8:15 now. Three minutes later Avedon appeared; Debra could see the anxiety on his face give way to relief when he spotted her. She recognized his parents—the father was a silver-haired version of the son; the mother was an elegantly dressed, large-framed, brown-haired woman. The three passed through the metal detector. Avedon introduced his parents; Debra introduced Nadine as an associate and led the way down the hall to the left to Department C, the Master Calendar Court.

Annette Prado was there. So were over twenty other attorneys—prosecutors and defense attorneys. The defendants—most of them in prison blue—were sitting in what in other courtrooms was the jury box. During the intense plea-bargaining exchanges between opposing attorneys that were conducted during pretrials, which took place two weeks after preliminary hearings, the atmosphere in the courtroom often reminded Debra of an outdoor bazaar.

At 9:45 the clerk announced Avedon's case. Annette stepped forward; Debra motioned Avedon to follow her.

"Ready for the People," Annette said.

"Ready for the defense," Debra echoed, aware that both she and the prosecutor were wearing almost identical navy suits. Annette was wearing a white blouse; Debra, a cream silk camisole.

The judge instructed them to go to Department A, next door. Entering the courtroom, Debra reminded Avedon in an undertone that a judge might not be available; she could sense his tension as they waited and was relieved both for herself and for him when, twenty minutes later, the presiding judge directed them to Department M on the second floor.

Claire's courtroom. Debra wasn't particularly surprised—Claire had said she expected jury deliberations on the case she'd been hearing to conclude on Monday. "It would be strange, wouldn't it, after all this," she'd said, "if I'm the one who hears your case?"

"Strange" was the operative word, Debra thought as she walked to the elevator with her client and his parents and her bodyguard.

There were fifty people in the jury pool. As the clerk called twelve names, Debra watched eight men and four women from the spectator's gallery take their places on the royal blue upholstered chairs in the elevated box at the right of the courtroom. Two seats remained empty; those were for the alternates.

Voir dire can be tedious. Debra had tried cases before judges who turned what should have been a one-day jury selection process into a four-day nightmare. Claire, thank God, was thorough but efficient and established a smooth pace in her courtroom.

As each juror responded to Claire's questions, Debra, using her own shorthand, noted the name and relevant information on a small Post-it note, which she affixed to the corresponding square on the juror sheet in front of her. If a juror was later excused, Debra would replace the Post-it with a new one. She also wrote notes about each juror on her pad. Avedon had a pad, too. So did Annette Prado, who was sitting at the prosecution table to Debra's right.

After general questions, including those about occupation, marital status, and previous jury service, Claire addressed the prospective jurors. "The defendant has a presumption of innocence," she began. "The defense doesn't have to prove anything or dispel suspicions or put on a case. The defendant doesn't have to testify. The State must prove beyond a reasonable doubt that a crime has been committed."

While Claire spoke, Debra assessed the jurors, watching their faces and body language as they listened to what the judge was saying. On three of the Post-it notes, she penciled a question mark.

" 'Beyond reasonable doubt' isn't 'beyond any doubt,' " Claire continued. "This is human justice, not divine. To convict, you must have an abiding conviction of the defendant's guilt—on later reflection, you won't have a nagging doubt. If anyone has a problem with anything I've just said, please raise your hand."

Debra looked at the jury—no hands were raised.

"I'm supposed to instruct the jury not to form opinions during the trial. That's impossible, unless you're robots." The judge smiled. "You can have tentative opinions, but never say, 'I've heard enough. I've reached a decision.' " She examined her notes. "The defendant is charged with forcible date rape of an acquaintance. The nature of this crime elicits an emotional response. Has any one of you witnessed this type of offense? Does any one of you know someone who has been a victim of this type of offense. Does any one of you . . ."

Several jurors raised their hands: One woman's neighbor had been raped. A male juror's wife worked in a hospital emergency room, where she saw rape victims. Debra made notes to have both prospective jurors excused. A woman's uncle had been accused of rape; charges had never been filed. Annette would undoubtedly excuse the woman. Debra glanced at Avedon. He had filled a page of his pad; he looked serious but not nervous.

Annette had submitted eighteen questions to the judge; Debra watched intently as prospective jurors responded to those Claire had decided to use:

Will you be uncomfortable with discussion of intimate details about so-called sexual behavior and anatomy?

Do you believe that a woman can put herself into a situation where she deserves to be raped? What if she wears revealing clothes? What if she drinks alcohol?

If the victim of a sexual assault did not make a prompt report, do you feel her testimony should not be believed?

Do you think a woman has to resist to the point of bodily injury before she can charge someone with rape?

Under the law, the testimony of a single witness is sufficient to convict someone of a crime if you believe that one witness. Will you be willing to follow that law?

Do you think people react differently under conditions causing pressure/fear/threat of bodily injury?

Have you ever made a serious mistake in judgment that could have resulted in placing yourself in physical danger or harm?

Do you believe that a woman has to do anything other than say no in order to refuse a man's sexual advances?

They were excellent questions, Debra thought. She had submitted only four, all of which Claire posed to the jury:

Do you think someone can be falsely accused of rape?

Do you think doctors should be held to a higher level of accountability for their behavior?

Do you think a man can be confused by signals he gets from a woman?

Do you think men and women communicate in nonverbal ways when they're together?

After the last juror had answered, Claire addressed Annette. "Do the People pass for cause?"

"The People pass."

She asked Debra the same question and received the same answer. "Peremptories are with the People," Claire said.

"The People ask the Court to thank and excuse Ms. Winslow."

Ms. Winslow was a gray-haired, retired teacher—in Annette's place, Debra would have excused her, too: while younger women were generally sympathetic to rape victims, traditional, middle-aged women were more disapproving and attributed blame to the victim, especially in a date rape. In a sense, Debra knew, these women were trying to preserve their belief in a just world: If you don't do anything wrong, nothing bad happens to you; if something bad happens to you, you did something wrong.

Claire excused the woman. The clerk called another name; a man took the vacated seat and answered Claire's questions.

Now it was Debra's turn. As a nervous public defender during her first trial, she'd said, "The defense thanks and excuses . . ." The judge had reprimanded her. Debra's face had turned red; she'd never made the error again. "The defense asks the Court to thank and excuse Mr. Abrams," she said now. Abrams was a lawyer; she didn't want lawyers—she wanted people with conservative views who would respond more emotionally than logically.

The final jury panel consisted of five men and seven women; both alternates were women. Annette had excused, among others, a male doctor, a postal worker, and an IRS agent. Debra had excused a man who'd been on a hung jury; a twenty-year-old woman—she would identify with Penny Bailor; and another man who Debra instinctively felt would be trouble. Sometimes, she'd learned, instinct was worth more than all her years of law school.

The clerk administered the oath. Then Claire said, "We'll adjourn until nine o'clock tomorrow morning, when the People will give their opening statement. At no time are you to discuss this case or permit it to be discussed with you, nor form fixed opinions or express any opinions. Please meet in the jury assembly room at eight forty-five and remember your seats here. Thank you."

"What do you think?" Avedon asked after the jury filed out.

"It's a pretty good mix." Not a perfect mix, but that never happened. Debra would have liked more men—they generally sympathized with the defendant and attributed blame to the victim. "Don't worry." She smiled. "See you here tomorrow at ten to nine."

Avedon left the courtroom with his parents. Debra collected her papers, put them in her attaché case, and stood.

"Where to now?"

Debra turned; she'd been so engrossed in the jury selection that she'd forgotten about her bodyguard. She felt a flash of resentment at being reminded that she was in danger—resentment that was illogical, she knew. "I have to make a call," she said. "Then maybe go downtown."

With Nadine at her side, Debra walked down the hall to a pay phone and called Glynnis, who told her Simms had phoned. She thanked Glynnis, hung up, and phoned Wilshire.

"Your secretary said you were in court," Simms said when he came on the line. "How's the trial?"

He sounded friendly, but she couldn't forget what Annette had told her—Simms hated rapists and their lawyers. "We finished jury selection. The trial starts tomorrow. About those case numbers—"

"That's why I called your office. You were right—they're public record, so I can give them to you. Got a pen?"

She took a pen and notepad from her purse and wrote down the numbers he dictated, wondering why he was being helpful. Maybe to throw her off guard. She thanked him and heard him grunt in response. "You mentioned five defense attorneys with rape trials scheduled for December. Did any of them receive threats?"

"Nope. I'm sure they will. It's not all that hard to find out who these attorneys are. You could do it, if you wanted to."

"Why would I do that?" she asked, then realized what he was suggesting: If she was the killer, she'd send the attorneys threatening notes to continue the false pattern she'd established. Again she couldn't decide if he was serious or just wanted to give her a hard time. "Have you found out anything about the complaining witnesses in the murdered attorneys' cases?"

"We're pursuing those and other leads."

"You keep saying that. In the meantime my life is in danger."

"You keep saying *that,* Ms. Laslow. I sympathize, but we don't have the manpower to protect you. Maybe you should get a private bodyguard."

"I already did."

"Then I guess you have nothing to worry about, do you?"

She could hear the surprise in his voice. As she hung up the phone, she thought again about his hatred for lawyers who defended rapists and wondered how far that hatred would take him, then told herself she was being silly.

Simms was a cop, not a killer.

Chapter Thirty-three

From the initial letters of each case number, Debra was able to determine the courthouse where the trial had taken place.

The cases Madeleine and Pratt had tried both began with BA—that referred to the downtown courthouse in the Criminal Courts Building on Temple. The SA in Kelly Malter's and Susan's case numbers indicated Santa Monica or West Los Angeles.

With Nadine at her side, Debra walked down a long, narrow hall to the district attorney's second-floor office. From the receptionist she ascertained that Kelly had tried her case in West L.A. Susan had tried hers in Department E—Judge Kranstler's courtroom. Debra spoke to the court clerk, a thin, blond man who quickly located the court file in his desk drawer.

"You can't take this out of the office," he cautioned her.

On the front of the file were the names of the prosecutor and defense attorney—in this case, Susan. Inside Debra found the complaint form the DA had filled out. On her notepad she copied the name of the defendant, Henry Lee; the complaining witness, Alicia Vaughan; and the court reporter.

The court reporter was out to lunch, the clerk told Debra. "Then she'll be in court till around three—that's when Judge Kranstler takes a fifteen-minute recess. Then back in court till four-thirty or so, depending on when the judge adjourns."

There was no point in waiting; Debra would try to catch up with the court reporter before the morning sessions began.

In the lobby Nadine retrieved her gun, then exited the building with Debra and walked to the parking lot. "What about lunch?" the bodyguard asked when they were sitting in the car.

Debra suggested an inexpensive health food bar on Fourteenth Street that several of the Santa Monica DAs frequented. Nadine selected salads and grains; Debra had fruit salad.

After lunch they drove to West L.A., where Debra examined the court file for Kelly Malter's case. The defendant's name was Vincent Morgan; the complaining witness, Emma Banks. This time Debra was lucky—the court reporter was in a small office, where she kept the paper and the disk of the case proceedings.

Neither the paper nor the disk would be legible to Debra without transcription. "How quickly can you transcribe it for me?" she asked the red-haired woman. "I need it ASAP."

"Two weeks is my usual minimum, unless I'm swamped. I could do it in a day or two, but there'd be an expedite fee on top of the regular fee, which is six hundred fifty dollars per full trial day. I remember the trial you're talking about—it ran five days."

Over three thousand dollars. As a public defender, Debra

had requested transcripts, but the county had picked up the cost. "Is there a less expensive way to get a transcript?"

"A county judge can request one. Or if the transcript's been made—say, for example, for a defendent who needs the transcript to appeal his conviction or sue his lawyer—you can get a copy for a hundred twenty-five dollars per day."

A bargain, Debra thought.

"Another thing: You could request a partial transcript—only the judge's jury instructions or the motions. Or only the testimony. That would cut down on the cost."

At around three thousand dollars each, four transcripts would be exorbitant. But Debra wanted them. She could ask Claire to request them, but Claire would have to justify requesting four transcripts. She could ask Simms, but she doubted he'd cooperate—he'd have to go through the DA's office, who would then go through a judge; and she was reluctant to involve him. She could ask the firm to pay, but even Jeremy, who had been generous about the bodyguard, would balk at an expense that couldn't be billed to a client. And Anthony's scream would be deafening.

"I have to think about this," Debra told the reporter. "If I order the transcript tomorrow, could you have it for Thursday?"

The woman hesitated, then said, "Sure. What the hell."

The last stop was downtown. Madeleine's client, Debra learned, was Wayne Rawling; the complaining witness, Janey Schultz. Wesley Pratt's client was Adrian Tchermack; the complaining witness, Nancy Wallace.

Pratt's trial had gone six days, but Madeleine's trial had been short—only three days—and Janey Schultz's father, who was suing the city for an inept prosecution, had ordered a transcript of the trial. And Debra knew the court reporter, who agreed to have the transcript of only the testimony and motions ready for Debra on Thursday and waived the expedite fee.

Debra would be spending almost two hundred dollars for one transcript; she wanted the other transcripts, too.

It was possible she'd be buying nothing. Or everything.

It was after four when Debra entered her office. Nadine had escorted her into the reception room and excused herself to go to the ladies' room; Debra had become accustomed to having the bodyguard around, but she welcomed the few minutes of privacy.

Glynnis had left several messages on Debra's desk. Jeff had phoned to remind her about tonight. Cynthia Ellis had phoned, too. Debra returned her call.

"I just wanted to know if that data helped," Cynthia told her.

"I'm not sure yet." Debra didn't want to advertise what she'd discovered. "But thanks again, Cynthia."

"One more thing. I'm embarrassed to tell you this." Cynthia laughed nervously. "That letter Ms. Chase received—I told you I didn't know what it said. That's the truth." Her voice dropped to a whisper. "But I *did* overhear her talking to someone after she got it—she was really angry, and her voice carried."

"What did she say?" Debra asked, careful not to sound irritated or impatient. She grabbed a pen and her yellow pad.

Still whispering, the secretary said, "Something like 'I know it's you' and 'You're crazy, and I'm going to tell the police.' " She was breathless when she finished.

"I appreciate your telling me this, Cynthia. Did you mention this to the police?" Did Simms know? Did he think Debra was the person Madeleine had called?

"No. I was afraid. What if the killer found out I overheard Madeleine talking to him? I don't know who she was talking to, but the killer wouldn't know that. Even if I told him I didn't know, he wouldn't believe me. What if he went after me?"

Debra could understand the woman's anxiety and told her so. "Do you remember anything else about the conversation?"

"There was one other thing, but I can't remember. I'm sorry."

"That's okay. If you do remember, will you call me?"

Cynthia Ellis promised that she would.

Debra introduced Jeff to Nadine, who said, "Pleased to meet you," and disappeared toward the back of the house.

"Big woman," Jeff said.

"She's an ex-marine, so watch your step." Debra smiled. "She's also a scriptwriter. And very nice."

"Is she coming along with us?"

"She's going home for a few hours. I gave her a key and asked her to be back by eleven."

Nadine had worried. "That's not what they're paying me for," she'd said. But Debra, desperate for some normalcy, had used Anthony's argument and insisted that she wasn't in mortal danger now—that would happen only if she won an acquittal—and that she'd be fine as long as she wasn't alone.

Jeff nodded. "I'll stay till she gets back." He looked around the room. "I see you had your window replaced."

"They did it today," she said, careful not to tell him "they" was Adam. "Nadine, we're leaving!" she called, and heard the bodyguard's, "Have fun!" as she and Jeff were walking out the door.

He led her to a red compact car across the street. "A loaner," he told her as he opened the door for her. "Mine's in the shop—the transmission mounts are gone. I'm dreading the bill."

Ten minutes later he parked in front of a new kosher

restaurant on Pico that served Mexican cuisine. Inside the
restaurant, a waitress seated them at a table in the center of
the room and took their orders.

"So did you drop the case?" he asked as he shut his
menu.

She tensed. "No."

He stared at her. "Do you have a death wish or something?"

"Obviously not. That's why I have Nadine." She took a
sip of water.

"Yeah, but why risk your life for a rapist? Rapists are
scum."

Agreeing to go out with him had been a mistake, she decided. She put down her goblet with more force than she'd
intended; the water sloshed over the rim. "He's not a rapist.
He's my client—a client who, by the way, I happen to believe is innocent."

"And if he's not? Would you still risk your life for him?"

She felt anger rising in her chest. "We know each other
two weeks, Jeff. We've gone out a total of three times. To
be honest, I find your concern excessive and a little abnor-
mal."

He looked as if she'd slapped him. "I like you, Debra. I
liked you the minute we met. And when I like people, I
care about their welfare. I didn't know that was a character
flaw."

She felt suddenly in the wrong, though she didn't know
why. They sat in uncomfortable silence until the waitress arrived with their appetizers.

"Can we start over?" Jeff asked after the waitress left.

Debra nodded and dipped a tortilla chip into her gua-
camole. "So where's your manuscript?"

"In the trunk of the car. I figured you'd look at it after
dinner, at your place. Unless you'd rather not?"

"No. That's fine."

They talked about books they'd read, movies they'd seen, places they'd been to. In the car on the way home an hour later, they were both quiet; she longed to bring the evening and the relationship to a graceful end and sensed he felt the same way.

He opened the car door for her after he parked, then got the manuscript from the trunk. She was wary as she approached her front door, looking to her right, then to her left; she unlocked the door quickly, ushered Jeff inside, shut the door, and bolted it. She missed Nadine.

"I thought you were getting an alarm system," Jeff said.

"I am. They're installing it on Thursday." She'd decided to go with the second company—their cost was several hundred dollars less than that of the first company.

She led Jeff to the den. Nadine was a polite house guest—she'd transformed the bed back into a sofa. Jeff sat next to Debra and, opening a dark brown accordion folder, removed an inch-thick stack of papers.

"My masterpiece," he said, handing her the papers. "Be kind." He was smiling, but his voice betrayed a hint of nervousness.

"What about the rest?" She'd seen more pages in the folder.

"Those chapters are still rough. I'll show them to you another time, after I polish them."

She didn't want there to be another time. "Why don't I look at them now," she said, "just to get a sense of where you're going," and after a moment's hesitation, he handed her another, larger stack of papers. She placed the title page to her left and glanced at the outline of the book's contents. The introduction was next; it offered a history of the criminal justice system. Each subsequent chapter, she saw, would deal with a different type of crime, presenting cases and interviews with attorneys expert in their fields. There were

chapters on homicide, burglary, arson, assault, domestic violence, drunk driving. And rape.

With the manuscript on her lap, she skimmed the introduction and read the first page of chapter one: burglary.
The writing was smooth and uncluttered, if not elegant, and
she found the attorney interviews interesting. She was on
the second page when she felt Jeff's arm on her shoulder.
She looked at him, surprised, and removed his arm.

He put his arm around her waist and moved closer to
her. "I really like you, Debra," he whispered.

"Don't." She pulled his fingers away, annoyed.

He put his hand on the back of her head and leaned toward her. She jumped up before he could kiss her; the
manuscript pages fell to the floor.

"I think you should leave, Jeff."

"You don't really mean that, Debra."

He was standing, too. He gripped her upper arms with
his hands. They were strong hands, and she couldn't move
away, but she twisted her head to the side, and his kiss
landed on her cheek.

"Stop it, Jeff!" She felt the beginnings of alarm.

He kissed her neck. She kicked his shin. He forced her
onto the couch and pinned her down with his weight.

"Stop it!" she screamed. "What are you doing?"

She shoved her hands against him, trying to throw him
off, but he was a stone. He clamped his hand around her
throat and kissed her. His mouth was hard, bruising. She
felt his tongue and pressed her lips together, stifling another
scream.

He removed his hand from her throat. She yelled, "No!"
as he slid his hand under her sweater. His other hand was
underneath her skirt, between her legs. She locked her
knees. He pried them apart. Thrashing wildly under him,
she screamed, "No!" as his hand inched upward. "Please,

no!" when he pushed her skirt up, and she knew that nothing would stop him, that no one would save her.

Suddenly he removed his hands and sat up. She lay for a few seconds, dazed, trembling, then hurriedly backed away from him and scampered off the couch.

"I could have done it." He was staring at her, panting, red-faced.

"Get out!" she whispered. Her throat ached from screaming.

"I would never have gone through with it, Debra. You know that. But I *could* have." He stood. "Would it have been rape, Debra? After all, you invited me in."

She smacked him hard across his face. "You bastard!" Tears stung her eyes. She bit her lip to keep from crying.

"I don't blame you for being angry, Debra, but—"

"Get out before I call the police."

"I did it for your own good!" His eyes had a feverish glint. "I did it to shake you up, to show you what your client did—this client that you're risking your life to defend."

"You're vile, Jeff." Her voice shook. "You're vile and reprehensible and I never want to see you again."

"Drop the case!" He was pleading now. "Drop it before it's too late."

"Get out," she said again. She was still trembling. Hugging her arms, she turned her back on him.

"I would never hurt you, Debra. You have to believe me."

A moment later she knew without looking that he had left the room. She listened for the sound of the front door closing; when she heard it, she walked to the entry hall and slid the dead bolt shut. Then she sat in her bedroom, holding Adam's gun, until Nadine returned.

In the morning she unfolded the *L.A. Times* and stared at the front-page headline:

RAPE ACQUITTALS BIZARRE LINK TO ATTORNEYS' MURDERS.

Chapter Thirty-four

"The motion to exclude the tape was denied at the preliminary hearing, Ms. Laslow," Claire said, scanning the papers in front of her. "I don't see why you're asking the Court to reconsider."

It was 9:15 on Wednesday. Annette Prado, wearing a dark gray suit and peach blouse that complemented her dark hair, was at the prosecution table; Debra and Avedon were at the defense table. The male clerk sat at an L-shaped desk to the judge's right; the court reporter, to the judge's left. Stage left and stage right, Debra thought—the courtroom was, after all, a theater where everyone played a role against the backdrop of the California State seal. Today the audience was larger than usual; the gallery was filled to capacity, a result of the *Times* article and radio broadcasts. The media were here, too—newspaper and television reporters, sketch artists, a television camera. Only the jurors were missing; they were waiting in the assembly room.

Debra stood, conscious that the camera eye was on her. "Defense counsel asks that all witnesses be excluded during motions." She wished there were some legal way she could permanently exclude Jeff from the courtroom. She'd been shocked to spot him when she'd arrived; she'd quickly averted her eyes, but her chest had tightened and her heartbeat had accelerated.

"Are there any witnesses present?" Claire asked the bailiff, who was sitting behind Debra, to her left. A moment later Claire said, "There are no witnesses, Ms. Laslow. Proceed." There was no hint of camaraderie in her voice or facial expression, no sign that she and Debra were friends.

Which was the way it should be. "The tape is prejudicial, Your Honor," Debra said, forcing aside thoughts of the article and Jeff and the irony that the night before beginning a rape trial, she'd almost been raped herself. "The jury will hear Ms. Bailor repeatedly—and without cross-examination—accuse my client of forcing her to have sexual relations. On the witness stand, she wouldn't be allowed to repeat those accusations."

"The tape is not prejudicial, Your Honor," Annette said. "It's crucial to the People's case, as it contains the defendant's adoptive admissions which corroborate the witness's charge."

"Would the Court consider ruling on this motion directly before the People plan to introduce the tape?" Debra asked.

"Without a ruling now we can't mention the tape in our opening statement. Defense counsel knows that." Annette smiled at Debra, who returned the smile and lifted her shoulders in an "I tried" motion.

"I'm going to allow the tape, Ms. Laslow," Claire said. "Bailiff, please bring in the jury."

Two minutes later the twelve jurors and two alternates entered the courtroom and filed into the jury box.

"Ladies and gentlemen," Claire said, "the *Los Angeles Times* ran a news item this morning, later broadcast on several radio stations, which has some bearing on this trial. May I see by a show of hands who read or heard this report?"

Six jurors and one alternate raised hands. "Mr. Ackerman," Claire said, addressing juror number one, who had raised his hand, "will you have any difficulty putting aside what you've read or heard this morning as you listen to the evidence presented and as you evaluate that evidence during jury deliberations?"

"No, Your Honor."

"Will what you've read or heard predispose you to find the defendant guilty or not guilty?"

"No, Your Honor."

"Thank you. Ms. Petrinko, will you have . . ."

Claire polled the six jurors and alternate and received seven "no" responses to both questions; Debra believed the jurors were sincere but wondered what unconscious pressure their unwanted knowledge would place on them during deliberations, when by voting to acquit, they'd be jeopardizing the life of the defense attorney.

Avedon had read the *Times* piece and voiced the same concern. "It's not only the verdict that worries me," he'd said. "I don't want you in danger. We can postpone the case until they find the killer."

Debra had told him there was no need—the firm had hired a bodyguard to protect her. And if the jury deliberated before the killer was caught and convicted Avedon—just an "if," Debra reassured him quickly—he'd probably have grounds for an appeal. She wasn't sure whether she'd turned down his offer from stubbornness or professional pride.

"You are not to read any news reports or listen to any news on the media until you've returned a verdict," Claire instructed the jury. "You are not to discuss this news report among yourselves or with anyone else or allow anyone to discuss it with you." She called on Annette to give her opening statement.

The prosecutor walked up to the podium and faced the jurors. "My name is Annette Prado, and I want to thank you in advance for your attention. I need to tell you up front that nothing I say or counsel says is evidence. The evidence presented to you will be in the form of witnesses, diagrams, and a taped conversation between Penny Bailor, the complaining witness, and the defendant."

The jurors would be thinking about the tape until they heard it, Debra knew. And there was nothing she could do about it.

"From the voir dire you had yesterday," Annette continued, "you know that this case is about one count of forcible rape. Date rape." She paused again and let her eyes survey the jury. "In a date rape, trust has been established by virtue of the relationship. You will hear that Penny had every reason to trust the defendant. He is a highly respected doctor. He was her employer. Penny is twenty-one years old. Her family is deeply devout. She was a virgin on the night of July twenty-third of this year. She will tell you that she liked the defendant and trusted him. She will tell you she was attracted to him and looked forward to having a pleasant evening together on that Tuesday night. She will tell you that they had dinner, and that after dinner the defendant invited her to his luxurious apartment, where he raped her." She stopped to let the statement sink in.

The jurors were listening intently. Avedon was listening, too. His lips were a grim line. Debra scribbled "Relax" on her pad and pushed it toward him. His expression softened.

"Now I have to be honest," Annette said. "Penny won't remember exactly the order in which everything happened that night. She was frightened. But what she does remember, and what she will tell you in detail, is that the defendant forced her to have sexual relations with him even though she repeatedly said no. Even though she was crying and pleading with him to stop. Even though she told him she was a virgin.

"Penny will tell you she didn't go to the police right away. She didn't tell her girlfriend, with whom she spent the night. She didn't tell her parents. She didn't tell anyone, because she was ashamed, because she was afraid of what people would think. Because she *blamed* herself for trusting the defendant and going to his apartment. Because she was angry at herself for making a mistake. But when she heard that the defendant was engaged, she knew she had to come forward. She didn't want what happened to her to happen to someone else.

"She will be honest. She will be candid. And after the close of the evidence in this case, ladies and gentlemen, I will ask you for a verdict of guilty. Thank you very much."

Annette returned to her table. Out of the corner of her eye, Debra saw Simms enter the room. She wasn't surprised, but her stomach muscles tightened. Now I have two fans in the audience, she thought, then wondered suddenly whether the killer was here among the crowd of spectators. Watching her. Waiting. The idea chilled her. With great effort she focused on the judge, who was asking whether Debra wanted to make an opening statement.

She cleared her throat and tried to do the same to her mind. "I do, Your Honor." She closed the button of her taupe suit—the same suit she'd worn on the day of her confrontation with Madeleine—and approached the podium. She felt a surge of excitement—this was what she loved, this was why she'd become a lawyer—and forgot everything else.

She introduced herself, then said, "Even before seeing Ms. Bailor, all of you probably feel sorry for her. To tell you the truth, I feel sorry for her, too. She's a confused person. But what you've heard is the prosecution's version of what happened on Tuesday, July twenty-third. That version had nothing to do with reality. The real victim is seated next to me. The real truth is that the witness wants to destroy Dr. Avedon."

"Objection," Annette said. "I think counsel is arguing."

Claire said, "It sounded like it, but I assume that defense counsel is ready to tell us what the facts will show?" When Debra nodded, the judge said, "Go ahead."

"Could the Court admonish the jury?" Annette asked.

Claire nodded. "In opening statements, lawyers are supposed to say what they believe the evidence will show," she told the jury, "not state their opinions. Continue, Ms. Laslow."

Simms was probably enjoying this; Debra could imagine a lopsided smirk on the detective's face. "The prosecution talked to you about evidence, but there is no evidence. There is no medical evidence. There is no corroboration. There are no bruises. There are no witnesses. There were people all around the apartment building, but no one heard Ms. Bailor scream. There was a guard at the lobby entrance, but Ms. Bailor said nothing to him. She didn't call the police right away. She didn't call the rape hot line. She didn't tell her best friend. She went back to work, knowing she would see Dr. Avedon every day, and she didn't say a word to anyone in the office. Not one word. She didn't tell anyone until three weeks after she had sexual relations with Dr. Avedon in his apartment, and when she did go to the police, it was only after she learned Dr. Avedon was engaged. That's when she quit her job."

Debra paused. "We all feel extremely sorry for Ms. Bailor, but the case hinges on her testimony, so I will have to question her vigorously. Listen carefully to her explanation for why she told the police only after Dr. Avedon announced his engagement. Pay close attention to her both on direct examination and cross-examination. And I believe you will have some doubts about Ms. Bailor."

Debra returned to her seat.

The first witness for the prosecution, Cynthia Staten, was in her mid-forties. She was tall and slim and had short brown hair and metal-framed glasses. The clerk swore her in and asked her to state and spell her full name for the record.

Annette said, "Dr. Staten, what is your occupation?"

"I'm a psychologist."

Debra took careful notes as the prosecutor established that Staten had practiced for seventeen years, had published several articles in major psychological journals on rape trauma syndrome, and was considered to be an expert on the subject.

"Dr. Staten, can you define the term 'rape trauma syndrome'?"

"It's used to describe a collection of the consequences of rape."

"What are some of the symptoms?" Annette addressed the psychologist, but her body was half facing the jury.

"There are two phases: the acute crisis phase—the phase of impact—and long-term reactions."

"Tell us about the acute crisis phase."

"Victims are in shock. They feel that everything has fallen apart inside. They report anxiety or fearfulness—shaking or trembling, a racing heart, tight muscles, rapid breathing, numbness. They have great difficulty falling asleep and nightmares in which they relive the rape."

Debra felt strange, listening. Jeff hadn't raped her, but her heart had been racing, her body shaking. She'd felt numb. She'd been unable to fall asleep for hours. She felt his eyes on her now and knew why he had come here—he wanted her to remember.

"Are there other symptoms in this phase?" Annette asked.

"Some victims are in denial. Some are unresponsive to their environment. Some become helpless or dependent. Many are filled with guilt and self-blame. Others have distorted perceptions and paranoia."

"Dr. Staten, from your experience with rape victims, do women raped by acquaintances suffer less than those raped by strangers?"

"No. In fact, the date rape victim feels she can't trust anyone—not even people close to her. She can't trust herself or her judgment. She blames herself more. In a recent study, forty-one percent of acquaintance rape victims who were college students believed that they would be raped again."

Annette paused—ostensibly to check her papers; Debra knew she wanted the jury to absorb the information.

"What about long-term reactions, Dr. Staten?"

"We call this the recoil stage. Victims have to restore order to their lives and regain mastery over their world. This takes time. Victims in this phase may experience fear, sadness, guilt, and anger all at once. Major symptoms include phobias, disturbances in physical functioning including sexual behavior, and changes in lifestyle."

"What kind of phobias?"

"Victims may be afraid to go out alone, or at night. Others may be afraid to stay at home alone. Many victims leave the lights on in their homes twenty-four hours a day."

"You mentioned disturbances in physical functioning. Can you give us an example?"

"Many victims aren't able to eat on a regular basis. Others eat continuously. Some experience changes in sleeping patterns, including insomnia. Many victims have a reduced interest or reduced enjoyment in sexual activity."

"Does a person suffering from rape trauma syndrome always have all these symptoms?"

"Definitely not."

"Dr. Staten, did you have occasion to examine Penny Bailor?"

"Yes, I did."

The jurors, Debra noted, had been following the testimony with varying interest. Now several of them leaned forward. "When was that?" Annette asked.

"I examined her in my office on Monday, October twenty-second, and on Tuesday, October twenty-third of this year."

"And what was the nature of your examination?"

"I evaluated her mental health and administered standardized psychological tests."

"And what did you observe?"

"Penny was fearful. She was easily startled by noises and sudden movements. She indicated that she didn't sleep well, that she suffered from nightmares about the rape."

"Objection." Debra stood. "Hearsay."

"Sustained."

"Did you observe any other symptoms?"

"Yes. I took Penny's pulse before we began our sessions and during the sessions. When Penny talked about the rape, her breathing and heart rate became accelerated."

"Dr. Staten, in your expert opinion, is Ms. Bailor suffering from rape trauma syndrome?"

"Definitely. Her behavior is consistent with that of other victims of rape trauma syndrome."

Annette smiled. "No more questions at this time."

Jurors number two and number seven nodded. Debra checked their seats against the jury list and noted their names.

Claire said, "You may question the witness, Ms. Laslow."

Debra took her pad with her to the podium. "Dr. Staten, you indicated that you've published numerous articles on rape trauma syndrome. Where could a person find one of these articles?"

"In a university library. Some of them have been included in a book on the subject," she added with a hint of pride.

"Do general bookstores carry the book?"

"Yes. If they don't have it in stock, they can order it."

"Is the book—Strike that. Is the language of your article understandable to the layperson?"

"Definitely. I had that in mind when writing my articles." The psychologist smiled.

Debra smiled, too. "Dr. Staten, is it possible for a person who has read your articles on rape trauma syndrome to fake its symptoms?"

"Objection. Calls for speculation."

"The witness has established herself as an expert on human behavior," Debra said.

Claire frowned. "Overruled. Answer the question."

"It's possible." The psychologist's smile had disappeared; her tone was grudging.

"A person could fake being startled by noises or sudden movements?"

"Yes."

"A person could report insomnia or nightmares?"

"Yes."

"A person could report eating disorders?"

"Yes," she said, clearly annoyed.

"Doctor, you mentioned that Penny's breathing and heart rate accelerated when she talked about the rape. Correct?"

"That's correct." Her tone was wary.

"And these symptoms are a result of anxiety?"

"Yes."

"There are situations other than rape that cause anxiety. Isn't *that* correct, Doctor?"

"Yes." She pushed her glasses back.

"And the anxiety symptoms caused by these other situations might be the same?"

"Yes."

"From your experience, does guilt produce anxiety?"

"Sometimes." The psychologist shifted on her seat.

Out of the corner of her eye, Debra saw Annette's frown. "What if a person is lying and fears discovery? Could that fear produce anxiety?"

"It's possible." She gave the answer reluctantly.

"Is it also possible that anxiety caused by guilt or by the fear of having one's lies discovered will produce symptoms similar to those experienced by someone with rape trauma syndrome?"

"It's possible. But—"

"And it's possible for someone to fake these symptoms?"

"Yes."

"Thank you, Doctor. No more questions."

Seated again at the counsel table, Debra glanced at the jury. The two jurors who had nodded earlier for Annette were nodding now for Debra. She reminded herself that jurors' mannerisms could be misleading. During one trial she'd been particularly anxious about an elderly juror who kept shaking her head "no"; later, after Debra had won an acquittal, she'd learned that the woman was suffering from Parkinson's.

Annette asked one question on redirect: "Dr. Staten, do you have any reason to believe that Penny was lying or faking?"

"No, I don't."

The psychologist spoke emphatically, but another glance at the jury told Debra they didn't seem convinced.

"Now's a good time to take a lunch break," Claire announced. "Court will resume at one-thirty." She gave the usual admonitions to the jury.

While the jury filed out, Debra collected her papers, then looked behind her. Some spectators were still there, but Jeff had left the room. So had Simms. The bailiff approached and handed her a folded slip of paper.

"A man asked me to give this to you," she told Debra.

Debra put the paper inside her pocket and ushered Ken out of the courtroom into the hall, where she was accosted by reporters.

"Ms. Laslow, have you considered withdrawing from the case?"

"Ms. Laslow, do you think your client can get a fair trial?"

"Ms. Laslow . . ."

She repeated "No comment" until she'd steered Avedon through the people crowding the hall to the stairs to the first floor, where she'd arranged for him to meet his parents.

"You were great!" Ken whispered as he followed her down the stairwell. "You demolished the psychologist."

She smiled. "I think it went well. But this is just the first round." She said good-bye to Avedon and returned to the second floor. In the courtroom she'd been consumed with the trial; now the excitement had been replaced by renewed anxiety. She was halfway down the hall to the district attorney's office when she remembered the paper in her pocket. She unfolded it and read it.

"Now the whole world will know about my sister's shame."

Stuart Bailor; Debra hadn't seen him in the courtroom. Though she'd done nothing wrong, her face felt suddenly warm. She walked the rest of the way down the long hall and, after speaking to the receptionist, made her way to Annette's office.

"Has your client decided to cop a plea?" the prosecutor asked when Debra entered the room.

"After this morning? Hardly." Debra smiled. "Annette—"

"I read the *Times* piece. Is it true that Madeleine and the others were murdered 'cause they won acquittals in rape trials? That you're the next target?" Her green eyes held concern laced with curiosity. "Is that why you got those threatening letters?"

Debra nodded. "I think so. I need a transcript of those rape trials." Now that the *Times* had made the rape connection public, Debra felt more comfortable asking for help; early this morning she'd realized that since Annette was with Sex Crimes, she could easily request the transcripts—more easily than Claire. And it would cost Annette, and Debra, nothing. "The court reporter for Susan Clemens's trial was Amanda Koessler. The defendant was Henry Lee. I have the case number."

Annette frowned. "Why do you need the transcripts?"

"I hope to find some link, some clue. I ordered a copy of a partial transcript for Madeleine's case—just the testimony and motions. I can't afford to pay for the others. I may not find anything, Annette, but I'm desperate."

"This isn't some sick joke, is it? You're really in danger?" She was silent for a moment, then said, "Let's start with Amanda. I'll have to give a reason for requesting the transcripts so the county will pick up the tab, but I'll come up with something."

Amanda Koessler was in the clerk's office. She was a short, plump woman in her late thirties with curly black hair.

"I need a trial transcript ASAP," Annette told her. "Just the testimony and motions." She and Debra had agreed that the voir dire and judge's instructions wouldn't be helpful.

Amanda frowned. "I can't promise. I'm backlogged, and I'm working nights as it is. But I'll try. Which case?"

Debra gave her the case number. "The defendant was Henry Lee."

"That was Susan Clemens's case, right?" Her tone was hushed. "You're in luck. The husband of the complaining witness paid for a transcript—said he was going to expose the whole 'goddamn criminal justice system.' He didn't even flinch when I told him the fee. I have the original at home.

I'm staying at a friend's tonight. I'm going straight to work from there tomorrow, but I'll bring it Friday."

Janey Schultz's father, Debra recalled, had paid for a transcript, too. After thanking the reporter and Annette—the prosecutor promised Debra she would immediately order partial transcripts for Kelly Malter's and Wesley Pratt's last rape trials—Debra returned to the hall near the courtrooms. She was thirsty. Bending down over a water faucet, she sensed that someone was staring at her. She stood up and saw Simms.

"Where's your bodyguard?" he asked.

"She's meeting me here at the end of court. She has a beeper." Debra had seen no point in having Nadine follow her around all day inside the building; the metal detector assured her that no unauthorized person had a weapon. And Anthony had been thrilled at the reduced fees.

"Nice work in there," Simms said. "I guess you must be proud of yourself, making shit out of that shrink."

"It's what I do." She started walking away.

"Hey, Ms. Laslow," he called. "Debra."

She stopped and faced him. "What?"

"You asked me to run a license plate check on Stuart Bailor." He took out a small spiral notebook. "Bailor drives a Honda Accord. Dark navy blue—which at night could look like black." He looked up at her. "License plate begins with 1ADO."

Chapter Thirty-five

Shira Frick was in her early twenties—pretty, with a clear complexion and dark blond hair styled in a French braid that reached the middle of her back. When she sat down on the witness stand, she smoothed the folds of her pleated black skirt.

She was nervous at first, speaking to a packed audience, and it was clear she'd never testified before—the judge had to direct her to speak clearly into the microphone and give only verbal answers; Debra felt sorry for her. But Shira relaxed as the prosecutor elicited general, innocuous information. She had been close friends with Penny for seven years, ever since high school. She was majoring in history and planned to attend law school. She lived with her parents and two younger siblings in the Beverly-Fairfax area, eight blocks from Penny.

"Ms. Frick, do you recall the night of July twenty-third of this year?" Annette asked.

Shira nodded. Claire instructed her again to say "Yes" so that the court reporter could record her answer.

"Did Penny Bailor spend that night at your house?"

"Yes. She slept in my room." Penny had arrived around eleven P.M. Shira had let her in; her parents were asleep.

"When Penny arrived, was she upset?" Annette asked.

"Objection," Debra said. "Question is vague and calls for speculation on the part of the witness."

"Sustained. Rephrase your question, Ms. Prado."

Annette said, "Did you notice anything odd about Penny?"

"Yes. Her eye makeup was streaked, and her eyes were red and puffy. She looked like she'd been crying."

"Did you notice anything else different?" Annette asked.

"She was unusually quiet. We usually laugh a lot and talk late into the night. But she just wanted to go to bed."

"Did you comment to her about her behavior?"

"Yes. I asked her what was wrong."

"And what did she say?"

Debra started to object but changed her mind. She wanted to save her objections for when they were needed.

"She said she didn't want to talk about it."

"What happened then?"

"We went to bed. Her back was toward me, but I heard her crying before I fell asleep." In the morning, Shira testified, Penny had still been quiet. Shira had gone to school, and when she'd returned at three-thirty in the afternoon, she'd found Penny in bed.

"Did Penny tell you why she was in bed all day?"

"Objection. Hearsay."

"Overruled."

"She said she didn't feel well, that her stomach hurt. I drove her home a little later."

"When did you next see Penny?"

"Three weeks later, on Monday, August twelfth. Penny called and asked if she could come over that night. She said she had to talk to me privately, that it was important."

"And what happened when she arrived?"

"We went to my room. That was when she told me that Mr. Avedon had raped her on July twenty-third."

Debra jumped to her feet. "Objection. Hearsay. Move to strike," she said, though she knew what Annette would argue.

"Your Honor, this comes under the 'fresh complaint' exception. Ms. Frick is the first person to whom Ms. Bailor spoke about the rape. This was before she went to the police. 'Fresh complaint' exception can apply for almost up to a year, so it can certainly apply for three weeks. I have the case law."

"The objection is overruled. The witness's answer will remain in the record." Claire nodded in Annette's direction.

"What did she tell you happened?" Annette asked.

"She said she had dinner with Dr. Avedon. Then they went to his apartment to listen to music. They were kissing and touching." Shira's voice dropped, and she was clearly uncomfortable. "He wanted to have sex, and she said no, but he forced himself on her even though she was crying and begging him to stop."

Debra looked at the jury—from their expressions, she could tell they were impressed by the witness's testimony.

"What did you do after Penny told you this?" Annette asked.

"I asked her why she didn't tell me the night it happened."

"And what did Penny tell you?"

"She said she was too scared, too ashamed. She blamed herself for going to his apartment and said everyone would blame her, too."

Avedon had been continuously writing on his pad. Debra scribbled on her own pad, "Look directly at the witness every once in a while," and moved the pad toward him. He nodded.

"Did you ask Penny anything else?"

"Yes. I asked her why she was telling me now. She said she couldn't live with the secret any longer. She had nightmares about the rape—"

"Objection."

"Overruled. Continue, Ms. Frick."

"She couldn't eat, couldn't sleep." Shira's voice became more urgent. "She was afraid to go to the police, but felt guilty about not reporting the rape, because maybe he would rape someone else."

"Objection!" Debra said, more sharply this time. "Move to strike. The witness is testifying to facts about which she has no knowledge. This doesn't come under 'fresh complaint.' "

Claire thought for a moment, then said, "Overruled. The answer will remain in the record."

Debra felt a rush of annoyance. "Your Honor—"

"Counsel, I've made my decision," Claire snapped. "The objection is overruled. Sit down."

Her face uncomfortably warm, Debra obeyed. She was surprised by the ruling but decided that, like Debra, Claire was probably nervous under the scrutiny of the media and the television camera.

Annette said, "What did you do then, Ms. Frick?"

"I urged Penny to tell the police. I told her to call a rape hot line. I told her to tell her parents."

"Ms. Frick, you testified that you've known Penny for seven years. Have you ever known her to lie to you or to anyone else?"

"No."

Debra used the fifteen-minute recess to freshen up and call the office for messages. When she returned to the courtroom with Avedon, Jeff was in the front row of the gallery. Simms wasn't here—she hadn't seen him since their talk in the hall. Also in the gallery were three men Debra had noticed yesterday. She'd assumed they were part of the jury pool; obviously they were court groupies. Ever since the O. J. Simpson double murder trial, America had become addicted to real courtroom drama.

After the jury was seated, Claire recalled Shira to the stand and reminded her she was still under oath.

At the podium Debra glanced at her pad, then at the witness. "Ms. Frick, you testified that you've been close friends with Penny Bailor for seven years. Is that correct?"

"Yes."

"And during those seven years, as good friends do, would you sleep over at each other's houses?" Debra smiled.

"Not recently. But when we were in high school, we did."

"So since high school you haven't slept at Penny's house?"

The woman thought for a moment. "No. Not that I can recall."

"What about Penny? Has she slept over your house? Aside from the night in question, I mean."

"Penny's slept over a few times."

"Would you please define 'a few,' Ms. Frick? Once a week? Twice a week? Once a month?" Debra kept her voice friendly.

"It would depend." Shira fingered the strand of pearls at her neck.

"Let me rephrase that. Penny slept at your house on July twenty-third. When did she sleep over before that date?"

Shira frowned. "Two weeks before that, I think."

"And the time before that?"

"Maybe a week before. Maybe two weeks. I can't remember."

"In the past six months, approximately how many times did Penny sleep at your house?"

"Objection. Relevance. Where is this leading?" Annette

asked, her tone a mix of impatience and sarcasm intended for the jury.

"I'm going to establish relevance, Your Honor." The jury, Debra could see, was interested.

"Overruled. Answer the question, Ms. Frick."

"Could you repeat the question, please?" After Debra repeated it, Shira said, "Approximately a dozen times."

"That makes it about once every two weeks. Whose idea was it to have Penny sleep at your house on the twenty-third of July?"

"Penny's."

"And the time before that?"

She hesitated, then said, "Penny's."

"Would it be accurate to say that each time Penny slept over your house, it was at her suggestion?"

A grudging, "Yes." Shira's hand moved from the short strand of pearls at her neck to her skirt.

"Did Penny tell you why she wanted to sleep over on the twenty-third of July?"

"Objection. Hearsay."

"I'll allow it," Claire said, and directed Shira to answer.

"She said she had a date, and that it would be easier to come to my house afterward than to go home."

"You testified on direct examination that you live eight blocks from Penny. Could you explain why it would be *easier* for her to spend the night at your house than go home?"

"Objection. Calls for speculation."

"Sustained."

A fair call. "When Penny slept at your house two weeks before the twenty-third, did she tell you why she wanted to sleep over?"

"She had a date."

"And the time before that? Did she have a date, too?"

"Yes."

"Isn't it true, Ms. Frick, that Penny arranged to sleep at

your house after her dates because her parents disapproved of whom she was seeing? Isn't that what she meant by 'easier'?"

"Objection. Speculation. The witness can't know what Ms. Bailor meant by 'easier.' "

"Sustained."

"I'll rephrase. Did Penny ask you not to tell her parents she was going out on dates on the nights she slept at your house?"

"Yes." Shira was beginning to have a trapped, angry look.

"Did Penny tell you what she'd given her parents to believe about those nights in question?"

"Yes."

"What did she tell them?"

Shira looked at Annette Prado, then back at Debra. "She told them that she and I were spending the evening together."

"That was a lie, wasn't it? You testified that Penny never lied, but in fact on the twelve occasions that Penny slept over your house, Penny lied. Isn't that true?"

"Yes. But it's not the same thing."

"You mean there are different kinds of lies?"

"She didn't tell her parents because she knew they'd be upset. But she wasn't lying about being raped."

"When Penny told you she was raped, she said it was her fault. Was that the truth, or a lie?"

"She said she should have been a better judge of character."

"When Penny told you on July twenty-fourth that she'd stayed in bed because she had stomach cramps, was that a lie?"

"She didn't feel well. She could have had cramps."

"You testified that you were in high school with Penny. Were you in the same classes?"

"Yes." A look of confusion crossed her face.

"Do you know for a fact whether Penny ever cut class?"

"Everyone cuts class."

"I wasn't asking about everyone," Debra said, her voice a little harder. "I'm asking about Penny. Did she ever cut class?"

"Yes."

"And did you ever find yourself having to make up an excuse for Penny's absence to her parents?"

Another reluctant, "Yes."

"So you lied for Penny. Did Penny's parents ever call your home on those nights when she slept at your house?"

"Yes."

Debra softened her voice. "And what did you tell them?"

"I said she couldn't come to the phone."

"So you lied for your friend. You lied for her in school. You lied for her to her parents. Isn't it true that you're lying for your friend here today?"

Nadine met Debra in the lobby at five o'clock and drove her home. Debra's answering machine was blinking madly; she listened to the messages as she put in a load of laundry (everyone she knew, it seemed, had seen the *Times* article), phoned her father, Julia, and Aunt Edith, then showered for her date with Adam.

While getting dressed, she noticed Jeff's manuscript at the side of her bed, where she'd left it last night after collecting the pages scattered on the den carpet. He hadn't tried to approach her at the courthouse, but he'd left an apology on her machine and asked if he could pick up the manuscript. She had no intention of allowing him into her house or of speaking to him again. She considered tossing the manuscript into the trash, but of course she'd have to mail it to him.

Adam took Debra to dinner in North Hollywood (again Nadine had protested; again Debra had insisted she'd be all right); afterward they drove to Universal City and strolled with hundreds of other people along City Walk, which was filled with shops, an outdoor skating rink, bookstores, and cafes with outdoor seating. At some point he took her hand; that felt right, and when he kissed her good night and his lips lingered on hers, that felt right, too.

She chatted for a few minutes with the bodyguard, who was at her laptop, then prepared for bed. Brushing her teeth, she reviewed the day and decided she'd done well. Avedon had thought so, too. As she walked around the side of her bed to pull down the comforter, she stubbed her toe on the manuscript.

Damn Jeff. Damn the manuscript. She wanted it out. She picked up the stack of pages, sat on her bed, and searched for the title page with his address. The pages were out of order; some were upside down. She aligned them and neatened the stack as she searched. Midway through she was startled to see a paragraph that began with "Kelly Malter." Frowning, Debra read the paragraph and learned that Jeff had interviewed the murdered attorney.

Obviously it was just a bizarre coincidence, but why hadn't he told her? She stared at the name, then put the page aside. Before, she'd been thumbing through the manuscript quickly; now she scanned each page, beginning with those she'd already turned over, and when she found Madeleine's name, her heart was hammering and her mouth was dry.

Susan's name was here, too. Debra searched through all the pages again but found no mention of Wesley Pratt.

Jeff Silver, the man who had pleaded with her to withdraw from the Avedon rape case, the man who had almost raped her last night, had interviewed three of the four murdered attorneys.

Jeff drove a black car.

Had their initial meeting at the restaurant been planned?

Had Susan known that Jeff had interviewed Madeleine,

too? Was that the information she'd changed her mind about sharing with the police?

Debra found the title page and scribbled down his address. Nadine was obliging when Debra explained what she wanted. She shut her computer down and drove Debra to Jeff's apartment on Barrington in West L.A.

Even with the bodyguard at her side, Debra felt nervous as she looked for the black Sentra, first in the underground parking garage, then up and down the block. Too late, she remembered that the car was in the shop for repairs. She apologized to Nadine, who told her not to be silly, it was no big deal.

Maybe she *was* being silly, Debra told herself when she was back in her bedroom, looking at the manuscript again. Jeff had asked her to read it; he'd known that she would come across the attorneys' names and wonder. Sighing, she lay on her bed and pressed her palms against the sides of her face. She remembered with sudden vividness how reluctant he'd been to let her see the other half of the manuscript. "It's rough," he'd said.

But in the end, he'd given her the pages. Maybe he had a logical explanation and had wanted her to find out.

Maybe he'd wanted to tease her with the knowledge. Or warn her.

Chapter Thirty-six

"I ordered the transcripts yesterday," Annette told Debra in an undertone Thursday morning before court. "You'll have all four Friday afternoon."

"You're wonderful." Debra smiled. "I can't tell you how much I appreciate your help."

"Are you kidding? We have to get this psycho." She squeezed Debra's arm. "I hope you find what you're looking for, Debra."

Annette walked over to a brown-haired woman Debra recognized as Penny Bailor's mother. Debra watched them for a moment. Then Avedon appeared with his parents; she spoke to him until the bailiff asked the jurors to step inside.

Naomi Bailor, Penny's mother, took the stand. She was wearing a navy double-breasted suit and a white sweater. She was short, and the clerk had to lower the microphone after administering the oath.

Annette established that Naomi was Penny's mother, that Penny lived with her parents and was a good daughter, that

Naomi had noticed on July twenty-fourth that something was troubling Penny.

"How are you able to fix the date?" Annette asked.

"The family was supposed to go to my sister-in-law's for my brother's birthday. Penny was looking forward to going—she loves her uncle—but Wednesday night she said she wasn't up to it."

"Did you ask Penny what was wrong?"

"Sure." The woman nodded vigorously. "I said, 'Maybe you have a flu.' She said no, she just didn't have an appetite. I asked was she having problems at work or with a friend. Again she said no."

"Over the next few days, did Penny's appetite improve?"

"No. She hardly ate. I caught her dumping food from her plate into the garbage. When I asked her why, she said she didn't want to worry me. But how could I not worry? A mother always worries about her children," she said, half turning to the jury.

"Aside from Penny's lack of appetite, did anything else about her behavior concern you?"

"She didn't sleep well. I'm a light sleeper, and I'd hear her going to the bathroom three times, four times. After work every day she'd stay in her room. When I checked to see if she was okay, she'd be staring at the ceiling. A few times I found her crying. I tried to get her to open up to me. My husband tried, too."

"Mrs. Bailor, on Friday, August sixteenth, a little over three weeks after the birthday dinner, did you find something that made you even more concerned about your daughter?" When the witness didn't answer, Annette said, "I know this is difficult."

Her eyes downcast, she said, "I was straightening up Penny's room and found a home pregnancy test in her wastebasket." She spoke in a low voice, and Debra could see from the sudden red in her face and neck that the admission had been difficult.

"What did you feel then?" Annette asked softly.

"I was shocked. I was frightened for her." She looked stricken, as if she'd just now made the discovery.

"Did you tell Penny what you'd found?"

"Yes. I think she wanted me to find it, so I would ask her about it."

"Objection," Debra said. "Nonresponsive and calls for speculation. Move to strike after 'Yes.' "

Claire sustained the objection.

"What did you do then, Mrs. Bailor?" Annette asked.

"I asked her if she was pregnant. She said no. That's when she told me"—her lips trembled—"she told me she was . . . raped by the doctor she worked for. She told him she was . . . a virgin, but he raped her anyway." Her shoulders heaved, and she began to cry. She took a tissue from her jacket pocket and wiped her eyes.

Debra could have objected—the testimony wasn't "fresh complaint," since Penny had told her friend Shira first—but she would have gained nothing and would have antagonized the jurors, whose faces showed strong sympathy for the mother. Debra sympathized with her, too—the woman believed her daughter. Or maybe she'd convinced herself to believe her.

"Did Penny tell you anything else?" Annette asked after the witness had composed herself.

"She wanted to go to the police. I begged her not to. 'You'll ruin your name,' I said, 'and for what? Who will believe you?' " She glanced at the jury, then back at Annette.

"But when Penny went to the police, you and your husband went with her. Is that correct?"

"Yes." She nodded. "She needed our support. And Penny was right. It's hard, very hard, being here today, but an animal like Avedon should be in jail." She started crying again.

"Objection!" Debra said. "Move to strike."

Claire sustained the objection and instructed the jury to disregard the witness's statement, but the damage had been done. And when Claire granted Annette's request for a recess so that the witness could compose herself before cross-examination, Debra knew that in spite of the judge's instructions, the jurors would take with them the image of the distraught witness's anger and tears.

After the jury filed out, Debra reassured Avedon. During the recess she called home and checked with Adam on the progress of the alarm installation; two men had arrived that morning before Nadine had driven her to Santa Monica, and Adam had offered to keep an eye on them. Everything was fine, Adam told her.

She was walking back to the courtroom when she saw Marty Simms talking to Annette. He noticed Debra, said something to Annette, and walked over to Debra, who had returned to the pay phones even though she had no other call to make.

"Sharpening your fangs for the cross?" he asked.

"Always. I'm surprised to see you here again today, Detective. Shouldn't you be looking for the killer?"

"I'm surprised at *you*. I thought you'd figure out I'm here doing that—the killer's probably in that courtroom every day."

"Then can I assume that you no longer suspect me?" Out of the corner of her eye she spotted Avedon. He was probably looking for her; she made eye contact with him and held up a finger to indicate she'd be right with him.

"You're in the courtroom every day, aren't you?" He inclined his head to one side. "I assume you followed up on the case numbers. Should I worry that you'll crack the case before me?"

She ignored his question. In a lower, more urgent voice

she said, "Have you checked into the four complaining witnesses?"

He nodded. "And their families."

"And?"

He smiled and shook his head. "Sorry."

She restrained her annoyance. "I can get the transcripts," she said, deciding not to tell him she'd arranged to do so. "The testimony will tell me about the witnesses' backgrounds and families. I can hire a private investigator if I have to." Simms was looking at her thoughtfully, assessing her. "Anyway, what horrible thing could I do with the information?"

"Okay." He glanced around him, then faced Debra again. "There's Emma Banks—she was the witness who accused Malter's client. Emma's a fifty-nine-year-old widow, and she's afraid of her own shadow. Just lost her job, too."

Most people thought rape victims were young. Debra knew that rape wasn't about sex—it was about rage, the need to control, to exert power, to intimidate. "What about her family?"

"A son and daughter. They have alibis for all four murders. The witness in Pratt's case—Nancy Wallace—is in her thirties. She just separated from her husband. No kids. The husband says he was out of town when Clemens and Pratt were killed. We're checking up. Alicia Vaughan—now that's interesting. Rich doctor husband, Beverly Hills home. The husband—his name is Karl—lunged at the defendant after the 'not guilty' verdict came in."

Alicia Vaughan, Debra recalled, was the witness in Susan's case. "Susan told me her client's DNA profile proved he wasn't the rapist."

"Tell that to Vaughan." Simms's face showed anger. "The guy who raped his wife told her he had AIDS. Yeah, real nice," he said when he saw Debra pale. "So far the wife's tested negative, but she won't know for another few months whether she's got it."

Debra nodded. "What about Madeleine's case?"

"Janey Schultz. Nineteen years old. The father, Norman, wouldn't let me talk to her. He's one angry man. Both men are here, by the way. They were here yesterday, too. So was Emma Banks, but I don't think she's here now."

Debra felt as if someone had punched her in the chest. Her heart thumped; her lips tingled. "Where are they?"

Simms scanned the crowd. "See that tall, heavyset guy with the brown plaid jacket—the one standing right next to the thin blond woman?" he whispered. "That's Schultz."

He was one of the men Debra had noticed the other day. "What about Karl Vaughan?"

Simms frowned. "I don't see— There he is. He's got salt-and-pepper hair, glasses. He's wearing a dark suit."

Debra nodded. She'd noticed Vaughan the other day, too. "Who's the silver-haired man on the bench? He was here yesterday, too." He looked familiar, but she didn't know why.

Simms squinted at the man, then shook his head. "Don't know. The killer could be someone not connected to any of these victims. He or she could be someone who hates rapists and their lawyers."

Like you, Debra thought.

From the podium, Debra could sense the hate emanating toward her from Naomi Bailor's eyes. In a gentle voice she said, "Mrs. Bailor, you testified that Penny is a good daughter. Is that correct?"

"Penny is a wonderful daughter," she snapped.

"Has she ever disobeyed you?"

"Objection. Ms. Bailor isn't on trial here."

"Sustained."

"Goes to the credibility of the complaining witness, Your Honor."

"The objection is sustained," Claire said with a touch of annoyance. "Ask your next question, Ms. Laslow."

Debra was annoyed, too. "You testified that a mother worries about her children. Can you tell us in what ways you worried about Penny?"

"Objection. The question is vague."

"Sustained."

"I'll rephrase. Were you worried because Penny was dating men of whom you didn't approve?"

Annette objected again.

"Goes to state of mind of the witness, Your Honor," Debra argued, and Claire, frowning, overruled the objection and directed the witness to answer.

"Yes, I worried," came the surly answer. "I didn't want her to make a mistake she would regret."

"Did you know that Penny went out on the evening of July twenty-third with Dr. Avedon?"

"No."

"And would you have approved of that date?"

"No." She was glaring at Debra. Her lips, when she wasn't speaking, formed a grim line.

"You testified earlier that you found a home pregnancy test kit in your daughter's wastebasket. Is that correct?"

"Yes."

"And you were shocked and terrified. Is *that* correct?"

"Yes."

"Were you angry?"

"Maybe," she said, her tone guarded.

"What's your opinion of premarital sex?"

"It's wrong. Our religion teaches us that."

"And does Penny know how you feel?"

"Yes, of course. It's how we raised her."

"And she would know that if she told you she was pregnant or that she'd slept with someone, you'd be angry?"

"Objection. The witness can't testify as to what her daughter does or does not know."

"Your Honor, the witness stated that she and her husband raised their daughter to believe premarital sex is wrong."

Claire thought for a moment, then overruled the objection; the witness answered, "Yes."

"Let's get back to the kit. Where in the basket was the kit? Was it on top of the other trash or in the middle?"

"What's the difference where it was?"

Claire said, "Mrs. Bailor, please answer the question."

"I don't remember where," she said with a hint of defiance.

"Do you have someone who helps clean your house?"

"Yes."

"How often does she clean your house?"

"Every Thursday."

"And you find once a week adequate help?"

"Yes. It's a small house, and there's just the three of us at home. My son is married."

"Is your daughter neat?"

"Very." She narrowed her eyes as if she sensed an attack were coming but didn't know from which direction.

"As part of her duties, does this housekeeper empty the wastebaskets, including the one in your daughter's room?"

"Yes."

"Do you ever empty wastebaskets in the house?"

"Yes."

"Objection. Why is counsel spending so much time on trash?"

There was a snicker from the gallery. "I intend to show relevance, Your Honor," Debra said.

"Do it promptly, Ms. Laslow. The objection is overruled."

"Mrs. Bailor, which wastebaskets do you empty?"

"The one in the kitchen. Sometimes those in the bathrooms."

"What about Penny's wastebasket?"

"Sometimes."

"You testified that your housekeeper empties the wastebaskets on Thursday and that you found the pregnancy test on a Friday. Correct?"

"Yes."

"You also testified that Penny is neat. Does she make her own bed? Hang up her clothes?"

"Yes."

"So if Penny makes her own bed and hangs up her clothes and the housekeeper cleaned her room on Thursday, why was it necessary for you to straighten her room on Friday?"

She took a long while and finally said, "I don't remember."

"Isn't it true that you weren't straightening your daughter's room that Friday? In fact, you were looking in her wastebasket to find something to explain what was wrong. Isn't *that* the truth?"

"Objection!"

"Goes to state of mind of the witness, Your Honor."

"The objection is overruled."

"Yes, I was looking." Naomi Bailor's face was flushed.

"Had you ever looked through Penny's trash before?"

"Why are you doing this?" the woman demanded.

Debra felt herself blushing and knew the jury was watching. Claire reprimanded the witness and directed her to answer the question. The answer was, "Yes."

"On those other occasions, were you looking for a home pregnancy test kit?" Debra asked.

Another, more sullen, "Yes."

"And isn't it true, Mrs. Bailor, that you were worried before this alleged rape that Penny had lost her virginity?"

Debra asked almost tenderly, not only because she didn't want to antagonize the jury, but because she felt terrible about the pain she was inflicting on the witness.

"Yes," the mother whispered. There were tears in her eyes.

On redirect Annette asked Penny's mother whether, with the exception of August 16, she'd ever found a home pregnancy test kit in Penny's wastebasket or in any other wastebasket in the house.

Naomi Bailor directed an emphatic, "No!" at the jury.

Claire announced an hour-and-a-half lunch break. As Debra stood, she cast a quick glance at the spectator's gallery but didn't spot Schultz or Vaughan. They'd probably left the courtroom already. The silver-haired man was still here, sitting in the front row.

After Avedon left, Debra approached the bailiff. "Do you know who that man is in the front row? He's been here every day."

The bailiff smiled. "That's Judge Werner's dad. He watches most of her trials. Always sits in the front if he can. He's so proud of her."

He looked older than in the photo Debra had seen on Claire's mantel—his hair had whitened, his face muscles had slackened, his frame had become gaunt. That's why Debra hadn't recognized him.

Debra's father had watched her first trial, and a few after that, but his schedule—teaching, leading Talmud classes, counseling families—didn't permit him to attend all her trials.

She was grateful her father hadn't been here this morning. She wasn't sure how proud Rabbi Ephraim Laslow would have been of his daughter today.

Chapter Thirty-seven

Lucy Montoya, the short, brown-haired detective to whom Penny had reported the alleged rape, took the stand. She had been with Sex Crimes for over eight years, she told Annette; she related what Penny had told her on the morning of Monday, August 19.

"What was Penny's demeanor when she told you she'd been raped?" Annette asked.

"Distraught. She'd talk, then cry a little, then continue."

"Did you ask her why she'd waited four weeks after she'd been raped before she went to the police?"

"I did. She said she was ashamed and frightened about telling her parents, about having people know. She also blamed herself—she said people wouldn't understand why she went up to the defendant's apartment and let him kiss her."

"Did she tell you why she was coming forth now?"

"Yes. She said she needed to find peace for herself and she needed to protect other women against the defendant."

"From your experience over the past eight years, Detective, did you find Penny's behavior consistent with that of other victims?"

"Yes. Quite a few victims file late—especially in cases where the rapist is someone they know, like a boss or a family friend or a co-worker. And a lot of victims blame themselves."

"And based on your experience, did you find Penny credible?"

"Yes."

"What did you advise Penny?"

"I told her to tape-record a phone conversation with the defendant. I felt that a tape with admissions from the defendant would provide corroboration."

"And to your knowledge, did Penny make such a tape?"

"Yes. She brought it to the station on August twenty-fourth."

Annette produced a tape cassette and approached the witness stand. "Detective Montoya, is this the cassette Penny gave you?"

"Yes. Those are my initials." She pointed to the upper right-hand corner of the tape.

Claire said, "Let the record show that the witness is indicating her initials on the upper right-hand corner of the tape."

Annette had the tape introduced as evidence and labeled People's Exhibit One. "I have no more questions at this time."

"Ms. Laslow," Claire said.

Debra walked to the podium. "Detective Montoya, in your eight years of experience with Sex Crimes, have you ever handled a rape case where the complaining witness was wrong in her accusation?"

"I've seen cases of mistaken identity in stranger rapes. But not many."

Like Susan's case, Debra thought. "And in those cases, had you found the complaining witnesses credible?"

"Yes. They believed they *were* telling the truth."

"And have you ever handled a date or acquaintance rape case where the complaining witness was later found to have lied?"

Lucy Montoya frowned. "Maybe two in all the years I've been investigating rape."

"And when you interviewed *these* complaining witnesses, did you find *them* credible?"

"Yes."

"So is it possible that Penny Bailor was lying to you?"

"It's possible," she said, clearly unhappy about giving her answer.

After Debra indicated she was done, Annette resumed the podium. "Detective, of the rape cases your department has investigated during your career, approximately how many were date or acquaintance rapes?"

"I checked the report on last year's rapes this morning. The figures showed nine attempted rapes and forty-five rapes. Of the forty-five rapes, eleven were stranger. The rest—thirty-four—were rapes by known people. Those figures pretty much agree with the figures in reports of other years. If anything, rapes have been increasing." She paused. "So based on thirty-four date rapes a year, that would be two hundred and seventy-two date rapes."

"Two hundred and seventy-two date rape victims," Annette repeated, looking at the jury. "So out of these two hundred and seventy-two women, only two were later found to have been lying?"

"Yes."

A good rebuttal, Debra thought as Annette left the podium. She couldn't tell from the jurors' expressions what impression the detective's testimony had made on them.

"The Court has other business this afternoon, so we'll adjourn now," Claire said. "Court will resume at nine o'clock tomorrow morning."

Avedon seemed more tense than usual. Debra waited with him inside the courtroom until the jury and spectators had filed out. "I think it's going fine," she told him.

"They all felt sorry for the mother. Hell, I felt sorry for her!" he whispered.

Debra nodded. So had she. "The bottom line is, Penny's mother doesn't know what happened. The shrink doesn't know what happened. The girlfriend doesn't know what happened. The cop doesn't know what happened. Only the two of you know what happened, and nothing I've heard so far has me worried." She smiled.

"Who are they putting on tomorrow?"

"Penny." And the tape.

"Are you putting me on the stand?"

That's what Annette Prado wanted to know, too. "We'll see."

Debra was becoming adept at pushing her way through the crowd and avoiding the media. She exited the courtroom with Avedon, who walked down the staircase to the first floor and his parents, and used a pay phone to page Nadine. The bodyguard phoned back and told Debra she'd pick her up in the lobby in ten minutes.

She waited in the lobby, then decided she needed fresh air. She was standing to the right of the building's entrance when she heard someone call her. Turning, she saw Jeff.

"Can I talk to you a minute, Debra?"

"I have nothing to say to you." Her fingers dug into the leather of her purse.

"I was wrong to do what I did. It was crazy. I realize that now. I know 'sorry' isn't enough—"

"It's not."

He sighed, then nodded acceptance. "About my manuscript, can you leave it at your side door and give me a call to pick it up?"

"You sound anxious about it, Jeff. Why didn't you tell me you interviewed Madeleine, Susan, and Kelly Malter?"

Color spotted his cheeks and neck. "You read it, huh? It's a weird coincidence, but I knew you'd wonder. That's why I didn't say anything."

"Some coincidence," she said, watching his eyes.

"I could say the same about you—you applied to all the firms where the murdered attorneys worked, didn't you? By the way, did you know your contractor is buddies with Penny Bailor's brother?"

Jeff was crazy. She turned her back on him and wished Nadine would arrive and wondered why her heart was thumping.

"I'm worried about you, Debra. I was trying to find out if the brother sent you those notes and tried to run you off the road. Last night I was talking to someone who knows him, and the guy said, 'If you want to know about Stuart Bailor, talk to Adam Bergman. He's known Stuart and the family for years.' "

In spite of herself, Debra found herself turning back to face him. "How did you know Stuart Bailor's name?"

"I heard the family name in court. It wasn't hard to get a lead on him—the Jewish grapevine's incredible, you know that."

"You're making this up."

"Check it out for yourself. I think Stuart encouraged Adam to be chummy with you. Maybe he got Adam to drop off the notes. Maybe Adam's the one who broke your window—he boards it up and looks like Mr. Nice Guy, when all the time he's keeping an eye on you."

"My brother's the one who referred Adam. Having him build my office was my idea, not his."

"I'm only trying to help you, Debra."

"I don't need your help!"

"Is something wrong?" asked Nadine. She'd come up to Debra and was frowning at Jeff; her hand was resting near her jacket.

"Just talking," Jeff said. "Take care of yourself, Debra."

"Was he bothering you?" the bodyguard asked, watching Jeff as he walked down the steps and headed for the parking lot.

Debra hadn't told her about the assault. She decided not to say anything now. "Do me a favor? Get his license plate. I'll go back inside and wait in the lobby." Where it was safe.

A few minutes later Nadine returned. Debra exited the building again. "Well?" she asked.

"A black Sentra, right?" When Debra nodded, the bodyguard said, "License plate 1ABO . . ." She paused and said, "Is that good or bad?"

Debra had Nadine drive her to the office, where she spent several hours catching up on other case files and checking her mail and messages. She spoke to Charles and described the progress of the trial.

"Sounds good," he said. "Anything new with the murders?"

"Not yet. Simms is working on some leads." She told him about Schultz and Vaughan. "Talking to Simms is unnerving. One minute he's treating me like a suspect. The next minute he's discussing the case with me." She shrugged.

She talked a while longer with Charles, then returned to her office. Richard wasn't in—that was a blessing, although she reminded herself that in Monday's meeting he'd supported her about the bodyguard.

At seven-thirty she decided to go home. Adam's truck was in front of the house; she wasn't sure how she felt about seeing him. She didn't want to believe Jeff; she couldn't disbelieve him.

He was in the living room when she walked into the house with Nadine at her side. Nadine excused herself and went to the den.

"The alarm guys are just about done," Adam said. "They'll finish tomorrow morning. How'd it go today?" He leaned toward her to kiss her. When she pulled back, he frowned. "What's wrong?"

"Do you know Stuart Bailor?" She spoke with more intensity than she'd intended.

"Yes."

It wasn't the answer she'd wanted. Her chest felt suddenly hollow. "Why didn't you tell me?"

"Why is it important?"

"Because his sister is the woman who charged my client with rape. Did you know that?"

"Not from Stuart, but I heard about it," he said quietly. "Why are you so upset?"

"You know that I've been receiving threatening notes. You know that someone tried to run me off the road. You take me to a shooting range and lend me your gun when all the time it could be your best friend who's harassing me."

"What do you mean, 'best friend'?" His eyes crinkled in bewilderment. "I haven't talked to Stuart in years."

Debra stared at him. "You're not close friends?"

"Stuart and I were in elementary school together, and our families were close. That was years ago."

"Still, you should have told me," she said, but her voice lacked conviction.

"I thought it would make things awkward between us. Everybody was pressuring you to drop the case. I didn't want you to think about the case every time you looked at me. Do you believe me?"

She studied his blue eyes and nodded. He took her hand and drew her close against his chest, then kissed her.

"Do you want to have dinner out?" he asked.

"Why don't we eat in? I'll defrost some steaks."

"Fine. What about Nadine?"

Debra smiled. "She's great at disappearing when I want her to."

She walked to the kitchen, removed two steaks from the freezer, and placed them on the counter. She was thirsty. She took a glass from the cupboard, opened the refrigerator, and smiled when she saw the pink square cake box on the middle shelf. She lifted out the box with one hand, a carton of nonfat milk with the other, and pushed the refrigerator shut with her hip.

Aunt Edith had probably dropped off the cake; she was always doing things like that. Debra would serve it tonight for dessert.

She cut the string with a knife, opened the lid, and screamed when she saw the bloodied knife in the box and the tongue lying next to it.

Chapter Thirty-eight

She realized almost immediately that the tongue wasn't human, but the knowledge didn't keep her from retching into the sink. Adam and Nadine had come running into the kitchen.

"It's a calf's tongue," Nadine said, looking in the box. "There's a piece of paper under it." She took it out.

"God, I'm sorry, Debra!" Adam's face was ashen. "I found the box on the front steps around noon. There was a note stuck under the string that said 'Keep refrigerated.' I didn't know."

Nadine placed the paper on the counter. With shaking hands, Debra unfolded the paper and read the message:

"My conscience hath a thousand several tongues, and every tongue brings in a several tale, and every tale condemns me for a villain."
Where is your conscience, Debra Laslow?

"I'm phoning the police," Adam said. "What's Simms's number?"

Debra gave him the number; a moment later he handed her the receiver. She spoke to a clerk, who told her Simms was out. Debra left a message: "Tell him it's urgent, please."

"Did your men see who dropped this off?" Nadine asked.

Adam shook his head. "I noticed it when I was going out to my truck. I put it in the fridge. I'll ask my men in the morning. I'll ask the alarm people, too. I'm sorry, Debra," he said again.

"It's not your fault."

They sat in the breakfast room, waiting in silence. When the phone rang, Debra jumped up and grabbed the receiver, but it wasn't Simms. It was Jeff.

"Have you checked into what I told you, Debra?" he asked.

"Yes. You're misinformed."

"You sound strange. You got another threat, didn't you? What's it going to take for you to come to your senses and drop this case? I know you probably won't let me come over—"

"You're right," she said, and hung up the phone.

"Who was that?" Adam asked.

"No one." He *was* no one, at least to her. She wondered why Jeff had assumed she'd received another threat. Unless he knew. . . .

The doorbell rang. Nadine went to answer it and returned with Simms behind her.

"You said 'urgent,' so here I am," the detective told Debra. "I thought I'd find a body."

Ignoring his sarcasm, she took him to the kitchen. He grunted when he saw the tongue but didn't seem horrified; she supposed he was used to seeing considerably worse in his line of work.

"Before you ask," she said "I was in court most of the

day. After that I was at the office. I had no car. My body-guard, Nadine, drove me to the courthouse and to my of-fice, then home. So I couldn't have delivered this to myself."

"I'm the one who brought the box into the house," Adam said. He had come into the kitchen and was standing near Debra.

"Who are you?" Simms asked, scowling.

"Debra's friend." He explained where he'd found the box.

Simms questioned Adam. Then he took the box and its contents and promised he'd try to have the lab raise prints.

Debra walked Simms to the door. "Could I ask a favor, Detective? Could you run a check on a Jeff Silver?" She saw him frown as she related what she'd discovered in the man-uscript pages and told him about the license plate on Jeff's black Sentra. She gave him Jeff's address and watched as he crossed the street to his dark blue car.

She was no longer in the mood for dinner; neither was Adam. After he left she changed into a nightshirt and lay in her bed. Every few minutes the image of the tongue flashed through her mind and she would feel bile rising in her throat.

On the night before her mother had died, Debra had sat at her bedside. Her mother, heavily sedated with morphine, had been only partially lucid. Debra had held her hand for hours, murmuring to her, listening to her utter fragments and words that made no sense. Every once in a while her mother would whisper, "I'm afraid of going where it's dark," and Debra's heart would break and she would tighten her grip on her mother's frail hand.

Though her bedroom light was on, Debra was afraid of going where it was dark, too.

There was an electric tension in the courtroom on Friday morning when Penny Bailor took the stand. Debra sensed it. The jury sensed it. Ken Avedon, she saw, sensed it, too.

She'd heard on the news that the television camera would be allowed to record the proceedings live, but as in the William Kennedy Smith trial, a blue dot would hide the witness's face.

Norman Schultz and Karl Vaughan were in the gallery. So were Jeff and Stuart Bailor and Simms; the detective had approached her outside the courtroom and told her there had been no prints on the box or knife. Richard was here, too; that was a surprise. Claire's father was sitting where he'd sat yesterday, in the first row.

The young woman on the witness stand barely resembled the girl in the photo Debra had seen on the job application in Avedon's office. Her hair was the same blond, but the tousled curls had been smoothed into an obedient, shiny mane brushed back off her forehead and held in place with a simple gray headband that matched her midcalf pleated skirt. The makeup had been virtually eliminated, except for a hint of blush and pink lip gloss. A small pearl pendant lay against her pink sweater. She looked pretty, vulnerable, wholesome. Virginal.

In a quiet, unwavering voice she answered Annette's questions about the schools she'd attended, her aspiration to get a business degree, her family life. The questions and answers relaxed the witness. More important, Debra knew, the prosecutor was intent on having the jury get to know Penny and see her not as an accuser, but as a person they could believe.

Responding to questioning, Penny explained that she'd quit her job as medical receptionist for another doctor and taken a job in Avedon's office because the pay and benefits were better.

"Is Dr. Avedon in this courtroom today?" Annette asked.

Penny answered, "Yes," and, following Annette's instruction, pointed to Avedon, an identification that Debra had always found theatrical—"the finger of accusation"—and effective.

"How long had you been working for the defendant before the evening of July twenty-third?" Annette asked.

"Seven months."

Penny described her working relationship with Avedon. He was a considerate employer, she said. He never quibbled about her taking time off for Jewish holidays or leaving early on Friday afternoons so that she would be home before the Sabbath. He was friendly and always had a smile. The entire staff liked him.

Penny had been testifying for an hour and a half; Claire announced a ten-minute recess, during which Debra found Annette and learned that the transcripts would be here by two o'clock in the afternoon. She looked for Richard but couldn't find him.

When the recess was over and the jury seated, Penny resumed the stand and Claire reminded her that she was still under oath.

"Were you attracted to the defendant?" Annette asked.

"Yes. He's bright, sophisticated. I liked his sense of humor. I liked the way he treated his patients. He's compassionate."

"So you had every reason to believe he was trustworthy?"

"Yes."

"Did the defendant indicate he was attracted to you?"

"Yes. He would compliment me on my appearance, and he would flirt with me—in a very pleasant way."

"And you enjoyed the flirting?"

"Yes." A hint of color appeared in Penny's cheeks.

"Whose idea was it for the two of you to go out to dinner?"

"I think it was mutual."

"Did you have any qualms about going out with the defendant?"

"Yes. I knew my parents would disapprove." The color in her face deepened. "They're Orthodox Jewish and very strict."

"Penny, why did you go out with the defendant if you knew your parents would disapprove?"

"I wanted to have fun. I wasn't interested in a serious relationship."

"You testified that you took off early for the Sabbath and for Jewish holidays. Yet here you are, going out with someone you knew your parents would disapprove of. Can you explain that contradiction?"

It was clever of Annette to raise this on direct, Debra thought; it would be far more damaging if Debra were to raise it on the cross.

"I was going through a rebellious period," Penny said. "I was having conflicts about who I was. But I always kept the Sabbath and the holidays out of respect for my parents."

On July twenty-third, after the last patient had left, Penny had changed into a dress she'd brought along—a black sheath with a low, round neckline and a hem three inches above the knee.

"Would you call what you were wearing a sexy dress, Penny?"

"Yes."

"Is this a dress your parents would approve of?"

"No." She folded her hands on her lap.

"Why were you wearing it?"

"I wanted to look special for Dr. Avedon, and we were going to a well-known restaurant. I wanted to fit in."

Again the prosecutor had defused the issue of what Penny was wearing by raising it herself. From her previous trial experience with Annette, Debra had expected no less.

Penny testified that she'd followed Avedon in her car to a restaurant on Wilshire in Beverly Hills. Over dinner he'd told her about his family—he had a married brother who was also a doctor—and about his love for medicine.

"Did he discuss previous relationships he'd had with women?"

"Yes. He mentioned he'd had long-term relationships with women that hadn't worked out. He told me he was interested in marriage and a family." He'd asked her about her family and background; they'd discussed mutual likes and dislikes.

"Did he say or do anything to make you nervous?"

"No."

"Did you have any acoholic beverages with your dinner?"

"Yes. I had white wine. He had a martini."

"Penny, did you and the defendant have any physical contact when you were in the restaurant?"

"He touched my hand once or twice. That was all."

"Whose idea was it to go to the defendant's apartment?"

"Dr. Avedon's. I agreed. We went to our cars and I followed him to his condominium building."

"What time was this?"

"About nine o'clock."

"And at this point, Penny, did you have reason to distrust the defendant?"

"No."

Annette introduced as evidence a sketch Penny had made of the layout of Avedon's condominium. Then she elicited a description of the apartment—its purpose, Debra knew, was to reinforce for the jury the fact that Avedon appeared to lead a conventional life and the fact that Penny had no reason to worry about her safety.

"Did you see photos in the apartment?" Annette asked.

"Yes. Dr. Avedon said one was of his parents. Another was of his brother and sister-in-law and their two little girls."

"What happened after you got to the apartment?"

"Dr. Avedon fixed us drinks. Then he put a disk on his player, and we sat on the living room couch and talked."

"Were the lights on?"

"He dimmed them, but they were on."

"Tell us what happened then."

She drew in her breath. "We started to kiss."

"Did you like being kissed by the defendant?"

"Yes." She kept her eyes riveted on Annette.

"Did you kiss him back?"

"Yes."

"Where were your arms?"

"Around his neck."

"And then what happened?"

"He took off my shoes and started to massage my feet."

"Were you wearing stockings?"

"No. It was a hot evening. I was wearing dressy sandals."

"Did you ask him to stop massaging your feet?"

"No. It felt nice."

"What happened then, Penny?"

"He massaged my feet for about ten minutes. Then he massaged my neck for about five minutes. Then he unzipped my dress halfway down my back and massaged my shoulders."

Debra heard a squeak that indicated someone was leaving his seat, then the sound of footsteps heading toward the exit. Turning her head slightly, she saw Stuart Bailor leave the courtroom.

"And did you ask him to stop at *this* point?" Annette asked.

"No. It was very relaxing. I didn't think it was a big deal."

"You trusted him?"

"Yes."

"You still liked him?"

"Yes."

"What happened then?"

"He was kissing my neck and shoulders. He unhooked my bra . . . and touched my breasts." She bit her lips. "I told him 'no.' "

Debra could see the tears welling in the witness's eyes. So, of course, could the jury.

"When you told him 'no,' did he stop?"

"No! He shoved me down on the sofa and pushed my dress up past my thighs." Penny started to cry. "He forced . . . he forced his hand between my legs. I was fighting him, and I kept saying, 'No, I don't want to do this! Stop it! No!' "

Debra thought of Jeff, who was sitting behind her, probably staring at her now, remembering what had happened only two nights ago. She could still feel his hand between her legs, on her breasts. She started to perspire and her palms were clammy as she forced herself to concentrate on the testimony.

"Did he hear you?" Annette asked.

"Yes. I was yelling. He said, 'I know you want it, so stop pretending.' I told him that I wasn't pretending, that I was a virgin, but he didn't care. He just didn't care."

She was sobbing; Debra had to steel herself not to feel pity for a woman who she knew was lying—and lying well, judging by her own visceral reaction and the stern faces of the jurors.

Claire handed Penny a tissue and asked if she wanted to take a break. Penny shook her head and wiped her eyes.

"What happened then, Penny?" the prosecutor asked in a tender voice after Penny indicated she was ready to continue.

"He . . . held me down"—her voice broke—"and raped me."

"Tell us exactly what he did, Penny."

Penny, who had started to cry again and whose hands were gripping the edge of her seat, gave the anatomically specific description the law required; Debra was glad Stuart Bailor had left the room.

"Did the defendant use a condom?" Annette asked.

"Yes. When I saw that nothing would stop him, I begged him to use one. I was afraid of getting pregnant or getting AIDS. He took one from his pants pocket and put it on."

"At this point, Penny, why didn't you get up off the couch and run out of the apartment?"

"I tried! I couldn't get out from under him. And I was afraid he'd hurt me."

"After he raped you, Penny, what did you do?"

"Objection!" Debra sprang to her feet. "Permission to approach the bench, Your Honor." When Claire nodded, she left her seat and reached the bench just as Annette did. "The prosecutor's use of the word 'rape' is prejudicial to my client."

Claire frowned. "What term do you want Ms. Prado to use?"

" 'Incident.' "

" 'Incident' is far too vague, Ms. Laslow."

"What about 'engaged in sex'?"

" 'Sex' connotes a mutually participatory act and would be equally misleading. I'm overruling your objection. I'll admonish the jury that the word 'rape' as used by the prosecution is not a legal term, and that the jury will decide whether a rape in fact occurred."

"Your Honor—"

"That's my decision, Counsel." Claire's voice was frosty. "Step back."

Debra returned to the counsel table as Claire admonished the jury; Annette repeated the question.

"I washed myself in the bathroom and tried to fix my makeup," Penny said. "Then I got dressed and left the apartment and drove to my friend Shira's, where I'd made plans to spend the night."

"What time was this?"

"About ten-thirty."

"Did you tell your friend what had happened?"

"No. I was ashamed. I felt I was to blame—I should never have gone to his apartment."

Annette carefully led Penny through a description of Penny's emotions—her fear that her parents would discover what had happened, her fear that she would become pregnant.

"Why were you worried about becoming pregnant if the defendant had used a condom?"

"I don't know much about condoms, how effective they are. I don't know whether they're foolproof."

"Did you go to work the next day?"

"No. I phoned in and said I was ill. I worked Thursday."

"How did you feel about seeing the defendant after he raped you?"

"I was scared, but I needed the job."

"Did you see the defendant on Thursday?"

"Yes, I did."

"What was his demeanor?"

"He was smiling and acting like nothing had happened. He said he had a nice evening and wanted to go out again."

"How did you feel when he said that, Penny?"

"I was shocked. I was angry. He raped me, and now he was asking me out again! I said no, I wasn't interested."

Seeing the defendant every day increased her stress and filled her with doubts about herself. Unable to live with her secret any longer, Penny finally told her friend Shira, then her parents, then the police, who advised her to tape a conversation with the defendant.

Annette showed Penny the tape already marked as evidence; Penny identified it as the cassette she'd used to tape her conversation on Thursday, August 22.

"At this time, Your Honor, I'd like to play the tape for the jury."

Claire glanced at her wristwatch. "I think it's a good time to break for lunch. Court will resume at one-thirty."

Avedon looked tense. Debra waited until the courtroom had cleared, then led him out the door and through the thinning crowd to the stairwell, where she murmured encouragements.

"It's the tape," he said again. "I don't know why I didn't just hang up. I just felt sorry for her, you know?"

"We'll deal with the tape. The prosecutor's almost done. Then it's our turn." She watched him walk down the stairs, then sat on an empty bench at the far end of the hall to go over her notes on Annette's direct examination.

At one-thirty court resumed. Claire allowed the prosecutor to distribute transcripts of the taped conversation to every juror and to Debra and Avedon. At Claire's suggestion, Annette gave a copy to the court reporter, too.

Along with the jury and the media and the packed crowd, Debra listened to a static-laced recording of the ten-minute conversation. The initial dialogue was casual—Avedon sounded surprised to hear Penny's voice, then pleased when she congratulated him on his engagement and wished him luck. "Friends again?" he asked. She told him she wanted to be friends, but she had concerns about what had happened on their date. Debra had read the transcript of the tape before, but hearing Penny's plaintive questions—"Why did you force me to have sex, Ken? Why were you so rough? Why did you rape me?"—was far more dramatic. She could see the damaging effect the questions and Avedon's lack of clear refutation—"I'm sorry you were upset"—were having on the jurors, many of whom were frowning.

"Penny, to the best of your knowledge, is that an accurate and true recording of the conversation you had with the defendant on August twenty-second?" Annette asked.

"Yes."

"Did you tamper with this tape in any way?"

"No."

"Penny, how do you feel about testifying here today?"

"I feel ashamed," she said, her voice barely above a whisper. "I feel stupid. I feel naked." Her lips trembled; she stilled them with her hand.

"Why are you testifying against the defendant here today?"

She cleared her throat. "I need to get control of my life. I want to be able to sleep at night and eat normally and not be afraid. And I feel morally responsible to tell what happened so that he won't do to someone else what he did to me."

Annette thanked the witness and returned to her seat. Debra stood and started walking to the podium when Claire stopped her.

"It's two-fifteen," the judge said. "I think this is a good time to adjourn. Court will resume on Monday morning."

"May I approach the bench, Your Honor?" Debra asked. When she and Annette were standing in front of Claire, Debra said, "I'd like to begin cross-examination of the witness."

"Ms. Laslow, I took into consideration the fact that because of your Sabbath, you have to leave at around three o'clock."

"It's forty-five minutes to three, Your Honor. I appreciate your concern on my behalf, but I'd like to begin the cross. I can stay until three-fifteen." She hated the thought that the last thing the jury would hear today and would replay in their minds over the weekend would be the tape and Penny's articulation of her fears that Avedon would rape again.

"The witness has had a grueling day," Annette said. "She could use a break."

Claire nodded. "We'll adjourn until Monday."

"Your Honor—"

"Ms. Laslow, over the past few days you seem to have difficulty in accepting my decisions and rulings. This is my courtroom. I decide what time we adjourn. Is that clear?"

There were seventeen volumes of transcripts divided between two cartons. Nadine, who had arrived promptly after Debra paged her, carried one box down the hall; Debra carried the other.

They were waiting for an elevator when Richard appeared. He greeted Nadine, whom he'd met in the office, then asked to speak to Debra. She placed the box she was carrying next to Nadine's, then stepped a few feet away with Richard.

"I'm concerned about that tape," he said in a low voice. "So is Avedon. He spoke to me after court adjourned."

Debra felt annoyed with Avedon for "tattling" on her. "The tape is bad, but we'll work around it."

"Use the underwear."

She stared at him. "What?"

"Avedon said the girl was wearing a black push-up bra that practically pushed her tits out of her dress. The panties were like a G-string."

Debra gritted her teeth, then said, "One, Penny Bailor is a woman, Richard. Two, the correct word is 'breasts.' Three, and most important, her underwear isn't an issue."

"Get off this feminist shit!" he whispered, then looked around to see if anyone had overheard. "Rule number one: You use what you can to win."

"We have a strong case without talking about bras and panties."

"The underwear makes it stronger. It tells the jury she was interested in more than dinner. It tells them she was interested in sex."

"It's sleazy, Richard. The fact that she had on sexy underwear doesn't mean she was asking to be raped."

"Be careful, Debra. Someone might get the idea that you think she's telling the truth." He cocked his head. "Maybe you do."

"Maybe *you* think any woman wearing sexy underwear *is* asking for it." She sighed. "Richard, I think she's lying. Either that, or she's convinced herself she's telling the truth. I'll do everything legally and ethically possible to defend my client."

"I backed you up about the bodyguard. Maybe I shouldn't have."

He was such a child; if this weren't so serious, she would have laughed. "I won't use the underwear. I'll win without it, Richard," she said, though she couldn't be sure.

And if she did win, she thought for the thousandth time, she would be killed, her tongue slashed. Fear raced through her.

"You continue to disappoint me, Debra." With an abrupt motion, he walked away.

"Want me to flatten him?" Nadine asked when Debra returned and picked up the box. "I could find a legitimate reason."

Debra raised her brows. "You overheard?"

She nodded. "I hate guys like that. Just say the word."

It was so tempting.

Chapter Thirty-nine

The alarm system was working well, Adam told Debra. There were hot screens on the windows and sensor pads in the halls and a panic button near her bed. The installers had left instructional material. Adam gave it to Debra and helped her select and activate a code; she used the numbers of her mother's birth date.

The anniversary of her mother's death—the *yahrzeit*—was on the twenty-sixth day of the Hebrew month of Cheshvan. This year that would fall on November thirteenth—this Wednesday. Debra had bought a twenty-four-hour memorial candle, which she would light on Tuesday night. This Sunday she and Aaron would go with their father to her mother's grave; next Saturday in the synagogue, she and Aaron would host a kiddush—a celebration—in honor of the *yahrzeit*. "What are we celebrating?" Debra had asked before the first *yahrzeit,* not without bitterness, and her father had explained that while they grieved for the wife and mother they had lost, they were celebrating because each year her soul was rising closer to God. The thought gave Debra some comfort.

Driving home with Nadine, Debra had contemplated letting the bodyguard go until Saturday night, when Debra would return from Aaron and Julia's (she'd arranged to sleep at their house Friday night so that she wouldn't have to walk when it was dark; her father would be sleeping at Aunt Edith's). She mentioned the idea now to Adam, but he urged her to have Nadine stay with her at Aaron's. Nadine agreed.

"We could sleep here," Debra said, wondering how her brother and sister-in-law would feel about having a bodyguard for a *Shabbos* house guest. "My brother lives only five blocks away."

Nadine shook her head. "You'll be a perfect target when you walk home. You said your father received the same threatening clips and photo you did, right? So whoever's after you knows where your dad lives. We have to assume he knows where your brother lives, too. Your car will be in the driveway, but if the guy sees you're not home, he may look for you at your father's or brother's. Does your brother have room for me?"

They had plenty of room and food, Julia told Debra. She would prepare both beds of the high-riser in the spare room.

"We observe the Sabbath strictly," Debra cautioned Nadine. "We don't turn on electricity—we don't watch television or turn on the radio or turn lights on or off. We leave some lights on, of course. We don't cook—everything's prepared before. You'll probably find it terribly restricting."

"Honey, I was in the marines. I've been in situations where I couldn't talk or move for hours. I can handle your Sabbath." She smiled. "Do *you* find it restricting, or boring?"

Debra shook her head. "I love it. I read. I spend time with my family. I use the day for introspection. It's also the only day I don't feel guilty about taking a midday nap." She smiled. "And I love the quiet. It's a peaceful change. No rushing around, no appointments, no faxes." No television news bulletins with her name and face broadcast to the entire world.

"No phones?"

"Only if it's a life-threatening emergency."

"Let's hope we don't have one."

"Your dad's cool," Nadine told Debra as she was changing from the dress she'd worn to dinner into sweats. The room was dark except for a night light and the closet light Debra had turned on before the Sabbath.

Debra smiled. Her father had enjoyed explaining the Friday night rituals and blessings to Nadine, who had listened avidly and asked many questions, both during dinner and afterward, in the living room. "I'm going to read in the den. What about you?"

"I'll secure the house, then probably go to sleep."

Debra felt guilty about imposing her rules on the woman. "If you want to use your laptop here while I'm in the den, just remember that I can't turn off the light or ask you to do it."

"That's okay. I'm blocked on act three. I think I'll try some of that introspection you talked about. Who knows?" She smiled and slipped a rubber band around her hair.

Debra went into the kitchen for a cup of tea and a slice of Julia's carrot cake, then walked to the den, where she'd deposited the boxes with the transcripts. Julia and Aaron were there, too.

"Nadine's nice," Julia said, looking up from the book she was reading. "Very pretty, too. Not my idea of a marine."

"She loved your cooking." Aaron was at his desk, poring over a tract of the Talmud. He'd been quiet during dinner, and Debra sensed he was angry with her. "I hope this isn't an imposition, Aaron," she said in a low voice so that Nadine couldn't overhear.

"It's no imposition."

"Then what's the problem?"

He sighed. "You have to ask?"

"We agreed we wouldn't get into this, Aaron," Julia said.

"No, go ahead," Debra told her brother. "Tell me."

"The fact that you need a bodyguard is the problem, Debra."

"Dad understands. Why can't you?"

"The hell he does!" Aaron shut the tractate and walked around the desk to Debra. "You want to risk your life, that's your business—or so you keep telling me. But what about putting all of us in danger, too? They know where Dad lives. They probably know where we live, too."

She had given this careful, painful thought. "He's not angry at you or Julia or Dad. He's angry at me. And he's never attacked any of the family members of the other attorneys who were killed."

"And you want to join them, huh?" He shook his head. "Mom's been dead for seven years, Debra, and you know what I think? Part of you is still trying to prove to her and to Dad and to yourself that you're successful, that you're in control of your life."

"Aaron, leave her alone!" Julia whispered.

Tears welled in Debra's eyes. She bit her lip and started to leave the room. Aaron put his hand on her arm and turned her so that she was facing him.

"I'm sorry," he said. "It's just that I'm so worried about you, Deb. Do you have any idea what this is doing to Dad? To all of us?" He drew her close and kissed the top of her head.

"Nadine's protecting me. We have nothing to worry about." Her mind flashed to the pretty pink box with the not so pretty bloody tongue; she was glad she hadn't told her family about it.

"But for how long?" Aaron asked.

"Jeremy said until they find the killer." She pointed to the boxes. "That's why I brought these." She explained about the transcripts.

"Can I help?" Julia asked. Aaron quickly seconded her offer.

Debra shook her head. "Thanks, but you wouldn't know what to look for. I don't even know, and there may be nothing to find."

Aaron nodded. He kissed Debra again, then said, "I'm going to sleep," and looked at Julia. "Coming?"

"In a minute."

He left the room. Julia got off the couch and put her arm around Debra. "You know how much he loves you, don't you?"

"I know." She sighed. "How's everything else?" she asked after a moment. On Friday nights while the men were at the synagogue, she and Julia usually talked privately as they set the table, but tonight Nadine had been here.

"I saw Dr. Herman last week. He didn't find any scar tissue and said we should keep on trying. He also said I should drink wine before we make love so I'll be relaxed. Apparently, tension elevates a hormone called prolactin, which prevents ovulation."

Debra nodded. She'd read about that in one of the many clippings Aunt Edith had given her to pass on to Julia and Aaron. "Have you ever considered in vitro, Julia?"

"Aaron told me you offered to help pay for it. It's too expensive, Debra."

"Let me worry about it. I'd much rather pay thousands of dollars to help you and Aaron have a child than buy living room furniture." She hesitated, then said, "He thinks I'm trying to show him up. I'm not."

"I know that. He knows it, too. But his pride gets the better of him sometimes. We haven't ruled out in vitro, but I'll try wine first." Julia smiled. "I tried something else, too. I was an attendant at the *mikvah* last week. This week, too."

The *mikvah* was a ritual bath where women purified themselves each month seven days after their menstrual cycle ended. Debra looked at her sister-in-law, puzzled. "Why?"

"I heard it's good luck for someone having trouble conceiving. It worked for Helen Lieberman. Maybe it'll work for me. Who knows?" She smiled again and kissed Debra good night.

Who knows? Debra had read about the prolactin in an article in *The Wall Street Journal*. The same article had reported about a Moroccan-born rabbi, an authority on Jewish mysticism whose followers believed he had healing powers. The rabbi had sat on a chair during a ceremony blessing the opening of a supermarket in Ashdod, Israel. A month later the market's four cashiers—one of whom had been trying unsuccessfully to conceive for twelve years—were pregnant. A year later six replacement cashiers were also pregnant, and the market owner discovered that all ten women had sat on the metal office chair the rabbi had used. News of the chair spread, and women with fertility problems traveled from all over the country to sit on the chair. Many of them subsequently conceived, including a thirty-three-year-old woman whose fertility specialist was shocked when she became pregnant after seven years of unsuccessful treatments. "I believe that if you have faith anything is possible," another woman had said.

Sighing, Debra crouched next to the first box and lifted out the transcripts. She made four piles—one for each case—and decided to start with Madeleine's. Madeleine had been the first victim; it seemed logical that something about her case had triggered her murder and those of the three other attorneys.

She placed the volumes—there were five—at the foot of the sofa and sat down. She took the first one and looked through the transparent plastic cover at the sheet that listed the courtroom (Department L), the judge (Harold White), the defendant (Wayne Rawling), the prosecutor (Barbara Romano), the defense attorney (Madeleine Chase), and the court reporter (Lynn Tamado).

There were about two hundred pages in each volume. Debra had read transcripts before, but never with such care. And this time she was trying to read not through the eyes of a defense attorney, but through the eyes of the victim or someone connected to her—husband, lover, father, mother, brother—or someone unconnected with the victim who hated rapists and their lawyers.

There was nothing revealing in the motions. From the prosecutor's opening statement she learned that Wayne Rawling, an independently wealthy, divorced college professor whose two children lived with their mother in San Diego, had raped Janey Schultz at knife point when she'd met him at his home to discuss her term paper for his modern European history class. There had been no medical corroboration, since Janey had waited three days before going to the police. According to Madeleine, Janey had entertained a fantasy of marrying Rawling. When he rejected her advances, she cried rape. The knife, like the rape, was a total fabrication. The police had found no evidence of any knife wound or scratch on Janey.

Debra had just begun the second volume when all the lights in the house abruptly shut off. Within seconds she could see Nadine's shape in the doorway and the solid mass that was her gun.

"Don't panic," she whispered to Debra, who was now standing near the bodyguard. "Someone shut all the circuit breakers."

"It's not the circuits," Debra whispered back. "Aaron sets

an electric timer to shut off the lights Friday nights. I'm sorry. I forgot to tell you." Her eyes had adjusted to the sudden dark, and she could see the calm intensity in Nadine's eyes.

Nadine looked uncertain, then nodded. "I'll check the house anyway, just to make sure. Stay here till I get back."

While Debra waited, she made her way to Aaron's desk and found a small sheet from a notepad, which she used as a bookmark for the transcript. Then she placed the transcript on top of the pile at the foot of the sofa and hoped no one would come into the den in the middle of the night and trip on the volumes.

"Everything's fine," Nadine whispered a moment later.

Not everything, Debra thought as she followed her bodyguard to the spare room.

At synagogue the next morning, Debra introduced Nadine as a friend, and though there were curious stares, no one said anything to Debra or Julia about the statuesque blond woman.

During lunch Debra participated in the conversation, but as soon as she finished helping Julia clear the dishes, she returned to the den, removed her makeshift bookmark, and resumed reading.

She read for over three hours, dozing off every once in a while until she finally fell asleep on the sofa in the middle of the fourth volume. When she awoke her neck and legs were stiff and the transcript had fallen to the floor. Yawning, she picked it up and searched until she spotted a page with a folded corner and dialogue that sounded familiar. Julia came and asked whether Debra wanted to join her and Nadine for a light meal.

"In a minute," Debra said.

Forty minutes later she had finished the fifth volume and learned nothing. "Damn it," she muttered. She tossed the volumes almost angrily into the box—she'd been so hopeful—and went into the breakfast room, where she found her sister-in-law sitting at the table, her face cupped in her hands as she listened intently to Nadine's description of her experiences in Haiti and Panama.

"Any luck?" Julia asked when Nadine had finished speaking.

Debra shook her head. "Not yet." She talked with Nadine and Julia; after her father and brother returned from the synagogue and her brother recited the havdalah and her father explained the ceremony to Nadine, Debra packed and helped the bodyguard take the valises and boxes back to the car. She kissed her family good-bye.

"Take care of my daughter," Ephraim Laslow said to Nadine.

Debra had forgotten about the newly installed alarm system and would have triggered it if Nadine hadn't reminded her about it; Debra hurriedly opened the entry hall closet and deactivated the alarm.

Nadine excused herself—"Introspection has led to inspiration," she said, smiling—and Debra resumed reading the transcripts. She'd decided to read them in chronological order. Susan's two volumes were next; she'd alleged that Henry Lee had been mistakenly identified as the man who had raped Alicia Vaughan after tying her up and burglarizing the Vaughans' multi-million-dollar Beverly Hills home. When Debra finished the transcript an hour and a half later, she still had no clue as to the identity of Susan's killer.

It was nine o'clock. She was tired of sitting, and her eyes were bleary and achy; she walked into the alcove. Adam was making significant progress. The desk was assembled, as were all the bookcases, and he had started sanding the wood. She was tempted to phone him and have him come over, but she had more transcripts to read.

She finished the five volumes of Kelly Malter's trial after

midnight. The prosecutor had argued that thirty-two-year-old Vincent Morgan had raped Emma Banks after she invited him into her home for coffee; Vincent and the fifty-nine-year-old Banks had become friendly while taking a computer class together. Morgan insisted that Banks, a lonely widow desperate for affection, had initiated the sexual advances; guilt and self-doubt and fear of discovery had made her cry "rape."

There was still Pratt's transcript—five volumes. That would take Debra at least three hours, especially this late at night when her concentration was hampered by fatigue. With the Malter transcript, she'd had to reread entire pages.

She checked her watch again, then opened the first volume and read the district attorney's opening statement. Pratt's client, Adrian Tchermack, had been charged with raping Nancy Wallace, a twenty-seven-year-old executive in a pharmaceutical firm. Tchermack was an executive for a rival pharmaceutical firm. Over a period of eight years the defendant and witness had developed a friendship at biannual marketing seminars. At the last seminar, Tchermack had offered to walk Wallace to her hotel room. When he'd invited himself in for a drink, she'd seen no harm. After the drinks, he'd grabbed her and raped her and threatened to ruin her career if she told anyone. For two weeks, she didn't.

Debra finished the fifth volume at three-thirty in the morning. She was filled with an aching depression, not only because she had still found no clue as to who had murdered Pratt and the others, but because she'd spent almost thirteen hours reading about women who testified in excruciatingly humiliating detail that they'd been raped by men who denied raping them. At times she'd found herself believing the witnesses; at times she'd found reasonable doubt.

He said, she said.

Chapter Forty

The cemetery was in a southeastern suburb of Los Angeles, off the Santa Ana Freeway. There was little conversation in the car on the way there; Debra's father had tuned the radio to a classical station, and she assumed that he and her brother were involved with their own memories, just as she was involved with hers. Aaron was in the back; she sat next to her father in what had always been her mother's place. She could do this casually now. Initially, after her mother's death, she'd found it unbearably painful; whenever she and her father would plan to go somewhere together, she would offer to drive, and her father, either because he understood her discomfort or shared it, never refused.

Forty minutes later her father drove past the black wrought-iron cemetery gates down a long driveway; to the right and left were tombstones of varying heights. At the end the driveway circled around a plot filled with the tiny graves of infants. She could never see this without feeling a catch in her throat. Today was no different.

Her father completed the circle and parked halfway down

the driveway. On the Sunday between Rosh Hashana, the Jewish New Year, and Yom Kippur, the Day of Atonement, the cemetery was filled with sons and daughters, fathers and mothers, husband and wives, who came to visit the graves of their loved ones. This morning it was just the three of them. Debra liked the feeling that their ceremonial visit would be private, undisturbed; other times she liked the instant kinship she felt with people who would stop and sigh and say, "How many years has it been?" and "I knew your mother."

On the other side of the driveway the cemetery was bordered by a row of trees. On this side, where her mother was buried, a graffiti-stained concrete wall blocked the view of the boulevard and muffled the noise of the traffic. There was no color here—no sheltering trees, no fragrant grass, just the pale gray concrete slabs of graves marked by marble tombstones in charcoal, white, light gray, or black, and the pale reddish brown earth.

The sun was bright. Debra had forgotten her sunglasses, and she squinted as she followed Aaron and her father to her mother's grave. Etched into the gray marble tombstone beneath the date of her mother's death were her mother's Hebrew name and a poetic epitaph her father had written. On the tombstone ledge Debra counted more than a dozen small stones of varying shapes, each one left by someone who had visited the grave. When she'd last been here, in September, the day after a heavy storm, the ledge had been bare. She took comfort knowing that so many people had visited since then, that her mother wasn't forgotten.

She read silently to herself in the book of memorial prayers while her father and Aaron, each holding his own slim black volume, did the same. She recited a prayer for entering the cemetery after an absence of over thirty days, a prayer for visiting a mother's grave, a prayer for the *yahrzeit* of a mother. There was a special prayer for those in distress; she recited this, too, and felt tears sting her eyes as she read of Rachel, Jacob's wife, who, childless for so long, wept, refusing to be comforted when her children's descendants were exiled. "Let the spirit of my mother be my defender," Debra murmured.

Her brother read the prayer for their mother's departed soul, the *"Kel moleh rachamim"*—"God, full of mercy." Debra bent down and selected a smooth pebble, which she placed on the ledge, careful not to dislodge any other stones. Aaron and her father did the same. She lingered a moment, running her fingers over the etched letters, then followed her brother and father to the car.

After exiting the cemetery, her father parked on the street. All three of them rinsed their hands, using a faucet just outside the cemetery gate. They drove home as they had come, in silence.

Aaron walked her to the front door. "Everything okay?"

"Pretty much." She hesitated, then said, "I need the phone number of the rabbi of Jeff's synagogue."

"I thought you weren't interested in him anymore."

"I'm not. But I need to check him out."

"Why?"

Why, why, why. "It's possible he tried to run me off the road last Sunday. He may be the killer." She told him about the references to the murdered attorneys in Jeff's manuscript (it was still in her bedroom—she'd had no time to mail it to him) and about his license plate number.

Aaron stared. "Come on! The rabbi said he's a good guy."

"So good he tried to rape me." She watched the color drain from her brother's face and was glad his back was toward their father, who was waiting patiently in the car.

A muscle twitched in his cheek. "You're serious, aren't you?" he said in a strangled voice. "When was this?"

"Last week." She told him what had happened. "He said he did it to try to shake me up so I'd drop the case."

"I'll kill him," her brother whispered. His hands had formed fists. "I swear I'll rip his head off."

"I shouldn't have told you." She didn't know why she had, except that the burden of keeping Jeff's assault a secret was becoming heavier and heavier.

"Of course you should have!" He caressed her cheek. "Why didn't you tell me right away? Does Julia know?"

She shook her head. "I didn't tell anyone. I felt . . . I don't know, ashamed. Guilty."

He frowned. "But you didn't do anything."

"I know." She felt like every rape victim she'd read about, and she hadn't even been raped. "Call the rabbi again. See if you can find out anything about Jeff. And be discreet, okay?"

"Okay. You want me and Julia to come over later?"

"No thanks. But you're sweet to offer."

He pulled her close. "I love you, Deb," he murmured into her hair. "If anything happened to you . . ."

"I love you, too."

Debra carried the transcripts into the living room, where she'd left the boxes. She filled the empty box first, then started putting the remaining volumes in the other box, the one that contained the transcripts from Madeleine's case. Changing her mind, she removed Madeleine's five volumes, put the other volumes in their place, and took Madeleine's back to the breakfast room.

"I thought you'd finished," Nadine said. She had come into the kitchen to rinse a coffee cup.

"I want to go over them one more time. I was drowsy yesterday afternoon when I was reading. Maybe I missed something."

Nadine left to use the StairMaster. Debra skimmed the opening statements—she'd read those carefully Friday night and remembered everything—but slowed down as she read the testimony.

She saw nothing in volume one. Nothing in volume two. Nothing in volume three. Volume four was the one she'd been reading when she'd fallen asleep; she read with extreme care, and when she reached page fifty-seven, she frowned. The material—the district attorney was cross-examining the defendant, Wayne Rawling—sounded new to her. So did the material on page fifty-eight. She couldn't understand why; then she remembered that her eyes had closed once or twice (or more?) before she'd fallen asleep.

She reread the transcript pages:

MS. ROMANO:	Mr. Rawling, during the past ten years, have any female students aside from Ms. Schultz been attracted to you?
A:	It happens.
Q:	Is that a "yes"?
A:	Yes.
Q:	And what did you do?
A:	I would discourage their attention if I thought it was inappropriate.
Q:	Were you attracted to Ms. Schultz?
A:	I thought she was a bright young woman, but she's ten years younger than I am.
Q:	Did you ever tell her she was pretty?
A:	I may have.
Q:	Did you tell her she had a great body?
A:	I don't recall.
Q:	If I told you we have other witnesses who overheard you making that comment to Ms. Schultz, would that help your memory?
A:	I may have made that comment.

Q:	Isn't it true that you often comment on the physical attributes of your female students?
MS. CHASE:	Objection.
THE COURT:	Sustained.
BY MS. ROMANO:	Isn't it true that your attraction to your female students has caused you difficulty in the past?
MS. CHASE:	Objection!
THE COURT:	Sustained. Approach the bench. Ms. Romano, you're on dangerous ground. Do you have another witness who's going to testify that she was raped by the defendant?
MS. ROMANO:	I have witnesses who will testify that he's made advances, but no other witness who will testify that the defendant raped her, Your Honor. And we all know what happened six years ago, don't we, Ms. Chase? It could happen again, Your Honor.
MS. CHASE:	Your Honor, I take umbrage at Ms. Romano's insinuation.
THE COURT:	Ms. Romano, restrain yourself. That matter has no bearing on this case, and I won't permit you to allude to it. If you do, I'll declare a mistrial. Is that clear?

What could happen again? Debra finished reading the fourth and fifth volumes. Then she returned to pages fifty-seven and fifty-eight. Barbara Romano had referred to previous problems. Had Rawling been accused of rape before? Had he been charged? Tried?

Had he been acquitted?

She was flushed with excitement and dread as she picked

up the receiver, punched the numbers for Wilshire Division, and left a message to have Simms call her immediately. While she waited, she paced around the house, coming back every few minutes to the transcript and staring at the two pages, wondering if what she'd seen was significant or immaterial, wondering what had happened to Wayne Rawling six years ago.

She realized with a jolt that calling Simms may not have been a good idea. Six years ago the detective may still have been with Sex Crimes, not Homicide. Six years ago he may have known all about Wayne Rawling. And hated him. And hated his attorney.

When the phone rang, she jumped at the sound, then hesitated and lifted the receiver from the cradle. "Hello?"

"Don't you believe in Sundays, Ms. Laslow?" Simms drawled.

"I'm sorry to bother you, Detective. I just wanted to know if you found out anything about Jeff Silver."

"That's an emergency? Shit!" he muttered. "No, I haven't found anything. He doesn't have a rap sheet. Anything else you'd like me to do for you today? Take out the garbage? Mow your lawn?"

"I'm sorry," she said again. "I'm just so anxious."

"And here I thought you were calling with the name of the killer."

Debra listened to the dial tone, depressed the phone button, called West L.A., and asked to speak to Laurie Besem.

"Detective Besem's out of town till tomorrow morning," said the woman who had answered the phone.

"Please ask her to phone me as soon as she gets in. It's urgent." Debra gave the woman her home phone number. "I'll be in court all day tomorrow. If I don't hear from Detective Besem before I leave, I'll phone her from the courthouse." Debra had a pager, but she couldn't very well have it on in the courtroom.

"I'll give the detective your message."

Debra thanked the woman and hung up. Plagued by sudden doubts—was she bothering Laurie for nothing?—she read the two transcript pages again. The implication that the defendant, Wayne Rawling, may have raped another woman was definitely there.

Norman Schultz had ordered a transcript of the trial, she remembered. What if Schultz had learned that the man he believed raped his daughter had raped before? Wouldn't that have sent him over the edge? Wouldn't that have made him enraged against the lawyers who got Rawling off?

Alicia Vaughan's husband had ordered a transcript of his wife's trial. Susan's case. Debra would have to reread that transcript, too.

Chapter Forty-one

Today Penny had on a white headband to complement the white long-sleeved blouse she wore under a round-necked, long jumper with tiny white clover leafs printed on a navy rayon. She seemed composed as she sat on the stand with her hands folded on her lap and nodded when the judge reminded her she was still under oath.

"Ms. Laslow, you may proceed," Claire said.

Debra hadn't seen Claire since Friday; she was still smarting from her rebuke but could discern no annoyance in the judge's calm voice. Approaching the podium, she was aware that behind her the gallery was again filled with spectators and the media and the regulars—Simms, Vaughan, Jeff, Schultz, Stuart Bailor. Richard was here, too. Emma Banks might be here, but Debra had no idea what she looked like. Was Nancy Wallace here, too?

Debra still hadn't heard from Laurie Besem. Entering the courtroom, she'd stared at Schultz, wondering, then moved her head quickly when his eyes met hers, but not quickly enough to avoid his glare. *If looks could kill,* she'd thought, feeling a rush of fear that she told herself could be un-founded.

She had a delicate job—attacking Penny's credibility with-out alienating the jurors, two of whom sat with pursed lips and avoided looking at Debra. She also had the aftereffects of a migraine. The aura was long gone, but her eye sockets ached, and she felt as if her head were filled with nuts and bolts that banged against her skull with every movement she made.

"Ms. Bailor," she began in a pleasant tone, "you testified that you started college in September and that you gradu-ated from high school three years ago. What did you do after high school?"

"I took classes for one semester. Then I got a job as an office receptionist."

"What kind of office did you work in?"

"A doctor's office. Dr. James Little."

"And how long did you work for Dr. Little?"

"About a year."

"And then what did you do?"

"I was a receptionist for Dr. Melvin Volkand."

"And how long did you work at that job?"

"Also about a year."

"And then you worked for Dr. Avedon for a little over seven months, is that correct?" She smiled at Penny.

"Yes."

"Did you apply for work for anyone other than doctors?"

"No."

"Objection. Where is this leading?" Annette asked with exaggerated weariness.

"I'll show relevance, Your Honor," Debra said.

Claire deliberated, then overruled the objection.

"Ms. Bailor, you testified that you don't recall who initi-ated your date with Dr. Avedon. Isn't it true that you did?" Her tone was gently chiding.

"I don't remember."

"Isn't it true that when Dr. Avedon agreed to go out sometime, you suggested a date for July twenty-third?"

"Objection. The witness has testified she doesn't remember."

"I'll withdraw the question," Debra said. "You testified that you enjoyed flirting with Dr. Avedon. Is that correct?"

"Yes." Color tinted her cheeks.

"Do you like flirting with men?"

"Objection."

"Sustained." Claire frowned at Debra.

"Did you flirt with the other doctors you worked for?"

"Objection!" Annette's voice was louder.

"Sustained."

"Did you go out with any of them?"

"Objection, Your Honor! Counsel is violating seven eighty-two," Annette said, referring to the rape shield law.

"Sustained. Ms. Laslow, pursue another line of questioning."

"Approach the bench, Your Honor?" When Claire nodded, Debra, with the prosecutor following, walked to the judge's bench. "I intend to show a pattern of behavior on Ms. Bailor's part. That pattern is an admissible exception to seven eighty-two."

"What kind of pattern?" Claire asked.

"I have an X-ray technician who will testify that Ms. Bailor told her she wanted to marry a doctor. I have a doctor who will testify that he dated Ms. Bailor when she worked for him and that she quit her job soon after he told her he wasn't interested in a serious relationship." Debra had contacted and subpoenaed both witnesses and asked them to be available today and tomorrow.

Annette said, "The defense hasn't submitted these witnesses as part of their discovery, Your Honor."

"I have no written statements from these witnesses, Your Honor. I wasn't sure I would call them until this weekend."

Claire pursed her lips. "Is the doctor going to testify that the witness falsely accused him of raping her?"

"No."

"Then I don't see the relevance of your pattern."

"We believe that Ms. Bailor was interested in marrying a doctor. We believe she consented to have sex with my client in the hopes of obligating him and involving him in a permanent relationship. We believe she accused my client of rape because she was angry that he had become engaged."

Claire frowned. "I think this is farfetched. I'm going to sustain the objection and order you not to broach this subject during your examination of the witness. You may not put the doctor or technician on the stand, and you may not refer to either one or to this hypothetical pattern in your closing argument."

Even Annette, Debra saw, was surprised by the ruling. Forcing herself to restrain her anger, she said, "With all due respect, Your Honor, you're undercutting my client's defense. I ask you to reconsider."

"Denied," Claire snapped.

"I ask that the record note my objection," Debra said, her hands clenched at her side.

"So noted."

Debra returned to the podium, hoping her face didn't reveal her anger and frustration. She flipped a page of her pad. "You testified that your parents wouldn't have approved of your going out with Dr. Avedon. Where did you tell them you were going?"

"I said I was spending the night with my friend Shira."

"So you lied. Is that correct?"

"I didn't want them to be hurt."

"Nonresponsive, Your Honor," Debra said, and listened while Claire instructed Penny to answer the question.

"Yes, I lied."

"You lie easily, don't you? You lie when it's convenient."

"No." Her tone was quiet, nondefiant.

"When you left Dr. Volkand, what reason did you give him?"

Penny hesitated and looked at the judge, who instructed her in a kind voice to answer the question. "I told him I was going back to college," she said. "Dr. Volkand was very nice to me. I didn't want to hurt his feelings."

"Can the Court direct the witness to answer only what is asked?" After Claire complied, Debra said, "So you lied?"

"Yes." Penny took a sip of water from the glass on the ledge in front of her.

"Did you tell Dr. Avedon that your parents would disapprove of your dating him?"

"No."

"So you lied again. Why didn't you tell him?"

"I was embarrassed."

"So you lie when you're embarrassed?"

"You make it sound like I lie all the time. I don't!"

"You testified that you were interested in having a fun evening, not a serious relationship. Is that correct?"

"Yes." Her tone had taken on a sullen edge.

"You also testified that Dr. Avedon told you he was interested in marriage and a family. Is *that* correct?"

"Yes."

"Can you explain why, knowing this, you consented to go to his apartment? I mean, you wanted fun. He wanted a serious relationship. Weren't you misleading him?"

"I didn't see a problem."

"Isn't it a fact that you lied when you said you were interested in having only fun?"

"No."

"Isn't it a fact that you envisioned yourself as *Mrs.* Avedon?"

"No!"

"You testified that you weren't nervous about going to Dr. Avedon's apartment. Is that because you've done this sort of thing before?"

"Objection!"

"Sustained." Claire frowned. "I think this is a good time for a ten-minute break." She gave the usual admonitions to the jury, who filed out of the room.

During the recess Debra phoned West L.A. This time Laurie was in. "Sorry I couldn't get back to you sooner," she told Debra when she came on the line. "What's so important?"

"I need a favor, Laurie."

"What kind of favor?" Wariness had crept into her voice.

"I need a rap sheet on Wayne Rawling." Debra explained about Rawling's transcript, about the reference to an earlier charge. "I'm sure you're aware that my life has been threatened. I have a bodyguard, but I'd feel better if the police found the killer."

"Everyone's working on it, Debra."

"I'm really scared, Laurie. Can you do it for me, please?"

"I'd be putting my ass on the line." She paused. "I guess it's no big deal. I have to interview two witnesses right now. Then I'll check for you. Call me after two o'clock."

At two o'clock Debra would be in court. But she couldn't push Laurie. "Do me another favor? Don't mention this to Simms."

Laurie laughed. "Honey, I have no intention of mentioning this to anyone, least of all Marty Simms."

"You're still under oath," Claire reminded Penny when she resumed the stand after the break. "Proceed, Ms. Laslow."

"Thank you, Your Honor. Ms. Bailor, you testified that

when you were in Dr. Avedon's apartment, after you both had drinks, he put on music and dimmed the lights. Then you and he kissed. How long were you kissing each other?"

"I don't remember exactly. Maybe five minutes." She took another sip of water.

"You testified that your arms were around his neck while you were kissing him. Where were his hands?"

"I don't remember."

"Were they on your waist?"

"I don't know."

"On the front of your dress?"

"I don't know."

"But it's possible?"

"It's possible." Her answer was barely above a whisper. Her face was pink.

"You testified that Dr. Avedon took off your shoes and started to massage your feet. Is that correct?"

"Yes."

"According to your statement to the police, you kicked off your shoes when you sat down on the sofa. Which story is correct?"

"Objection to the word 'story,' " Annette said.

"Sustained. Rephrase."

"Did you kick off your shoes or did Dr. Avedon remove them?"

"It's hard to remember. I guess I kicked them off. I talked to the police closer to the time this happened."

"So you remember it differently now?"

"Yes."

"And will you remember something else differently a few months from now?"

"Objection."

Claire overruled.

"I don't remember about the shoes, but I remember that Dr. Avedon raped me!" Tears filled Penny's eyes.

"Move to strike as nonresponsive," Debra said, unimpressed by her anger or tears. She was angry, too—in falsely accusing Avedon, Penny was damaging the credibility of genuine rape victims.

"Strike the witness's last comment," Claire ordered.

"You testified that Dr. Avedon massaged your feet. What about your legs?"

"I guess so. Yes."

"That's not what you testified on direct examination. Which is true? The feet and legs or just the feet?"

"The feet and legs."

"You remember it differently now, is that it?"

"Yes."

She paused for effect. "On Friday you remembered that Dr. Avedon massaged your feet, and three days later you remember it better?"

"Asked and answered," Annette said.

"Sustained."

"What is Dr. Avedon's specialty, Ms. Bailor?"

"He's an internist."

"Not a chiropractor?" Three jurors smiled, she saw.

"No."

"Did you complain of feeling tense that evening?"

"No."

"So would it be fair to say that the massage was more romantic than therapeutic?"

"Yes."

"He massaged your feet and legs. How far up your legs did he massage? Past your calf?"

"Yes."

"Past your knee?"

"A little."

"And that didn't concern you?"

"No."

"And then he massaged your neck and unzipped your dress halfway—to do what?"

"To massage my shoulders."

"To massage your shoulders," Debra repeated, half facing the jury. Her tone and the lift to her brows conveyed her skepticism. "How far did he unzip your dress?"

"Halfway."

"Past your bra?"

"I don't think so."

"Well, when he unhooked your bra, did he have to reach down inside your dress? Remembering that you're under oath."

Penny thought for a moment, then said, "He didn't have to reach inside my dress." She sounded unhappy.

"You just remembered that now?"

"Yes."

"So in fact, he unzipped your dress three-quarters of the way down or more. Is that correct?"

"Yes."

"Were you lying when you testified on Friday that he unzipped your dress halfway?"

"I was mistaken."

"But you're clear about this now?"

"Yes."

"You testified that you said 'No' when Dr. Avedon touched your breasts and that you told him you were a virgin. Is that correct?"

"I didn't say it. I yelled. I begged him to stop."

"Was this before or after the sexual intercourse?"

"Before." Her lips trembled. She raised her hand to her mouth.

"You're sure it wasn't after?"

"I'm sure."

"You made a mistake when you said Dr. Avedon took your shoes off. You made a mistake when you said he unzipped your dress only halfway. How are you so sure you're not making a mistake now?"

She returned her hand to her lap. "I know when I told him."

"Isn't it a fact that you had consensual sex with Dr. Avedon and told him afterward that you were a virgin because you were scared and wanted to make him feel responsible?"

"No."

"Isn't it a fact that you hoped to marry him?"

"No."

"Remembering you're under oath, didn't you tell Dr. Avedon's nurse that you wanted to marry someone just like him?"

"I meant someone kind. Someone with a sense of humor."

"I didn't ask you that. Did you or did you not tell the nurse that you wanted to marry someone just like Dr. Avedon?"

"Yes. But Dr. Avedon isn't Jewish, and I'd never hurt my parents by marrying a non-Jew."

Debra felt a thrill of satisfaction. "You've never dated non-Jews?"

"Ms. Laslow." Claire's voice was stern. "I warned you to drop this line of questioning."

"Your Honor, the witness herself has opened this line of questioning. It goes to her state of mind."

Claire was frowning. She was silent for half a minute, then said, "I'll allow a limited range of questions. But be careful."

"Thank you, Your Honor." She faced the witness. "Have you ever dated non-Jews?"

"Yes. But not seriously."

"When you worked for Dr. Volkand, did you go out with his associate, Dr. Sanger?"

"Only a few times." She took another sip of water.

"Whose decision was it to stop dating?"

"It was mutual."

"Isn't it a fact that it became mutual when Dr. Sanger told you he wasn't interested in a serious relationship?"

"No."

"When you worked for Dr. Little, did you go out with him or any of his associates?"

"No."

Not the answer she'd expected. She thought quickly, then said, "Was Dr. Little or any of his associates single?"

Another "No."

Debra paused so that the jury could absorb the information. "You testified that you continued working for Dr. Avedon because you needed the job. Couldn't you have obtained a different job?"

"I was afraid having three jobs in less than three years wouldn't look good."

"I see. So when did you quit?"

"On the Friday after I taped the phone call."

"That would be August twenty-third. Were you in the office on Monday, August twelfth, when Dr. Avedon brought champagne to celebrate his engagement?"

"Yes."

"And did you phone your friend Shira Frick from work that day and tell her you had to talk to her?"

"Yes."

"In fact, that's when you told her Dr. Avedon raped you. But that was a lie, wasn't it?"

"No."

"Isn't it true that you lied because you were enraged by Dr. Avedon's engagement to Miss Hobart?"

"No. I was troubled that she was going to marry him."

"Did you communicate your concern to her?"

"No."

"Did you at any point congratulate her?"

"Yes. She came to the office the next week."

"So you congratulated her on becoming engaged to a rapist?" Debra asked, her voice heavy with irony.

"I didn't know what to do! I couldn't tell her."

"Isn't it true that you accused Dr. Avedon of raping you to get revenge because you felt humiliated?"

"No."

"Ms. Bailor, you underwent a psychological examination suggested by the prosecutor. Is that correct?"

"Yes."

"Were you asked to be evaluated by a psychologist retained by Dr. Avedon?"

"Yes."

"And did you agree to be evaluated by this psychologist?"

"No, but—"

"Isn't it true that you refused to be evaluated by another psychologist because you were afraid you'd be exposed as a liar?"

"No."

"You've been lying all along, haven't you? You lied to your parents. You lied to your best friend. You lied to the police. You lied to Dr. Staten. You're lying right now, isn't that true?"

"No."

"You've avoided looking at Dr. Avedon during the entire time you've been testifying. Is that because you can't face him while you're lying?"

"No!"

"I have no more questions for this witness."

Annette took the podium. "Penny, why did you decline to be examined by the defense psychologist?"

"I found it humiliating talking to the police and to Dr. Staten. I didn't want to be subjected to all those questions again. I was told I didn't have to."

"Were you afraid the defense psychologist would think you were lying?"

"No."

"Penny, why have you avoided looking at the defendant?"

"Because I'm humiliated when I see him. Because I'm reminded of what happened." She wiped her eyes with her fingers.

"Penny, is everything that you've testified to in this courtroom true to the best of your knowledge?"

"Yes."

"Did Kenneth Avedon rape you on July twenty-third?"

"Yes."

"The People rest, Your Honor."

Chapter Forty-two

"I know what you're doing," Debra said.

She was standing in Claire's chambers, in front of her desk. Annette was at her side. When Debra had requested a meeting, Claire had insisted that the prosecutor attend, too—"I don't want even the hint of impropriety," she'd told Debra.

"Be careful what you say, Ms. Laslow," Claire said now.

"You're consistently ruling against me. At first I thought it was because of the television camera—that makes me nervous, too. Then I thought that after your confrontation with Nancy Argula, you need to show that you're not soft in your courtroom."

"Neither the media presence nor my disagreement with Ms. Argula has any bearing on my judicial deportment or my rulings. How dare you suggest that I would allow either one to cloud my judgment!" Her blue eyes flashed with anger.

Annette looked uncomfortable; she probably wished she were elsewhere. Debra wished she could be elsewhere, too.

"You're trying to diminish the effectiveness of my defense, Your Honor. You want me to lose so that I won't be the killer's next target."

"That's absurd." Claire's face had paled and looked almost white against her dark hair.

"I know you have my best interests at heart. But in fairness to my client, I think you should recuse yourself from this case."

"I have no intention of recusing myself from this case, Ms. Laslow. I intend to see it through to a verdict."

"Your initial ruling against me in regard to establishing a pattern in Penny Bailor's behavior is a clear example of bias. I should have been allowed to question the witness along those lines."

"The record will show your exception to my ruling." Her voice was calm, controlled.

"The jury is not unaware that your demeanor toward me has been cold and impatient. I'm worried that those impressions will affect them, consciously or unconsciously, during deliberations."

"Then you'll have grounds for an appeal." She stood. "I'll see both of you back in court." She nodded at Annette.

"Your Honor—"

"This matter is no longer up for discussion. The problem is not my demeanor, Ms. Laslow. The problem is twofold. One is your presumption that our personal friendship would influence my judicial responsibility. It has not. The second is your expectation that I would allow our friendship to allow you more latitude than the law permits."

Debra shook her head. "You're either lying, Claire, or you're fooling yourself."

"Debra," Annette warned quietly.

Claire placed her hands on the desk and leaned her weight on her arms. "When you are trying a case before me, Ms. Laslow, you will accord me the respect that these robes bestow upon me and you will address me as Your Honor."

"I apologize, Your Honor." Her face burned with anger and embarrassment.

"You insult not only me, but the Court with your unfounded allegations. If you raise them again, I will place you in contempt. Is that clear?"

"Very clear, Your Honor."

Vickie Hobart, Avedon's twenty-nine-year-old fiancée, was a strikingly pretty woman with long wavy blond hair and large green eyes that dominated her face. Responding to Debra's questions, she testified that she had met Avedon two years ago through a friend; they had dated a while, broken up, and met again at a party hosted by mutual friends. Two months later they became engaged.

"While you were dating after you met at this party," Debra asked, "were you aware that Dr. Avedon was seeing other women?"

"We were both seeing other people. But we finally both realized that we were in love and wanted to get married."

"Did you know that Dr. Avedon spent an evening with his receptionist, Ms. Bailor?"

"Not at the time, but Ken told me about it later."

"Did he tell you anything about the evening?"

"Objection. Hearsay."

"Sustained."

It was a fair ruling. "Vickie, did you have an intimate physical relationship with Ken both before and after you met again at the party?"

"Yes. We slept together."

"Did he ever force you to have sexual relations with him?"

She shook her head. "Never."

"Was there ever an instance when he was in the mood for sex and you weren't?"

"You mean like when I had a headache?" She smiled. "It doesn't happen often. But yes, it's happened on occasion."

"And how would he react?"

"He'd say, 'No problem.' That would be that." She shrugged.

"He wouldn't cajole you into having sex?"

"No."

"Would he get angry?"

"No. It wasn't a big deal."

"How did you feel when you learned he was charged with rape?"

"I didn't believe it then. I still don't believe it."

"Thank you. I have no more questions." Debra returned to her seat and watched Annette Prado step up to the podium.

"Ms. Hobart, you testified that you stopped seeing the defendant at one point. Why was that?"

"Nothing specific. We just weren't sure of what we wanted or that we were right for each other."

"And what made you decide now that you and the defendant are right for each other?" Annette smiled at the witness.

"We'd dated other people in the interim, and when we met again we realized how much we'd missed each other."

"But you didn't get engaged right away. You got engaged two months later. Is that correct?"

"Yes."

"Was there a specific event that made you get engaged?"

"No. We just decided we wanted to get married."

"Did the defendant propose to you?"

"Yes." She smiled.

"What day was that?"

"Friday night, August ninth."

"Ms. Hobart, did the defendant tell you he wanted you to

be his fiancée because he was worried Ms. Bailor was going to accuse him of rape and he thought having a finacée would look good?"

"No."

"You said you were incredulous when you heard he'd been charged with rape. You didn't have any doubts at all?"

"None."

"Not the teeniest, niggling worry?"

"Nothing at all. I trust Ken. I had every confidence that he'd be acquitted. I still do."

"Have you scheduled a wedding date?"

"Yes. January first. We plan to marry in my family church."

"Have you reserved the chapel?"

"Not yet. Because of the trial, it's difficult to make plans."

"Did you order wedding invitations?"

Very clever, Debra thought. She could see where Annette was going with the questioning. So, she noted, could several jurors.

"No, for the same reason."

"Did you buy a wedding dress?"

"I've tried some on, but no, I haven't bought one yet."

"For the same reason?"

There was a hint of sarcasm in Annette's voice that wasn't lost on Debra or the jury.

"Yes."

"Have you registered for gifts?"

The witness sighed. "No. We'll do all that after the trial."

"You stated a few minutes ago that you have every confidence that the defendant will be acquitted. Is that correct?"

"Yes."

"In that case, why wait to reserve the chapel or order invitations or buy the dress or register for gifts?"

"It just seemed a safer thing to do, considering the circumstances." She pushed her hair behind her ear.

"Isn't it true, Ms. Hobart, that this engagement is a sham?"

"No."

"Isn't it true that you have no intention of marrying the defendant? That you agreed to stay engaged until the trial is over because he persuaded you that breaking the engagement would reflect badly on him?"

"No."

"I have no more questions for this witness."

On redirect, Debra asked, "Do you plan to marry Ken?" and Vickie Hobart's voice rang with sincerity when she said, "As soon as possible," but the jurors' faces told Debra that Annette had planted some doubts.

After a ten-minute break during which Claire, outside the presence of the jury, ruled that she would now allow Debra to question Eric Sanger and the X-ray technician within a limited scope, the doctor took the stand. He'd been reluctant when Debra had spoken to him in his office. He was reluctant now as he discussed his relationship with Penny. The reluctance to portray the former receptionist in a bad light wasn't altogether bad, Debra decided—it made him appear genuine.

He testified that he'd gone out with Penny a few times— nothing serious, he said.

"Was it your impression that Penny was interested in a serious relationship?"

He shifted on his seat. "Yes."

"And how did you respond to that?"

"I told her I thought we shouldn't go out anymore."

"And how long after that did Penny quit work?"

"About a month later."

Debra wanted to ask him about his physical relationship with Penny, but Claire had previously ordered her to steer clear of the subject. "No more questions."

"No questions at this time," Annette said, and reserved the right to recall Sanger, who was visibly relieved to leave the stand. On cross-examination, she had two questions for Yvonne Wilson, the X-ray technician who had testified on direct examination that Penny had told her she wanted to marry a doctor:

"Do you have any reason to believe that Penny was interested in marrying Dr. Sanger?"

"No," said Yvonne.

"Do you know why she quit her job?"

"She said she was taking a position that paid more."

The prosecutor also had several questions for Diane Zolar, the twenty-seven-year-old nurse in Avedon's office who testified that Penny had told her a month after she joined the office staff that she wanted to marry someone "just like Dr. Avedon."

"Ms. Zolar, was it your impression that Ms. Bailor meant that she wanted to marry Dr. Avedon or someone with his qualities?"

"I can't say."

"Are you married, Ms. Zolar?"

"No."

"Have you ever said you wanted to marry someone like Dr. Avedon?"

She blushed. "I might have."

"Did you mean that you wanted to marry Dr. Avedon or someone with his qualities?"

"Someone with his qualities."

Annette smiled. "Thank you. No more questions."

The last witness Debra called to the stand on Monday was Dennis Jessop, Avedon's next-door neighbor, who testified that he'd been home on the night of July twenty-third from seven o'clock and hadn't left until the following morning.

"Where is your apartment in relation to Dr. Avedon's?"

"My bedroom and his living room have a common wall."

"Can you hear what's going on in his apartment?"

"Sometimes." He smiled.

"On the night in question, where were you from nine o'clock to eleven o'clock?"

"I was watching TV in my bedroom."

"Did you have your television on loud?"

"Nope. I don't like it loud."

"Did you hear screams coming from Dr. Avedon's apartment?"

"No."

"Any sounds of people arguing?"

"No."

Debra yielded the podium to Annette.

"Mr. Jessop, did you hear music from the defendant's apartment on the night in question?" the prosecutor asked.

"No."

"Would it surprise you to know that the defendant was playing a compact disk on his player between nine and eleven o'clock?"

"Not really. The building walls are pretty good."

Damn, Debra thought. She kept a poker face.

"Did you leave your bedroom during those two hours?"

"Well, sure." Another smile. "I used the bathroom a couple of times. And I fixed myself a sandwich in the kitchen."

None of this had been in the statement Debra had read, but there was nothing she could do about his testimony.

"How long did it take you to fix your sandwich?"

"Ten, fifteen minutes. I had to defrost the roll—I like rolls—and the deli. Plus I sliced a pickle and a tomato." He was clearly enjoying testifying.

"And what time was this, sir?"

He thought for a moment, rubbing his chin, then said, "I'd have to say somewhere between nine-thirty and ten-thirty. My favorite Tuesday night show's on from nine to nine-thirty. After that, I don't much care what's on."

"So if a woman was screaming in the defendant's apart-

ment between nine-thirty and ten-thirty, is it possible that
you wouldn't have heard it?"

"It's *possible,*" he said. "Yeah."

"No more questions."

She didn't need any, Debra thought glumly. The next-
door neighbor had been a disaster. Tomorrow she would
put on Avedon.

"You just missed Detective Besem," the West L.A. receptionist told Debra. "She finished for the day."

Debra wasn't surprised. Her afternoon had been filled
with disappointment—Claire's scathing remarks, followed
by Annette's victories with Avedon's fiancée, nurse, and
neighbor. All of which had been noted by Simms, who'd
said, "Losing your touch, huh?" when he'd seen her after
court adjourned; and by Richard, who had glowered but
said nothing. Avedon had been concerned, too, even after
Debra had made all the right reassuring sounds.

She paged Nadine and waited again in the lobby. She
liked Nadine but was tired of the routine, tired of needing a
bodyguard, of being unable to drive by herself where she
wanted, when she wanted. Minus the fear, it reminded her
of her high school years when she'd had to depend on her
mother or older brother to take her places. She'd hated
being dependent; she hated it more now.

She had Nadine stop at the Ralphs supermarket on Third
and La Brea and filled a cart high with groceries, which
Adam helped unload when she got home. She offered to
prepare the steak dinner she'd canceled after she'd discovered the gruesome gift in the pink box, but he'd promised
his parents to have dinner with them tonight. She said she
understood, but she was disappointed. He stayed for a
while, keeping her company in the kitchen while she fixed
a salad and pierced potatoes for baking; she loved having

him around, loved the way his eyes watched her, the way she felt when he touched her, kissed her.

Aaron phoned. "Jeff's rabbi gave me the number of a rabbi in Chicago where Jeff used to be a member. I called the Chicago rabbi and told him I needed information for someone who's interested in dating Jeff."

"And?" She put down the jar of garlic powder.

"Silver worked for the DA's office for seven years. Apparently, he had a long list of consecutive losses and suffered a nervous breakdown—the rabbi says Jeff couldn't take the pressure of the job. Anyway, he quit and moved to L.A."

"Did the rabbi know what kinds of cases Jeff tried?" Debra asked, although she already knew the answer.

"He was embarrassed to say the words. Sex crimes."

She had dinner with Nadine—steaks, salad, and baked potatoes—then went into her bedroom to watch television. When the phone rang, she thought it would be Julia or Adam.

It was Laurie. "You were right about Rawling, Debra. Six years ago good old Wayne was charged with forcible rape, one count. He was acquitted. No other priors."

She felt a surge of excitement. "Do you have a case number?"

"I already checked it for you. The trial was downtown. I spoke to the clerk—they still had the DA's file in the downtown office. You're lucky they didn't send it to County archives—that's like the Bermuda triangle."

"No kidding." As a public defender, Debra had often requested files to check priors and learned that the files were missing. "Human error," they'd tell her. "Did you get the name of the victim?" Rap sheets didn't list the names of rape victims; case files usually did.

"Sorry. All the paperwork referred to her as Jane Doe—I don't blame her for having the DA keep her identity private." Laurie paused. "I can check the court file, but my guess is I'll find the same Jane Doe listing. The DA was Bernie Ottenberg, by the way. Know him?"

"Before my time. Six years ago I was clerking for a federal judge. Who was the defense attorney?"

"Madeleine Chase. Weird, isn't it? It gave me goose bumps."

All roads lead to Madeleine.

It gave Debra goose bumps, too.

Chapter Forty-three

On Tuesday morning Kenneth Avedon, wearing the same brown tweed sports jacket and beige vest that he'd worn the first time he'd come to Debra's office, swore to tell the truth, the whole truth, and nothing but the truth.

Debra had met with him before court began and given him her speech: Answer only what's asked of you; try to maintain a serious but not grim expression; if you don't understand a question, ask for clarification; don't react to the DA's sarcasm or innuendo—her job is to rattle you; don't fidget on the stand; don't avoid eye contact with the jurors, but don't stare at them.

Tell only the truth.

She'd also reminded him at the close of court yesterday and again with a phone call early this morning not to drink carbonated beverages before he testified—if he did, he might burp.

She led him smoothly through a description of his background and saw his initial nervousness quickly disappear. His voice, always pleasant, resonated with a sincerity that was amplified by the microphone. From the corner of her eye, she could see he was making a good impression on the jury.

"When did you first meet Penny Bailor?" Debra asked.

"Last January, when she interviewed for the job."

He'd been impressed. She was bright, pretty, and well dressed and had a friendly voice and cheerful disposition—all the qualities he was looking for in a receptionist. She also had an excellent recommendation from her previous employer.

"At what point did your relationship with Penny become more personal?" Debra asked.

"She was shy when she first hired on, but after a week or two, once she knew the office routine, she was outgoing. We'd joke a lot, and somewhere along the line—I think it was in April or May—we started flirting with each other. Nothing serious."

"Were you attracted to Penny?"

"Yes. She's a very attractive young woman."

"And did she indicate she was attracted to you?"

"Yes." He paused. "Her hand would linger on mine when she'd hand me a file. She'd brush up against me. She'd make sexual innuendos." He sounded uncomfortable making these revelations—as if it weren't the gentlemanly thing to do.

"Now on Tuesday, July twenty-third, you and Penny went out to dinner. Whose idea was that?"

"Hers. The day before we were laughing about something that had happened in the office. I said, 'Maybe we'll have dinner together sometime.' And she said, 'How about to-morrow night?' "

"Did you pick her up from her house?"

"No. She said her parents were overprotective and very religious and they'd disapprove of her dating a non-Jew. She said she'd bring a change of clothes and follow me to the restaurant."

"Did she say anything else about her parents?"

"Yes. She said she wasn't very religious and that this had caused friction between her and her parents for some time."

Over dinner they'd talked about their families. After dinner he'd suggested that they go to his apartment.

"And what did Penny say?"

"She said, 'Are we going to play doctor, Doctor?' Then she laughed."

Debra paused for a moment to let the jury reflect on the comment, then said, "And how did you interpret that comment?"

"Objection. Calls for speculation," Annette said.

Debra hadn't spoken to Claire since yesterday; she was careful to keep her voice polite. "Your Honor, I'm asking Dr. Avedon to testify to his own reaction."

"Overruled."

After Debra repeated the question, Avedon said, "I understood that she was interested in having sex."

"What happened when she arrived at your apartment?"

"She kissed me. I put on some music, and we sat on the sofa and talked. She was playing with my fingers, and she put her hand on my thigh. After about twenty minutes, we started kissing."

"Then what happened?"

"I asked her if she'd like a foot massage. She said yes, so I massaged her feet. Then I massaged her neck and unzipped her dress to massage her shoulders."

"Did she seem to be enjoying what you were doing?"

"Yes. She was sighing and making little contented noises and saying, 'That feels so good.' "

Again Debra paused. "And then what happened?"

"I unhooked her bra and moved my hands to her breasts."

"Did she tell you to stop?"

"No. She leaned back against me and put her hands on

top of mine. Then we undressed each other and made love."

"At any point did Penny ask you to stop?"

"No."

"Did she scream?"

"No."

"Were you wearing a condom, Ken?"

"Yes. She asked me to. I would have anyway."

"When did Penny tell you she was a virgin?"

"After we made love, she started to cry. She said this had been her first time and she was afraid of getting pregnant even though I'd used a condom. She said her parents would kill her if they found out."

"And how did you feel, Ken?"

"I was shocked. I'd had no idea. No idea at all." His face shone with fresh bewilderment.

"And what did you do?"

"I held her and told her she wouldn't get pregnant. She stopped crying and we talked a while. Then she got dressed and drove to her girlfriend's, where she'd planned to spend the night."

She'd phoned in sick the next day and he'd assumed she was feeling guilty about losing her virginity and shy about seeing him. On Thursday she'd seemed fine. He'd asked her out again for Saturday night, but she'd told him she was afraid her parents would find out and be angry. He'd intensified his relationship with Vickie.

"Three weeks after your evening with Penny, on August twelfth, you told your office staff you were engaged. What was Penny's reaction?"

"She was upset. She was cold. Barely civil. Later that day I realized why—she'd had some fantasy about our getting together."

"Objection," Annette said. "Calls for speculation. The witness cannot testify to Ms. Bailor's thoughts."

"Sustained. The jury will disregard the last statement."

"Let's talk about the phone conversation Penny taped," Debra said. "Were you aware that you were being taped?"

"No."

"On the tape Penny said, 'Why did you force me to have sex? Why were you so rough?' *Did* you force Penny to have sex, Ken?"

"No. She enjoyed it—at least she acted like she did. She participated."

"Were you rough?"

"We were both passionate. I wouldn't call it 'rough.' "

"But you didn't deny her accusations. You said, 'I'm sorry you're upset.' and 'I didn't mean to be rough.' Why did you say that if it wasn't true?"

"I knew she felt guilty about losing her virginity and scared about her parents finding out. I figured she was blaming me because it was easier than blaming herself. To tell you the truth, I felt sorry for her. I didn't want to upset her more by denying what she was saying."

Debra paused for a few seconds. "At one point in the conversation Penny said, 'Why did you rape me?' What did you say then?" The jury had heard the tape and read the transcript, but she wanted to remind them of Avedon's denial.

"I said I didn't rape her. I said I was hanging up."

"Were you angry at this point?"

"Yes. I wasn't sure anymore what was going on, but I didn't want to take the blame for something I hadn't done."

"Ken, how do you feel right now?"

"I still can't believe this is happening. I feel as if I'm in the middle of a nightmare."

"Did you rape Penny?"

"No, I didn't."

* * *

Laurie Besem had given Debra the name of the court reporter for Rawling's first trial. Before the morning session
began, Debra had phoned downtown. and learned that the
reporter had moved out of state four years ago. No one had
a current address.

Six years ago Madeleine had gone to work for Blackmeyer. During the fifteen-minute break, after telling Avedon
how well he'd done and reviewing what he could expect
during cross-examination, Debra ran to the pay phone and
called Cynthia Ellis.

"I need another favor." Debra explained that she wanted
to know the identity of the woman who had accused Rawling of rape six years ago.

"Even if I was allowed to tell you, I couldn't," Cynthia
said. "About a month ago—right after his trial—Mr. Rawling
came and insisted on removing his entire file—he said he'd
paid enough for it and was entitled to it. Ms. Chase had me
get all his papers right then and put them in an envelope."

"What about his address? Can you give me that?"

"I'd lose my job if Mr. Rawling told Mr. Blackmeyer or
anyone else here that I'd given out information about him.
I'd like to help you, I really would." She sounded troubled.

"That's okay, Cynthia. I understand."

"I have no idea who that woman was—I wasn't working
here then—but that time I overheard Ms. Chase yelling on the
phone about that letter she received, telling the person he
was crazy?" The secretary dropped her voice. "She also said
something like 'You can't blame me for what happened six
years ago.' So I guess she was talking about the same thing.
When you mentioned six years, that made me remember."

And Madeleine, Debra recalled, had scribbled "6 yrs.?" on
one of the pages in Avedon's file. After thanking Cynthia,
she phoned West L.A.; Laurie wouldn't give her Rawling's
address, either. Debra had deposited another quarter when
the bailiff opened the courtroom door and announced that

court was about to resume. She retrieved her quarter and, hurrying down the hall and through the crowd that had assembled, came face-to-face with Stuart Bailor.

"She didn't say that, about playing doctor," he said in a quiet, mournful tone. "She didn't do what he says she did. That's not my sister he's talking about."

"I'm sorry." She saw the bewilderment and pain and anger in his eyes; she understood his need to hold on to his illusions.

She turned to her right. Karl Vaughan was staring at her, hate smoldering in his eyes. She averted her head, expecting to find Schultz staring at her, too. She didn't see him, but she knew he would be inside the courtroom, watching her.

"Mr. Avedon, when you went out with Penny, were you planning to become engaged to Miss Hobart?" Annette asked.

"Vickie and I hadn't made a commitment to each other."

"Prior to July twenty-third, when had you last gone out with your finacée?"

"Objection to the term 'fiancée,'" Debra said. "It's misleading as to the relationship Dr. Avedon had with Ms. Hobart at the time he went out with Ms. Bailor." Deliberately misleading. Annette was also deliberately addressing Avedon as "Mr." instead of "Dr.," just as she had consistently referred to him as "the defendant"—to strip him of his status and credibility.

Claire thought for a moment, then sustained the objection. Annette rephrased the question.

"I don't remember exactly," Avedon said. "Not that same week—Vickie was out of town. We went out before she left."

Don't volunteer information, Ken, Debra felt like hissing. But it was too late. And why hadn't he mentioned this to her?

"So your fiancée—I'm sorry, *Miss Hobart*—was out of town on July twenty-third?" Annette asked.

"Yes."

"Did you go out with anyone aside from Penny while Miss Hobart was out of town?"

"No."

"How long was Ms. Hobart out of town?"

"She left on July fourteenth—I remember it was Bastille Day." He smiled. "She came back on July twenty-ninth."

"So she was away for a little over two weeks—fifteen days, to be exact. She testified earlier that you and she enjoyed an intimate physical relationship. Is that correct?"

"Yes."

"So you must have missed the physical intimacy when Ms. Hobart was away. Is that correct?"

"Yes."

Debra could see from the tension in Avedon's jaw that he realized the trap he'd stepped into. The jury could see it, too. She nodded encouragement.

"So what happened? Did you need a little action while Ms. Hobart was out of town? Were you feeling a little horny?"

"Objection!"

"Sustained. Rephrase the question, Ms. Prado."

"I'll withdraw it. So here you are, three weeks away from becoming engaged to one woman, and you have sex with another woman. Is that correct?"

"Vickie and I didn't have a commitment at that time."

"And three weeks later you did," Annette said in a voice that conveyed volumes. "You testified that after dinner, Penny said, 'Are we going to play doctor?' Where were you when she allegedly made this comment?"

"We were standing in front of her car."

"Was anyone near you?"

"No. We were alone."

"So we have only your testimony that she made that comment?"

"Yes."

"I see." Another pause for the benefit of the jury. "You testified that after Penny calmed down, you talked a while. Then she got dressed and left for her girlfriend's. Did you accompany her to her car?"

"No. I wanted to, but she didn't let me."

"You didn't walk her to her car," Annette repeated. "She'd just given up her virginity for you and you were reassuring her. Why wouldn't she want you to walk her to her car at ten-thirty at night in an unfamiliar neighborhood?"

"Objection. The witness can't know what Ms. Bailor was thinking," Debra said.

"Overruled."

"She said she'd feel embarrassed if she saw the doorman or security guard. She felt they'd know what she'd done."

"You're very clever, aren't you, Mr. Avedon?"

"Objection!" Debra exclaimed.

"Sustained."

"You testified that Penny was feeling guilty on Tuesday night but seemed fine when she came back to work on Thursday. You didn't detect any signs that she was still upset?"

"She was a little quiet. I figured that was natural."

"Because she'd lost her virginity?"

"Yes."

"And when you asked her out again and she said 'no' because she was worried that her parents would be angry, did you find it odd that she hadn't worried about them before?"

"No. I thought she was being more cautious."

"I see. Did you ask her out another time?"

"No. I respected her decision."

"And Ms. Hobart was back in town by then." Annette smiled. "You testified that when you announced your engagement, Penny was cold, barely civil. How long did she stay like this?"

"It was pretty constant."

"A week? Two weeks?"

"Yes."

"Was she like that pretty much until she quit?"

"Yes."

"Referring to your taped conversation with Penny on Thursday, August twenty-second, when Penny said, 'Why were you so rough?' you responded that you were sorry that she was upset and that you'd been rough with her. Is *that* correct?"

"Yes, but—"

"Just answer the question, please, Mr. Avedon," Claire instructed.

"You didn't deny her accusations because you felt sorry for her, because she was feeling guilty about having had sex and you didn't want to make her feel worse. Is that correct?"

"Yes."

"Well, at this point, according to your own testimony, Penny wasn't feeling guilty—she was angry at you for getting engaged. So why were you worried about her feelings?"

"I still felt bad for her. I thought her feelings were all mixed together—her guilt about having lost her virginity together with her being upset that I was engaged."

"Isn't it true that you said you were sorry about being rough because in fact you forced Penny to have sex with you?"

"No."

"Isn't it true that you said you were sorry she was upset because you knew you'd raped her?"

"No. I didn't rape her."

"Isn't it true, Mr. Avedon, that you wanted to have sex and wouldn't take no for an answer?"

"No."

"Isn't it true that Penny didn't want you to walk her to her car because you'd just raped her? I have no more questions at this time, Your Honor." Annette left the podium.

"Redirect?" Claire asked.

"Yes, Your Honor." Debra walked up to the podium.

"Ken, there's an old song that goes, 'Your lips say no, no, but there's yes, yes in your eyes.' Do you believe that when a woman says 'no' she means 'maybe'?"

"No, I don't. I believe 'no' is 'no.'"

"Do you believe that if a woman allows you to kiss her and touch her body, she's giving you permission to engage in sexual intercourse?"

"No."

"Ken, did you rape Penny Bailor?"

"No, I didn't."

"Call your next witness," Claire said.

She could call the psychologist who would testify that Avedon's profile didn't match that of a rapist. She could call the security guard who would testify that Penny hadn't said anything when she'd left Avedon's building. She could call ten or more witnesses who would testify to Avedon's sterling character. She didn't believe they were necessary for his defense, but she could call all these witnesses and prolong the trial and give the police more time to find the killer; she could postpone the moment when the verdict would be read. Not just Avedon's verdict—hers, too.

She hesitated, then said, "The defense rests, Your Honor."

Avedon seemed shaken when he stepped off the stand. Debra smiled at him and said, "You did great," and waited, once again, until the courtroom cleared before she escorted him downstairs.

She found an empty bench and reviewed the closing argument she'd prepared. Now she incorporated several points that had come up during Avedon's testimony. She was a perfectionist and knew she'd never be completely happy. Finally she put her papers into her briefcase and looked at her watch: 1:20.

She was in the rest room, replacing the lipstick she'd chewed off, when she noticed that the woman next to her was staring at her even as the water flowed over her hands into the basin.

"You were very good in there today," the woman said. Her hair had been tinted brown, but the color was faded and two inches of new growth were metal gray. Her eyes were tired.

"Thank you." Debra capped her lipstick and put it in her purse.

"He was good, too. The doctor. Very convincing." She pumped liquid soap onto her hands and forearms and worked up a lather. "I can see why the jury would believe him. Do you think you'll win?"

"I'm sorry. I really can't discuss the case." She shut the flap of her purse and flipped the latch.

"Of course not. I know that." She rinsed her hands and dried them with a paper towel, then turned toward Debra. "The man who raped me was convincing, too. But not nearly as convincing as his lawyer. She's dead now, like the others. But of course, you know that, too." Her hand had disappeared inside her purse.

Debra froze. This is Emma Banks, she thought, and she has a gun and she's going to kill me right here. Feeling as though the air had been sucked out of her lungs, she lifted her purse and was prepared to swing it into the gun and knock it from Emma's hand; but the gun was a brush.

The woman drew it through her hair. "I lost my job. They said I cried too much. They said I made people uncomfortable."

"I'm sorry." Debra took a few steps backward.

"Are you?" She stared at Debra again. "You'd better go. You don't want to be late for court."

Chapter Forty-four

"This is about credibility," Annette Prado told the jury. "If you don't believe Penny, you have to acquit the defendant. If you believe her, you have to find him guilty." She paused and let her eyes survey the twelve men and women, all of whom were watching her with rapt attention.

"Penny has been brutally, painfully honest. You may not like her. You may think she did some stupid things." Annette made a dismissive gesture with her hand. "But ladies and gentlemen, that's not the issue here. The issue—the sole issue—is the following: Is Penny telling the truth?

"I need to prove three things. The first is that two people had sexual intercourse. The second is that these two people were not married to each other. The third is that the intercourse was against the will of the female and that there was a use of force. Rape, ladies and gentlemen, is lack of consent and use of force.

"Why didn't Penny report the rape right away? She told you why. She felt ashamed. She felt stupid. She blamed herself for going to the apartment of someone she trusted. Her employer. A respected doctor. She did what thousands of women in her situation do—she tried to bury what had happened. Ultimately, though, she couldn't, because her secret was destroying her life, and she told her friend and her parents and the police.

"Throughout her testimony, Penny has been painfully honest. She told you she went to the defendant's apartment. She told you she kissed him and let him massage her feet and neck. She told you she let him unzip her dress. Why did she do all of this? Because, like everyone else, she wants romance. She wants affection. But Penny didn't want to have sex. When the defendant touched her breasts, she said no. When the defendant pinned her onto the couch, she said no. And when the defendant forced himself on her and violated her, she screamed, 'No. No. No. No. No.' "

Annette is damn good, Debra thought again; she kept her face impassive and looked at Avedon. She couldn't tell what he was thinking. She tried not to think about the others—Vaughan, Schultz, Jeff, Simms. Emma Banks.

"Defense counsel has tried to portray Penny as a liar," Annette said. "If she was a liar, why didn't she make up a better story? Why didn't she say she didn't let him massage her? Why didn't she say he forced her to let him unzip her dress? She could have told a better story, but she didn't. She told the truth.

"Counsel has made a big issue of pointing out inconsistencies between Penny's testimony and her statements to the police. Let's examine those inconsistencies. Penny told the police she kicked off her shoes when she was on the defendant's couch. On direct examination she said the defendant removed them. She didn't lie—she remembered less clearly an event that took place almost four months ago. That's a natural mistake, and about what? A pair of shoes?" Annette paused. "It does nothing to diminish Penny's credibility. It doesn't change the fact that she was raped.

"Counsel emphasized that Penny didn't mention on direct testimony that the defendant massaged her leg as well as her foot. Counsel then spent a great deal of time establishing that Penny let the defendant unzip her dress more than halfway down her back. Are we talking about inches here, ladies and gentlemen?" Annette shook her head. "Penny told you she enjoyed the massage. She told you she wasn't concerned because she trusted the defendant. She also told you that when the defendant touched her breasts, she said, 'Stop.' When he forced his hand between her legs, she screamed, 'No!' Don't let defense counsel distract you with talk about feet and legs and inches from the real issue—the fact that the defendant raped her."

Debra scribbled notes on her yellow pad and listened.

"Shira Frick, Penny's friend, testified that Penny wasn't herself when she arrived at Shira's house that night. Penny's eyes were red and puffy. She was unnaturally uncommunicative. She cried herself to sleep. The next day she couldn't go to work. Penny's mother told you that her daughter wasn't eating, wasn't sleeping, that she was spending all her time in her room, crying.

"Dr. Staten testified that after examining Penny, she determined that Penny was suffering from rape trauma syndrome. Counsel tried to trick you here, too, by suggesting that Penny was afraid to be examined by a defense psychologist who would discover she was lying." Annette stepped closer to the jury box. "Penny wasn't afraid. She didn't want to subject herself to more pain, more humiliation, more intimate questions about the most terrifying, degrading experience of her life. And what defense counsel didn't tell you is that the law protects Penny from having to be subjected to this kind of examination. The law states Penny doesn't have to do it. Defense counsel didn't tell you about that law, and you're all smart enough to figure out why."

While Annette paused, Debra saw that several jurors cast quick glances at her. She kept her face blank.

"Counsel wants you to believe that Penny told the defendant she was a virgin after they had sex because she wanted to make him feel responsible," Annette continued. "Counsel wants you to believe that Penny set out to trap the defendant into marrying her. Ladies and gentlemen, if Penny wanted to marry the defendant, why didn't she accept his offer to go out again? Why didn't she pursue the relationship?" She leaned forward and gripped the railing. "She didn't do it because she never had any intention of marrying the defendant. She didn't go out with him a second time because he raped her. And she went to the police not because her fantasy blew up when he became engaged, not because she wanted revenge, but because she was afraid he would rape someone else. And she got him to admit on tape that he forced her to have sex.

"In jury selection we asked you whether you could convict the defendant based on the testimony of one witness. All of you answered that you could do so. Ladies and gentlemen, everything Penny has told you, as embarrassing and painful as it was, is the truth. I ask that you ignore the defense's attempts to hide that truth. I ask you to find the defendant guilty of rape. Thank you."

During the ten-minute recess, Debra stayed at the counsel table, making notations on her closing argument. When the recess was over and the jury had returned, she crossed the room and, conscious that the spectators and the camera and the judge were watching her, stood in front of the jury.

" 'Are we going to play doctor, Doctor?' That's what Penny Bailor asked Ken Avedon after they'd enjoyed a pleasant dinner on a date which she initiated. That's what she said when she agreed to go to his apartment. That's what she said before she had consensual sex with him. 'Are we going to play doctor, Doctor?' " Debra paused. "Ladies and gentlemen, you may feel sympathy for Penny Bailor. That's only natural. But you must lay that sympathy aside. You must regard the defendant with presumption of innocence and take that presumption of innocence into the jury room and examine the evidence." She rested her attention on a woman in the back row who, she'd sensed throughout the trial, had seemed skeptical of the prosecution witnesses.

"Ladies and gentlemen, what did we see? No evidence, just the unsupported testimony of one witness. The prosecutor told you that's all you need to convict my client—one witness's testimony. But that witness has to be telling the truth. And she's not.

"Penny proved she was a liar. She proved it several times. She admitted she lied to her parents. She lied to her girlfriend. She lied to the police. She lied to the psychologist. She lied to you, ladies and gentlemen. And she got caught in those lies. The prosecutor said to you, 'Big deal. Who cares whether Penny kicked off her shoes or let my client remove them? Who cares whether a foot or a leg was massaged? Who cares how far she let her dress be unzipped?' Ladies and gentlemen, it's not the shoe or the leg or the unzipped dress that's important. What's important is the fact that Penny lied about them. The judge will instruct you that a witness who is willfully false in one material part of his or her testimony is to be distrusted in other parts of the testimony. That you may reject the whole testimony of a witness who has willfully testified falsely as to a material point." Debra paused and surveyed the jurors.

"Why did Penny tell you that she let my client kiss her and massage her leg and unzip her dress and unhook her bra? She did it because an accomplished liar knows that to be convincing, she has to throw in some truth. But everything she told you about the rape is a lie. And she's practiced that lie. She's told her story so many times, she has it down perfectly. But ask yourself, Why did she go to my client's apartment? Why did she let him touch her leg? Why did she let him unzip her dress and unhook her bra? For a massage?" Debra shook her head. "Ask yourselves, Why didn't anyone hear her scream? Why did she ask for a condom instead of running away? Why didn't she tell the police or her friend or call a rape hot line? Why did she go back to work, where she knew she'd have to see my client every day? And why, ladies and gentlemen, did she tell her story only when she learned my client was engaged?

"Now I'm not sure what was in Penny's mind on the night of July twenty-third. She cried after she and Dr. Avedon made love. Were her tears genuine? I don't know. Maybe they were. Maybe she was scared because she'd gone too far. Maybe they were part of her plan to make my client feel responsible, to trap him into a permanent relationship. You've heard Penny testify that she's gone out with other doctors. She wanted to marry a doctor—a doctor just like Ken Avedon. She quit one job because the doctor she'd been dating didn't want a serious relationship. She quit that job for another position with my client—an unmarried doctor.

"Why did she turn him down for a second date?" Debra shrugged. "I can't read her mind. Maybe she wanted to play hard to get. But her plan backfired. And when she found out that the person she'd had sex with—the person who comforted her when she cried and said she'd given up her virginity for him—when she found out that this person made a commitment to someone else, she decided to get revenge. Because she couldn't face the fact that she'd acted rashly. She had to blame someone else. And she blamed my client and punished him in the only way she knew how— she accused him of rape.

"The prosecution played a tape for you in which Penny accused my client of being rough on her. He knows she's upset. He knows she's having a hard time with his engagement. He doesn't want to set her off, so he says, 'Penny, I'm sorry you're upset.' But when she says, 'Why did you rape me?' he says, 'I didn't rape you,' and he hangs up.

"Centuries ago, an Egyptian named Potiphar had a beautiful wife who lusted after a man named Joseph. She wanted him. And when he refused to sleep with her, she wanted to punish him, and she punished him in the best way she could: she cried rape and had him thrown into jail. Ladies and gentlemen, Penny Bailor told my client she wanted to play doctor. She played the game. And when she lost, she didn't like it. She didn't like it at all. Thank you."

Walking back to her seat, Debra kept her eyes straight ahead, refusing to look to her left at the gallery, where she knew Vaughan and the others were watching her.

Annette approached the jury box again. "Penny never made that statement about playing doctor, ladies and gentlemen. She wasn't playing a game. She told the truth. She didn't lie—she remembered some things more correctly. Defense counsel says Penny cried rape to take revenge. What does Penny gain? She gets to be humiliated in front of strangers. She has to discuss in graphic terms the most intimate details of her life. She has to repeat these details endless times, and she subjects herself to a grueling cross-examination. Some revenge." Annette shook her head.

"Defense counsel asked you, Why did Penny go to the defendant's apartment? Why did she let him kiss her? Why did she let him unzip her dress? Ladies and gentlemen, Penny will be the first one to tell you she made a mistake. We all make mistakes. We all do unsafe things. We walk outside with our purses on our shoulders. We leave windows and doors unlocked. But does that mean that we give up our rights as being a victim of a crime? If I go into an unsafe neighborhood and I'm mugged, I may be guilty of stupidity, but no one will say to the mugger, 'You had a right to take her purse. She asked for it.' No one will exonerate the mugger. With rape, it's different, isn't it? With rape we say, 'Well, she went to his apartment, so she asked for it.' Ladies and gentlemen, Penny didn't ask for it. Ken Avedon thought he was going to have sex that night. He took Penny to dinner and thought he deserved to have sex. And when he didn't get it willingly, he forced Penny to comply. And that is rape."

Looking at the jurors as Annette returned to her seat, Debra found it impossible to know what they were thinking. She watched their faces intently a moment later as Claire began her instructions in a voice free of inflection:

"You must not be influenced by mere sentiment, conjecture, sympathy, passion, prejudice, public opinion, or public feeling," the judge said. If there were two reasonable interpretations for circumstantial evidence, she continued, "one of which points to the defendant's guilt and the other to his innocence, you must adopt that interpretation which points to the defendant's innocence. . . ." In regard to the tape, jurors were the "exclusive judges as to whether the defendant made an admission" and had to decide whether the statement was completely or partially true.

The tape was a problem, Debra admitted to herself as Claire discussed "reasonable doubt" and "criminal intent"; she felt she'd dealt with the tape effectively, but she wouldn't be in the jury room when they discussed the tape or asked to have it played again and heard Penny repeatedly say, "Why? Why? Why?" She listened as Claire explained that if the defendant had a "reasonable and good faith belief" that the woman had voluntarily consented to engage in sex, no criminal intent existed, "and you must find him not guilty." And Debra, who had shifted her attention to Claire, had seen nothing in the judge's eyes or manner that conveyed any tacit message to the jury.

They were to vote as individuals, Claire cautioned. They were not to hesitate to change an opinion if they thought it was wrong; on the other hand, they were not to decide with the majority.

"Remember," she said, "you are the judges of the credibility of the witnesses."

At home, Debra lit the memorial candle for her mother. She stared at the flame as she recited a phrase in Hebrew. She would have liked to stay here with her thoughts and memories, but she hadn't been to the firm for days. She stood in front of the candle a while longer; then Nadine drove her to the office, where she talked to Charles and Glynnis and returned several calls. The rest she would do tomorrow morning.

At seven-thirty she went home. She checked on the candle—the flame was flickering faithfully inside the glass, bathing the room, which was dark except for the candlelight, with a soft yellow glow. There were several messages on her answering machine. One was from Cynthia—she didn't identify herself, but Debra recognized her voice as she dictated the address for Wayne Rawling and said, with breathless urgency, "Please don't say I told you."

The address was in Westwood. On the way there, Debra explained to Nadine about Rawling and why she had to see him. She wasn't sure he would talk to her, but she had to try.

They were approaching Rawling's residence when Debra saw the flashing red police lights. She knew even before Nadine parked across the street from the police vehicles, before she read the brass numbers near the front door, that this was Rawling's home.

There was an ambulance in the driveway; its lights were flashing, too. With her bodyguard at her side, Debra hurried across the street and approached a uniformed policeman standing at the end of the brick walkway. "What happened?" she asked.

"This is a crime scene, ma'am. Stay back."

"I just want to know what happened." She looked to her right. Another uniformed policeman stood near the ambulance. Next to him was Stan Cummings. "Detective Cummings!" she called.

He looked in her direction, frowned, then said something to the policeman. A moment later he was at Debra's side. "What are you doing here, Ms. Laslow?" he asked in a voice that held more than curiosity.

"I wanted to talk to Wayne Rawling."

"You know him?"

She shook her head. "Madeleine Chase defended him twice for rape—the first time six years ago, the second time just before she was murdered. I wanted to find out who the first complaining witness was."

"Rawling has been shot." Cummings was studying her thoughtfully.

She felt her chest constrict and glanced again at the ambulance again. "Is he alive?"

"Barely."

"Who—" She cleared her throat. "Who shot him?"

Cummings pointed to the black-and-white police vehicle. "We caught him trying to run out the back."

Debra followed the detective's finger. In the glare of the streetlight she saw a man seated in the backseat of the car.

Norman Schultz.

Chapter Forty-five

Wayne Rawling had been taken to the emergency room at the UCLA Medical Center. He was now in intensive care, Debra learned when she arrived at the hospital at seven o'clock on Wednesday morning. Nadine had insisted on accompanying her. "We still don't know that you're safe," she'd told Debra.

"Is Mr. Rawling conscious?" Debra asked the uniformed policeman guarding the entrance to the intensive care unit.

"Sorry. I can't comment on his condition." His hand rested casually near his weapon. His expression revealed nothing.

"I'm Debra Laslow, an attorney. Is Detective Cummings here?"

The officer looked at her with interest. "He's inside with Mr. Rawling."

"Would you please tell him I'd like to speak to him?"

He hesitated, then said, "Okay." A moment later he returned with the detective.

"How can I help you, Ms. Laslow?" Cummings sounded polite, but tired. His face, filled with stubble, looked darker.

"I need to speak to Rawling."

Cummings shook his head. "I can't let you do that."

She moved closer so that she was out of earshot of the officer. "Did Schultz admit he killed all four attorneys?"

"Schultz hasn't said one word since we picked him up. He's been booked at West L.A. on attempted murder."

"I need just a minute or two with Rawling."

He squinted at her. "Why?"

She'd asked herself the same thing. "Reassurance that Schultz is the killer, I guess." She'd been living with fear so long that it was difficult to give up its ghost. "You can listen to whatever I have to say to Rawling. I have no secrets."

Cummings frowned in contemplation, then said, "Okay. Just you," he said, indicating with his eyes that Nadine couldn't accompany Debra. "And just for a minute. He was shot in the chest. He lost a lot of blood before surgery, and he's pretty weak."

Debra followed him into the intensive care unit and past the nurses' station to a private room at the left.

"Wait here," he said. "I'll see if he's up. The painkillers knock him out. Even when he's awake, he's not all that co-herent."

A moment later, Cummings beckoned and Debra stepped inside. Rawling had dark brown hair and a strong chin smeared with pink-streaked saliva. His eyes were closed. He was very pale, and except for the rise and fall of his chest, Debra would have thought that he was dead. An oxy-gen tube was connected to his nostrils; an IV dripped into the vein of his right arm; more tubes emerged from under his blanket. Debra heard a soft, gurgling sound and won-dered what was being suctioned.

She approached and stood at his side. "Mr. Rawling, my name is Debra Laslow." He didn't respond; she continued anyway. "I know you're in pain and can't speak. I promise not to stay long."

Rawling's eyes remained closed and he made no movement.

"Is he asleep?" Debra asked Cummings. When the detective shook his head, she turned back to Rawling. "Mr. Rawling, I'm an attorney. I'm defending a man charged with rape"—she saw a wince pinch his face—"and I could be the next target of—"

"I . . . know," he rasped. His eyelids flickered open, then shut.

"The man who shot you, Norman Schultz. Did he tell you he killed the other attorneys?"

"Didn't . . . say." His eyelids opened again. "Set . . . up."

"Schultz was set up?" she whispered. She saw an almost imperceptible nod of Rawling's head. "By whom?"

"Don't . . . know."

"Six years ago Madeleine Chase defended you. What was the name of the complaining witness?"

He turned his head aside and looked at the wall.

There was no reason for Rawling to tell her; she couldn't justify her need to know, except for her instinct, which told her there might be a connection. "Someone's trying to kill me," she said. "I'm grasping at straws, trying to find out who."

"Try . . . forget . . . past," Rawling said.

"Please," she whispered. "What's her name?"

"Ms. Laslow," Cummings said, coming up to her. "I'm going to have to ask you to leave."

"But—" She nodded. She took a step away from the bed when she felt Rawling grab her hand. She flinched and turned toward him.

"Not . . . my fault . . . what . . . happened . . . later."

"What happened later?" Debra leaned down to hear better.

"Detective . . . said . . . my fault." He coughed up phlegm; his chest heaved. His grasp on her hand tightened. "Not . . . true." He shut his eyes again.

"Which detective?" Was it Simms? she wondered, her heart beating faster. Had he been on Rawling's prior rape case?

"Didn't . . . want . . . shoot."

"Who didn't want to shoot? Schultz?" Had her questions prompted Simms to goad Norman Schultz into shooting the man who had allegedly raped his daughter? "Mr. Rawling?" she prompted. "What's the woman's name? Please tell me."

Rawling coughed again, then released her hand as his head slumped to one side and he fell into unconsciousness.

Adam was in his truck when Debra returned home. He walked to Nadine's car and opened the door for Debra. "I was worried when you weren't home," he said when she stepped out of the car.

She told him where she'd been.

He nodded. "I heard about Schultz. The news stations have been playing the story practically nonstop since last night. So it's over, thank God?" He drew her close.

"I don't know. From what I could understand, Rawling said Schultz was set up. I don't know what that means—did someone else shoot Rawling and draw Schultz to the scene? Did someone goad Schultz into shooting Rawling?" She'd been alternating between the two possibilities on the drive back from the hospital. "I don't even know if I understood Rawling correctly." Cummings was following up on what he'd heard; he told Debra he'd let her know as soon as he learned something.

Adam frowned. "But even if Schultz was set up with Rawling's shooting, Schultz killed the other attorneys, right? That's what the news said."

"I don't know that, either."

Nadine's pager beeped. Debra unlocked the front door; Nadine and Adam followed her inside. Nadine went to the kitchen to use the phone.

"That was the security company," she told Debra when she returned. "They have another assignment for me starting now."

"But I still need protection. You said so yourself." I'm whining like a child, Debra thought.

"Apparently, someone from your firm phoned last night and said my services wouldn't be needed any longer. I guess they heard about Schultz and figured the police had the killer."

"I guess." It was Anthony, Debra knew. She was going to the office now anyway. She would talk to Jeremy and explain the situation and get another bodyguard.

"I hate to let you down, Debra. But I have no choice—I have to report to my new job in half an hour."

"I'll be all right." She hugged Nadine. "You were a great bodyguard. And don't worry—I'm not in immediate danger. The jury hasn't returned with a verdict yet." She forced herself to smile.

This time there was no mistaking what she saw when she opened her office door—Richard was at her desk, using her computer. And he had no bouquet of roses to camouflage his activity.

"What are you doing?" she asked, walking toward him.

He tried a smile. "My computer's on the blink, and I needed one right away." He moved his hand to the keyboard, but she'd reached the desk and grabbed his hand. "Are you crazy, Debra?"

On the screen were listings of all the firms to which she'd applied and all the notations she'd made. "You've been snooping through my files. Why?" She didn't try to hide her anger, her loathing. She was through pretending.

"You're making a big deal out of nothing, Debra. This is a firm. We share information."

"This is my personal file, not a client file."

"Well, maybe you shouldn't be using the firm's computer for your personal business."

"Are you the FBI, Richard? The IRS?" When he didn't answer, she said, "What you did is inexcusable."

He stood. "How about what you're doing, applying to other firms without telling anyone here? Letting all of us think you're part of the team when you have no intention of staying?"

She pressed the Enter key; the lists disappeared. She removed her floppy disk—obviously he'd searched through her desk drawers to find it—and put it inside her briefcase. "I'm a free agent, not an indentured servant. I have the right to consider another firm without broadcasting my intentions to you or anyone else. The last I heard, most people—doctors, lawyers, plumbers, accountants, actors, teachers—don't leave one job unless they have an assurance of another one." She glanced at the computer screen, now an innocent blue. "I still don't understand why you were snooping through my files. Who told you I was looking for another position?"

"No one. I just had a hunch." He walked over to her bookcase.

She didn't believe him. She remembered what Simms had said: Madeleine had planned to meet with Richard on the Friday after her confrontation with Debra. "Madeleine Chase told you, didn't she?" From the surprised expression on his face, she knew she was right.

"I took you under my wing, Debra. I tried to help you. I felt betrayed when I learned you wanted to leave."

She snorted. "You've been harassing me from the day I came here. You belittle my religious beliefs. You set obstacles in my path. You're constantly making sexual references which I find juvenile and obnoxious. You're the reason I want out."

"Maybe you should get out. You can't handle the real world, Debra. You should give up practicing law and go back to a shtetl and be a good little wife and mother."

"I hope that someday I *will* be a good wife and mother. As for my professional skills, I'm a better lawyer today than you'll ever be."

"Do you think Avedon will agree when the jury finds him guilty? I sat in that courtroom. You didn't give it your best. But maybe you didn't want to win—not when you knew you'd be the killer's next target if you did." He paused. "You know, if Avedon *is* found guilty, he could sue you and the firm for legal malpractice. Have you considered that?"

"Richard, I'm not going to answer your ridiculous allegations or defend my professionalism. I will see the Avedon trial through to its conclusion. And then I will hand in my resignation."

"Blackmeyer turned you down, and that was before your involvement with the murders. Hoffinger turned you down, too. Face it, Debra—if you leave here, your legal career may be over."

"I'll have to take that chance. Would you excuse me, please? I have work to do." She sat down, opened her briefcase, and pulled out several folders.

He stood for a few minutes, watching her, then left. He was probably going directly to Jeremy, she knew, and Anthony.

She realized with a pang of apprehension that getting a new bodyguard was probably not going to happen. She consoled herself with the fact that she'd retained her dignity, but dignity wouldn't stop a bullet and would be of small comfort in the grave.

* * *

There was a white Cadillac behind the teal green BMW in Rawling's driveway. Debra couldn't remember seeing either car last night. Last night she hadn't paid attention to the house, either. It was a salmon-colored two-story structure with a Spanish tile roof, large mullioned picture windows with white trim, and twin wrought-iron balconies in front of the second-story windows.

She parked her Acura across the street, walked to the front door, and rang the bell. She heard footsteps, then a woman's Spanish-accented voice asking, "Who's there?"

"I'm Debra Laslow," she said, smiling for the person eyeing her through the peephole. "I need to speak to Mr. Rawling's aunt about what happened to her nephew. I understand she's here."

From Cummings Debra had obtained the name of Rawling's mother's sister, Cora Tarrigan—the wounded man's next of kin in Los Angeles. After several attempts, Debra had located the right Cora Tarrigan at a Beverly Hills address and learned from an initially hesitant husband that Cora was at her nephew's house. Rawling's parents, the husband had added, lived in Minneapolis; they were flying in sometime today.

"One minute, please," the woman said.

It was more than a minute before Debra heard another set of footsteps and heard an older, warier, unaccented voice. "I'm Wayne's aunt, Cora Tarrigan. How can I help you?"

"May I come in, Mrs. Tarrigan? I'm sorry about your nephew—I spoke to him this morning, and I wanted to ask you a few things."

"This isn't a good time. I'm getting some things for my nephew and taking them to him at the hospital."

"I understand. But it's urgent that I talk to you now."

"You're not a reporter, are you?" The flinty edge of suspicion had entered her voice. "I won't talk to any reporters."

"I'm an attorney. I can show you my business card." Debra took a card from her purse and slipped it under the door.

A few seconds passed. "What do you want to talk to me about?"

"I'd rather explain inside."

There was another wait. Then the door opened and Debra faced a tall, slim woman with short, steel gray hair. She was wearing a pair of black slacks and a cream-colored angora sweater.

"I can give you ten minutes," Cora Tarrigan said, and led the way to a living room darkened by closed shutters. She sat on a dark brown cotton sofa and pointed to a brown-and-black-print armchair on the other side of the glass-topped black wrought-iron coffee table. "I brought my housekeeper along to straighten up. The police left quite a mess."

Debra sat on the chair. "I appreciate your talking to me, Mrs. Tarrigan. As I said, I'm an attorney. I'm defending a client charged with rape." She saw distaste flutter across the woman's face. "If you've been reading the papers, you know that someone has murdered four other attorneys who won acquittals for clients charged with rape."

"I thought your name was familiar. But why are you here?"

"The first murdered attorney was Madeleine Chase. Madeleine defended your nephew on a rape charge and won an acquittal for him."

"I'm not going to discuss my nephew." A warning glint appeared in her blue eyes. "If that's why you've come, you're wasting your time."

"Please, let me finish." Debra leaned forward. "I discovered that Madeleine had won another acquittal for your nephew on another rape charge six years ago. I need to know the name of the woman he was accused of raping."

"You said you spoke to my nephew. Why didn't you ask him?"

"He couldn't talk very long. He was weak and I didn't want to upset him." Half a lie, half a truth.

Cora Tarrigan studied Debra, then said, "You're lying. Wayne didn't want to tell you, did he?" She rose. "I think you'd better go, Ms. Laslow. My nephew is fighting for his life. Your coming here and prying is cruel and insensitive."

"My life is in danger, too," Debra said, hearing the melodrama of her words. "What harm would it do if you told me the woman's name?"

"They arrested the killer. Wayne is trying hard to put all this behind him. Why can't you leave this alone?"

"I don't think Norman Schultz killed those attorneys. Your nephew told me he thinks Schultz was set up."

Cora Tarrigan's eyes flickered with indecision.

"I've been getting death threats," Debra said. "Someone tried to run me off the road. Someone left a box with a tongue and a bloody knife at my doorstep. They're warning me that I'm next." After trying unsuccessfully to reach Cummings to ask for police protection, she'd hired another female bodyguard at her own expense; she would be at Debra's office at five.

Cora paled and sat down. "Why are you so sure that what happened six years ago has something to do with the murders?"

"I'm not sure, but your nephew said that what happened later wasn't his fault. He said the detective blamed him."

Rawling's aunt sighed. "I don't know." She stared at her hands and played with a pearl ring on her left hand, as if she would find an answer there.

Debra waited. From the back of the house, she heard the hum of a vacuum cleaner.

"The girl's name was Emily Patterson," the aunt finally said, still not looking at Debra.

"Do you know where she lives?"

Another silence. Finally the woman glanced up. "She's dead. She killed herself not long after the trial."

"My God!" Debra whispered. She shut her eyes briefly.

"Wayne took it badly," his aunt said with a hint of defensiveness. "We all did. But it wasn't his fault. She just . . ." Cora Tarrigan raised her hands and dropped them back onto her lap. "It was sad, so very sad."

"When was this?"

"The trial ended at the end of May. This was in July."

"Do you remember the name of the detective on the case?"

Cora Tarrigan shook her patrician head.

"Was it Marty Simms?"

"I really don't know."

Debra's pager beeped. "Excuse me a minute." She removed the pager from her jacket pocket and looked at the numbers on the tiny screen. "May I use your phone?"

"Of course." Rawling's aunt stood and led Debra to a small breakfast room and pointed to the wall phone.

"Thank you." Debra punched the numbers; a moment later she heard her secretary's voice. "It's Debra. What's up?"

It was probably Richard, demanding to know where she was. She'd made a halfhearted attempt at starting to get her files in order for her impending departure; unable to concentrate, she'd told Glynnis she had an important meeting and driven here.

"I'm glad I reached you," Glynnis said. "The jury's reached a verdict. You have to get to the courthouse right away."

Chapter Forty-six

"Has the jury reached a verdict?" Claire asked the foreman, a tall, heavyset man with a somber expression on his jowly face.

"We have, Your Honor."

"Have you signed and sealed it?"

"Yes, Your Honor."

Avedon looked pale. Debra had reached him in his office; fifteen minutes later she'd met him and his parents outside the courtroom. "I don't know," she'd said when he'd asked about the rapidity with which the jury had reached its verdict—they'd deliberated for six hours yesterday and three hours this morning. Annette seemed confident, Debra thought. And how do I look?

The foreman handed the sealed verdict to the bailiff. The bailiff handed it to the clerk, the clerk to the judge. Claire unsealed the verdict and read it silently to herself, then returned it to the clerk.

"Will the defendant please rise," the clerk said.

Avedon stood. Debra stood, too; her nails dug into her

palms. She wanted to win for Avedon, and for herself, be-cause she always wanted to win, and for Richard, who was here in the courtroom.

She wanted to lose.

"In the matter of the People versus Kenneth Avedon, the jury finds the defendant not guilty to the charge of forcible rape."

Debra heard an angry gasp behind her. Her head began to throb and her hands tingled as she listened to Claire thank the jury for performing their job so diligently; she heard Avedon's "Thank you" and felt his hug and said, "I'm so glad for you, Ken," but she felt as if someone else were talking.

She looked at the bench. Claire nodded and smiled quickly at Debra, then stepped down and exited the room. Eventually Debra would have to leave the safety of this room, too. Was the killer still here? she wondered. Had he chosen the time, the place?

Annette came over to her. "Great job." She extended her hand to Debra, who lifted hers automatically and said, "You had me worried," and smiled even though someone was waiting for her to be alone, and now she had no body-guard.

"I'm glad they got the killer," Annette said, and Debra didn't correct her.

In the hall she saw many people she didn't know and some she wished she didn't—Emma Banks; Karl Vaughan; Penny Bailor, circled by her brother and mother and an older, bearded man Debra assumed was her father. She pushed her way past reporters, repeating, "No comment," until she escaped into the rest room, where she swallowed two tablets with faucet water that she drank from her cupped palm and noted dispassionately the blind spots on two of her fingers. Several women entered the rest room.

Debra locked herself in a cubicle and sat for twenty minutes until the aura receded.

"I'd like to see Norman Schultz," Debra informed the male officer at the West L.A. station after she'd identified herself. "I want to represent him." She handed the officer her business card.

"I'll tell him." The officer took the card with him as he left the small reception area.

While she waited, she wondered whether Laurie Besem was here. She hadn't had a chance to talk to Laurie—she hoped the detective didn't regret having told her about Rawling. Not that she was responsible for the man's having been shot. . . .

The officer returned. "Sorry. He won't see you."

"Tell him I know he didn't shoot Wayne Rawling."

He gave her an "I'm not your messenger" look but said, "Okay." When he returned again a few minutes later, he nodded and escorted her up the stairs to the second floor and Schultz's jail cell.

Schultz was on the bottom of the bunk bed, his hands clasped beneath his head as he stared at the underside of the top bunk.

"Mr. Schultz, I'm Debra Laslow," she said through the bright orange bars. Her head still hurt, but she could talk clearly.

"The rapist lover. What's this bullshit about representing me?" He hadn't changed his position.

"Rawling told me you were set up. He didn't know by whom. If you know, if you have any idea, I could help you prove it."

Schultz snorted. "You want to save your ass. I saw you at Rawling's last night. You thought they found the guy who killed those lawyers—you must have been feeling pretty good, huh? Now you're scared shitless. Now you know this guy's still out there."

"I *am* scared," she said. "Why did you go to Rawling's?"

"I'm not on the witness stand. I don't have to answer your questions, Ms. Lawyer."

"You're right. But I'm sure you'd like to get out of here, to get back to your family, to Janey."

Schultz sat up quickly and hit his head on the bunk frame. "Shit!" He winced, then hissed, "Leave my family the hell alone! Janey's suffered enough! I don't want her going through any more ugliness." His face was mottled with anger.

"Your staying in jail isn't helping her."

"Why the hell should I help you? It's people like you who let guys like Rawling do their dirty things." He paused. "Your client, Avedon. Think he'll get off?"

So he hadn't heard yet. She hesitated, then said, "They just acquitted him."

"You could've lied." He eyed her appraisingly, then said, "I don't know who set me up. But I didn't shoot Rawling. God knows I wanted to, but I didn't."

She nodded. "What happened?"

"I got a call at eight. I couldn't make out the voice—it was muffled. This person said Rawling was going to come after Janey. I bought a gun after that bastard raped her—I taught her how to use it. I loaded it and drove to Rawling's house."

"How did you know where he lived?"

"Oh, I knew." Schultz's smile was grim. "I used to drive by his place a couple of times a night, to make sure he was home. I'd park in front of his house and think about what I'd do to him if he came outside and I got my hands on him. Do you know Janey?"

Debra shook her head.

"God, she was the happiest person in the world before it

happened! Now she won't even leave the house." Tears welled in his eyes. "Anyway, when I got there, the door was open and Rawling was on the entry hall floor. He'd been shot in the chest, and there was a lot of blood. I thought he was dead. You know what? It wasn't like I'd imagined it." He wiped his eyes.

"Did you call the police?"

He shook his head. "I knew they'd think I did it. I must've froze for a minute or two—I mean, I knew I'd been set up. So I found the back exit and left. But by then the cops were there. And I had my gun on me. 'Check it out,' I told them. 'You'll see it hasn't been used.' They read me my rights and cuffed me and put me in the squad car." He shrugged. "I figure as soon as they run some tests, they'll know he wasn't shot with my gun."

"Who do you think called the police?"

"I've been thinking about that while I was trying to sleep in this fancy hotel room." He glanced at the bare walls and the toilet at the far wall. "Somebody—the person who called me—must've been watching Rawling's house, waiting for me to show up. He must've been in his car. When he saw me drive up, he used a car phone and called the cops."

That made sense. "Did you see any cars when you arrived?"

Schultz nodded. "I didn't think much of it at the time. But yeah, I saw a car. A black Honda."

She thanked Schultz. "I meant that about representing you. If you need help—"

"I think you need help more than I do."

She was fastening the harness in her car when she saw Marty Simms and Stan Cummings walking together from the police lot on Butler toward the orange-tiled station entrance. She ducked down, and when she was sure they'd entered the station, she drove away.

From her office she phoned the *Times*. She'd been there in the past to research information in the archives area that used to be called the morgue but was now called the library, but the *Times* library, like other large-city newspaper libraries, was no longer open to the public. She spoke to a researcher, gave the woman her credit card number (the fee would be six to ten dollars), and explained what she wanted.

"How long ago was that?" the woman asked.

"Six years ago, in July. There may have been one or more articles." Debra wasn't sure whether Emily Patterson's suicide had made the front page or been buried in the obituaries. "I'd like a fax of everything you find, if that's possible."

"If it was six years ago, it'll be in our database. I'll check for you. If I find something, I'll phone you, get a printout, and fax it to you."

Debra went to Charles's office—she didn't want him to hear from someone else that she was leaving—but he hadn't returned. She was in her office working on a file when Glynnis buzzed and told her Simms was on the line. Debra asked the secretary to tell the detective she wasn't in. Fifteen minutes later the *Times* researcher phoned—she'd found two articles. Debra thanked her, hung up, and hurried to the facsimile machine. When the transmission was completed, she grabbed the pages but waited until she was in her office before she read them.

The first page was a small two-inch article in the July 17 Metro section. Her chest tightened as she read:

Emily Patterson, a twenty-two-year-old graduate student, was found dead in her Culver City apartment last night, a victim of an apparently self-inflicted gunshot wound.

Gerald Patterson, the dead woman's father, told West L.A. detectives that his daughter had been distraught about the outcome of a recent trial in which she testified. "It killed her," he said, choked with emotion, but declined to comment on the particulars. An autopsy is pending.

Gerald. Why was that name familiar? The second page was the obituary, dated six days later. Funeral services for Emily Patterson, she learned, had been held on a Saturday at a church in Burbank. "Patterson," Debra read, "is survived by her parents, Gerald and Beatrice Patterson, and her sister Claire."

Debra stared at the page. Claire Werner's father, she remembered, was Gerald; that's why the name had sounded familiar. It was an eerie coincidence, so eerie it chilled her, but of course, that's all it was—a coincidence. Because Claire's sister hadn't killed herself; she'd died of cancer, just like Debra's mother. And her name was Lee, not Emily.

Lee could be short for Emily.

Her head still felt wobbly. Her eyes ached; she rubbed them and looked at the obituary again.

Claire's father had been in the courtroom every day, watching the trial. Watching Debra.

Madeleine had written "G.P.?" on a page in Avedon's file.

But this was a different Claire.

With the pages tucked inside her purse, she tossed a quick, "I don't know when I'll be back," at Glynnis and left. Without traffic it was forty minutes to Norwalk and the county building where records of births, deaths, and marriages had been moved from the downtown hall of records on Broadway. She kept the car radio on her favorite classical station, but she wasn't aware of the music and she drove without thinking, changing from the San Diego to the Century and then to the 605 as if she were on automatic pilot.

At the Imperial Avenue address she parked her car. She was walking trancelike, unaware of her surroundings, and bumped into a person who stared at her and growled, "Watch where you're going, lady!" and was unmollified by Debra's apology.

In room 208 on the lower level, she approached the clerk behind the counter. After she filled out a pink application requesting the decade she wanted to search—Claire, she remembered, had married fourteen years ago—she presented her license for identification. The clerk handed her a microfiche, which she inserted in one of the viewers in the public area.

She found the year she wanted on the microfiche. Claire had mentioned her ex-husband's first name. Debra couldn't recall it, but as she scrolled through the numerous entries for "Werner" and saw the name Paul, she nodded. That was it. Paul Werner. She told herself she was ridiculous, driving seventy miles round trip to satisfy her curiosity, but she was filled with a gnawing dread; and when she scrolled down the Pauls and found, listed next to him, "Claire Patterson" and verified the information on the certificate the clerk showed her after she gave him the registration number, a certificate that listed "Gerald R. Patterson" as the bride's father, the pain above her eyes was so intense that she thought she would faint.

She tried thinking of innocuous explanations for what she'd learned but was left with the numbing possibility that Gerald Patterson, the silver-haired father of the judge who was Debra's friend, could be a killer. The "why" was painfully clear—his younger daughter, Emily, had killed herself after Rawling was acquitted of raping her. When Rawling was charged with rape again, and was acquitted again, Patterson may have snapped and killed the person he held responsible for his daughter's death—Rawling's attorney, Madeleine Chase. And other lawyers like her. Susan, Kelly Malter, Wesley Pratt.

And me, Debra thought. If he's the killer, he holds me responsible now that Avedon's acquitted. She thought about the black car that had tried to run her into the mountain. She didn't know what kind of car Patterson drove but remembered that on the night of the WRIT meeting, Claire's father had suddenly canceled dinner plans. Had he canceled so that he could follow Debra home from the Sportsman's Lodge and frighten her into dropping Avedon?

From a pay phone she called West L.A. and asked for Laurie.

"I hope you're not asking for another favor," the detective grumbled when she came on the line. "I'm in deep shit with Simms because of you. He found out I told you about Rawling's prior."

"What's he saying—that I shot Rawling and goaded Schultz into driving to Rawling's place last night to take the rap so I could cover my murderous tracks?" That's what Patterson could have done. Annette could have told Claire that Debra was looking at the four transcripts; Claire could have told her father. He must have panicked that someone would discover his connection to Rawling and Madeleine.

"Something like that. I don't think he's serious, but he's making a lot of noise."

"I had a bodyguard with me last night, Laurie. She was with me when Rawling was shot."

"Tell that to Simms. He's looking for you. He phoned your office—they said they don't know where you are."

"I'll phone Simms. I do need another favor, Laurie. I need the license plate and make of car belonging to Gerald Patterson."

"What's he got to do with this?"

"This is an unrelated matter." Debra hated lying to Laurie, especially since the detective had just bent the rules to help her. But if Debra was right about Patterson, she had to prepare Claire before she told the police.

"Do you have a date of birth?"

"No. He's in his late sixties. A widower, about five feet ten inches. I think he lives in Burbank," she said, recalling the information from the obituary. It was possible that Patterson had moved since then—six years had passed. Six years filled with painful memories that had been revived and had led to murder.

"Okay. I'll check it out for you. Is tomorrow okay?"

"Not really. I'm checking on a witness who accused my client of driving under the influence," Debra said, improvising as she spoke. "I think the witness is lying, but my client will be bound over for trial tomorrow unless I can come up with enough information so that the judge will dismiss charges. Is there any way you could get me the information right now?"

She sighed. "I guess. Just make sure I don't find out tomorrow that the witness has been shot and that you were at the scene. Where can I reach you?"

"At my office. I'm heading there now. By the way, who was the detective on the first Rawling case?"

"Roger Hickman. He's retired. Why?"

"Just curious." The Hickman who was Simms's friend? she wondered. The Hickman whose son she'd demolished in the Lassiter pretrial? She thanked Laurie and hung up, feeling a twinge of unease.

Jeremy was at his desk, studying a sheaf of papers. He stood when Debra entered. "Congratulations on winning the Avedon case."

"Thank you." He was always formal, but she could tell from his strained smile that Richard had spoken to him about her. And Glynnis had told her that "Mr. Knox is anxious to see you, dear."

"I admire your courage." Jeremy had moved from his desk and was standing next to her. "You had every reason to withdraw from the case, but you didn't. You must be relieved that the case is over and that the killer is behind bars."

"Very much." She wondered where Patterson was now.

"Richard told me you're planning on leaving the firm," he said in a mournful tone, as though someone had died. "Is the problem one we can work out?"

You can fire Richard or muzzle him. You can teach him to treat me like an equal, not an object. "I don't think so. Richard and I have difficulty communicating. We see things differently." She'd saved the catalog of sexy lingerie as evidence, but even if she showed it to Jeremy, what would she accomplish? Richard wasn't about to change; Jeremy wasn't about to fire Richard. Even if he did, he'd resent Debra.

"I'm sorry to hear that. You're an excellent attorney, Debra. You can be assured that I'll give you the highest recommendations. And if there's anything I can do for you, please let me know."

She thanked Jeremy. On the way back to her office, she asked Glynnis whether Charles was in.

"No, dear. He's still in court," the secretary said. "But I told him about the acquittal when he phoned, and he said to tell you how happy he is that you won the case and the killer's in jail." Glynnis smiled. "Now you can get on with your life and stop looking over your shoulder." She patted Debra's hand. "By the way, Detective Simms called five times. He sounds angry."

Debra returned to her office. She booted her computer and was staring at the screen, trying to concentrate, when Laurie phoned.

"A black Honda, license 1ABC432," she told Debra. "You owe me."

Schultz had seen a black Honda parked across the street from Rawling's house. A black car had followed her from the WRIT meeting. It was a confirmation of what she'd expected; still, she was filled with incredulity and fresh dread.

She'd felt the same way when the doctor had come to the house and reported that her mother had less than twenty-four hours to live. "What do you mean," Debra had said, "twenty-four hours?" even though her mother had been failing before her very eyes.

She thanked Laurie and said, "You don't by any chance have a photo of the guy, do you?"

"I knew you'd ask, so I got the DMV to fax me Patterson's driver's license with the photo. I'll fax it to you."

For the second time today Debra waited anxiously by the fax machine. The facsimile of a facsimile wasn't great, but Debra recognized the face that stared at her—it belonged to the man who had sat during the entire trial in the first row of the spectator's gallery.

Now she had to tell Claire.

Chapter Forty-seven

Or did Claire already know?

The thought jolted Debra as she drove to the courthouse. Was that why Claire had been so hard on her in the courtroom—to keep her from winning and being her father's next victim?

Rawling had been tried downtown, not in Santa Monica. Had Claire been aware that he'd been charged with raping another woman, that Madeleine had defended him again? Had she made the numbing realization about her father after Debra had led her to discover that Madeleine and the others had been killed because they'd defended rapists?

Claire was a judge; she was committed to justice. But would she have turned in her own father?

Maybe Claire didn't know about Rawling. Maybe Gerald Patterson wasn't a killer. Maybe this was all a bizarre, horrifying coincidence.

Debra's cellular phone rang. She picked up the receiver and heard Glynnis's voice telling her that the bodyguard had arrived and that Marty Simms had phoned again and insisted on seeing her.

"I told him you were going to the Santa Monica Court House," Glynnis said. "I told Mr. Silver, too, when he phoned. I hope that's okay."

It wasn't okay, but Debra said, "That's fine, Glynnis, thanks," and asked her to have the bodyguard wait.

In the lobby she surrendered her purse and reclaimed it after she passed through the metal detector. Climbing to the second floor, she took comfort in the knowledge that if Patterson was the killer and he was here—and she doubted he was—he'd had to give up his weapon.

Department M was locked and empty—hardly surprising, since it was five-thirty—but Debra had phoned ahead and Claire's clerk, Brian, had told her the judge would be in her chambers for another hour. Debra knocked loudly; after a minute Brian opened the door, his briefcase in his hand.

He was leaving for the day. "Claire's around," he told Debra, "but I don't know where. I told her you were coming. Why don't you wait in her chambers?"

She walked through the courtroom where she'd spent the past week and exited. Claire's chambers were to her right. She knocked on the door, just in case Claire was inside. When no one answered, she entered. She was struck by the serenity of the room and saddened by the knowledge that she was about to ruin it forever.

She took out the facsimile of Patterson's license; she still found it difficult to believe that the pleasant-looking man in the photo was capable of murdering and mutilating four people. She looked at his signature—his writing was neat, tight, controlled. Too controlled? she wondered. Her eyes went to the line above the signature: RSTR: DAY ONLY.

She frowned. RSTR was an abbreviation for "restricted." Her own father was restricted to driving with corrective lenses. According to this license, Patterson was restricted to driving in the daytime. She stared at the line, her heart thumping as she remembered with dizzying clarity what Claire had told her.

Her father had night blindness. He couldn't drive at night.

She reminded herself that Patterson *had* driven at night—he'd hit a lamp pole, Claire had said. But with his impairment, could he have been the driver of the black car that had followed Debra through the winding canyon road that Sunday night?

Simms, she thought; blood rushing to her temples. Simms had a dark blue car. Simms had reacted impassively to the contents of the pink box on her kitchen counter. Simms's friend Hickman had been the detective on Rawling's first case. Hickman might have told him when Rawling was arrested again, acquitted again. Was that why Simms had been intent on building a case around her? He'd found out that Debra knew about Rawling. Had he made a phone call to Schultz with the intent of framing Debra for Rawling's murder, too?

She had to find Claire. Claire would know what to do. Wondering whether the judge was in the bathroom, she crossed the room and knocked. "Claire?" No one answered. Debra turned the knob and pushed open the door. The room was empty.

She left the judge's chambers and walked down the long hall that extended the length of the second floor. "Claire?" she called. "Claire?" The walls echoed her urgent whisper, but no one was here. Brian had been wrong—Claire had left.

Should she talk to Annette? Was the prosecutor still in the building? Debra returned to the courtroom and walked to the exit. She had pressed the door release and was about to step into the hall when she saw Simms thirty feet to her right. He saw her, too. He smiled at her, but she could see the coldness in his eyes. "She tried to escape," he'd claim. "I had to shoot." She moved back quickly, yanking the door shut, and heard the comforting sound of the bar sliding automatically into place.

Seconds later Simms was pounding on the heavy door; she could hear his muffled yelling. Her heart was pounding, too, as she hurried through the gallery and swung open the half door that separated it from the counsel tables. When she saw Claire, wearing her robe, sitting in the front row of the jury box, she stifled a scream.

"Brian said you were coming to talk to me," Claire said. "He said you told him it was urgent."

"God, you scared me!" She put her hand to her chest. "I was looking for you. Where were you?" Simms was still pounding. She looked back and saw his face, flattened against the door's window.

"I was in the jury room. I wanted to see it from the other side." The judge sighed. "I wanted to see how they let Lee's rapist go. You know, don't you?"

Debra stared at Claire, at the haunted expression on her face, and blanched. Was the killer Claire's father after all, not Simms? But how had he driven down that serpentine road?

"Claire," she whispered, her eyes widening in shock even as she told herself that it couldn't be Claire, Claire was so just, so honest, but it *was* Claire, and Debra was nauseated, trembling with fear of the woman who was a murderer, fear for the woman who was her friend. Simms's pounding had stopped.

"You think I'm crazy, don't you? I'm not. This"—Claire swept her hand in a semicircle that encompassed the judge's bench, the witness stand, and the jury chairs to her right—"this is crazy."

"Claire, let me help you." Her knees were shaky and her heart was thumping so loudly that she could barely hear herself speak. She held on to the railing for support.

Claire inclined her head to one side. "Did you speak to Wayne Rawling?"

Debra nodded.

"I heard he's going to live. I'm not surprised. Animals like him don't die. They go on and on, preying on innocent victims."

"Norman Schultz is in jail for attempted murder," Debra said, struggling for calm. Where was Simms?

"Schultz will be out soon. The police will verify that the bullet didn't come from his gun. I feel terrible about Schultz, but Annette told me you had the transcripts. I knew you'd figure things out. I needed more time." She frowned. "Did Rawling tell you it wasn't his fault that my sister killed herself?"

"Yes," Debra said, hoping her answer wouldn't agitate Claire.

"Of course he'd say that. My father comes to all my trials and tells me at least once a day that it's my fault Lee shot herself. He's right, you know," she said, her tone earnest. "My mother thought so, too. I'm the one who convinced Lee to press charges. 'Trust the system,' I told her. 'Testify,' I urged. So she trusted the system, she trusted me. And the system brutalized her. The system raped her again. And there was nothing I could do about it."

Debra opened her mouth but found she had nothing to say.

"You found out Madeleine was Rawling's attorney in Lee's trial, didn't you? She taunted me. Every time she tried a case in my courtroom, she smirked at me. I hated her." Anger contorted her face, then quickly disappeared. "Still, I was always fair. But when she won an acquittal in the Schultz trial, and my father sent me clippings of both trials, I knew what I had to do. You see that, don't you?" Her voice was imploring.

"Come with me now," Debra said soothingly. "Come with

me to Annette. Tell her what you've told me. She'll help you." It was better than having Simms arrest her. Did he suspect Claire or her father?

"Will she bring Lee back? Will she kill the demons that haunt me every night?" She paused. "I didn't plan to bring the others to justice. At first it was just Madeleine. But that wasn't fair, either. Because it's not only Madeleine. It's all of them, all those attorneys who make their clients look like saints and the victims look like whores. And the saints go out and rape again."

"Not all men accused of rape are guilty," Debra said, her voice gentle. "Avedon is innocent. Susan's client was innocent, too. The day you . . . the day Susan died, she told me the DNA results proved that her client hadn't raped Alicia Vaughan. You made a mistake, Claire."

"You're wrong." Her voice was sharp, stinging; an angry glint appeared in her eyes. "They're all guilty. I warned them all. 'The tongues of dying men enforce attention.'"

"Let me go with you to the police, Claire. They'll find out anyway. Rawling will tell them you're Lee's sister. He'll identify you as the person who shot him last night."

"Rawling opened the door for a woman with long curly red hair who was getting signatures for an environmental protection agency. He doesn't know I'm Lee's sister. I wasn't at the trial. I talked to Lee every day, but I couldn't get away from my judicial responsibilities in San Francisco." Her voice was flooded with bitterness and self-loathing. "Anyway, I don't care if the police find out after this. I warned all those lawyers. I warned you, too, Debra. Why didn't you listen?" With an abrupt motion, she stood. From the folds of her robe she removed a gun and aimed it at Debra's chest.

For a moment Debra couldn't breathe. "How did you get that past the metal detector?" she asked in a detached way, as if this were happening to someone else. She could scream, but who would hear her? Simms may not have seen

Claire through the window. Even if he had, if he thought Patterson was the killer, he'd probably left the building. And the courtroom was barred; no one could get in without a key.

"I told them I was being stalked, that I needed it for my protection. They believed me, of course. I'm a judge." Her smile was ironic. "Lee used this gun to kill herself. It's fitting that I'm using it now, don't you think?"

"You don't want to do this, Claire," Debra said with a calmness that amazed her.

"You're right. Why do you think I wanted you to lose? Why do you think I made sure to get this case assigned to my courtroom?" Her voice resonated mournfully in the high-ceilinged room.

"Let me go, Claire. Come with me to Annette."

She shook her head. "It wouldn't be fair to the others." She flipped off the safety. "Sit on the witness stand."

"Simms followed me here, Claire. You heard him pounding. He'll be back with a key." With her left hand, she groped for the swinging half door. If she could get behind it and drop down—

"Do it now! And put both your hands where I can see them."

Debra obeyed. The dead coldness in Claire's voice and the blank stare in her eyes terrified her more than the gun. This wasn't Claire; this was someone else.

"You can try to run," Claire said in a matter-of-fact voice, "but I'm a good shot." With her gun still aimed at Debra, she stepped down from the jury box. "Get on the witness stand," she said again.

I have to keep her calm, Debra thought. With her eyes on Claire and the gun, she stepped sideways toward the witness chair. She stumbled as she climbed the stairs and had to grab on to the seat to steady herself.

Claire approached the podium. "State your name and oc-cupation."

"Claire—"

"The Court directs you to answer the question!"

"My name—" Debra cleared her throat and stared at the gun. "My name is Debra Laslow. I'm a criminal defense at-torney."

"Ms. Laslow, is it true that you recently defended Kenneth Avedon on a charge of forcible rape?"

"Yes."

"And did you win an acquittal for your client?"

"Yes."

"Isn't it also true that you willfully and deliberately made the complaining witness out to be a liar?"

"No."

A vein in Claire's jaw twitched. "Isn't it true that you hu-miliated her by exposing the intimate details of her life?" She had left the podium and was standing ten feet from the witness stand.

"I didn't intentionally humiliate her." Debra wondered what she would feel when the bullet pierced her chest. She thought about her mother, whom she missed so terribly, and the dark that frightened her so much. She wasn't ready to die.

"Isn't it a fact that you manipulated information to under-mine the credibility of the witness?"

"I practiced criminal defense and abided by the ethics of my profession."

"Objection! The witness isn't being responsive. Did you or did you not manipulate information to undermine the credibility of the witness?"

Claire's eyes were feverish, Debra saw as she answered, "Yes." She licked her lips. Her hands were trembling.

"Isn't it true that in defending your client, you perverted the justice system?" Claire took another step closer to Debra.

Debra hesitated, then said, "No. I worked within the ethical boundaries of the justice system."

"Isn't it true, Ms. Laslow, that the justice system has no ethics! That there is no justice!"

"You can't take the law into your own hands," she said, realizing she had nothing to lose. There was no mollifying this mad stranger in front of her.

"Nonresponsive! Move to strike."

"Claire, you can't—"

"I have no more questions for this witness."

"You called Rawling an animal. If you kill me, you're no different."

"The witness is excused."

"Susan's client was innocent, Claire. You committed murder. You have to turn yourself in."

"Step down!" She was holding the gun with both hands; her feet were apart.

Now, Debra thought; Claire is going to shoot me now. She stepped off the stand slowly. "Don't do this," she whispered. "Please, don't." She glanced at the window to the courtroom but saw no one. "Simms is here!" she exclaimed, hoping to divert Claire's attention.

"I'm not stupid, Debra."

She extended the gun and aimed it at Debra's chest for what seemed like an eternity. Her face contorted with pain. With a sudden, swift movement, she dropped her left hand and turned the gun to her temple.

"Claire!" Debra screamed.

She raced to her and grabbed at her right hand, trying to wrest the gun away, but clutched air. She heard the deafening crack, smelled the acrid scent of gunpowder, and held Claire as she crumpled to the floor.

Blood trickled from the bullet hole and her mouth.

Chapter Forty-eight

Debra sat in the courtroom, watching the jurors file in and take their seats in the box.

When the last juror was seated, the bailiff said, "The Superior Court of Santa Monica is now in session. The Honorable Judge Judith Simons is presiding. You may remain seated. Come to order."

It was a different judge, but the same courtroom. Debra hadn't been here since the night, a year ago, when Claire had shot herself and died in Debra's arms; this morning she'd been overcome with emotion and had to steel herself before she pushed open the door and entered. She'd darted a glance to her right, at the space between the witness stand and the counsel podium, but of course there was no blood.

In her dreams she sometimes still saw the blood—Claire's blood, Susan's blood. Debra had mentioned this to the therapist her father had urged her to see. "It takes time to get over something that horrific," the therapist had said.

Adam had said the same thing last night when she'd

awakened him after her nightmare. He'd held her and soothed her and made love to her; she'd fallen asleep in his arms. She twisted the gold wedding band on her left finger and thought for the hundredth time how lucky she was to have found him. She'd whispered her joy to her mother two months ago when, following tradition, she'd visited her grave and invited her soul to attend their wedding.

The wedding had been bittersweet. Debra had been overwhelmed by her love for Adam and had rejoiced in the dancing and celebration. But she'd ached to have her mother at her side as Adam lowered her veil and her father blessed her before he walked her down the aisle; she'd yearned for her as she'd stood under the canopy and listened to her father, his voice husky with emotion, perform the ceremony; yearned for her as she'd accepted wishes of *"Mazel tov!"* from a teary-eyed Aunt Edith and Uncle Morrie and from her grandparents and all her other relatives and parents' friends, some of whom voiced what she knew everyone was thinking—"If only your mother could have lived to see this day." She had come to accept that she would yearn for her mother forever.

Adam had offered to come with her to the courthouse today, but she'd told him she'd be fine. She'd refused her father and Julia, too. "This isn't the place for you," she'd told her sister-in-law, who was four months pregnant. Aaron insisted it was the wine that had relaxed his wife and helped her conceive. Julia liked to think it was her helping out as an attendant in the ritual bath. Debra remembered the words of one of the women who had sat on the miracle chair in Israel: "I believe that if you have faith, anything is possible."

"Calling case number SA 011 . . ." the judge announced. "The People versus Kenneth Avedon."

Debra stared at Avedon's back. He'd smiled at her nonchalantly in the hall; he'd smiled at her after the preliminary hearing, too, at which he'd been bound over for trial on one count of forcible rape. This time there was no fiancée; Vickie Hobart had broken off the engagement two weeks after Debra had won the acquittal. Debra had wondered then.

Simms was in the gallery. Debra had seen him when she'd entered the courtroom. He'd come over, smiling his crooked smile, and she'd braced herself for a snide comment about Avedon, but he'd said, "This must be tough for you, huh?" and she'd said, "Yes," and he'd nodded. He'd never apologized for suspecting her, not when he'd returned to the courtroom that day with the other officers (he'd suspected Patterson, not Claire), not at Claire's funeral. He'd said only, "I guess I was wrong," when he'd returned her brown Coach purse a few days after Claire was buried next to her sister's grave. Debra had given the purse away. She'd canceled her purchase of the gun.

"Ready for the People, Your Honor," Annette Prado said.

Debra had wanted to prosecute the case—partly to pay penance, partly to redeem her pride—but of course, she'd had to recuse herself. She'd taken a week's leave from the downtown Criminal Courts Building where she was now a deputy district attorney so that she could be here every day, watching Avedon, forcing him to see her.

Penny Bailor was here, too, with her brother. She'd avoided looking at Debra, who had written her a note when Avedon had been arrested again but could never undo what had been done. Debra would have to live with that knowledge.

She wondered occasionally how Jeff was doing. She'd returned his manuscript but hadn't answered any of his calls or letters of apology; finally the calls and letters had stopped. Aaron had heard from the rabbi that Jeff had moved back to Chicago. Debra didn't hate him—she'd come to accept that his friendship for her had been genuine, that fear for her safety may have brought back all the trauma that had led to his breakdown. She didn't hate him; but she couldn't forgive him, either. The best she could do was to try to understand.

"Ready for the defense, Your Honor," said the attractive blond woman at Avedon's side.

Debra still believed in the criminal justice system. She still believed that it was better for ten guilty people to go free than for one innocent person to be convicted. She still believed that everyone charged with a crime was entitled to a zealous representation by his defense counsel. She just couldn't be one of those defenders.

Not now, anyway.

"Miss Prado, do you wish to make an opening statement at this time?"

"Yes, Your Honor." Annette Prado approached the podium. "Ladies and gentlemen, I want to thank you in advance for your attention this morning. Rape is a private crime, without corroboration. Rape . . ."